THE ORNATRIX

KATE HOWARD

THE ORNATRIX

*Beauty is in the eye
of the beholder*

Duckworth Overlook

First published in the UK in 2016 by
Duckworth Overlook

LONDON
30 Calvin Street, London E1 6NW
T: 020 7490 7300
E: info@duckworth-publishers.co.uk
www.ducknet.co.uk
For bulk and special sales please contact
sales@duckworth-publishers.co.uk,
or write to us at the above address.

NEW YORK
141 Wooster Street
New York, NY 10012
www.overlookpress.com
For bulk and special sales please contact
sales@overlookny.com, or write us at the above address.

The right of Kate Howard to be identified as the Author of
the Work has been asserted by her in accordance with
the Copyright, Designs and Patents Act 1988.
A catalogue record for this book is available
from the British Library
Cataloguing-in-Publication Data is available
from the Library of Congress

ISBNs:
UK: 978-0-7156-5097-4
Typeset by Charlotte Tate

Printed and bound in Great Britain

For Sue, with thanks

'Why do women who are not born fair
attempt with artificial Beauty to appear so?'

Buoni, Problems of Beauty and
All Human Affections

'Whoever washes the head of an ass, wastes the soap'

Italian proverb

PROLOGUE

It happened because Mona Grazia saw a bird in flight. If the sky had been empty, everything would have been different.

She was supposed to close her eyes to ugliness. Look only on beautiful things. The wild lady slipper orchids on the terrace by the workshop; the smiling face of San Fortunato above the church altar. Things to feed her eyes and her soul, because goodness and beauty cannot be parted.

There were no looking glasses. Even if the dyer could afford such vanities, Mona Grazia did not need one to know that grief had ploughed two deep lines across her forehead.

The last year was hard on the people of San Fortunato. Disease came from a nearby town, turning the summer winds to poison. The village sank into quiet despair and the dyer's business grew as stagnant as the vats in his workshop. Everyone stayed behind closed doors, speaking in whispers. They hoped to trick the sickness into thinking no one was at home.

Mona Grazia had two good reasons to hide: two small sons with hazelnut hair and clear brown eyes. Boys of Arcadia, running barefoot with small golden bows and a sheaf of toy arrows, too busy laughing to notice the boar scampering ahead, too young to know their beauty and beautiful because they did not know it.

At least, that is how Flavia always thinks of them.

It is a strange lesson. In dangerous times jewels are buried under yard stones to keep them safe. When trouble has passed they are dug up and polished and found to be much the same. But small boys with clear brown eyes are no ordinary treasure. They cannot be locked in a strong room or swallowed whole to keep them from thieves. As Mona Grazia found out that summer – the greatest gifts are those we cannot keep. No prayers were good enough for her sons. The fever swept them out of her arms and lay them dead on the kitchen table, ready to be sponged and sewn into her two best sheets.

In the autumn she swept the leaves that fell on their small square of stone, waiting for heavier skies and despair's proper scenery.

The new year brought hope. Stirring the dyer's supper, Mona Grazia felt a familiar clench in her belly.

A cautious creep along the scales of fortune.

The dyer wept when he learned, his discoloured hands clasped tight.

It is a scene he replays, when Flavia asks him.

Mona Grazia welcomed the ache in her knees as she knelt before the priest, emptying herself of sin so she would think only of good things. She paid for a special mass, and when the last words echoed on the plaster walls she passed her beads through her fingers and said over again: 'Inside and outside, only beauty.'

Early springtime. A quiet day: the dyer was in his workshop below with the steam from the vats drifting lazily. The window of Mona Grazia's bedroom was open to the breeze; a stool placed beneath it. She settled with a pile of rags, washed and ready to stitch into swaddling bands. It was the hour

when most of the villagers folded themselves back into bed
for a while and the street outside was empty. Mona Grazia's
ears held nothing except the rustle of thread through cloth
and the gentle suck and release of a half-drawn curtain.

When the thread grew short she pulled the last stitch tight
and bit into it, working her teeth from side to side. As it came
apart a loud chirping noise began outside the window. Fas-
tening her needle into the end of the swaddling band, Mona
Grazia looked out. Down in the street, lying in the groove of a
cartwheel track, was a broken nest. Around it a tangle of
chicks, puckered and featherless, their eyes swimming behind
see-through lids. Hopping among them, the mother bird
chirped her denunciation of treacherous winds or small boys'
mischief.

An ugly scene. Mona Grazia did not mean to see it. She
tried to think of lady slipper orchids and smiling saints, but
one glance was enough. She flung a hand to her cheek and let
out a cry.

Startled, the bird fluttered upwards, its wings bowed dark
against the sky. Mona Grazia watched it go and the child, tight
in her belly, took its shape on her skin.

PART ONE

'One desires the hands to be white – especially the
upper side – large and a little full, the palm a little hollow and shadowed with roses; the lines distinct, clear,
well-marked, not muddled, not crossed.'

Firenzuola

1

To anyone who can bear the stench of him, Maestro Bartofolo shares the great secret of his trade. While his companion reels towards the nearest draught of fresh air, he points a bruised finger to the sky and his pale round face breaks into a smile.

'My friend, good dyeing takes patience. Grinding, sifting, soaking, drying, painting. No task done slackly and no half measures. To make the colours regular and the cloth smooth takes an indecent measure of time.'

For days he has been preparing. First boiling and settling the dye, carefully cleaning off the scum that forms on the surface every morning and night. When he is not steaming the skin from his face he pounds out fenugreek and linseed to add richness to the colour. As soon as the vat is ready to cool he will paint the first coat of red onto each of the kidskins, letting them dry until they are soft to the touch. He will do this three more times. Painting, stretching and drying, deepening the hue each time until it is as strong as ox-blood. Then he will dry them for good in a spot well chosen for its southerly breeze. Finally, once the finished skins have been checked by the guildmaster at Avigliano, Ser Aldo's servant will be summoned to collect them so they can be perfumed and cut to the size of his master's hands.

Maestro Bartofolo will not ask for payment then. He will wait until Ser Aldo is ready to loosen his purse strings, and be thankful for whatever comes his way.

As he always says, leaning forward genially as his companion stuffs two fingers up his nostrils, 'Good dyeing takes patience.'

He uses verzino to make the red. As a journeyman he worked with chermisi: the crimson dye from the crushed bodies of insects that soaks the cloth of the rich. Though the silkworm still flourishes in the East, he is not used to such finery now. His fingers have grown unaccustomed to powdered alessandrino, the deep blue beloved of dukes and courtesans. Instead he uses oricello from the lichens of the forest, or verzino from brazilwood. Woad is even cheaper, and indigo is the truest colour of the dyer's trade. Maestro Bartofolo wears his deep blue apron with pride.

Flavia once asked if she could have an apron the same colour, because her hands are clamped around the stirring stick just as often, and she gulps the stinging fumes until her eyes water. But Maestro Bartofolo shook his head and said she must be happy with his old brown cape, worn back-to-front to keep the splashes from her dress.

Flavia does not care about the splashes. She just wants an indigo apron to wear with pride, even if there is no one to see it.

As the last of the verzino bubbles rise to the surface, Flavia and her sister work on the kidskins. Cold water spills over hands that are pink and shrivelled, rinsing and squeezing until the skins are pulpy smooth. As they work, Pia tuts over her wrinkled fingers, which are small and neat with nails as smooth as shaved almonds. Flavia is rougher, wringing the last drops with her face screwed tight.

The alum water heats slowly on the second fireplace. As Pia slaps the skins on the table Flavia goes to fetch the brushes. They are valuable. Soft hogs hair from the workshops of the dyer's own Maestro, kept on the top shelf of the cupboard, above the dust. Pia usually makes Tommaso fetch them, so she can fuss over his hose, which are always ripped at the knee, or scold him for his knotted hair, as though he is already her husband and she his thistle-tongued wife.

Flavia prefers to fetch a stool.

She takes the brushes to her father and he thumbs through each of them in turn, looking for loose hairs. Then he hands back the largest one with a slow wink, and Flavia smiles for the first time in three days. Though she cannot be trusted with the verzino she is allowed to put on the first coating of alum water, spreading it over the skins so they take the dye more smoothly. It is always risk, letting a woman loose on the dyer's art, but the guildmaster does not visit them often and Flavia has always been good with the brush. She is much quicker than Tommaso, who is too busy making cow eyes at Pia and dribbling great splashes down his apron.

As Pia stretches the skins tight, Flavia dips the brush lightly into the alum water and lets it drift, watching as it glistens and quickly sinks in. The leather is good, level and unmarked where the flesh is cleaved. By the hunting season Ser Aldo's hands will be nested in a soft second layer, as warm and close as his own skin. If he likes the gloves he might send her father some thread for dyeing with verdigris or leaves from the oriola shrub, because no one makes green like Maestro Bartofolo, except Pia when she has to clean the fat off a sheepskin that has been soaking for a week. Then she is such a sickly colour it is hard to tell her from the oriola leaves.

When the painting is finished the sisters carry the kidskins into the courtyard to hang them on the drying rack. Wiping his hands on the front of his apron, Tommaso lopes after them and stands next to Pia, yanking the delicate skins this way and that. When Flavia leans across to slap his hand he yelps like a beaten puppy until Pia coos and places a kiss on the flesh between his thumb and his pointing finger. This makes Tommaso grin like a man with love in his heart and sawdust in his head.

As they all seem to be making animal noises, Flavia lets out a grunt and goes back to the workshop.

Behind the steam Maestro Bartofolo stares into the vat as though it holds a great secret. He always looks down as he stirs, his round face tilted to the bubbles, eyes red from the woodsmoke. He stares into the colour, whistling softly to himself as his breath parts the vapour.

Though it is shaded by trees, the workshop is boiling. Besides the verzino there are two other dyes brewing, and the fires pump a cutting heat as the smell of urine rolls out of one of the vats. Flavia forces herself to give the mixture a good stir. Woad and sheep's piss make good dye but bad perfume. It is said you can smell a dyer ten miles before you can see him, more if the wind runs ahead of him. Her mother often complains about it.

'Have you finished?' Maestro Bartofolo nods his head to the courtyard.

'Yes. Shall I call Pia and Tommaso?'

'Give them some time together.' He speaks quietly, turning the stick in wide circles.

Flavia feels a sound like 'pah' shaping her mouth and struggles to keep it closed. Pia and Tommaso always have time together. At meals, after meals, in the workshop, walking to the village or into the hemp field. Soon Pia will have the rest of her life to gaze at Tommaso and talk about how much sawdust they can both fit into their heads.

'Go and help your mother, child.'

'Papa?'

Her most plaintive voice, which is not as persuasive as Pia's. Her sister escapes a lot of things by whining.

She pulls off her back-to-front cape and wipes her hands on it, adding a smear of purple to the other stains.

Back in the courtyard, Pia has abandoned the kidskins and is fussily retying the shoulder stitches on Tommaso's tunic. He stares at the square of white flesh above the top of her undershirt, which has been unbuttoned and tucked down into her bodice since she left the workshop. As Flavia goes into the house a giggling shriek rips through the courtyard and the 'pah' she tried to swallow explodes through her lips like an unblocked bellows.

* * *

The *sala* is very plain. There are no dried flowers or little lace embroideries like Zia Dolce and Zia Modesta have pinned to their rafters. There are no servants either. The last one was a young widow from the village but Mona Grazia did not like her. She said the widow brought more dirt with her than she took away, so Maestro Bartofolo timidly dismissed her after a week.

The bowls they used at lunchtime are scoured and stacked, the spoons put away and the stools tucked beneath the table at strict intervals. Mona Grazia neither loves her labours nor shares them. A clean, orderly space with no people, in the time between tidying one meal and preparing another. This is as close as Flavia's mother comes to happiness.

Up the staircase and along the passageway, Flavia traces the warp of the floorboards. Her mother often takes herself upstairs in the afternoon, worn out with cauldrons that are never smooth enough no matter how furiously she rubs them with sand. Stopping at the far end, she puts one hand to the beam that frames the doorway, running it lightly down the grain until a sharp piece of wood jabs her finger.

The shutters are mostly closed but a little light creeps in.

Mona Grazia sits on the edge of the bed. Tight coils of chestnut hair are flattened on one side and her head is bent to the floor, shoulders hunched as her knuckles press into the mattress. In the half-light her face has the look of yellow wax into which eyes have gradually sunk. Maestro Bartofolo says they are green, but to Flavia it is not of the oriola shrub, more the soupy waters of a pond that has seen too little light.

'Flavia.'

Mona Grazia sighs the first part of her daughter's name as she turns to look at her. Not at her face, she never does that, but somewhere around the line of her chin.

This is the shape of their reunion. After a night's sleep, a day's work, or a moment's absence, the dyer's wife must look, and sigh, and let sunken eyes show how much sorrow her daughter has brought.

'Were you sleeping?'

Flavia does not call her Mama. Mona Grazia does not like it. She cannot, unlike Pia, push her lips into a sweet double 'a'.

Another sigh, and a slow shake of the head, as if sleep were a precious object mislaid rather than a simple act of lying down when tired. Mona Grazia pushes her fists deeper into the mattress, looking at Flavia's feet.

'Did you clean your shoes before you came in from the workshop?'

She eyes the scuffed trim of her daughter's clogs, which are bearded with powdered brazilwood.

'I don't remember.' Flavia's voice belongs to the pigsty not the honeypot; there is no doubling of sweet lips to soften it. She falls back into the passageway as Mona Grazia stands, still glowering at the clogs as though she can see right through them, because the dyer's wife thinks clean soles no less important than clean souls. Luckily there is not enough light to mark shadow from soil, and as Mona Grazia lifts her head to her daughter's chinline her eyes glaze over again.

'We need more water. Go and ask Pia.'

'Pia is busy. I will go.'

Flavia answers in retreat, moving quickly down the passageway.

'No, it must be Pia! Flavia, I will not have you going out there!'

Mona Grazia's words swarm towards her but Flavia is already clattering down the staircase and through the *sala*. She grabs a jug on her way into the courtyard where Pia is still giggling around Tommaso. Pushing roughly between them, she makes sure to strike the jug against her sister's elbow. Pia cries out in pain but Flavia is already cutting through the ragged vegetable lines beside the workshop.

Behind her, Mona Grazia's voice rises and fades.

* * *

Maestro Bartofolo calls it the Casa Nascosta, the house that nestles in the woods. The stones on the ground floor are old Roman, better cut than the ones higher up. The windows were thin as arrows when they first arrived. A watchtower, said the old villagers, but there is nothing to watch from it now. It was left to rot, eaten up by the woods for more years than anyone in San Fortunato could count. There is no road, just a mule track rising into the island of trees, and even that trails away before reaching the house. Like a preacher distracted in the middle of his sermon, it bumbles backwards and forwards until it forgets where it was going.

When they moved down here from San Fortunato there were just four crooked walls, a roof strangled by ivy, and a crumbling courtyard. The walls are stronger now but the trees are as thick as ever. In winter patches of field appear through the branches, but in summer they are completely hidden. The trees press hard against them and Flavia does not love them. Silent allies in Mona Grazia's war of concealment, she would happily take a torch to every last one.

The nearest stretch of river is down a pathway trampled into great ruts by Maestro Bartofolo's mule, but there is a quicker way. Like the house, it is hemmed in by pine and oak and tangled bushes. Flavia likes to do battle with them, breaking the twigs as they drag at her skirts. Her arms are covered with thistle scratches that take weeks to heal. Broom is kinder, and she holds out her hand to its feathery touch, shivering as it glides over her palm and breathing deep as the branches thin towards a strip of wheat field rising up to the sky and framed below by a sparkling band of water.

If they lived on the riverside of a town Maestro Bartofolo would be rich enough to wear silver buttons on his tunic. At the Casa Nascosta he must carve them from wood. There is never enough water. Now in the middle of summer the river is low and there are wide cracks where it makes an ugly mosaic of its bed.

Reaching the bank, Flavia slips off her clogs and stockings before scrambling down. From the baked soil she steps into a cold, labouring stream that barely reaches to her knees. She levels the jug, glancing by habit at the water and the dark shape beneath her, its twisted edges floating into the reflected sky.

There is no glass or silver disc in the house to show what she is. Pia is always preening herself in the copper plate but her mother has forbidden Flavia from doing that.

It is one order she is happy to obey.

Like Mona Grazia, she keeps her eyes glazed against the rippled cap and the dark plaits falling stiffly over her shoulders. She looks instead at her hands gripping the base and lip of the jug. Not small and dainty like her sister's, but not awful. The fingers are long, which she likes, though etched with dark brown, because red verzino and indigo are not so pretty when mixed together. At least her skin is dark, so the stains don't look too bad. Pia says she will never be fair because she likes to sit in the sun wherever the trees part. Flavia laughs at her then, because that is like saying a donkey will never look like the Madonna because its hooves need clipping.

Pia has paler skin and lighter, wispy brown hair. Flavia does not know if this makes her pretty.

When the jug is full she takes it back to the bank, sitting on the grass as she picks up her stockings. They are stiff about the soles, the wool warped into the shape of her feet. She throws them aside and stretches herself full out. The grass tickles her neck and there is a welcome sting of sun on her forearms. The sky is a sheet of blue; not a single cloud and nothing to see except the swifts that tumble in endless circuits. On the nearest hilltop is the village of San Fortunato, its bell tower rising over the orange tiled roofs. Further west, the walled towns of Todi and Montecastello squat on higher hills making giant stepping stones up the valley.

Sometimes, when the sun is high and there is no mist around, she can make out the city to the north. It winds itself up a steep ridge, russet towers reaching skyward like a fleet of fists raised in war. Her father worked there once, but San Fortunato and a few pitted roads are the sum of Flavia's travels. To be surrounded by so many people that you cannot move, to hear a clashing chorus of pedlars and horsemen, men cursing in the streets and women gossiping between high balconies: such things are near beyond imagining.

The river laps sluggishly in its bed. Flavia closes her eyes for a moment, longer, drifting into half sleep until time makes itself known through the church bells.

On the second stroke she is kicking her feet into her stockings, knowing she has truly given Mona Grazia cause to exercise her whisk broom. She can already see her mother's arm cutting the air, and does not notice the small dark figure silently crouching a few feet away. She is pulling on her clogs when a stone whistles past her head and smacks into the river, sending an arc of droplets onto her skirt.

Quickly, she turns away from whoever has thrown it. Lifting the jug to her head she marches stiffly towards the trees and is already halfway up the slope when a familiar voice calls out.

'Aa–ee–aa!'

There is no mistaking it. A collection of noises that come more from the nose than the mouth. Someone she can look at because his own face is as spoiled as hers.

'Alfeo, you frightened me!'

Springing up, he walks towards her. His upper lip, scored as though split by a blade and hitched high into his left nostril, parts further into a smile. Two sun-shrivelled arms reach out as he tilts his head to signal for the jug. Alfeo always prefers to gesture when he is sober. When drunk, he does not care how he sounds.

'I ran away Alfeo, and Mama will be very cross when I get back.'

They all speak to Alfeo like this, as though the gap in his mouth has let his brain trickle out. His head looks like some half-finished vessel, the potter having dozed at his wheel. The rest of him is as skinny and brown as a southern peasant from his years carting grain along the north road.

Alfeo takes the jug and puts it lightly on his head, which is flat enough to make a good platform.

'Did you go to the house?'

He nods, forgetting the jug is on his head and spilling water on his shoulder.

'She said you were here.' Or so Flavia hears it. She thinks of Christmastide, when Alfeo sings carols that belong more to the barnyard than the church while she and Pia double over with laughter and Mona Grazia slaps the back of his warped skull and says the devil is piggy-backing on his shoulders.

Her mother always says Alfeo isn't real family but that is shame talking. He was born to a young servant of Maestro Bartofolo's father, who was fifty years old when he took the girl into his carved oak bed. The old man and the oak bed creaked together, and sometime later Alfeo was born. Mona Grazia says he grew out of aged seed, like the sickly blackcurrants of late autumn, and this is why he has a hitched lip and a squashed brow. Flavia wastes no sympathy on him. Alfeo is allowed to drive his cart wherever he pleases. Even if he is too ugly to have a wife, no one is afraid to look at him.

They follow the scent of woodsmoke as much as the light. Night time is still far from the open fields, but here it settles early and the Casa Nascosta spills tallow light from its windows. When they reach the courtyard Flavia loops her arm through Alfeo's, comforted by the smell of the willowherb he likes to chew into great mashed wads.

Mona Grazia has been busy in her absence. The smell of braising pigeon fights its way through the dye smoke and the voices from inside have a tenor of waiting appetites. To the footsore traveller the Casa Nascosta might look like a welcome refuge, but when Flavia walks into the *sala* and her mother turns quickly to the hearth there is no such feeling.

* * *

Flavia sometimes teases her uncle that he could earn a good living as a fool. It is not just spite that makes her say this. Alfeo knows how to juggle with pieces of fruit and he can walk around on his hands, a trick made all the more funny by his deformity. Though it is beyond Mona Grazia to lift the corners of her mouth, the rest of them cheer when Alfeo throws a pickled chestnut from one side of the room and runs across to the other side to catch it in his mouth. They slap the table with laughter when he begins choking on the same chestnut, which has to be ejected by a great wallop from Mona Grazia, who then decides that one wallop is not enough and carries on hitting Alfeo long after he has coughed the nut into the fire.

None of them notice when the dyer's wife whips away the dirty plates and begins an ecstasy of cleaning louder than a summer thunderstorm. With looks and sighs Mona Grazia tries to make an end of the evening, but Maestro Bartofolo has a cask of sloe wine that has yet to know the pleasure of his tongue and together with Tommaso and Alfeo he sets about it with rustic delight. As soon as Mona Grazia takes herself upstairs the dyer gives Pia and Flavia a cupful each. It sets fire to their throats and makes them cough, but when the burning stops Flavia reaches for more. Soon the wine and the candles are making a warm haze of the faces around her: her father, round and pale as a cloud-covered moon; Tommaso, his hair washed clean and settled merrily round his cheeks; beside him delicate Pia, bright and pink-faced; then Alfeo, brown and squashed like a trodden acorn. All of them clear eyed and smiling, no downward glances or hands cupped over a smirk.

None of them thinking there is a monster in their midst.

The wine makes a furnace of Flavia's stomach. For a while she is almost happy. Then Tommaso turns his big eyes to Pia and a familiar grimace tightens her jaw. With a scrape of her stool she rises unsteadily to her feet and begins clearing away the cups. Yanking Alfeo's from his hand, she tuts at a pool of purple liquid on the table.

'Really, Zio Alfeo, you must learn to drink from a straw if you cannot control your dribbling.'

Alfeo looks up blearily.

'Flavia!' Her father's voice, never loud, has the threat of anger about it. 'Both of you girls, upstairs.'

'Papa.' Flavia nods and grins at Pia's sulky drawing away from Tommaso.

Their room is at the back of the house. A bed, a stool, a small cupboard and a chest are all crammed under the eaves, forcing greater proximity than either of them want.

Still cross, Pia tears off her dress and gets quickly into bed, making an overwrought turn to the wall. Because the air is warm and there is no need to dash to the covers, Flavia takes her time, cupping her hands to the water bowl and splashing some of the heat from her cheeks. She pulls up the edge of her skirt and rubs at her teeth until they are a little less furry. The cap is tossed aside and her plaits torn loose until her hair forms stiff waves down her back. She does not bother to comb it. Mona Grazia would be disgusted if she saw how little attention she pays to these things, but Flavia knows that a donkey is just a donkey. No one cares if it is well groomed or not.

Slipping out of her dress, she stands in her undershirt at the window. Unlike the others it has never been widened and the arrow's breadth is little more than a keyhole to the night sky. In summer the breeze gets caught in the trees long before it reaches this room and there is barely a whisper now.

Flavia puts her face to the opening and looks to the stars, swirling in clouds as high as the barrelling swifts. She wonders if her mother also looked at the night sky when she was in her belly, because hundreds of freckles scatter themselves like stars over her arms and nose when she sits in the sun. Then she wonders why nobody minds these spots, and why a man with a lip hitched up through his nose can walk through the streets when a girl with a mark on her face cannot.

The stars don't offer any answer. She stands at the window until the fire in her stomach grows weak.

Pia has taken most of the blanket with her. Flavia finds a corner and tugs hard. Her sister's grip is not that of a sleeper, and after a few more tugs Flavia is obliged to launch a knee into the small of her back. Ignoring Pia's squeals, she grabs a fistful of blanket and wrenches it over to her side. Now it is Pia's turn to wrestle, but Flavia is stronger and more stubborn. Eventually Pia flops onto her back, letting off sighs deep enough to make up for the lack of breeze.

Flavia is still busy congratulating herself when her sister rolls back towards her, putting her lips close to her ear.

'In a month you will have this bed all to yourself.'

Then she turns again to the wall, and there is no answer Flavia that can think of because Pia is right. Any lack of blankets will be richly replaced by dreams of her new life. Tommaso will soon be keeping her warm every night in the new bedroom being prepared for them behind the *sala*. The embroidered sheets Mona Grazia has been sewing for years are pressed smooth and ready to be stretched out beneath the headboard of their grandfather's old oak bed.

This is the one thing worse than living in the Casa Nascosta. Worse than lurking behind trees or never seeing a stranger's smile. Worse still than the memory of her little brothers with their faultless beauty, or the ragged shadow that floats across her face and makes no sense to God or man.

2

They did not always live in the Casa Nascosta.

Before the guild made him master of all colours, the dyer worked as a journeyman in the city. It was the only place he'd ever used the valuable chermisi dyes or handled velvets and damasks. In the city everyone wanted to paint themselves brighter than their neighbours. They gorged on colour. Stygian black was favoured by notaries, widows, men of learning. Noble boys strutted around in tunics the colour of sunflowers. For the matrons, nothing rivalled an overdress of cardinal red to embellish their gowns in the winter months.

Nobody could have such a wardrobe without the smelly dyers. Bartofolo made good money there, learning his trade among sails of drying silk and the steam of a hundred vats. He might have spent many years creaming the scum from glistening alessandrino and milking the vanity of his butterfly clients, growing ever more used to the weight of a fat florin in the palm of his hand. But the city was no place for a man of gentle temper. Bartofolo was lost among the tenement blocks where he lodged. Their shaded passageways leaned into him and he struggled to guess whether a darkened figure was friend or not. More than once a chance encounter left him bleeding from the head while his purse clinked out of earshot.

As soon as his training was finished, Bartofolo was eager to return to the drowsy village of his birth. He wanted to honour his childhood promise to one Grazia da Pesciano, daughter of his mother's cousin and an excellent spinner of wool. Everyone called her Mona Grazia because she walked like a lady, with her back straight as a lance and her head held high. Bartofolo wanted nothing more than to raise sons with Grazia's chestnut hair and bright green eyes. In the autumn of his twenty-fifth year he went back to San Fortunato, made good on his pledge, and never again returned to the city of bright coloured cloth.

Bartofolo spent his journeyman's savings on a house at the edge of the village: a slim three storeys with terraced land leading down to a rocky olive grove. The windows were wide and faced west towards the hills. In the garden there were fruit trees, small and fragrant. They were trimmed hard every spring and bore apples and quince in the autumn that Mona Grazia baked into thick-crusted pies.

They were never alone. Threads of kinship criss-crossed the narrow streets of San Fortunato, and the lives of its inhabitants were so closely knit it was sometimes hard to say where one person ended and another began. No outsiders came to live there and few people ever left. They came and went by way of the crib and the grave. Everyone was aunt, uncle or cousin, and the years rolled past like an endless family gathering. If a small collection of houses could yawn and roll over on its side, that is what San Fortunato would have done. The young worked in the fields and the old settled by fires in the winter or in the small church square in the summer. They sat in the shade of vines, knotted hands bent around knotted sticks, and if rumours reached them of distant wars or the death of kings, they would grunt or sigh as though an unsought dream had disturbed their long night's sleep.

Flavia was not hidden then. When she was born and the midwife discovered that no amount of scrubbing with a milky rag would clear the purplish mark from her face, the men of the village shrugged and the women wept, for everyone must pity the mother of an ugly child. No one said the devil had spat in her face; no one talked of bad blood. The villagers were used to the whims of nature. Springtime lambs were sometimes born with a limb too many and one of the village cats was famed for shedding kittens with no ears. After everyone had come to look and to weep or shrug as nature dictated, the matter was forgotten and the occupations of sitting and stick-holding quietly resumed.

But Mona Grazia was not reconciled.

She remembered the broken nest, saw in the thwarted pigment a grieving bird in flight.

When Flavia was very new to the world Mona Grazia would gaze for hours at the vibrant splash: a pair of wings arcing over and under her left eye as the beak drifted up to the bridge of her nose, the tail shooting red tendrils across her cheek. When the gazing stopped, she would leave her daughter's crib and take a brush to the back doorstep, scrubbing the stone until the bristles wore down and her knees swelled up.

As Flavia grew and the bird spread further across her cheeks, Mona Grazia found herself staying up past sunset, polishing door bolts and measuring out cloth squares to cover the windows. She was so busy with needle and broom one morning she failed to notice her daughter totter out of the front door and up the street to the village square. There the little girl found herself wrapped in the arms of Zia Caracosa, a wet nurse of unimpeachable filth who was happy for any number of toddlers to urinate on her lap.

From that day on Flavia became a frequent visitor to the squalor that was Zia Caracosa's home. There was always something interesting to play with on the floor, among the

dead spiders and scraps of rotten meat. The air was rich with
the smell of unwashed babies and the thin grey milk the wet
nurse worried constantly from her teats. On Saints' days Zia
Caracosa sometimes gave Flavia a doll made out of old spice
sacks. Fleas often hopped out of the stuffing and they made
her pillows smell of cloves but she loved them all, and wept
stridently whenever a disgusted Mona Grazia threw them on
the fire.

The birth of another daughter brought little comfort to
the dyer's house. Though Pia was a whole child with no
greater evil inside her than a noisy pair of lungs, she failed to
patch the woe of her mother's life.

If Flavia's childhood was troubling, her girlhood was a
rising terror. To Mona Grazia's mind the stricken bird flew
straight at the veil of life, its beak cutting clean through the
narrow beam of light that is life's happiness to a place thick
with grief. Though she did not want it in her house, she would
not inflict it on the world at large. Flavia was warned not to go
pestering Zia Caracosa or talk to the pedlars on the church
steps. If ever an unknown figure appeared on the road to the
village she was dragged from sight. Mona Grazia stitched a
square cloth veil into an old straw hat, to be rolled down like a
blind whenever her daughter left the house. Flavia managed
to snag the veil on every passing branch until it was torn
loose.

When she wasn't yanking invisible cobwebs from the
rafters or scrubbing the underneath of tables, Mona Grazia
went to the church. She swept the dust from the altar into
triangular piles and transferred it, pinch by pinch, to a little
earthenware pot.

She prayed that God would wipe away the stain that no
human hand could clean.

Sometimes she would travel on foot to the convent of Santa Giuliana on the slopes of the city. The journey forced her to share Alfeo's cart for an uncomfortable length of time, but the blessed Giuliana had cured disfiguration and was therefore a saint worth talking to.

The dyer's wife stayed a long time in the public chapel. A mirror of itself, its two halves were separated by a wall and a range of small iron grilles. One door was for the nuns; the other opened to the street. No one side could really see through to the other, and the movement of veiled figures behind the ironwork appeared as mere shadows from another world.

It was close to heaven for Mona Grazia: to draw a veil not only over one's face but over an entire existence. It was her greatest wish that Flavia be taken into the convent while her bodice was still flat on her chest. Returning from Santa Giuliana, she would demand that Maestro Bartofolo put their daughter upon the mule and deliver her to the abbess without delay. But the dyer had different ideas. Unlike Mona Grazia he had accepted his child's face with the fleeting dismay of a housewife who finds her pudding burned on the crust but otherwise edible. He wanted Flavia thickening her thumbs on the stirring stick, not soaking up the cold of a chapel floor.

It should have rested there; but Mona Grazia was a stranger to rest, and what she did not have, she could not share. She mixed the altar dust with holy water and pinched Flavia's nose as she drank its bitterness down. In between ever greater ecstasies of cleaning, she wept and raged at the hapless dyer. Her eyes, which had once been clear as emeralds, grew as dull as a dead fish.

Just after Flavia's eleventh birthday, her father began walking out into the woods every evening, returning hours later with torn sleeves and blistered hands. He did this for months, pausing only in the coldest frosts. The following spring saw them all traipsing down past the hemp field and the little hedgerow where Alfeo set his bird traps. From there they turned onto the stony mule track. When the track ended, Maestro Bartofolo led them into the woods, swiping at the nettles and holding back branches for Mona Grazia with a low bow.

The dyer pretended it was an adventure, but Flavia did not like the way the trees looked down on her like a gathering of priests at a terrible confession. When she saw the walls of the Casa Nascosta, black with rain, no prison could have looked grimmer.

Maestro Bartofolo said they were moving there because the other villagers complained about the smell of the woad dye. Flavia did not believe him but it did not matter what she thought. There was no going back. When Maestro Bartofolo wanted company he went to his brothers' houses or the tavern at Avigliano. Pia saw her village friends twice a week and on feast days. As for Mona Grazia and Flavia, they rarely went as far as San Fortunato. Life was the Casa Nascosta, the workshop, and the woods. Few invitations were made to their home, and strangers were more likely to come there by chance than design. That was how Mona Grazia preferred things. If the dyer's wife had been as wealthy as a duchess she would have built a castle of towering walls and thick oak shutters to keep Flavia hidden. In the island world of the Casa Nascosta, she had the next best thing.

* * *

The day before the wedding and Flavia has the taste of ashes in her mouth. Mona Grazia made her drink down a full cup of watery altar dust and she is still grimacing from its bitterness.

Summer is burning itself out and the leaves are mindful of change, but the sapping of green to russet has no place among the preparations. Flavia counts at least five different sauces being stirred and sipped. At the table Zia Modesta scoops the sunny yolks from a pile of boiled eggs while Zia Nuta mixes a bowl of goats' cheese and raisins to fill them back up again. Mona Grazia cuts almond dough into the shape of angels. There has never been a feast at the Casa Nascosta. At first Mona Grazia said no and the dyer did not strike a stick against his wife's reluctance, but he leaned on the door for as long as it took, and because Maestro Bartofolo is a patient man every last pinch of spice and spoonful of sweet preserve is now being emptied into this one day.

Standing in front of a small mountain of herbs, Flavia stares out at the courtyard. The steaming hides have gone, as have the racks of drying cloth and the stacks of firewood. Some of the thornier shrubs have been uprooted from the boundary, though the trees are as thick as ever. Tommaso and Maestro Bartofolo spent the previous week sawing tabletops from a trunk of ash. They are now set out in a square, laid with dried bouquets of yarrow and cornflowers. In the middle stands a little bower woven from beech saplings, where Pia and Tommaso will reign over games and dancing.

The workshop itself is almost empty. The barrels of sheep's piss have been moved into the woods. The dyer says only a thief with a wooden gullet will be able to steal them without losing his dinner. There is just a small vat of oricello cooling for Maestro Bartofolo's cousin. Ever morbid, Zia Elissa has weeping ulcers on both legs and a mind to be buried in a bright purple cape. Though the rest of their customers will wait, Zia Elissa brooks no delay.

Flavia cannot remember a time when steam wasn't coming out of the vents in the workshop roof. She does not like her hands busy with sugared treats when they should be strangling water from a length of wool, and her body is playing such tricks on her she wishes for nothing more than an hour stirring a dye into its settled shade.

Last week there was a strange tightening in her chest when she watched Mona Grazia embroider a string of poppies round the collar of Pia's nightgown. It was there again when her aunts came to weave ribbons onto the pillowcases. The older women seemed to be sharing a secret among themselves, stitching and sewing in tacit silence. Watching them from the corner of the room Flavia's heart flickered in time with the candlelight, but if she imagined herself a bride in that moment it was against her will. Mona Grazia once said there are only two parts to womanhood – before marriage and after marriage – and she already knows that neither of these belong to her. She has lived over seventeen winters, two more than Pia. Tomorrow her sister will marry Tommaso, and when all the guests have drunk so much they cannot tell the night sky from the ground beneath their feet, the pair of them will lie together on the oak bed where Maestro Bartofolo's father once held the young servant in his age-slackened arms.

Flavia can only hope the product of their love will be as ugly as Alfeo.

As soon as the herbs are chopped, Flavia takes them across to her mother, who makes a sound like a punctured pig's bladder and says there is not enough rosemary for the ham. Since her cousins came, Mona Grazia has slackened her grip on

Flavia, and there is barely a murmur as she slips off to fetch some more. Hurrying through the courtyard, Flavia almost knocks Maestro Bartofolo off the stool where he is perched tying honeysuckle vines round the top of the bridal bower. Recovering his balance, he tuts with mock dismay.

'Careful child. If I go crashing through this thing, your mother will not help me pull the twigs out of my backside.'

Flavia forces a smile to her lips as she walks through the sickly smell of blossom and round the back of the workshop. Everyone is so cheerful it is almost a relief her mother isn't stringing daisy chains around her head and singing 'O Rosa Bella'.

Pia is the worst. All day she has been practicing dance steps, jumping and clapping to invisible minstrels with flaring skirts and a maddening smile on her face. While everyone else stirs, plucks and grates, Pia simpers among them with idiotic questions. Should she loop her wispy brown locks into a knot or leave them woven with star flowers? Should she wear Mona Grazia's silver brooch on the collar or the shoulder of her gown? And how on earth will she get through the bassa danza without tearing her new slippers? Flavia can easily imagine introducing a fist into her sister's face if she has to hear any more about ribbon lengths and toe loops. Then Pia will have to sit in her bridal bower with a swollen nose and know what it is to be stared at for the wrong reasons.

'Hello Flavia.'

She starts as Tommaso leans out of the sprawling fig tree. With no man's work to do, he has been sent to gather fruit. Flavia peers into the basket and stifles a giggle. Small hard figs are mixed with those that are full to bursting, their juices summoning wasps from miles around.

'Do you think this will be enough for Mona Grazia?'

Tommaso shakes the basket around and thumbs through the hopeless fruit, squirting more juice through the weave before licking his fingers with delight.

'Oh,' Flavia grins. 'I think we can do even better than that. I'll help you choose some more.'

As they pick together, Tommaso talks happily about the lute player walking all the way from his home town as a gift from his guardian. Flavia largely ignores him, concentrating instead on finding the very worst figs the tree has to offer, until Tommaso peeps through the branches that separate them.

'I am glad you'll be my sister, Flavia.'

She stares back at him through the leaves. Tommaso's smile is broad and buoyant. Eyes that usually trail around after Pia are settled warmly on her face.

Suddenly she feels very sorry for making him pick the wrong fruit, and for all the little slights and shoves she has given him, just because on the day he first arrived at the Casa Nascosta he made cow eyes at Pia when she brought him warm milk and began following her around like he had a bell upon his neck and she a bucketful of grain.

'Thank you Tommaso. And I am glad you will be my brother, for I have none living now.'

It surprises her, how easily these words are spoken. How she might, if she tries very hard, catch sight of a life after tomorrow. When Tommaso has had his fill of the oak bed he might just notice when she saves him the best cuts of meat and makes ointments of sorrel juice to clean the dye from his hands.

As Tommaso picks the last of the useless figs, Flavia grabs a few good ones and puts them on top of the basket.

'There,' she smiles. 'And if Mama sends you for more,

I will come picking with you again, and we shall find some better.'

Grinning, Tommaso disentangles himself from the tree and snatches Flavia up, his arms full about her waist as he lifts her from the ground and plants a kiss on her cheek.

His lips are dry like the crack of stale bread at communion and it is over in a moment, but the kiss sends a thrill to every nerve in Flavia's body. From ice to fire quicker than any gulp of sloe wine. As she flies into the air her stomach flips over like a fried *crespella* tossed from its pan just before it burns.

There is only one thing to do. As soon as Tommaso puts her down she kicks out, not seeing but feeling her foot make contact with the edge of his thigh. She turns clumsily, knocking the basket over and sending the fruit flying into the dirt. As she runs, the figs balloon and burst beneath her feet.

* * *

The empty workshop is the safest place. Maestro Bartofolo is still wrestling with the honeysuckle so Flavia creeps low to the doorway and darts inside. Ducking under a table, she draws her knees up to her chin and buries her face.

Once before she crouched like this. Last summer when Maestro Bartofolo cut his hand slicing through a cow's hide and dripped more blood than the crucified Jesus over the church altar. Then she ran into the woods and hid for hours, not daring to move until her father came looking for her with his hand strapped tight to his chest.

This is different, but the heart-thudding change from something normal to something strange makes her press against the wall with eyes and guts squeezed tight. The kiss and the kicking of Tommaso make her cheeks glow redder than cochineal, and she lets out a low groan as her mother stalks into the courtyard calling her name. Mona Grazia is better than Zio Anzolo's prized hunting dog when it comes to tracking her eldest daughter.

Springing up, Flavia walks quickly over to the bubbling vat of oricello. She grabs a stick and begins to stir.

'What are you doing in here?'

Her mother is already in the doorway. She looks even more shrunken than usual, her neck sloping seamlessly into her arms with scant interruption for shoulders, her hands bunched under her apron. Every part of her seems to be dribbling earthwards like a candle making its passage down the wick. Flavia is surprised to find herself in a moment of pity; then Mona Grazia's eyes form their usual glaze around the curve of her chin.

'Flavia!' Her mother's bark belies her melting features. 'Stop that at once! You must help Zia Dolce shorten Pia's skirts so they won't catch on her heels when she dances.'

She speaks with the urgency of a deathbed summons, as though a finger's breadth on the length of Pia's wedding gown will bring the whole day to ruin.

Flavia squeezes the stirring stick between her hands.

'I was just making sure the dye is smooth, Mama. Cousin Paola is coming tomorrow and she will want to know when her mother's wool is to be ready.'

'Paola will not be interested in household matters at Pia's wedding feast!' Flavia swears the steam is coming as much from her mother's ears as from the vat, but she can hear Tommaso talking to her father in courtyard and she cannot face walking past him.

'I just want to tell her the oricello is deep like Zia Elissa wanted it, and that her cape will look very pretty when it's finished.'

Tommaso's voice fades away and Flavia lets out a long, slow breath that sends ripples across the surface of the dye.

'You will not be seeing anyone tomorrow, Flavia.'

The stick seems to double in weight as Flavia blinks up. Her mother's gaze is still on her chin.

'But they are all from the village. They have seen me before.'

'Not all of them,' Mona Grazia sighs and shrinks a little more. Her fists are tight beneath her apron. 'There will be people who have never seen you, Flavia, and who cannot be expected to—'

She cuts her words in half as Flavia jams the stick into the vat, sending a spray of purple up the wall.

'I could wear my veil!'

A bitter compromise. Her voice is louder than she wants it to be.

'No, Flavia. The veil is for prayer or confession. Put that stick away now, and fetch Pia's gown before we lose the day.'

Her fists are two white bulges behind the apron. For a moment Mona Grazia looks straight at the bird. Just long enough for fear to chase the anger from her eyes. The fists come together, a conjoined bulge of hand-wringing, as the dyer's wife silently begs her daughter's mark not to fly clean from her cheek and peck away this narrow day of happiness.

Mona Grazia leaves the doorway but the light she was blocking does not come back. Flavia does not move for some moments. The stirring stick squeezes up against her thumb, forcing the prickle of a splinter beneath the nail, throbbing like an old quarrel. She stares into the purple oricello as it stills, and does not flinch from the reflection as it settles.

Her image sharpens in the middle of the vat. Slowly she dips a finger and thumb into it, drawing out a liquid pinchful of dye. It slides warmly and without hesitation through her outer skin. Again she plunges a hand into the vat, taking in more colour until the stain is deep. She lifts a finger to her face and smears it evenly across her good cheek. Peering at her reflection she giggles at the bruised symmetry.

There are no thoughts to this action, or what follows. As though a skilled puppeteer holds command over her limbs, she takes a large bowl from the work table and scoops up as much of the oricello as it will hold. Next she clambers onto a stool and takes one of the hogs hair brushes from the top shelf. Pulling her cap low over her brow and wrapping her apron around bowl and brush, she hurries out of the workshop and through the courtyard, into the bustling *sala* and up the staircase.

By the time she reaches her bedroom her heart is doing somersaults.

She sets everything down next to the chest. The wedding cassone, Pia calls it, as though it is a great painted thing to be heaved by servants through paved streets while people cheer the bride to her grand new home. The lid sits back on its hinges, revealing a stack of linens and clothing that Mona Grazia has been collecting since her second daughter was born. Flavia begins laying them out on the bed. Thick woollen stockings, plain undershirts, lace-trimmed handkerchiefs. More than one daughter will ever need. Soon there is no more room on the bed so she spreads the rest on the floor. She smooths out the pretty nightdress with its poppy-edged collar, the pillowcases with their trailing ribbons. Finally she takes out a pale yellow gown, light summer wool with green embroidery twirling across its bodice. Pia's wedding dress.

Everything laid out in front of her. A lifetime of wifely pleasures in clean, pressed cloth.

Flavia picks up the paintbrush and begins stirring it around the oricello. She watches her hands, thumb-thickened and hard-wearing. So far she has mostly used them for good. Apart from the odd shove or slap, she has kept them away from stains that cannot be cleaned.

She starts with a plain linen square. Resting her right wrist on her free hand, she dabs the paintbrush into the middle of the cloth. The dye speeds along the warp and weft as she makes a series of curved strokes. In seven movements it is finished.

A meaning of a shape. The ink, slower now, creeping unevenly through the cloth.

She tries again.

With each new attempt the brush moves more fluidly and the lines are cleaner. After the smaller pieces are finished she kneels on the floor. The nightgown sucks up a lot of oricello and more drips onto the boards beneath, but she is pleased with how it looks.

The light starts to shift long shadows around the room but Flavia's eyes bore through them. When every piece of Pia's cassone has been anointed, she spreads the skirts of the wedding dress across the floor and traces a finger over the green embroidery. She crushes the fine hogs hair bristles into the grain of the dye and stirs again. The final sweep of the brush goes all the way from the bodice to the middle of the skirt, using the last of the oricello.

She stands back to look at it. The unmistakeable mark bleeding deep and wide. Even Mona Grazia will not be able to

scrub them out in time. Every last piece of her sister's wedding chest now carries the purple stain of a bird in flight.

The best one is on the dress itself. It has no mistakes and
looks ready to fly right out of the bodice and through the window. It won't, of course. That is the beauty of it. Flavia would
marry Tommaso in that dress or any other but her sister will
not feel the same, and though it is very quiet in the room,
somehow she knows that when she turns around Pia will be
standing behind her.

She takes her time, picking up the bowl in her skirts and
fussily rubbing the hem of her apron around the outer lip. She
squeezes the brush to stop any drops falling. She hums as she
does this.

When at last she turns, Flavia makes sure there is a smile
on her face.

Pia's hair is strewn with white flowers and her face is
empty of blood. Her mouth is a tunnelling pink 'O', shaped
for the sound that would like to come out of it. A shout of pri-
mal woe.

Taking one last look at the flock of birds still seeping into
the floorboards, Flavia's lips tremble as her gut kicks into
helpless laughter.

3

Perhaps Mona Grazia was praying to the wrong saint.

Santa Giuliana may have cured disfigurement, but Margherita da Cortona understood it better.

Margherita was born in a little town to the west of the city. Wilful and reckless, her faults were forgiven through the sweetness of her face and the blush of her rosebud lips. Few were surprised when she entranced a young cavalier from the neighbouring town. Seduced by his declarations of love, she ran away with him and lived as his mistress for nine years, until the day the cavalier's hunting dog came home covered in blood and whining for the dead. Margherita followed the dog to find the body of her lover in the nearby woods, his purse gone and his guts ripped wide open.

Few would have guessed it then, but the cavalier's murder was a blessing for Margherita. She now regretted the perfect features that had torn her from the path of Christ. Freed from her adultery, she decided to make amends. Poverty and chastity were not enough to right the wrongs of her former life. Impatient for time to wither her looks, she took a razor and gashed at her nose, cheeks and lips until the sin of beauty was cut from her face. By such deeds did she set herself on the course of sainthood, because no woman can be called holy who stirs the loins of her confessor. If Venus plays midwife to a girl, her choice is twofold: to be consumed by her beauty and greedy for adulation, or to scour it from her face and free her soul from the mirror's measure.

But Mona Grazia never called on Margherita, and Flavia has made no prayers at all since the day before the wedding.

* * *

It is often hard to tell night from day in the Casa Nascosta but the chill is as telling as any hourglass, and the woodland birds have not yet woken when the dyer's wife walks into her room. Barely awake, Flavia peers through the gloom as her mother pulls undershirts, stockings and aprons out of the chest and stuffs them into a sack before walking back out without a word.

She scratches the crust of sleep from her eyes in disbelief, because her mother never puts anything anywhere without brushing, pressing and folding it first.

'Flavia.'

Her father's voice.

Rolling onto one side she scrabbles around the floor for her clogs then clatters through the dark to feel for her dress on its rafter peg.

Maestro Bartofolo is in the passageway with a candle, his face watery yellow in the blackness. The crisp tang of urine that always hangs about his apron is strong in the still air and Flavia blenches as he holds out a woad-mottled hand and places it over hers.

'Finish your dressing and come downstairs. Alfeo will be here soon.'

'Papa?'

Maestro Bartofolo's hand tightens; the calluses on his finger pads interlock with her own.

'He is to take you up to Santa Giuliana. They are expecting you.'

The cold flaps into the open back of her dress.

'Are you joking, Papa?'

Maestro Bartofolo looks back at her, his eyes as round and pale as his face.

No, not joking, it is too dark for that. But the idea of stepping up to Zio Alfeo's cart and stepping down in a place she has never been before is so ridiculous she wants to laugh as she did when Pia found her ruined cassone. That time it did not stop until Zia Modesta shook her so hard her fingers left two trails of black marks up Flavia's arms.

'The convent is a place close to your mother's heart.'

His voice is weary.

'She believes life with the sisters will be good for you, that you may come to learn their ways. And perhaps, even if you find no great goodness within you, you may come to imitate goodness so well that no one will know the difference.'

'Am I to become a nun, Papa?' Flavia bites at the inside of her mouth against a swell of panic.

'Dear child, no.' The crescent smile fills Maestro Bartofolo's cheeks and Flavia has to stop herself burrowing gratefully into his piss-soaked apron.

'You will serve the sisters and spend as much time in prayer as your knees allow. At Christmastide I will speak to the Abbess about your return.'

There is something tight in his voice as he says these last words. The same as when he said they were moving to the Casa Nascosta because their neighbours did not like the smell of woad.

* * *

She is used to dressing in the dark but her hands are shaking so she can hardly loop the buttons through their catches, and the plaits she twists into being are lumpy and uneven. As the shapes in the room get clearer, her eyes fall on the outline of her old sack doll, the last one Zia Caracosa made her before they came to the Casa Nascosta. It is very ragged and squashed. The smiling face Zia Caracosa stitched is faded almost to nothing and the arms are hanging by threads, but she has slept curled around it every night since Pia's wedding. She tucks it down the front of her dress and goes over to the window.

In the blue gloom a circle of light makes its way up the mule track. Flavia watches it turn towards the house and thinks of Christ carrying his lantern to light the world, but it does not feel like a saviour is coming through the trees.

Below, the huddled voices of her mother and father set her heart into wild rhythms. Alfeo's yowl of greeting is followed by the scrape of the door. The voices start again, still huddled. There is no more time to think before her father calls up the stairs.

All three of them are waiting in the *sala*. Pia and Tommaso are not yet awake, thankfully. Her sister has not spoken to her since the day before the wedding. She twists her head so much to avoid looking at Flavia it is a miracle she hasn't fall down the well. As for Tommaso, he runs through his brief range of facial expressions, and because none of these are bitter or angry he seems much the same as usual, but few words come out of his mouth and he makes sure never to be alone with her. Flavia avoids him too. Her chamber is above theirs and the noises that come through the painted birds tell her he has made a proper wife of her sister.

Mona Grazia pours out three bowls of warm milk. Alfeo slurps noisily, Maestro Bartofolo softly. Flavia sits on the other side of the hearth and let hers cool. The taste of broken sleep is on her tongue and her stomach is the size of a walnut.

She watches her mother walk over to the cupboard and take out the one thing she hoped never to see again.

'You are not to startle the good sisters of Santa Giuliana or make them question God's charity by removing your veil in their presence.'

Mona Grazia holds up her old straw hat. It has a new square of cloth stitched along the brim with two pieces of thread for tying around the back of her head. The material is thicker than the old veil and as stiff as her own two plaits.

Flavia stares at the tallow features that look ready to slip off the end of her mother's face. Alfeo drains the last of his milk noisily as she waits for the sunken eyes of Mona Grazia to meet her own, but they are fixed to the floor so she snatches furiously at the hat and pulls it on. Mona Grazia is now a little bent shape made of tiny squares where the warp and weft of the veil parted company. The shape moves closer and Flavia feels the edge of a small paper package pushed into her hand.

* * *

They are outside. Maestro Bartofolo leading the way and Alfeo behind. Through the courtyard, past the garden and the straggling fruit trees. Now into the woods, silent except for the swaying of trees and the leafy rustle of unseen creatures. Above their heads the branches knit at jagged angles.

The mule track seems shorter than usual. In no time at all they are out of the trees and into a grey morning light. The sky is covered in clouds and a light rain patters on the sacking over Alfeo's cart. Here the view from behind the veil isn't so bad. Flavia can see the line of the road stretching into the valley, the

sleepy rooftops of San Fortunato behind them. She squeezes
Mona Grazia's little package deep into her skirt pocket, wish-
ing herself small enough to crawl in beside it. So much time
has been spent running for open ground. Now the finger is
pointing her out of the door and she cannot breathe for fear.

Alfeo loops the reins over the horse's neck. The thump of
its hoof sends a sudden wave of terror through her. She looks
back to the woods with the fearful longing of a rodent who
has lost sight of its burrow. Digging her clogs into the mud
she fights the urge to scurry back up the track.

Maestro Bartofolo holds her elbow as he helps her into
the cart.

'At Christmastide, Flavia.' The words sound steady but her
father keeps his head close to his shoulders and she knows it
is not the cold that makes him turn quickly back towards the
Casa Nascosta.

* * *

Every part of her is as taut as a minstrel's bow. Only her ears
are open to the steady dig of the horse's tread and the rolling
creak of the cart. She feels the expanse of sky above her head,
the heavy clouds that threaten to suddenly lose their cargo
of rain. As they move further away from the Casa Nascosta
she begins to sneak glances from under her veil at the layers
of landscape, from roadside bushes to twisting fields hedged
by poplars and the rise and fall of stumpy olive groves. The
fading folds of countryside meander like rucked cloth. The
hills are shy behind the mist but their ridges are visible,
comforting.

Alfeo does not say much. Apart from pointing out the
occasional eagle he limits himself to extended forages around

the inside of his ear with the nail of his little finger, which Flavia suspects he keeps long for this purpose.

They have not yet covered many miles but every one of her bones is jolting against its neighbour as the cartwheels meet the rutted road. She digs her elbow into Alfeo's ribs and makes him pull to a stop. Stretching her legs to the ground, she walks over to the verge, lifts her skirts and squats down. The long grass tickles her bottom and she shifts further up the slope, loses her balance, and puts a hand down in the puddle between her feet. From the cart Alfeo giggles and Flavia curses him.

It is only a week since the wedding but autumn already feels like a torn curtain and the wind needles uncovered flesh. Her straw hat is wrong for the time of year and she has to keep one hand on her head to stop it whipping loose. Even Alfeo has sense enough to keep his hood pulled over his flattened head as he steers round the worst of the ruts.

Further north the landscape is uglier: full of brutal little shrubs and brown fields stripped of crops. A few peasants trudge along with packs of grain on their backs, their faces set to the road. The houses they pass look empty, though the tap of a bucket against a well and the occasional shout to beast or wife speaks of habitation. Occasionally a pillow-flattened face appears at a window as the cart labours past, but most of the reapers sleep the sleep of the dead, nestled in clean straw as they dream of empty fields.

They make another stop, at a turn where the road meets a steep hill track. Here Alfeo loosens his teeth on a crust of rye bread before wandering off to throw stones at a group of crows pecking at the last of the crops. Flavia unwraps a piece of cheese that Mona Grazia left for her. It stinks even more than the goat that made it but she is hungry enough to gulp it whole without breathing. Afterwards she walks a little way up the ridge, where a small roadside shrine is decked with sprigs of yellowish flowers. Behind an iron grille, set deep into a stone column, sits a painted statue of the Virgin.

She was here once before, years ago. It was the furthest she had ever been, with Pia and Mona Grazia and Zia Dolce. Alfeo had been missing for two days on his way back from the city, and while the men of the village searched, the women came here to call on Santa Maria. It was the only time Mona Grazia ever said a really short prayer, but it worked all the same because Alfeo turned up the following day with a crooked grin and a lame horse.

The Maria behind the grille has straight black hair and pink cheeks, but sometimes she is blonde and pale like the wall painting in the church, or brown-haired with chestnut skin like the village banner rolled out at Eastertide. Flavia does not know which is the real one, but they all look very pretty, and she likes the painted smile on the shrine Virgin, even if she does have a chip on her nose. Pia always liked the blonde one above the altar. She prayed to her for clear skin.

Flavia stares at the terracotta-coloured hole where the paint has flaked off the shrine Maria's nose. She has had barely a moment's regret for the oricello birds on her sister's wedding cassone. Empty of penitence said Mona Grazia and she was right. Not even when she learned how her father led Pia to the bridal bower, hastily stitched into Mona Grazia's best dress, her face all puffy from crying. Lying on her bed as the guests ate and sang, Flavia was light as air. Careless of punishment or forgiveness and happy to know herself now beyond any comparison with those two little boys chasing their wild boar.

A monster after all.

When the cart sets off again each turn of the wheel brings a new distancing. As the miles tick past Flavia starts to feel very cold, and understands why the children of her cousin Zuana fell into a deep sleep whenever Zuana's husband got drunk and beat her with an iron hook, because it is pointless to stay awake, shivering and worrying, when sleep can take it all away. Leaning into Alfeo's shoulder, she closes her eyes and lets the world dim and drift.

PART TWO

'Eyes must be big, full, not concave or hollow, as hol-
lowness makes for a proud look, while fullness makes
for a beautiful and modest look.'

Firenzuola

4

All around, darkness.

Somewhere close by a bell clangs. Once, twice, then a stop. Then again, quieter. Not regular but plaintive, a weakening cry reviving and fading.

The air is bitter and the top of her nose hurts on the inside. When Alfeo lifts her down she is not sure if she will stand or fall. Her legs are two wooden props and unless she plants them in exactly the right place they will fold in two. Sleep drunk and shivering, she hangs on the edge of her uncle's cape. Perhaps he has forgotten about Santa Giuliana. Perhaps she is back home with the empty cart and an island of trees just ahead of her.

But the chimes don't belong to San Fortunato.

She lifts up her veil.

A black stretch of wall.

It rears out of the darkness like a hillside breaching the night fog, a reluctant gate set deep into the stone.

Beyond the brim of her hat the moon comes and goes through slow-moving clouds.

Alfeo raps hard on the gate. She is glad he doesn't call out.

Leaning against the edge of the cart, Flavia hopes the wall will not open up for her. She pretends the rustling of skirts on the other side is just the flap of her veil in the breeze, anxiously fooling herself until the gate shutter flies open and a candle-coloured face is pushed into the frame.

'Yes?'

A stern voice, deep, but not a man's. Alfeo makes a few nasal squawks, flapping his cape as he gestures towards Flavia and looking a bit like Mona Grazia's prize rooster. A series of rattles and slidings and the wooden frame swings out. Flavia shrinks back behind her veil as the gatekeeper steps out of the wall, plucks her by the sleeve and pulls her inside. There is barely time to grab her sack of belongings from Alfeo before the gate is slammed hard as if the devil had come to beg a drop of cream.

More rattling of bolts and locks. Flavia peers back through the open gate shutter at Alfeo, his brown face lost behind cloth and gloom and his rotten teeth giving no further clues. All that remains is the scent of mashed willowherb and a garble of vowels that make up a question she has no answer to.

Because when will she come back? At Christmastide? That didn't sound right when her father said it. Now time has fallen over itself and she is inside this other wall, in a place beyond reach of Mona Grazia's prayers and altar dust. She thinks of her mother's sunken eyes and the way her father turned quickly back up the mule path, the oricello birds on her bedroom floor and the winter's darkness on a summer day.

A sneer burrows its way out of the terror and weariness. She leans into the opening and whispers.

'Zio Alfeo, the day I come back to the Casa Nascosta is the day I enter your bed as your loving wife, so be sure to kick the goat out of it first!'

A herb-scented titter shoots from Alfeo's mouth as the gatekeeper nun leans across and closes the shutter. More keys are turned and the candle is swept away.

* * *

A big square room with pitted tables and a hearth big enough to sleep in.

The gatekeeper nun walks over to the remains of the fire and begins scraping around the bottom of the stockpot. Without asking, Flavia pulls out a stool and slumps down.

'Your veil. Take it off.' The nun's hand moves in a sideways motion, the way Mona Grazia pushes Pia's hair from her eyes when it comes loose.

Flavia pauses. Her father said obey the nuns, her mother said to keep herself hidden.

'You will not need to cover your face at Santa Giuliana.'

She draws a quick breath, fumbles with the cord around the back of her head.

The hat falls away and she looks at the square face of the gatekeeper nun, who regards her steadily, without approval or disgust.

'Our walls are thicker than cloth,' she turns back to the stockpot. 'The sisters will get used to you.'

Less exhausted, Flavia would rather climb down a well shaft than take her supper from such a formidable figure. The richness of the nun's gown is terrifying in itself. Maestro Bartofolo says black is the hardest colour to make because any variation in the dye will make it look dusty and worn, yet this nun bleaches the night sky by comparison. If she ever came by chance to San Fortunato the villagers would think death itself had marched out of the underworld.

The beans are dry and overcooked, but Flavia rattles the spoon around the bottom of the bowl until the gatekeeper nun takes it away from her. Again she is on her feet, back into the night and moving from stones to earth as they head towards a low grey block.

The cold softens a little as they step inside, merging with the drowsy air of penned animals and stalls thick with manure. She is pointed to a ladder resting against the edge of a loft shelf.

'You will not need a candle for this part.'

Because the gatekeeper nun looks like she is about to pluck, pull or prod her again, Flavia moves quickly to the foot of the ladder and begins to climb, one-handed with her sack clasped to her chest. Finally she swings herself onto the shelf and peeks back down.

The nun nods briefly then takes the last of the light with her.

* * *

It is cooler up here and draughty where the roof tiles part. Flavia scrambles to her feet, immediately banging her head on a low beam and falling heavily on to her knees.

Several groans erupt nearby, followed by a curse as rich and ripe as the stall floor excrement.

'I'm sorry,' she whispers. 'I was trying to stand up.'

'You don't stand, clay brain, you crawl,' comes the slurred voice closest to her.

Miserably she shuffles on hands and knees in the direction of the voice until she touches the edge of stuffed sacking and her nostrils fill with the smell of night breath. Several dark mounds are wrapped tightly in a single blanket. None of them make room for her so she creeps sideways onto the sacking with her knees and elbows hanging into open space, her cape pulled tight around her. Suddenly she is very glad she has Zia Caracosa's doll squeezed between her undershirt and her dress. As the dark mounds shift and settle behind her, she presses her head into the rough cloth and wraps her arms round her middle, trying to breathe without making a sound.

It is so dark she could almost think herself home, but the noises tell her she is not. Picking apart the silence, layers run in and out like rats through straw – there one minute, gone the next. A splash of water and the creak of a stone wheel; nearer by, the slow pad of feet at watch. There are chimes too, not the plaintive toll she heard earlier but a confident strike that is made when there is news to be told. And over it all, a buzz of something immense, a distant swell of life.

The voice of the city.

Shivering under her cape, Flavia sidles further into the mattress until her back is pressed against the flesh of her neighbour. Though she never hugged Pia in the coldest nights she would not mind being bundled into thick warm arms now, not to feel the space between herself and what she knows quite so wide.

Then it comes. Out of the darkness and through the broken roof tiles. Not a cry or a laugh, but an instrument, plucked, its notes tumbling softly through the air. Flavia lifts her head a little. A tune she has never heard in church chanting or village carols. No composition of nature either, though it is closer in melody to the woodland birds.

She strains to hear it, a silvery thread running high above the music. A single voice, gently curling itself round the plucked strings before soaring into a high and perfect note.

5

The loft is empty when she wakes up.

A musty light. Petulant rain spits through a hole in the roof, flattening the carpet of straw. In clouds her breath rises to the rough underside of the tiles. To the front of the loft is the beam where she struck her forehead: an ugly stretch of cracked knots just waiting to hit someone with the force of their own blindness. Laundered undershirts drip from an upright post; a scuffed leather shoe with a missing strap hangs wearily from a nail.

Her marked cheek was pressed into the pallet when she woke. She hopes they have not seen it. Whoever they are.

She has some of the blanket over her now, a coarse serge bearing the stains of a sumptuous incontinence. Flavia throws it off. Sitting on the edge of the pallet, she roots through her little sack, more for comfort than anything else. Careful not to crack her head again, she goes over to the drying post and uses one of the undershirts to wipe the mud stains from her dress. A washing bowl is on the floor and she plunges her hands into its oily water. Cold droplets run down her forearms as she smooths it over her face, tracing the seams from her nose to the corners of her mouth, pinched with distaste. She rewinds her plaits.

'Did you see her Madalena?'

A voice, down in the barn. The one who called her a clay brain last night. A bucket thuds to the floor and Flavia's hand closes tight around the end of her plait.

'Looked horrible.'

The second voice is like the first, full and thick as ripe cream.

'And that dress. If that's what northerners wear they're as mad as a bucket of frogs.'

'What can you expect from people who build houses on a lake?'

Laughter, and the spurt of milk hitting the side of a pail. Flavia creeps over to the edge of the loft and peers down. Below, two heads press into two cow bellies, the nearest one eclipsing a low-backed undershirt and semicircle of bronzed flesh mottled with dark moles. Flavia leans forward until a groan in the loft floorboards sends her darting back to the pallet.

'Clay brain, that you?'

The ripe voice of the servant called Madalena is followed by a twofold snigger as the wind whips through the broken tiles.

Flavia keeps quiet.

'Must've been a rat then. Skinny one, with freckles.'

More laughter and renewed spurting.

Flavia crawls further into the eaves. After a few more sneers the girls carry on talking as if she is not there. She leans stiffly against one arm until they have finished and the spurting sound is replaced by the scraping of barrels outside.

At the back of the pallet is her straw hat. The brim is bent and the veil has come partly loose. She picks it up, pulls the outlying threads through her fingers. Then she remembers Mona Grazia pushing the paper package into her hands while the milk grew cold. She rummages around her skirt pocket and pulls it out. On the front, two lines intersect in charcoal. Flavia's heart beats faster as she unfolds the paper, wondering what Mona Grazia has given her to guard against fear and doubt in her new life.

The paper flattens out to reveal a pinch of grey altar dust.

She begins to cry. Not prettily like Pia does, dipping her head as her shoulders tremble. When Flavia cries it is like a pig with a knife in its throat, loosening such streams of mucus that Maestro Bartofolo says it is a pity the alchemists cannot spin it into gold, for he would then be as wealthy as the Duke of Spoleto. She wails so loudly she does not notice when a woman's head pops over the top of the ladder.

'Good God child. Is it your wish to bring a flood onto the poor beasts below?'

Startled, Flavia wipes her nose on her sleeve and looks into a pair of eyes even more bloodshot than her own must be. A frayed knot of hair perches on a face worn like Mona Grazia's though not perhaps rubbed up against the same bitterness.

'Suora Benedetta wants you working.'

'Suora Benedetta?' Flavia speaks down at her hands, sensing the woman's eyes on her mark.

'The gatekeeper nun. She says your father is a dyer. Handy with a pestle?'

Flavia stares at the indigo stains around her knuckles and shrugs a nod.

The sky is paler now the rain has stopped. Flavia keeps her cloth cap pulled well forward so only her swollen nose can be seen. She keeps pace with the worn-faced woman, who gives her name plainly and does not call herself Suora. Susanna is not dressed in the rich black robes of Suora Benedetta. She wears a short jacket and a blue striped skirt, patched around the hem, which is short like Flavia's and shows her ankles as she moves.

They leave the rough ground around the barn, their clogs clipping in unison through the archway to a large courtyard. Flavia steals glances at the patchwork stones, bigger than the Casa Nascosta but less tightly knit, the gaps between them sprouting ryegrass. An open shutter reveals a dust-covered floor and the flicker of a rat's tail disappearing behind a sack of grain. Further along, a staircase leads to a covered walkway looking over the courtyard, its ledge lined with potted flowers. Small windows are cut into the upper wall and several voices float through them, clear and precise, as though the speaker has given thought to both content and delivery before setting their tongues in motion.

'You won't see much of the choir nuns at this time of year,' Susanna glances up at the windows. 'They play games in their cells, or warm their slippers in the parlour. You will not tend them either, they have their own servant nuns.'

They round the edge of the building, away from the flowers and the clean floating voices. Flavia moves more freely as they leave the courtyard and pass once more into open ground. Shy glances to the left and right yield layers of information: the crumpled vegetables and string beans limp on their canes; browning fruit trees in a stony orchard. Pictures of a new world, each one margined by the edge of her own cap. Another boundary, beyond everything else, is the wall around the convent. It meanders alone or joins the surrounding buildings before coursing doggedly onwards, a seam of moss at its lower edge like the hem of a skirt dragged through a swamp.

At a place where two corners meet is a single-storey building whose sagging shutters lend it a sleepy, demoralised look.

Susanna leads her inside and Flavia's nostrils are immediately stung by a mustardy heat. A tall nun comes towards them and she lifts a cautious glance to a sweat-soaked face as crumpled as her robes.

* * *

The dispensary is a stuffy room, crammed with thick-bottomed jars and glass vials smeared with different coloured oils. It is like a smaller, much messier version of Maestro Bartofolo's storeroom.

For the first time Flavia feels the knot in her stomach loosen a little. Though her shoulders ache from scrubbing at years of grime it is good to feel the yoke of work again. She can hear Susanna and the dispensary nun in the next room. Sometimes they come in to rattle among the shelves. Suora Dorotea is haphazard and constantly drops things but Susanna is calm and quick, her hands moving deftly among the curing herbs. When she sees Flavia unafraid to scour her hands with sand and stone she gives her a faint smile. Flavia is almost sorry when she tells her to go and get her supper.

Alone now, she finds her way over to the kitchen. She eases herself quietly through the doorway, trying to keep as far as possible from the grey figures of the servant nuns who dart between tabletops and steaming hearths with fretful lines on their foreheads.

A bowl of something thick and inelegant is thrust into her hands by one of the nuns. Flavia finds herself a stool near the waste bin. She dangles her feet and watches the sisters work. Occasionally one of them shoots her a look before turning away quickly, as though she has seen something by accident. These looks are worse than the village games at San Fortunato, when the boys chased the girls with muddy sticks and tried to prod their arms and necks. If she was hit then, a splinter might jab and break loose but that could be pulled out. The eyes of the grey nuns are harder to get rid of.

She takes her bowl and wanders outside.

The light is beginning to fade. Behind the kitchen a shallow incline leads up to a section of the wall where the roots of a poplar tree make little steps in the soil. Folding over the back of her skirts to make a cushion, Flavia perches on the thickest one and spoons the rest of her supper into her mouth. At the bottom of the bowl is a chicken bone which she snatches up. Sucking hard on the joint, she draws her knees up to her chin and looks to where the branches of the poplar arch over the wall. She runs her teeth around the bulb of the joint. From the dining hall come the sounds of a gathering over warm plates and laughter that is not like that of the village, where peasants wheeze and spit out their mirth.

Flavia's ears are usually covered by her cap. Pia says it is better that way because they twist at the tips and poke between her plaits when her hair is greasy. She would not be without them though. Sitting on the poplar root in the evening light they are open to everything. The noises of the grey nuns from the kitchen, the voices in the dining hall, the creak of the miller's wheel behind the wall . . .

The sound of a door clicking open.

She peers into the gloom. To a place where the back wall of the cloister makes way for a small door.

A sly turn and the slap of an iron catch, swiftly muffled as though a hand has been pressed against it. Not the way the gatekeeper nun opens and closes things.

There is nothing for a minute or so, and Flavia wonders if her ears are playing wanton tricks on her because she opened them too much. Then, very slowly, the panels of the door shimmer and narrow as it swings open.

* * *

A solitary figure. Slow like a night hunter, slender shoulders moving side to side. A cloak of dark blue trails behind slippered feet. The hood is drawn forward and rucked in places, outlining the shape of piled hair.

Glued to the shadows, Flavia holds her breath as the figure walks to the outer wall and takes a small object from its pocket. A flicker of light strikes the blade before it plunges into the stones, scraping from side to side. The crut-crut sound of a woodland bird at mating time.

The knife comes out of the wall and gloved fingers take its place, slowly easing a square block of stone out of the wall.

Flavia does not move. There is a belch of food and fear working its way up her throat, and she is not well hidden in the poplar roots. Her throat quivers and she burps quietly into her lap.

The figure leans into the place where the hole is made.

She is too far away to hear, and can only watch as the head disappears into the hole. Any words spoken through it are buried in the wall but she does not dare move except to shrink further into the roots as the head re-emerges.

The figure stands for a moment, both arms braced against the wall. The hood of her cape seems to tremble though the air is still.

A striking of bells from the chapel. The voices from the dining hall grow louder and somewhere above them a shutter is unlatched. Quickly the figure returns the stone to the wall then stoops to the ground, gathering a handful of dirt and pressing it around the edges.

The cloak swings back into the gloom.

* * *

The bells are for Vespers, but it is well past that hour when Flavia dares to move from the poplar roots.

Like the Casa Nascosta, it is easy to find it once you know it is there: a squarish block the size of a small dinner plate. The mortar round it is hollowed out, a deception of dirt squeezed into the cracks.

Still as winter rime, she presses an ear to the stone and listens for sounds from the other side.

Nothing.

She takes a twig from the ground and jabs it around the edges, loosening the dirt until the stone begins to shift. The moon is building by the time she takes the weight of it in her arms and sets it down.

She crouches, wary, knowing that a hole can work both ways.

Fingers scaling the stones like a thrifty abacus counter, she creeps up until she is level with the opening.

If there are eyes staring back from the other side there is no light to them.

She pushes her head further in. The edge of the hole peels at her cap and grazes her chin.

Through the gloom, an empty dirt road. It merges into cobbles that rise in an ambling see-saw, sprouting a row of small houses either side.

The beginning of the city. Rolling outwards and upwards.

Her eyes scale the rooflines, stopping here and there at

houses bigger than the whole of San Fortunato. She had not realised that buildings could grow in layers, like olive trees on a sloping terrace. Great blocks of stone with flag-bearing towers cast a proud gaze on the houses below, as if to say that these smaller dwellings belong to the hedgerows and not their world.

There are lights too, the pallor of stars, far brighter than the sickly tallow of home. And over it all, the murmur of life coiling into the night sky: fervent and ceaseless.

* * *

It is almost dark. The edges of the hole press coldly into her cheeks but she does not want to go back to the loft and the girls with their tough words and fleshy backs. Her eyes bore through the gloom until they ache. She is shivering from something stronger than cold. Squeezing her hands under her armpits, Flavia keeps her face to the city and tries to imagine who among these black and grey nuns has cut her way through to the other side.

6

Just before Flavia moved to the Casa Nascosta, the priest gave a lesson to the village children. Sitting in the shade of the church wall, he called one of the older boys to the front, gave him a long stick and told him draw a circle in the earth. The boy readily dug a channel out of the packed dirt, his country brow thick with concentration. When he had finished the priest told him to find the end of the circle.

The boy stuck his finger into the earth and swept it round and round. The other children were asked to try, but they could not find it either. Flavia pushed her way forward and stared very hard at the circle, because she had seen the boy start and finish it, so there must have been some way in and some way out. But eventually she too gave up.

Then the priest said to them: imagine how long it will take you to find the end of this circle, because that is how long you will burn in the inferno if you live an impure life and do not repent of it when your season on earth is finished.

It is one of the few lessons Flavia remembers. She thought of it as she circled the woods of the Casa Nascosta. She thinks of it now, tight within the wall of Santa Giuliana, because that has no end to it either.

* * *

A pattern has emerged. A life of sorts.

The loft dwellers get up first. They light the fires in the kitchen, ready for when the servant nuns come to make the choir nuns' breakfast. Wracked from early prayers, it is dangerous to cross the grey nuns first thing in the morning and Flavia always makes sure her fires have good kindling at their heart.

Most of their work is overseen by Suora Benedetta. The gatekeeper nun is sturdy as a Roman bridge. Barking orders, she puffs out her cheeks until the hairs on her upper lip stick out like porcupine quills, then unleashes a barrage of commands at whoever is nearest. Susanna says that if Suora Benedetta had not had the misfortune to be born a girl she would have done well for herself as a captain of soldiers.

Flavia works most days in the infirmary, where she is firmly ensconced as chief pounder of mustard seeds and peppercorns. It is busy now the thin winter air creeps into the marrow. She helps Susanna and Suora Dorotea pack poultices for rheumatism; for frostbite they make ginger tisane and pastes of dried mullein flowers. Flavia sometimes leans over Suora Dorotea's shoulder to her Book of Common Ailments, full of recipes written out in the sister's spidery mess of a hand. It is proudly bound in calf hide and stamped with an image of Santa Giuliana holding an apple, because the sainted healer Hildegard of Bingen said cooked apples were the first treatment of any sickness.

Though the priest at San Fortunato taught her and Pia a few words it is impossible to read Suora Dorotea's scrawl so Flavia just copies Susanna, who spins recipes out of her head and knows how to cure a sickness before the patient even knows they are ill. Susanna is less frightening than the nuns and much nicer than the rest of the servants. Flavia

wishes she could sleep in the infirmary with her instead of
Madalena and the others, with their thick ropes of hair and
their words of spite. But Suora Dorotea only lets Susanna
stay there because her lungs are too weak for the freezing
loft.

There is another pattern at Santa Giuliana. One that has nothing to do with the infirmary or any of the tasks that pop into
the head of Suora Benedetta.

It belongs to Flavia and the hooded figure who opens up
the wall.

It does not happen every night.

Sometimes Flavia waits for hours and sees no one. Sometimes she arrives just as the figure disappears back into the
cloister. The shadows grow colder each time, and sometimes the frost glows on the branches. Still Flavia sits and
waits.

The figure always leans against the door, as if to seal up the
convent behind her. Then she walks smoothly to the same
place in the wall, slippered feet punching the hem of her
cloak. The flick of the knife before it dives between the stones.
The gloved hand resting on the lip of the hole, then stretching
all the way inside – the way Flavia used to stretch through the
arrow thin window on dead summer nights. Then the hooded
head disappears into the hole and there is a shivering around
the shoulders as though her breath is quickened by urgent
conversation, though Flavia is never near enough to hear
what passes between the figure and whoever must be standing on the other side of the wall.

Sometimes the hood wavers when it retreats from the
hole and the figure bends itself forward, a faint moan shivering in the air. Flavia is frightened then, especially if the

moon is full because creatures that are not of God's making stalk the earth at such times. Crouching in the poplar roots, she shrinks into herself, her sleeve gripped tight between her teeth. Then the rage that makes the figure a stranger to this world seems to melt. The monster tucks itself quietly away and Flavia unclenches her jaw.

Afterwards she sits in the cold and thinks about Tommaso. Sometimes she sees him dressed in a shining gold cape and armed with a sword, like the one Ser Aldo has strapped to his saddle when he rides along the road. She imagines Tommaso coming to the wall, a basket of ripe figs in one hand and a broad smile on his cheeks. Climbing skillfully over the top, his calf muscles flex as he jumps down. He will take her hand then, and draw her close, and this time she will be ready, and not kick him or run and hide under a table.

7

Alfeo smiles behind the grille. His gums host even fewer teeth than before. Those that are left are as rotten and stumpy as trees in swampland. In his hand is a leather strap. Attached to other end of it is a disgruntled goat.

'Empty bed now?' Flavia sneers.

The goat has a wad of dried excrement attached to its tail.

'You should call it Pia.'

Alfeo laughs. He holds his breath, pushes his stomach out until it swells his jerkin, and begins waddling around holding his back.

'Got even fatter has she?'

Alfeo leans over, miming great heaves from his gullet.

'Eh, eh.' He clasps his hands together in a rocking motion and draws his lips into a slurping noise.

Flavia feels her own stomach shrink as Alfeo spits a wad of chewed willowherb into the grass.

'What does my father say?'

Alfeo shrugs.

'Nothing?'

Another shrug. Alfeo mimes the sweep of the stirring stick.

'You should go.' Flavia's voice is cold as she signals to Suora Benedetta to close the shutter.

'Ai!' Alfeo calls out as it is brought to bear on him, jamming a small square envelope through the gap before the bolts are driven home. Flavia snatches at it but the gatekeeper nun is too quick.

'I know your uncle is not to be trusted with word of mouth but there are no secret notes at Santa Giuliana.'

Flavia sullenly presses the envelope into her palm. Behind the closed gate, Alfeo's feet crunch towards his cart.

Scratched on the front of the envelope are the two inter-secting lines. Mona Grazia's cross.

Suora Benedetta tears open the envelope and a small pinch of dust is taken by the wind.

* * *

'Firewood?' Flavia asks sullenly.

'Christmastide decorations,' sniffs Suora Benedetta. 'Not that we need any more.' She pushes open the chapel door and Flavia peers inside, blinks, and peers again. The outside world has been ushered in. Branches of holly and several small pine trees are strewn among other greenery, covering the altar and draping the pews. For a moment Flavia thinks the woods of the Casa Nascosta have followed Alfeo up the valley.

'You have a little time before Vespers. Arrange it as well as you can. The abbess will not be satisfied until she is reading psalms from a treehouse.'

She is a long time dragging round the cuttings, pulling them awkwardly down the nave as holly and pine needles stab at her face and neck. She sets the little trees upright against the stone columns and hopes they will not fall on the choir nuns' heads during the Vouchsafe, O Lord prayer.

She feeds ivy cuttings through a wooden partition along the side wall before straightening the Virgin's berried wreath, which has slipped down over her eyes. With a bunch of left-over twigs she sweeps up the fallen needles, gathering them into her skirts as she goes. She has almost finished when the door swings open and one of the choir nuns marches in with a train of novices, their white headbands tinged yellow from the lamps. Flavia stands as still as the Virgin. Apart from Suore Benedetta and Dorotea she has avoided the black nuns as much as possible. She creeps behind the partition of laced ivy and lets the pine needles drop quietly from her skirts.

One by one the others come in. They take their places either side of the altar on benches rising in tiers to the chapel walls. The grey nuns are there as well, but they sit apart from the others, further back where the candles are less regular. On a high bench sits a group of young choir nuns, each of them very pretty, with pale skin that glows like a polished coin. Their habits are made of smooth wool and trimmed with brooches that catch both the light and the disapproving glare of Suora Benedetta. They look like angels in spite of their dark wings.

Flavia has not stared at anyone for a long time. Like Mona Grazia she usually lets her gaze fall and dig itself into the dirt. Now, though, she cannot stop herself. As the young choir nuns tilt towards their prayers, Flavia thinks she could happily sell both thumbs for half of their grace.

The murmurs die out and the chapel stills. The shadow of the priest settles behind the public altar on the other side of a narrow grille in the wall. As he chants the Gloria, the little novices turn to their prayer books, anxiously searching. The candles dance to the words and the nuns' voices rise in an indifferent tune. More words come from behind the grille, more fingers search for the right place on the page.

The handle to the chapel door turns from the outside.

The fingers stop searching and all eyes go to the late arrival. From behind her screen, Flavia pokes out as far as she dares.

The dark blue cloak of the figure from the wall.

Her hood hangs deep over her head, just a brief flash of white as she turns to close the door behind her.

She does not creep like a latecomer. As she makes her way towards the benches her cloak swings nonchalantly around her slippered feet. Despite Suora Benedetta's glower she walks at a gentle pace, shoulders moving in a familiar prowl. When she reaches the altar she does not lie down as the nuns do. Pausing in front of the black and grey rows, she fingers a strand of stray ivy trailing from the rafters before taking a seat in the first row beside a startled-looking novice.

The psalms have begun again. The nuns turn back to their readings. The latecomer turns and whispers something in the novice's ear, then reaches across and takes hold of her prayer book, gently easing it from the girl's hands and settling it on her own lap. Patting the novice gently on the knee, she folds her hood up over the top of her hair, and turns her face to the heavens.

She is not like the other choir nuns. Their light is soft. Clouds and cotton sheets. This creature has a hard light, marble and glinting gemstone.

There is a name for this colour. Candida. Pure white. Bright enough to attract the moths from miles around.

Her skin is not the only thing glowing. There is also the sheen on her flush-red lips and the strands of pale auburn hair falling around her shoulders, coiled as tight as the screw of an olive press. Her cloak has no ornaments. It doesn't need them. Flavia has seen damask samples from Maestro Bartofolo's guildmaster, but nothing like these leafy swirls against the sateen weft of deep blue.

The woman's eyes stay closed until the end of the Gloria. Then they roll open, brilliant and blue with a great black wolf stalking through them. They move along each row, coming to rest on the pretty young nuns and their clustered brooches. When one of them returns her glance and looks quickly away, the red lips curl in triumph and Flavia wonders if this truly is a creature of night-time transformation. Change seems to run through her. If a hymn is dull, she sits with the stolen prayer book on her lap and barely opens her mouth. But when the tune wakes she snatches it up, her voice so clear it scales the air until there is no ceiling between earth and the angels.

Singing or silent, she is a revelation of beauty. It does not seem possible she belongs to a world of people who sweat and burn and itch. As Flavia stares, a painful admiration runs through her chest. Eventually she has to turn away, slumping back behind the screen and onto the floor. She wants to shout out, in joy and fury, because what she has seen has brought her both. Now she realises: Mona Grazia will never let her go back to the Casa Nascosta.

The time for her return will be shifted back to Eastertide, Michaelmas, someday, never. The grief of lost boys flies across Flavia's face. Whether she holds that face to the sky or the woad vat, her mother will never hang up her scrubbing brush and set her feet upon the hearth. More than that, she can never return because of the thing that sits and sings so perfectly among the choir nuns. If someone so flawless can be walled up inside Santa Giuliana there is no hope for anyone else. The cripple or halfwit, the girl with the bird on her face: they will stay here, locked away from the world until age shrivels their deformities and a little patch of earth is picked loose for them in the convent graveyard.

A Recipe to Make the Face
Look Youthful

Take two ounces of acqua vitae; bean flower water and
rosewater, each four ounces; water of water lilies six
ounces; and set it in the sun for seven days. Strain it
through a fine linen cloth. Wash your face with it in
the morning, do not wipe it off.

Gilia la Bella I

They were expected. Her father and his new wife, first on a boat and then by road – and all of it a distance she couldn't begin to imagine. Jacopo said it was better he kept her in the north but Gilia had an idea of Ghostanza Dolfin ever since she sent her a present of tiny glass beads, each with a little flower closed up inside it. Antonia threaded them into a necklace and said only the fairies could make such a thing. Jacopo's wife Ricca frowned at that and said fairies were fallen angels and subjects of the devil but Gilia thought they were probably just lost and a bit rascally.

There would have to be a wedding feast. The same as when Ricca came to them from Foligno with her brothers and her father and a donora of two thousand florins (she is not supposed to know this last bit but Antonia told her because she was the one who undressed Ricca on her wedding night, and Ricca was crying and saying she would have preferred the florins went to Santa Giuliana so she could live there and not have to marry Jacopo or anyone else). Ricca was a poor bride for all her wealth, said Antonia. Pasty as uncooked dough. Gilia laughed at that, and had to be shushed, Antonia tugging her sleeves up a little too hard so they chafed at her armpits. Still, it had been a good wedding feast (though Jacopo said how would she know) and there should be another one now because that was fair.

At least Antonia was with her. She had spoken to Alfonso and the others in the kitchen and they had promised to make it nice with pheasant capelletti and zanzarella and melon tarts, even if they were only five at the table. Jacopo said she could wait for them to arrive in the courtyard though Ricca wanted her rested. Gilia scooped up Parassita before he could change his mind and ran to her favourite bench next to the pink and white rosebush. Parassita wriggled all the way and had to be held by the neck and the bottom. Jacopo huffed after them a little while later, and tried to sit on the bench but was just as fidgety as Parassita so took instead to walking around the courtyard, tapping his stick in the dirty bits between the stones and looking every few minutes at the large gate that led to the street. Her brother was sweating a lot because the sun was right on top of his head and he was wearing his smart winter doublet.

Gilia sat for a long time with Parassita stretched out next to her and tried to look right. She had her best dress and her beads and the silver brooch her mother had left her – Ricca said she must wear that to 'make it understood', though she did not say what was supposed to be understood or who was supposed to understand it. She smoothed out her skirts and crunched her curls and wondered how she was supposed to be. Parassita was happy just lying on her side and licking a curled paw but Gilia didn't want to be found that way when they arrived. The kitten looked up when the bells of the Chiesa del Gesu rang out though she was used to them by now and no longer ran under the rosebush when they struck.

Jacopo turned to the sound of the bells and said, 'not now, they will have broken at Assisi most likely'. He looked annoyed and pleased at the same time. But then there were hooves and shouts from the other side of the gate and Jacopo didn't look annoyed or pleased any more, he looked scared.

They ate the capelletti and the melon tarts and the zanzarella broth – they were good but only a small bit of Gilia's stomach had room for it. Jacopo drank a lot of wine and got red in the face, which was interesting because he was sitting next to their father's new wife and she was whiter than frost and it was hard to imagine the two of them now mother and son. Ricca looked at her plate a lot and Gilia thought that was a shame because her father's new wife was beautiful and a plate was just a plate. Her father clearly agreed because he stood up in a wobbly way and said something about his Ghostanza being a legend of emeralds and water that he had dreamed of for a long time and Ghostanza smiled a bit and Jacopo went even redder. Her father couldn't see very well because his eyes were teary, so nobody except Gilia really got to enjoy how beautiful she was.

After they had all finished eating, or pretending to eat, her father wobbled up again and put a pearl ring on Ghostanza's finger. Ricca's face did something a bit strange and Ghostanza seemed to notice because then she said she had a gift for Ricca too and unwrapped a small square block of wood and passed it to her. Gilia craned to see it, though no one said she might. Ricca took the block as though it was a piece of dirty linen and held it away from her which meant Gilia could see the picture on it. It was a very young girl with wavy hair twisted into plaits. Her clothes were white and there was a pimpernel tucked over one ear.

'Who is it?'

Gilia had not meant to speak. Ghostanza looked straight at her and Jacopo glowered.

'Is it the Virgin?' Ricca blinked at the painting.

'Of course it is not the Virgin!' Ghostanza laughed. 'It is me in my youth, perhaps a little younger than Gilia is now.'

Ricca put the painting down on the table. Gilia leaned in front of her and stroked a finger along the bottom edge where there were small letters in black.

'That is the name of the artist,' said Ghostanza.

Gilia paused at a small line of gold swirls at the bottom edge of the portrait.

'You can read that, surely, a clever girl like you?'

A slow swivel of the head. Her father smiled and said what was the point of it and she thought Ghostanza would laugh again like she did at Ricca, but instead she looked sad and a bit angry. She pushed back her chair and came to where Gilia was sitting then she leaned over and took her pointing finger, lifting it from word to word.

'It says: Inside and outside. Only beauty.'

*   *   *

Antonia was not there when she woke up. She did that more now, left a candle by the bed then went away sometime after Matins to lie on her pallet. Gilia had told her not to. She always woke in the hours between her dead sleep and her morning sleep, hungry or thirsty or sometimes just frightened of so much silence and herself alone in the middle of it. Parassita was gone too, most likely curled around the embers of the kitchen fire, dreaming of mice.

She lay for a moment, staring at the wood panelling of the ceiling above her bed, trying to decide if she could bear the cold floor between herself and the little supply of biscuits Antonia kept in the bedchamber cabinet. She still had her bead necklace on, the petals of the little flowers each locked in their own shell. She put it in her mouth and sucked on it. The candle made shadows in the panelling and gave shape to many things. A swan, his neck long and curved, a great eye in a woody knot. Faces too, the dead saints her mother had loved. Agata behind the bars of her cell, Apollonia in the flames. Santa Lucia was Gilia's favourite, flying sideways between panels on her way to heaven.

The beads were slippery in her mouth. She pulled them out looked over to the cabinet with its biscuit stash.

'Antonia!'

Best to shout it. A nightmare yell to bring her maidservant scurrying. She popped the beads back in, tried to suck them into something sugary. Santa Lucia looked down at her, the grain of her timber face twisting into a smile.

The footsteps were long in coming. Soft too. Antonia must be barefoot because her clogs could wake the dead.

Then an oil lantern in the doorway. Except it wasn't Antonia, and there wasn't a lantern. Just a candle in front of a stark white face.

Ghostanza sat down on the end of her bed. She had a lute in her hand, a big-bellied black thing with strings down its middle, fine as hair.

'I call him Ibn Yunus,' she rubbed her sleeve across the lute's belly. 'Do you sing?'

Gilia shook her head. Antonia used to sing some funny-sounding carols until Ricca decided they were not Godly. Her mother sang, Jacopo said, but she couldn't remember how that sounded.

Ghostanza's fingers wandered the black neck of the lute.

'Back home, the sky would be ablaze with torches at this hour,' she said.

Her lips were glossy in the candlelight and when she started to sing they stretched in a circle so her mouth was a dark red hole.

'Poor Cara Rossina ... Forced to marry her ancient suitor ... On the night of their wedding she did take her looking glass ... And crush it into a thousand pieces ... In her husband's wine she sprinkled the glittering dust ... In the evening he died, in the morning she was hanged ... Poor Cara Rossina.'

When the song was over Ghostanza put the lute back on the bed. Gilia reached over to the smooth darkness of it, catching a fingernail against the strings. They sent a noise across the room and the walls gave it back to her once. She glanced up at Ghostanza, expecting her to be angry, but she was hunched on the edge of the bed, still, with her face pressed into the palms of her hands. Gilia watched her a while but Ghostanza did not move at all so she wriggled out of the sheets and up beside her and cupped her own hands together, bringing them close to her face until they covered every part of it.

She breathed in slowly, feeling the suction of skin against skin. When she took her hands away Ghostanza was looking at her.

'Give me your arm.'

It wasn't a question. Ghostanza reached for Gilia's wrist and pulled up the sleeve of her nightshirt.

'Look.' She pressed a finger into the flesh between Gilia's wrist and elbow and watched the mark disappear as quickly as it was made, the flesh rising back to its proper shape.

'So young,' she said. The red of her lips was smeared either side of their outline, making her smile look sad.

Gilia didn't know what to say. She wasn't as young as Parassita, but she wasn't old like Jacopo and Ricca, and she certainly wasn't ancient like her father.

Ghostanza pulled Gilia's wrist to her face, holding the palm of her hand just under her nose as she breathed in.

'Summer flavours,' she said.

8

An idle day. Madalena's bronze shoulders mirror the sun as she draws a hoe along the soil. Under the flowering peach trees a group of choir nuns sit in a circle and read aloud the rude bits of Boccaccio. Their cloaks are strung with cornflower chains. Some have taken off their veils, letting their hair slide free from nets and clips.

Flavia watches them. Leaning against the wall of the infirmary with a stalk of long grass, she grips the root between her teeth and sucks in the pulp. In the orchard, two of the nuns get up to dance, their pointed shoes lifting in wide arcs as they circle each other.

Flavia slaps at a fly perched on her forearm, annoyed at the distraction. Since that evening in the chapel, she cannot stop looking at the choir nuns. She has even learned how to walk with her head up, copying Susanna, who always wandered through the cloister with her haggard face and striped skirt and did not care at all. Flavia cried long and messily when Susanna went home to the city, her lungs finally clear enough to brave the damp of her home. Suora Dorotea cried too, because Susanna was close to witchcraft in her curing of illness, and now she only has her scrawled Book of Common Ailments and Flavia's pestle to help her.

The nuns in the orchard finish their dance and fall laughing against one another. Flavia laughs too, just to see if she can make the same tinkle of bells, but her 'huh' sounds like a pig in rutting season and she stuffs the grass stem back between her teeth. One of the nuns glances towards the infirmary before turning back to her companions with a loose swish of black hair.

Flavia is used to this. She is entirely invisible to the prettier nuns. She could run naked through the parlour and the ivory needles would not slow in their embroidering twirl.

The choir nuns brush each other's capes for loose grass. A cluster of wide eyes and thick lashes, little mouths folded into a trim pout, brows clean as snow. Flavia would have thought each of them perfect if she has not seen that candida face tilted to the heavens. These women are not the meaning of beauty. They belong to the world of carved frames and silver brooch settings: a lovely thing that is made to display what lies at the centre.

La Perfetta.

Flavia lets the words roll around her tongue like warm honey.

La Perfetta likes the orchard. Flavia has seen her sitting in one of the peach trees, her stockinged feet dangling, her flashing red hair held in place by a golden thread net. Her eyes everywhere at once: on the top of the wall; darting to a low grille where the waste flows out. Slowly she has drawn in the prettier choir nuns. They respond easily, bringing her small bouquets from the flower garden tied with hair ribbons.

She does not dare look at La Perfetta as often as she looks at the choir nuns. Her eyes are sharper, more wolflike, than theirs and her beauty can be dangerous to watch.

La Perfetta isn't her real name. It is what Susanna called her when Flavia asked about the figure in the dark blue cloak, though Susanna didn't say it like it tasted of warm honey.

She has other names, depending on who you ask. Suora Benedetta calls her La Veneziana, the Venetian, but Madalena calls her La Strega, the witch. Flavia has never met a Venetian or a witch, so that information does not help her.

In any case, La Perfetta's real name is none of these things.

She is Ghostanza Dolfin, and she arrived at Santa Giuliana shortly before Flavia. She brought with her three enamelled chests and a host of rumours. A new widow, she lives among the choir nuns but has not taken their vows.

She never leaves the convent.

Suora Dorotea probably knows more than anyone else. For three days now she has been tending Ghostanza Dolfin after she tripped and injured her wrist. Ever since then, the dispensary nun has barely been seen. One of the grey nuns has been sent to come and help Flavia, who tries unsuccessfully to follow Suora Dorotea's messy Book of Common Ailments. Fortunately there is only one patient in the infirmary: an ancient, leathery-skinned nun who is reluctant to cross the eternal threshold before which she has long been hovering. Flavia washes her wasted body and combs her dandelion white hair. She finds it soothing, even more so when the leathery nun is unconscious and entirely in her hands, a flaccid kidskin to be washed and wrung, dried and tended until it is a thing more beautiful to be behold. Then she forgets everything, even the glaze of La Perfetta's skin and the questions she wants to ask her.

* * *

'It is intolerable. Intolerable!' Suora Dorotea's shriek almost startles the leathery nun out of her stupor.

The dispensary sister is soaking wet. A keen tang of urine drifts from her veil and her face is blanched with anger.

'Is something wrong with Mona Ghostanza?' Flavia tries hard not to stare; it is not the first time Suora Dorotea has returned in dishevelment from a visit to La Perfetta.

'Not at all! Her wrist will heal sooner than her temper,' Suora Dorotea's hands shake as she tears off her apron, 'I have done my best to be certain of it. In any case, it will not be long before someone else takes charge of her care.'

The dispensary sister looks as though she would happily be laid alongside the leathery nun to enjoy a slow, gentle death.

'Here!' She takes a chamberpot from the shelf and thrusts it at Flavia. 'Tell Ghostanza Dolfin that the next thing to be thrown at Santa Giuliana will be herself, head first from the tallest window!'

* * *

It smells different in this part of the convent. The passage to La Perfetta's room is narrow and windowless and full of scent. Like the wild flowers that Pia used to put in their bedroom, but much thicker: a violent fragrance that pulses through Flavia's head. Jasmine and lavender, and others she does not recognise, flagrant as rich cochineal dye. Struggling for breath and balance, she wonders how anyone can live among such smells with no air to cleave it.

The passage is empty and dark except for the far end, where a curtain hangs slightly ajar with a narrow strip of light at its side. Flavia stumbles forward, her hands gripping the edge of the chamberpot so hard she thinks it might break long before Ghostanza Dolfin has a chance to throw it at her.

The smell is strongest here. Her eyes are watering as she raises a fist to the doorway.

The first tap gets no answer. She hovers, listening to the silence.

Another tap; another silence.

Her grip loosens and she takes two steps back along the corridor.

Then a rustle, and a low-voiced, 'Wait.'

Through the curtain the light is everywhere, piercing her eyes like cosmic plenty. Not the natural light of day, but the kind that must be made by man or God when everything else is dark: the great bonfire or the pocket of heaven that opens up on the night of San Lorenzo when stars charge across the sky.

There are dozens of candles on every surface, not tallow but clean white wax, more than the villagers of San Fortunato will burn in ten years. Through pursed eyelids the room begins to assemble itself. Glossy chests are ranged around the walls and piled high with cushions. At the far end of the room a canopied bed strains to support a mattress as thick as a tree trunk and so wide that the figure stretched across its centre seems to be drifting in a luxurious pool.

Flavia walks carefully towards the bed, stepping around broken shards of chamberpot and a bright puddle of urine.

The figure does not move. Her arms are spread wide, the right one strapped to a splint, the fingertips purple and puffy. White legs bend at right angles, sheets twisted around them, as though their owner is running from a nocturnal evil. She is dressed only in an undershirt, rucked up to her thighs. The bright red curls are tangled around her cheeks and neck; her eyes are open and fixed at the canopy above the bed and the shadow of her face stutters at the wall as one of the candles slips into its socket. If Flavia hadn't heard her voice she would think her dead. There is no rise and fall of the chest, no flicker of acknowledgement, no scramble to cover herself.

She moves closer.

La Perfetta's face is not as it was in the chapel. Then it dazzled and glowed. Now it is the colour of an invalid: pallid, not candida. There are small blood bursts around her nostrils and her eyelids are swollen, with smoke-grey crescents around the tear ducts. Lines too, from nose to mouth, a crinkle around the unsmiling eyes.

Flavia feels the outline of the bird pulsing on her cheek. She tugs at the side of her cap as the eyes of Ghostanza Dolfin snap sideways.

'Christ. What has she sent me?'

Her voice has no song in it now. Flavia dips her head towards the chamberpot. She wishes it were big enough to crawl into.

'Put it down there.' A purple finger extends from its strapping and points to the edge of the bed. Flavia ducks down and settles the pot, relieved that she will not have to help La Perfetta balance on it. Without straightening her back she stoops to pick up the broken pieces of terracotta, mopping up the puddle with the hem of her skirt.

La Perfetta watches her narrowly.

'Shall I leave you now, Suor . . . Mona Ghostanza?' Flavia stands with the broken shards wrapped in her apron.

'Leave me?' Ghostanza struggles onto her good shoulder. 'Am I supposed to live like a pig here? Or perhaps a strained wrist is considered no handicap in this house of cripples.'

'No Su . . . Signora . . . But perhaps Suora Dorotea is ready to come back now . . . '

'I'll not have that shrivelled fig in here.' A grim smile flashes across the white face. 'Though I imagine she is less dry since I gave her a dousing. How did she smell?'

Flavia blushes the same colour as her birthmark. Then she sees the challenge in La Perfetta's face, the long white teeth inching out of her lips as she waits for an answer. Clearly Suora Dorotea got a headful of chamberpot because she is drabber than a poor man's funeral. La Perfetta needs better entertainment.

'Almost as bad as sheep's piss.' The words are out of Flavia's mouth before they have talked to her brain; but they must be the right ones because La Perfetta lets out a shriek of laughter and flops back on the bed.

'And you would know, little *bruttina*,' the tousled head rolls back towards her.

Blushing still, Flavia forces herself to meet the mocking gaze.

'That disgusting mark of yours! Like a bird shat elder-berries on your cheek.'

Another peel of laughter. The legs wriggle gleefully, kicking the sheets to the foot of the bed.

Flavia stares at her.

She would like to say that these are filthy words – worse than sewer water served in a jewelled goblet – but she is caught in awe and shame and a strange sense of relief. No sighs or pitying smiles. No snatched glances and covered giggles. Ghostanza Dolfin has called her a donkey to her face.

The laughter dies as quickly as it came. La Perfetta lies still, staring at the canopy over her head. The sneer floats away from her face, leaving it as deathlike as before. Flavia waits quietly until La Perfetta's eyelids close and begin making the juddering, globular movements that happen when a person watches their own dreams. The rise and fall of the rucked undershirt and the sweating coils of hair speak of a slovenly, sumptuous spirit. Mona Grazia turned inside out.

For the Falling of Hair

Take the ashes of pigeon dung in lye and wash the head with it, also walnut leaves beaten with bears' suet restores the hair that is plucked away. Also the leaves and middle rind of an oak sodden in water and the head washed thorough therewith is very good for this purpose.

9

It takes less than two days with La Perfetta to understand why the servant nuns are frightened to come to her rooms, and why Suora Dorotea has not been near since the chamberpot christening.

Flavia watches in silence as she tosses the red brocade gown on a chair and walks to the other side of the room, spreading her skirts wide across the bench seat of a curve-legged table. Her hands wander among the pots and jars, more than in Maestro Bartofolo's storeroom, though smaller and prettier. Bone-handled brushes too, and harsh silver combs bearing strands of bright red hair. And in the midst of it all a wooden box covered with pictures of plump children with tiny wings running along a blue band of water.

'You may tidy in a moment.'

La Perfetta fumbles awkwardly around the items on the table, her strapped wrist pushing a square glazed pot towards the edge. If Flavia was at the Casa Nascosta she would have leapt forward to push it to safety, but she has already learned to do nothing without being told exactly how and when. Although La Perfetta's wrist is healing her mood is fragile as she waits for her stepson to send what she calls her 'proper assistance'. Besides, she has not given Flavia permission to touch anything other than the dressing on her wrist, and Flavia is almost as scared of these precious objects as she is of the woman who owns them.

For the first time she has been allowed into the small parlour just beyond La Perfetta's bedchamber. The oil burners
push their incense in here as well and the steam of riches rises
from everything. There are half-finished embroideries and
trinkets beyond counting: a large onyx ring set with pearls;
ivory hair clasps; a pair of golden dice. A lute, a creature of
ebony and stretched gut, is propped against a plump little day
bed. They must be doubly precious to La Perfetta because
each of them has a name. The dice she calls Da Lezze ('who
can ever forget a beautiful man?'), smiling to herself as she
rolls them in her hand. The onyx ring is Alessandro Gritti
('impetuous, lithe'). Guillot Bardou doubles as the ivory hair
clasps ('a perfumed wig and a tight pot belly'), while the
ebony lute is Ibn Yunus, ('tall as his ship's mast and black as
the pitch that held it in place'). At first Flavia finds it strange,
this christening of valuable things, but then she remembers
that her grandfather took the trouble to name Alfeo when he
is not worth two bent sticks and a tattered apron.

Even more stunning are the two pet birds La Perfetta
keeps in a large cage. These birds are not from the woods, or
the little noose traps Alfeo collects each morning from the
hemp field. One of them has a yellow face with blushing red
cheeks and long green tail feathers. The other is brilliant blue
with a black collar. The blue bird hops around excitedly about
when Flavia presses a finger to the bars, but the yellow bird
keeps its blushing cheeks close to its wing. Among the biscuit
crumbs on the cage floor are several glossy green feathers.
Both of them flutter on their perch when a patter of feet in the
passageway is followed by the sound of the pretty choir nuns
giggling outside the doorway.

Ghostanza grimaces as she stands.

'Tidy, don't steal.'

She walks towards the sound of the choir nuns, the same look of disgust on her face as when Flavia leans close to plump her pillows.

Flavia waits until Ghostanza has gone, listening to the sound of her and the pretty choir nuns fading down the passageway. When she is sure she is alone she moves closer to the red brocade gown on the chair. It is stronger and brighter than anything from her father's workshop. A city colour, not just plain-dyed but patterned with the shape of hares and hounds. No bleeding of one colour into the next. It can only be cardinal's purple, from the tiny chermiso insect: each little creature harvested from the oak tree where it gorges on sap. A hundred times more costly than the madder root Maestro Bartofolo uses. As for the yellow embroidery on the sleeves, this cannot be dyed by the weld plant, which turns sickly orange in candlelight. Only saffron makes the colour of the sun. Mona Grazia's whole store cupboard contains two wrinkled stems that she was given when each of her sons were born.

The scent of the oil burners makes Flavia sway and the cardinal's purple is just as strong. She cannot stop herself reaching for the gown. Softer than the peaches from their old garden in San Fortunato. She presses it to her breast and whirls in a circle as the skirts flare wide.

Flavia has never danced. Her legs are made for stomping from one place of work to the next. But she has watched Pia skip around the courtyard and the choir nuns circling and clapping. She tries a few paces, keeping a cautious eye on the doorway as her clogs strike the stone floor.

Something flashes across the room.

She skids to a halt, her arms spread wide. The red of the gown sways inside an oval surface nailed to the wall above the table. She drops her hands. Inside the oval, the redness folds over, revealing the tired grey threads of her day dress.

Cautiously she walks towards it. The picture in the oval keeps changing and she can plainly see her own stained hands clasping La Perfetta's gown, the faded bodice of her dress, the undershirt knotted tight at her throat, the ends of her stiff plaits. She only has to tilt her head and she will meet it properly for the first time: the thing Mona Grazia prayed every night to be taken away; the thing Tommaso saw close up when he kissed her.

She leans forward.

In the centre of the glossy oval the bird mark stares back at her.

It is stronger than she has ever seen it, in the river or leaning over the vats: a deep mottled purple that sprawls from the bridge of her nose towards her ear, taking most of her left eye with it. It lies flat upon her skin, the rest of which is bronzed and freckled and nothing like the candida gleam of Ghostanza Dolfin.

The eyes that stare from under her cap are different too. Mid-brown and hitched together by a frown, no hint of laughter in them. She tries to smile, but her eyes do not follow her mouth. They just make the bird do a funny wriggle.

Her hands twist around the gown as though she is wringing it dry. Only fear of Ghostanza stops her striking a fist into the glass.

She spins away. Looking for an empty space but horrified to find another face, stern as the devil and studded with eyes that peer from dark places.

A man in a black cap stands quietly behind her, like a nightborn incantation. The impossibility of his appearance makes her mouth open and close like a landed fish and she totters backwards, finds herself sinking into the little day bed. That too feels wrong. Her buttocks meet nothing but more feathers and she thinks she will slip right through them and onto the floor. She struggles to sit upright, pulls her cap down and peers around the edge of it at the same time.

Away from the glass, she is glad of her eyes again. What seemed dark and ungodly moments ago is not so frightening now she uses them properly.

His hair is straight and to his shoulders, the colour of dirty straw. Though overfilled, his brow is soft looking. The shortest of beards, blond then red as he moves between the parlour candles.

He looks down at her. The shape of the bird is still sharp in her mind but he is quite dishevelled and this calms her a little. Beneath the dusty cape his shirt is yellow from bad washing. He has no ornaments except a silver ring, worn deep into the skin of his middle finger. His face is gaunt and ruddy in places, differently moulded from the peasants of San Fortunato.

'How do you find my patient?'

The words are gentle. Like the priest of San Fortunato who speaks for God they are not for refusing, but Flavia is still too bewildered to know how to answer.

'Forgive me,' a slight bow, which she has no idea how to return. 'I am Maestro Vitale.'

He looks at her all the while.

'It is not customary, of course, my being here. But Ghostanza Dolfin has a talent for the unusual. I am certain that getting a physician to attend her, even in Santa Giuliana, is not the full extent of her skills.'

'Physician?' A dry-mouthed question, met with a nod.

'You are a servant here,' his eyes wander to the red brocade gown still in her hands. 'That is plain at least.'

He does not say it unkindly but Flavia scowls when she
replies.

'I am Flavia di *Maestro* Bartofolo, master dyer of San Fortunato. I have never seen a physician before and that is the
only reason you surprised me. Are they usually so dusty?'

There is a shape of amusement to his eyes and the beginning of a smile which Flavia does not trust.

'Never once?' he asks.

'I was treated by Zia Caracosa when I had a fever, and
Papa once went to see a woman in Avigliano when he cut his
hand, but then she was sent away for talking to toads.'

The smile broadens into a full laugh, exposing translucent
teeth which make the gaunt face strangely elegant.

'Well, I do not talk to toads. The occasional dog perhaps,
when I find myself sharing my supper in the marketplace.'

Flavia feels a little shiver of laughter in her chest, and
stares down at her lap. She realises she is still holding La Perfetta's dress. The physician looks at it too.

'It is not a crime to like pretty things, Flavia di Maestro
Bartofolo.'

She must be as red as the dyer's crushed chermisi.

'I am not made that way,' she snaps. 'Nature abhors artifice.'

One of Mona Grazia's sayings.

'Those are courageous words, considering in whose parlour you are sitting. I wonder what Ghostanza Dolfin would
say to them.'

Flavia opens her mouth, because Mona Grazia has a list of
truisms longer than a hermit's toenails, but Ghostanza must
have heard her name spoken because a murmuring of voices
from the passageway is parted by a sudden cry.

'Servant! Where is my Ornatrix? Ornatrix!'

A giggle like the clink of glass beads through the doorway.

Flavia turns a questioning face to Maestro Vitale. He is not smiling any more.

'It seems you have been chosen, Flavia.'

Still puzzled, Flavia makes to go to Ghostanza but the physician signals her to stay. He walks back into the bedchamber and Ghostanza's voice rises in a cry of surprise and takes on a songbird tone.

Flavia sits back on the little day bed. From across the room comes a flutter of wings and a keen squawk. The yellow bird with the blushing cheeks is on the far end of the perch, flapping its wings against the brilliant blue one. Undeterred, the blue bird briskly and methodically plucks out the remaining tail feathers of its companion.

PART THREE

'We like small feet, slender but not skinny, climbing neatly from the ankle. Homer said Thetis's were like silver. I say they should be white like alabaster if one were to see them bare.'

Firenzuola

10

Ghostanza was lying.

When she turned her song to the heavens the glow on her face was not the light of God. That face sits quietly in the square glazed pot on her dressing table. Cerussa she calls it. A dazzling white powder, brighter than the starch of a nun's headband against the veil. With water it becomes a smooth paste to cover the face, neck and hands. A face that can be worn at one time and not another.

Flavia peeps past the window curtain while Ghostanza settles at the curve-legged dressing table. Down in the garden a new flower bed is cut in two by a paved path and trimmed with neat box hedges. Behind it is the vegetable patch, where Madalena ploughs at a patch of bare earth, sleeves rolled up and knees to the sod. Ghostanza takes up the pot of cerussa, pokes around inside it, and puts it back down.

'The gatekeeper nun is quite wrong.'

She pulls her hair into a knot and peers into the looking glass, grimacing as she pushes the side of her nose flat to inspect a blackhead then swiftly evacuating it between two fingernails. Flavia moves away from the window.

'God is not affronted by a little colour. I shudder to think of a world where every woman looks like Suora Benedetta. Our very existence would be in peril, for men would find us so repulsive they would have to learn how to make babies among themselves.'

Flavia's cheek muscles tense as Ghostanza gestures for her

rabbit-fur mantle. Ghostanza's flippancy is just a few degrees
cooler than her anger, and there is never much warning of an
explosion. Recently she has become annoyed at Suora Benedetta, who checks everything that arrives at Santa Giuliana
and is grudging in passing on Ghostanza's packages to her,
each one carefully wrapped and smelling of a different world.
Flavia must be careful now. The dressing table is La Perfetta's
altar. Pots and brushes instead of the gospel and the cross.
She must not anger her high priestess.

Ghostanza flashes a brilliant smile into the glass then lifts
her upper lip to check the colour of her gums. She has slept
badly and the light is harsh but she insists on seeing the worst.
Like a warrior who favours his weaker arm in mock battles
before facing his enemies, she must know her flaws before
they are seen by others.

'Or am I wrong, *bruttina*? Perhaps there is a top for every
pot, a three-legged peasant back home who thinks you the
most beautiful thing he has ever seen?'

Alfeo's squashed features float into view as Flavia tucks
the mantle around Ghostanza's shoulders. She suppresses a
shudder but Ghostanza does not notice.

'Da Lezze, now there was a top. Maestro of the chapel of
the ducal basilica. He earned one hundred and fifty ducats a
year and borrowed the rest.'

Da Lezze of the golden dice. Perhaps that was why he
borrowed. And the others: Guillot Bardou, the ivory hair
clasps; Alessandro Gritti, the onyx ring? What tops were
they? Ghostanza never speaks of them, only the money they
earned and the things they gave her. As for her husband, he is
named in many of the parlour items: silver card boxes, pearl
bridles, a little games table and the silk cushions all carry the
name of Corrado Tassi, bounteous giver.

'Well, it is not important now.' Ghostanza unlids a large jar of pale ointment. 'Here, ornatrix.'

She thrusts a thin wooden spatula at Flavia.

'Smoothly, remember.'

Her voice grows tight as she stretches her neck and tilts her face to the ceiling.

Flavia loads the spatula and spreads thick swatches of the ointment across Ghostanza's face until just her nostrils are left uncovered.

She still does not know why Ghostanza calls her ornatrix, though she prefers it to *bruttina*.

Ghostanza, still tilted, upends a small sand-timer on the table. La Perfetta does not like to be disturbed when her mask is on, so Flavia hovers beside her for a moment, surveying the dressing table.

She has just about learned what everything is. The pretty leather box and its tools for removing unwanted hair and ear-wax. And all the pots and jars for lips, cheeks, hair, breast and hands; some for softening and some for scouring. There is veal suet for dry hands, which smells bad and has to be masked with perfume; oil of roses that smells good when applied to the neck but needs covering with powders to stop it looking like a patch of sweat. She recognises the brazilwood verzino that gives colour to Ghostanza's lips, and other shades she has pounded in the mortars of Maestro Bartofolo's workshop. Some of these make a salve Ghostanza calls fucus, an artificial blush to cover the cerussa. At first she gaped as Ghostanza awkwardly applied these layers with her good hand, demonstrating which brush to use, when to coat thickly or sparingly. The fierce training has had some effect, and Ghostanza appears almost satisfied at times, but Flavia is very far from a maestra of this strange new art and further still from understanding what it all means.

There is only one thing on the table she has not opened: the painted box covered with little winged boys. Out of all Ghostanza's possessions it is the loveliest. Minute brushwork details each eyelash on the boys' faces as they run along their stream; around the edges baby deer and strutting peacocks stop to look at them.

There is a gold-framed keyhole at the top, the key to which Ghostanza keeps around her neck. Whatever is inside, she guards it more carefully than anything else she owns.

As for her night-time visits to the wall, and the person she has cut her way to, that remains a mystery as well. Ghostanza has rarely left her rooms since she hurt her wrist and the only person to visit from outside the convent is Maestro Vitale. The physician came two days ago to change Ghostanza's dressings and restock a jar of mandrake juice for sipping when the pain is bad. Ghostanza wanted a stronger mixture of hemlock and vinegar but Maestro Vitale said it was too dangerous. For a moment Ghostanza looked angry, then she smiled with her eyes half closed and said she knew of an excellent tailor near the Porta Sant'Angelo who would make Maestro Vitale a new cape for nothing. She reached out her good arm and touched his hand as she spoke. Maestro Vitale's face went as taut as the hide of his bag. He left soon after, and Flavia, shyly lurking in the parlour, did not get to ask him what an ornatrix was.

'Where is the sand?' Ghostanza's voice is muffled beneath the salve.

'Halfway down.'

'Well hurry up, we only have three more hours to prepare.'

Flavia now knows that in Ghostanza's mind three hours is a very short time. Especially today. First she must clean her face with egg whites so the pastes that come afterwards spread evenly and do not clump together like cold butter on bread. Flavia is forever sneaking off to the hen house, taking care to hide from Suora Benedetta as she eases the warm eggs from feathered backsides. She takes six of them now, breaking the whites into a large earthen pot and beating in a spoonful of slippery mercury before putting it over the little parlour fire.

The sand timer is empty. She takes up the spatula again and shaves the ointment from Ghostanza's face, spooning the grey clumps into a saucer. La Perfetta's eyes are puffy beneath the glaze, but she seems happier now things are progressing and does not slap Flavia's hand when she accidentally drops a grey splodge on her lap.

When the mixture on the fire has thickened, Flavia soaks it into a cloth and takes it to Ghostanza's face, rubbing hard until the skin is red raw. La Perfetta says heat and coarseness are twin avenues to perfection. Like a master builder denuding and replastering the same stretch of wall, her skin must be peeled and anointed over and over again. So it is today. An hour more scraping and scrubbing before Ghostanza Dolfin declares herself ready for reconstruction.

'You see, I am now a *tabula rasa*, a blank slate.'

Ghostanza looks in triumph at her shaved eyebrows. Her plucked hairline makes for a high forehead as white as a goose egg. The mirror glows back with a spectral face: none of life's pleasures or hurts written on it.

Flavia spoons a little cerussa into a cup. Its creamy blankness glows in the candlelight as she adds water.

She begins to stir.

This is the part she loves most. A blush of magic as the powder becomes paste. More exciting than the crust of Christ's body on her tongue when wheat becomes flesh.

Ghostanza dips a finger into the paste and declares it satisfactory. Flavia takes a clean sponge and begins to dab and smooth, first around the plucked hairline, then in and out of the nostrils, around the eyes, over every rise and fall from the top of Ghostanza's brow to the base of her neck, until no speck of skin can be seen.

She takes a small miniver tail brush from the leather box and paints a deep red salve onto Ghostanza's lips. For the cheeks, a powdery fucus is applied with a fresh sponge. Although she sometimes draws a line of kohl around her eyelids, today Ghostanza decides to leave them unpainted. She talks happily for a while about the women of Venice, who are such experts in the art of cosmetics they would fall down in shock if they saw how the midland women go about the business. Dull, dark, square, more hair on their wrists than teeth in their mouths. Necks fit for the oxen's yoke, no triangular waists, no high-wedged slippers.

Knowing nothing so much as her ignorance, Flavia keeps quiet whenever Ghostanza compares her home city to where she is now. Besides, La Perfetta's remembrances are usually made to the glossy oval glass and Flavia doubts if she senses another living thing in her presence at these times.

Ghostanza's hair still needs to be rebraided, curled, and pinned. Flavia oiled and brushed it the previous evening, so when she loosens the knot it slips down her shoulders in a silky rope.

Like her face, Ghostanza's hair has two states: dressed and undressed. Its brilliant hue does not come from God either.

Down the parting it is more faded brown than red, but no one will see that once the braids are in place. Flavia concentrates hard on making them all even, then winds and pins them to the back of her head, leaving the little end wisps loose. She does this for all of Ghostanza's hair except for two long strands either side of her temples. These she curls with irons, being careful not to burn her fingers for the hundredth time. Lastly, she pins a thin lace veil to the top of Ghostanza's head.

Ghostanza gives a curt nod, watching the oval glass as the ringlets bounce.

At least dressing is easier. There are not many more layers than Flavia's wardrobe of undershirt, stockings and daygown. The only additions are a plain silk covering for the neckline that Flavia attaches to the top of Ghostanza's bodice with gold pins, and a long-sleeved black overdress that hides the splint on her arm. For decoration, Ghostanza settles on a sapphire hairpin and a matching shoulder brooch. Grinning, she picks up a large crucifix and Flavia fastens it around her neck, surreptitiously feeling the clasp of the little gold key chain as Ghostanza slips her feet into a pair of suede slippers.

'It serves my purposes to appear plainly today.' Ghostanza plucks at a loose thread on her skirt.

'Plainly?' Flavia does not try to keep the disbelief from her voice. To her mind La Perfetta has been smeared, plucked, oiled and dressed in a manner to which no Christmastide goose was ever subjected.

'Oh this is nothing, *bruttina*.' Ghostanza adjusts the sleeves of her overdress and smiles indulgently. 'My friends and I used to pass the whole day in the hands of our maidservants. Only the lighting of the lamps would call us into society, and when we stepped from our homes whole crowds would gather to watch us. Believe me, if an event was worth attending we would never walk about unaided.'

She scuffs her slippers lightly over the floor.

'We would break our necks rather than socialise flat footed as a peasant. Only a woman who needs two servants to support her is worthy of admiration in Venice.'

She lets out a quick breath as Flavia makes some final adjustments to her sleeves.

'Bring some more pins with you.'

'Y–you want me to come with you?' Flavia looks aghast at Ghostanza, crossing her arms over her chest and feeling two damp patches seeping through her undershirt.

Ghostanza looks at her with a faint grimace.

'Yes, well, not all the way up to the grille. You can sit behind the listener nun where it's darker. I may need you if the interview is a long one, so bring brushes and cloths and cerussa. If I retire at any stage, you are to follow me into the hallway and we shall see to things there.'

'Ghostanza!' A light scurrying sound is followed by the lustrous face of one of the choir nuns. 'Suora Benedetta says your stepson has arrived.'

Ghostanza is still for a moment. The grimace she gave Flavia hardens into something that even the cerussa cannot hide as she gathers up her skirts, marching out of the room with the nun bouncing after her like a nervous lapdog.

Flavia dives towards the dressing table. In front of her the oval looking glass shows a face half covered with unravelling plaits. She is patchily flushed and the bird has deepened to a sickly purple.

Quickly she rams pins, brushes, pots and rags into her skirts before turning from the glass in disgust.

11

'Have you learned nothing here?'

Ghostanza looks past the shoulder of the man, idly scanning the fresco behind him of Lazarus being turned away from the rich man's table.

The visitor's parlour is cut in half by a wall and a locked door. People speak to each other through a series of iron grilles, sometimes whispering when they don't want to be overheard by the listener nun perched by the fireplace. Further along, a boisterous family are visiting a novice nun. One of the children, a little girl with fluffy black hair, reaches through the bars and squeals in delight when the novice playfully clasps her arm.

They look much happier than La Perfetta's guests.

'What shall I say when Gilia asks after you?'

Ghostanza retracts her gaze from the fresco and looks at her visitor.

A youngish man, overweight but neat in appearance, a shiny black walking stick resting against his knee. His beard is a near perfect reflection of his stiff brown hair.

From her seat next to the listener nun, Flavia watches Ghostanza turn her head to one side, a shiver on the edge of her lip, hidden from him.

'What do you mean, Jacopo?'

'I mean that you have shaved scant degrees from your opulence, and none whatsoever from your powders. Quite apart from general propriety, it is not suitable for a girl Gilia's age to see her stepmother always so ...' He waves a small circle in front of his face, which does not fit the gesture. Beside him is a young woman in an uncomfortable-looking gown, a faint scattering of pockmarks on her forehead. She nods her approval. Ghostanza ignores her.

'What of prayer?' he asks.

'I pray,' says Ghostanza, lightly.

'And does He answer you?'

'Indeed,' she bows her head so her ringlets tremble. 'He tells me that I cannot work to my soul's best advantage within these walls, that I should return home if I am to perform His will.'

'Really?' This time the woman speaks, her pockmarks squeezed sideways above raised eyebrows. 'I was always told that the churchmen alone can communicate with God. For any woman, not least one such as yourself, to hear His voice with her own ears ...' she shakes her head, 'this is a spiritual malady. I am sure my husband will agree.'

She lowers her eyes towards Jacopo who nods firmly, his jowls trembling in agreement.

Ghostanza's shoulders tighten then fall on the gust of a long outward breath.

'How is your wrist?' Jacopo asks stiffly.

'Healing, thank you. Though I think you ought to send me a different physician.'

'Has Maestro Vitale not always treated you well?'

'Well enough,' Ghostanza sighs. 'But to have such an ill-dressed man in attendance. Never shaven or combed. I don't mind his being a Jew but he might sponge his cape once in a while.'

The words drop into Flavia's stomach like cold lead. She thinks Ghostanza must be joking. She has never a met a Jew though Pia once told her they have beards down to their toes and live in caves of gold. But Jacopo does not correct Ghostanza. Instead he picks up his walking stick and examines it as though it is a thing newly found, peering down its length for warps and notches.

'Maestro Vitale is much demanded by the Collegio and the Comune, not to mention how much I have to pay the abbess to let him in here, so be thankful he has mended you quickly, and for his discretion the last time he treated you.'

Jacopo is grim in these last words. Ghostanza's ringlets begin to tremble.

'Your father would have sent a cleaner man,' she says quietly.

'Do not be so sure of it!' Jacopo ejaculates a fine spray of saliva into the air. Several heads from the visiting family turn in their direction.

They are silent for a moment. Jacopo's face has gone deep purple, the kind of verzino Maestro Bartofolo would be proud of.

'Why have you come here?' Ghostanza's voice is cold as stone.

'To tell you that these night-time visits will stop. I will not have you ruining everything.'

Jacopo digs the walking stick into the floor. Ghostanza's back goes rigid.

'What on earth do you mean?' she examines the back of her gloved hands but her voice hits a false note. Jacopo leans close to the grille, fury in his jawline thickening his beard.

'Alessandro Bontempi's daughter is a novice here. She says you have been seen in the gardens, at night. That hole will be sealed immediately! This convent will get no more money from me until it is done.'

'Is that all?'

Ghostanza's words could freeze hot ashes.

'No, that is not all. Until I am satisfied you are living as God intended, there will be no more packages sent from that bloody place. You will learn to wear the face God gave you . . .'

The last words have barely left his mouth before Ghostanza is on her feet. She casts wildly around the room then takes hold of a tall brass candleholder, spins it sideways and thrusts it deep through the grille. Jacopo, twisting in alarm, overturns in his seat and crashes to the floor.

'Murderess! Help! Help us!' Jacopo's wife is on the floor beside him. She tries to drag him backwards, but every time she lifts one of his arms it flops heavily back onto the floor.

Flavia runs up to the grille. On the other side Jacopo lies groaning. Though he doesn't appear to be badly hurt, his legs wriggle helplessly as an upturned woodlouse. The listener nun desperately flaps her arms at Ghostanza, which is as useless as trying to shoo a bee swarm away from a honeypot because she is still thrusting the candlestick towards her stepson. With one final cry she launches it through the bars where it strikes the far wall of the visitor's section, scoring a gash in the fresco and chipping off the rich man's finger as he points Lazarus out of his house.

The other visitors and the novice have shrunk against walls either side of the parlour. The children wail in tune with Jacopo's groans and his wife's shrieks. Voices rise through the passageway and Suora Benedetta bursts in.

'Get her back to her room!' the gatekeeper nun growls at Flavia.

Ghostanza seems to have spent her rage. She stands motionless before the grille, her fingers curled around the iron bars and her teeth partly bared. She does not resist when Flavia takes hold of her arm.

'Look! Look what company she keeps!'

They are almost at the doorway when Jacopo's wife cries out. Her eyes have a hold of Flavia's face with the force of talons.

'See, the whore has run to her own. Both of them were sent by the devil!'

* * *

Ghostanza walks casually over to the dressing table and peers into the looking glass.

'Mona Ghostanza...' Flavia realises she is trembling inside and out. The backs of her hands are white.

Ghostanza peels off her gloves. 'No ... that is not worth troubling myself. I must be blamed for living when his virtuous stone Sybil of a mother does not.'

She sighs into the glass and stretches her neck one way then another. The cerussa is starting to peel around the edge of her chin and she clicks her fingers at Flavia.

'My charming choir nuns are coming to play cards after prayers. I shall need more of this.'

Flavia picks up the square glazed pot and scoops out a large pinch into a clean cup. Her hands are still shaking. Some of it is fear, but not all. To feel a stab of joy at such violence when a normal soul would sicken, perhaps this makes a truth of what Jacopo's wife said.

'Careful,' snaps Ghostanza. 'Not so much. Do you think this is powdered eggshells you are playing with? And wash your hands before you touch it!'

She snatches the pot back and slumps down on her

elbows. Flavia looks at the curve of her fingernails, polished with a chamois cloth and neatly filed.

'If that pig keeps his word . . .'

She turns to Flavia, her eyes alert behind the white mask.

'You will have to go to Il Sicofante.'

'What is Il Sicofante?' Flavia absently wipes her hands on her apron.

'He is not a "what", *stupida*, he is an apothecary. He will not have all the ingredients I need, but he is the only one who knows even half his trade in the city.'

'The city?'

'Of course in the city!' cries Ghostanza, flinging herself upright so Flavia can begin undressing her. 'Do you think I know anyone who does not live in a city? Get this shroud off me,' she wriggles impatiently.

'But I cannot leave Santa Giuliana.' Flavia takes off the black overdress and begins tugging at the ribbons criss-crossing the back of Ghostanza's gown, loosening the bodice as the latter tears off her brooch.

'Why on earth not? I've seen the other servants heaving their great arses in and out of the gate.'

That is true. Madalena often steps out of Santa Giuliana with her basket swinging. The servants come and go as they please, but they never invite Flavia. Her place is in the convent until Maestro Bartofolo tells her otherwise. Daughters stay where they are put. They do not go chasing wild boar with toy arrows unless they want to get pierced themselves.

'Of course you cannot go like that. Il Sicofante will not do business with someone who looks like a leper's handkerchief, and I must have the best he has. The cerussa will be inferior, but it must do for now. I need to make fucus as well, and there is a special recipe for my hair that he will not know about either, but I shall tell you the ingredients. You will need a list. I do not trust you to remember it all.'

Shrugging off her gown, Ghostanza picks up a piece of seedcake from her little games tables and pokes it the bars of the birdcage.

'When will I go?' Flavia's ears are tingling with excitement but Ghostanza does not answer. Ignoring the yellow bird with blushing cheeks, now bloodied and almost featherless, she talks in a high-pitched voice to its brilliant blue victor.

Flavia begins tidying up. The remains of Ghostanza's preparations are never attractive. The sponges she used to apply the cerussa are grey and hard, and must be wrung out and replaced in their glass container ready for the next day. Stained rags litter the floor, and on the dressing table are different sized tweezers still clasping the sticky roots of eyebrow and nostril hairs. The pots and mortars where Flavia makes up her recipes are rimmed with egg whites and goose-fat. She wonders what Ghostanza's night-time visitor would say if he saw from what sewage his sweet rose grows.

Across the room Ghostanza brushes the seedcake crumbs from her hands and picks up her lute. She pulls her thumb across the strings and they bite back discordantly, angry at their neglect. She wanders into her bedchamber with it and stretches herself out beneath the floating canopy, strums a few chords then launches into a song about a man who turns into a beetle so he can spy on his beloved, only to be swept up by a zealous housemaid. All thought of the apothecary seems to have vanished, and it is quite possible the pretty choir nuns will arrive later this afternoon to find her in her undershirt still singing songs about beetle-men.

But even if that is so, the Venetian cerussa will run out sooner or later. If her supplies are stopped by Jacopo, Ghostanza will be lost without it. And if she wants to have her glowing face back she will need the help of her ornatrix.

An anxious thrill moves across Flavia's body at the idea of stepping through the convent wall. Mona Grazia cannot stop her. The only barrier is her face. If the apothecary won't see her, Ghostanza might ask Madalena or one of the other servants instead.

Picking up the cup she used to mix the first batch of cerussa, Flavia pokes a finger around inside.

Ghostanza is still singing next door but she moves quietly all the same.

The mixture is hardening and she can almost taste its bitter metallic scent. She dribbles some water into it, softening the clots with her fingers. With a clean sponge she dabs at the cerussa until it is half covered. Leaning towards the looking glass, she presses the sponge lightly to her cheek.

A white circle appears beneath her left eye. The bird is half inside it, swooping high into a summer cloud.

She dabs again and again, over her eyelid, across her cheek and the top of her nose, from beak to tail, until it has disappeared.

It looks very strange. The rest of her face is tanned and freckled, so the circle of white makes no sense. Still, it is a glimpse of how she might have looked if Mona Grazia had not looked down at a broken nest when she should have kept her eyes on her sewing.

Quite a small face. The features equally so, except for her eyes and a plump, petulant lower lip. A working face, lines of labour digging into her forehead. Eyebrows thick, with soft down running over the bridge of her nose. Not the face of a pretty choir nun, but not a monster either.

If Tommaso had seen her like this he might not have been ashamed to sit with her in a honeysuckle bower while their guests ate and sang.

A Recipe to Make the
Eyes More Lustrous

Make a tincture of the berries of the Belladonna,
known also as nightshade. Place three drops in each
eye morning and night. In this way the orbs will glow
and the pupils widen.

Gilia la Bella II

Ricca was tiringly stupid. She could only give lessons in the disappointments of womanhood. So said Ghostanza, laughing and pulling Gilia inside her long overdress.

'Will you end your days like her, little chicken? A bitter face and a rattling of household keys for music?'

No was the answer. 'No,' said Ghostanza, lightly pinching Gilia's chin with her thumb and forefinger and waggling it until her head shook back and forth, because Gilia had flesh that could rise and rise again no matter how many times she pressed her fingers into it. 'Summer flavours,' said Ghostanza every time she pulled her close, best enjoyed straight from the orchard and better that way than soaked in honey for the long winter months.

There was a little time then, when her stepmother was happy, to feel her heart beating red and quick, before Ghostanza stopped laughing and pushed her away again, because Ghostanza was never one thing for very long. She turned from amusement to anger then back again, and remembered neither her amusement nor her anger when she was its opposite. She had no time for Jacopo or Ricca, and did not smile as much when her father called her his legend of emeralds and water. She did not even like Parassita, who was a 'vile little thing' to be brushed away with a strict sweep of the hand. Only Gilia was allowed to keep her company for very long. Without knowing how, she crept between the harsh words and the moans of boredom to be pulled for a while next to Ghostanza's fierce beating heart.

Sometimes when they were together it seemed as though her stepmother was drinking her in. Not just the pressing of her bouncy skin or running her fingers through Gilia's tightly curled hair. Something more than that.

'It is a secret of beauty,' said Ghostanza as she looped a hand around Gilia's puppy-thick waist. 'Fresh-minted skin, a curl of lashes around an innocent eye. You must always have youth at your side, their lifeblood becomes yours.'

In the waking hours between Gilia's dead sleep and her morning sleep Ghostanza would bring Ibn Yunus to her room.

Most of the songs were dark like Poor Cara Rossina who crushed up her mirror. All of them were written for her by a man named Da Lezze who was a great maestro and had a fine moustache and cheekbones made for smiling. When Gilia was hungry Ghostanza fed her capers and pistachios, and a sweet mostarda of quinces on her favourite plate. She oiled her hair as she ate, rubbed her feet with wax and rosewater before slipping them under the covers.

During the day Ghostanza sat at her dressing table which was put in the brightest room in the house. It used to be Jacopo's study but Ghostanza said he could read his musty books in any musty room and instead of hitting her with a birch as he would have if Gilia had said it, her father smiled in a teary way and looped the ends of his beard around his fingers.

Ghostanza encouraged Gilia to watch her there. 'This is how you fix a scent so it will not stale'; 'this is how you use cloth and kermes to colour your cheeks'.

Other things she talked about, the pestle groaning against the mortar as her coloured powders spewed out. But the noise set Gilia's teeth on edge and she took to stuffing candlewax in her ears so she never got to hear very much of Ghostanza's lessons and anyway her stepmother talked mostly to her oval looking glass when she was at her preparations. Gilia sucked on her beads while Ghostanza sifted, stirred and dabbed at her pots and her face until she was white and smooth.

'How do you stand it?' Ghostanza asked when she was finished stirring and dabbing. 'Never going out? Never being seen?'

Gilia pulled the wax from her ears and Ghostanza looked annoyed that she had to repeat herself, but even more annoyed that Gilia could not answer her even without the wax.

She had never really thought about it. Apart from confession at the Chiesa del Gesu she had her room and the passageways and the courtyard, and sometimes the *sala grande* and the vegetable garden behind the Palazzo, but mostly just her room with the things that were inside it and the things that came alive to her in the panelling over her bed. Sometimes she wished herself out of her room, and if she stared too hard at the wood it made shapes that were much stranger and uglier than Santa Lucia, but she didn't say any of that to Ghostanza. She wished she had kept the candlewax in her ears because her stepmother's questions were like a great hand reaching into her head, pushing things around that ought not to be moved, and squeezing what was known and normal into a small forgotten place.

Ghostanza was angry with Gilia for not answering. She was also angry with the passageways and the courtyard of the Palazzo Tassi because they were not enough for her. As soon as she had finished making herself white and smooth she would put on her flat shoes and walk servantless out of the house and through the big gate.

Jacopo got very purple when that happened. The only time Gilia heard him shout at their father was the day Ghostanza disappeared from the Palazzo Tassi for hours and hours and only came back when the Chiesa del Gesu had already rung Vespers and they were halfway through the meat course. Something must have come of it because the next time Ghostanza put on her flat shoes and went out of the house Ricca whispered something to Antonia who put down her needlework and went out straight after her. That was sillier than Jacopo himself huffing after Ghostanza with his tapping stick because Antonia was too tall and clumsy not to be noticed and all she saw was Ghostanza standing on the cathedral steps talking to some of the other matrons and looking a bit around the Piazza Grande.

'Why does she go?' Gilia asked Antonia. She hated it when Jacopo was purple and shouting because then Ricca would be sullen too, and her father would stay all day in his study and look even older when he came out again. It was the part of Ghostanza she did not like. The part that moved the furniture in her head around and made her sleeping and night-waking hours feel vague and drifting, until she wasn't sure if it was a bed or a seafaring raft that carried her through those times.

'She has to be seen,' said Antonia, jabbing at her needlework. 'Take her admirers away and she will die.'

'Admirers? Like Jacopo and his butterflies?'

Jacopo admired butterflies so much that he caught them and suffocated them and pressed them between parchment though it didn't work very well because their wings always fell to pieces and all that was left was a bright-coloured smear.

But Antonia just smiled and shook her head in a way that made Gilia want to yank her nose.

* * *

'Who are your admirers?'

Ghostanza sat in front of her dressing table, pressing pink powder onto her eyelids. Like Antonia, she smiled as if to say, 'that is not for you to know,' and said nothing at all. Gilia looked hard at her stepmother in the oval glass and something in her expression must have caught Ghostanza's eye, because eventually she put down her powder sponge and turned to face her.

'They are people who see me,' she said.

'I see you,' replied Gilia sullenly.

Ghostanza rubbed her fingers, smearing the pink powder around her palms so they looked like one of Jacopo's squashed butterfly parchments.

'And what about when you are asleep, or with Ricca, or your dolls? Who is to see me then?'

Another of Ghostanza's questions, squeezing Gilia's old world into a smaller, tighter space.

'Dear child,' Ghostanza leaned towards her, reaching for her hand. Gilia snatched it away and held it behind her back.

'It cannot be helped. If a woman is not seen, she does not exist.'

'But what if I promise to look at you all the time, and not sleep or look at Ricca or even Antonia. Then Jacopo wouldn't get so purple and Papa wouldn't look so old . . .'

Ghostanza tried not to laugh. She covered her mouth with her sleeve but her eyes were stretched and shiny. Eventually she gave up and slapped her hands together, her shoulders shaking. Gilia looked at her and didn't know whether she wanted to yank Ghostanza's nose or climb inside her long overdress and feel herself as special and cherished as all the pretty things Ghostanza kept in the painted jewellery box on her dressing table. Then Ghostanza stopped laughing, and all of a sudden she didn't look happy at all.

'It would not be enough, Gilia. An admirer does not only look at you. He lives through you, sees the world only by way of what you would find pleasing or displeasing until you own him utterly.'

Gilia thought for a moment. She remembered how Jacopo had a look on his face when he was chasing butterflies around the vegetable garden and again when he laid them out dead on the parchment. It was a look he never had when he was with Ricca.

'How do you find an admirer?' she asked.

'You do not find them. They come to you.'

'But how?'

Ghostanza sighed and wafted her hands over the little pots and jars on her dressing table.

'You must be beautiful on the outside, and believed to be beautiful on the inside too.'

Gilia looked at the pots of pink and blue, yellow and white. Butterfly colours.

'Who are your admirers?' she asked again.

'Oh,' smiled Ghostanza, 'there are many young men in this city.'

'Name one.'

But Ghostanza just put a finger to her lips.

12

The city towers rise over terraced rooflines. Holding out her hand, Flavia measures the tallest of them against the length of her finger. After a few more paces it will not fit behind it.

'Keep up, clay brain.'

They are only just out of the gate but Madalena is already ahead.

Flavia's toes are pinched together. Like everything else, her shoes have been borrowed and the shape of them does not match her feet. At least the dress fits better. Ghostanza borrowed it from a reluctant Suora Umiliana, one of the pretty choir nuns who is almost as thin as Flavia and keeps all her maiden dresses wrapped in a cedar chest. Ghostanza says the wool is inferior but it is the best thing Flavia has ever worn: dark violet – a mixing of indigo and madder that her father sometimes made to imitate the more expensive pavonazzo dye – with a skirt that reaches so far down she has to scoop it up with one hand to step out of the gate. The dress is finished with a plain cream mantle, trimmed with a band of silk – another loan from Suora Umiliana, who made Flavia take a bath in the laundry vat before touching it. Flavia also washed her hair with some of Ghostanza's rose oil soap and pinned her plaits under a newly starched cap.

Her face was a bigger problem. Ghostanza was torn between the risk of her ornatrix being turned away and the dread of using up more of her precious cerussa. In the end she grudgingly donated a small pinch, which Flavia mixed with soil until it almost matched the shade of her own skin. Though Ghostanza shuddered to see her cerussa polluted to a gravy brown she was satisfied when the bird mark disappeared underneath the mixture. To be certain, they finished off Flavia's costume with a light gauze veil.

Madalena was surly when they met by the convent gate. Flavia worried she would refuse to take her, but the servant said nothing and Suora Benedetta opened the gate for them without too many questions. Having grudgingly heard some choice entreaties from Ghostanza, the gatekeeper nun expelled Flavia into the street as briskly as she had once plucked her inside.

For the first hundred yards it is hard to know the distance of things. The cart ride with Alfeo seems long ago and she slept for most of it. After months in Santa Giuliana it is strange to walk forwards with no wall in front of her. She is frightened of tripping over her skirts in case she falls into the vastness of the life that has suddenly opened. The air is too plentiful. She sucks it in like a drowning man breathing his first lungful of water, panicking and gulping until she finds a steadier rhythm.

Over the dirt road and onto cobbles, past the row of little houses she saw through the hole in the outer wall, winding up the hillside. The sweat creeps down her neck, dampening her undershirt.

'So you're running around after La Strega now?'

Madalena turns, grinning unpleasantly. Her worn teeth part company in the middle of her mouth.

'Why do you call her that?' Flavia tries to frown beneath the cerussa. 'She isn't a witch.'

'And what would you know about it?' chuckles Madalena.

'She doesn't have a toad, or a cat. She doesn't have anything except two birds, and lots of ladies have those.'

'Ha! Doesn't matter what she keeps. It's what she does. See that house up there?' Madalena points upwards and Flavia follows her finger to a wide building with neat long rows of square then pointed windows.

'Palazzo Tassi. And there,' her finger moves to another, squarer block with russet coloured towers rising above it, 'Palazzo Alfani. Big families here. La Strega comes from some lake town on the arm of Corrado Tassi, things go rotten after that.'

'What do you mean?'

'She cursed Jacopo's wife. No babies for her. Cursed her husband too, no more Corrado Tassi now is there?'

The final giver of Ghostanza's precious things. Did she treat him well then, or did she mock him until he shrivelled under the stone dates of his birth and death?

'Why would she hurt her husband if it means she has to live at the convent now?'

'Ah,' Madalena nods back to the big square building, 'La Strega sees Ridolfo, pretty boy from the Alfani family. Sees him and wants him.'

Madalena gives her bosoms a self-satisfied adjustment. 'We've all seen her creeping about at night in that cape of hers. Can't keep away from him.'

'Ridolfo Alfani?' For some reason Flavia's mind flicks to the small golden key around Ghostanza's neck. Questions crowd into her mind like bees queuing for the hive.

'Cousin of mine worked at the Palazzo Tassi,' Madalena continues. 'Strange things there.'

'Such as?' Flavia takes a sharp breath as a blister bubbles on her heel.

'A black cat found under a rosebush. Eyes gouged out. Who else but a strega does that kind of thing? And she put a hex on my brother when his mule splattered mud on her skirt. He woke up the next morning feeling like his head had been split in two.'

'My uncle feels like that when he's been to the tavern.' Flavia says snidely, regretting it as soon as she sees Madalena's face darken.

'I told you. She's a witch, sure as I'm fat and you're a clay brain.'

Madalena strides off ahead, her backside rotating like a cartwheel beneath the thick serge of skirts which are ringed with deepening shades of mud.

* * *

The Porta Eburnea, gateway to the city. It squats over their heads, vast and grey. Flavia has a sudden urge to crawl into the gutter that passes beneath it. She keeps her face to the slow-moving river of sludge while Madalena jokes with the gatekeeper, grinning as he fondles her buttocks in the manner of Mona Grazia kneading her dough into crucifixion cakes.

They are inside.

In the village there aren't enough houses to block you in so the fields are never hidden. Here it is as dark and closed as the Casa Nascosta. The sky narrows to overhead strips and only the ache in your legs tells you if you are going up or coming down.

Madalena beckons her around a corner and they funnel right and left through tight alleys overstrung with stagnant laundry. The air is very thick now and the incline seems to double with each pace. The path widens until they reach a square filled with noise and dirt. A herd of pigs charge around a corner, trotters slipping. Chickens run free, throwing up feathers that spin vertically among boots and cartwheels.

Everyone seems to be shouting. Pedlars cry out in competition and men roar out jokes that would make Alfeo blush. Even the women call to one another from opposing windows.

Flavia is glad to crouch behind Madalena as she pushes her way forwards, up another street and into a bewildering arena. Vast buildings surround them now, their walls as mountainous as the ark. A church tall enough to house the heavens looms over a packed marketplace where the traders weigh and slice and pack and shout, and blacksmiths strike metal beside a giant two-tier fountain. In and out of the crowd, pedlars selling fans and buttons are joined by tough-armed women with baskets of food.

Flavia has never known the press of bodies around her. It is thrilling and terrifying – the changing gallery of faces and the cries of greeting, reproach and irritation. By habit she tilts her face to the side, but no one pays her much attention. There is a moment of panic when Madalena disappears into the crowd, and Flavia is pitifully relieved to spot her coarse dark plaits in front of a clothes stall.

'There,' Madalena points towards a smaller, neighbouring piazza. 'Few paces along you'll find him. Meet here when the market closes.'

She begins rifling through a bundle of old skirts.

* * *

It is better out of the marketplace. The swarming stops almost as soon as it began, and she finds herself in a quiet circle of three-storey buildings. They are not as grand as some she has walked past, but very pretty still, with finches in little wooden cages on some of the balconies. One house in particular has a proud look to it, its polished shutters evenly spaced. The sign of the pestle and mortar that Ghostanza told her to look for is pictured in a series of little blue and white frescoes beneath the eves.

Dry-mouthed and breathing sharply, Flavia makes a final adjustment to her veil.

13

She will think about it later, reaching for comparisons. Cool like the church of San Fortunato when the heat was clawing and the hills shimmered in the distance. Order imposed with the burning of incense and the steady chant of the liturgy.

Silver lanterns give a gentle glow to pale blue walls lined with tight rows of glazed jars and wooden boxes. In the centre of the shop is a long marble counter, smoother than a rich man's tomb and shot through with cobwebs of dark grey. At either end of the counter sit granite mortars, scales and weights. Trays of biscuits and glossy-looking cakes are laid out at the front.

In the far corner of the shop a young man in a white apron sweeps the floor. A large Adam's apple pokes out of his neck and lank brown hair falls either side of his cheeks. His nose is upturned, the nostrils arching reproachfully as he ferrets his broom around the edge of the counter.

'Can you help me?'

The man's neck elongates a little, but he carries on urging the dust from one place to another.

'Are you the man they call Il Sicofante?'

'Who wants him?'

The man's voice rasps as rudely as one of Alfeo's ripe fig-farts, the kind that make Pia blush and Mona Grazia throw him bodily out of the house.

Remembering Ghostanza's instructions, Flavia draws herself up to her full height, which is about as tall as the man's throat.

'Ghostanza Dolfin requires certain preparations that Il Sicofante is to make for her. No one else is to serve me.'

Ghostanza assured her of copious grovelling wherever her name was spoken, but the lank-haired man merely shrugs then shuffles behind the counter to an arched doorway. Parting the curtain he rasps, 'Maestro, customer,' then turns back to Flavia and makes an ugly low bow. Flavia shudders as he moves slowly around the counter and retreats into a passageway at the far end of the shop.

'Cimon, you wretch,' a voice booms out, 'you had better not have your hands in the sugar bin!'

A clatter above her head like a herd of horses making their way down the staircase. The footsteps grow louder and Flavia barely has time to adjust her veil before the apothecary bursts through the curtain, sweeping a large velvet cap from his head.

He has offered his greeting too quickly. As soon as he sees Flavia's country face and borrowed dress, his smile fades and the cap is tossed onto the marble counter. A pair of silk-sleeved arms interleave in front of his doublet and he slouches in the doorway.

Flavia's breath steadies a little. As the apothecary's eyes wander over the pile of dust she peers at him through the gauze. He is a curious mixture of large and small, as though two Creators with different ideas of a man's shape have put him together. The arms and hands are long and finished with an array of gold rings. His head is small, with close cropped curls of brown hair that glisten like a newborn conker. The waist belongs more to an adolescent than a man, but his thighs are large almost to obscenity. Trapped in tight green hose, they put Flavia in mind of a grasshopper, tensed to spring a great distance. His shoulders and neck are also muscular, and a face that only has room for delicate features is crowded with a beaked nose and thickly lashed eyes.

His brief smile had revealed teeth as big as tombstones. Now there is nothing but boredom on his face as he flicks at a meandering fly.

'You have broken my sleep for nothing. The apothecary in the Via dei Priori serves the artisans.'

Flavia was expecting this. Ghostanza warned her that Il Sicofante is well paid by the nobles, that his favourite patrons are the women of the Alfani family.

She pulls a piece of folded parchment from her sleeve.

'If you will provide such preparations as are on this list,' her voice is little more than a whisper, 'Ghostanza Dolfin will pay double what you pay the Alfani matrons. And if your work is pleasing she may see fit to dispense some secrets of her own to the improvement of your art.'

Flavia has never commanded anyone in her life, least of all a man whose doublet is worth more than her father could earn in ten years. The words are not her own but she knows she has remembered them properly because the huge teeth are resurrected and Il Sicofante suddenly bounds towards her. Before she has time to shrink back, her shoulder is grasped by long ringed fingers and she is whisked behind the counter, through the doorway, and into a room of stunning blood red.

* * *

The cool pallor of the shop is obliterated. Here everything screams at her. The painted ceiling and the tiled floor, the silk wall hangings and the feather-plumped couches, all such a boiling crimson that it hurts her eyes to look at them. A million insects must have been ground into dust for such a room, the dyers growing as fat as the wriggling kermes, squeezed and pulped into cochineal.

The only relief is a series of frescoes between the wall hangings: small, pastel-coloured pictures of young women dotted along the length of the room. Some of them are dancing, weaving silk ribbons around themselves; others play a game of chess, or work at their embroidery. One lays on a field of daisies while a small boy fans her face.

They are all beautiful. One of the chess players has a deep red mouth and black hair in a loose plait over her shoulder. The embroiderer is crowned by curls of gold, her white breast only partly covered by her robes. There are redheads too, with pink lips and violet blue eyes, their tresses falling freely to their thighs. Every one of them is lovelier than the next.

Flavia slips between the glow of the lamps as Il Sicofante scans Ghostanza's list.

'Your mistress has a particular sense of what suits her beauty,' he frowns. 'Ah, but who would not place their limbs on the rack for the privilege of serving Ghostanza Dolfin?'

He looks again at Flavia, his head tilted and his forefinger lightly strumming his lower lip. She thinks of Maestro Bartofolo planning how best to cut up a calf skin. The cerussa on her cheek feels heavy.

'Sit.'

She cringes when he pushes her into a soft chair, shakes her head when he offers her a tray of sweetbreads. Unperturbed, the apothecary springs lightly round the room on his great thighs, adding some drops of strong-smelling oil to the burners, searching out little baked delicacies to place reverentially at her side. Now he is not so much a grasshopper as a clever spider who brings a web-wrapped fly to his mate in order to couple with her while she undoes it. Flavia is still thinking about spiders and flies when he begins asking about Ghostanza and her life at the convent.

She has been warned on this point: the apothecary will suck out a woman's secrets like a hot poultice. She answers him vaguely or not at all. He smiles in a way that leaves his eyes behind, then asks after Flavia's health, which is such a strange question from a man in a silk doublet she laughs loudly and sends her gauze veil shooting upwards.

'My feet hurt,' she says quickly, trying to draw his attention from her face.

Before she knows it, Il Sicofante is on the floor, one hand cupping her foot as he pulls off her shoe with sympathetic tuts and remonstrations.

'This type of shoe is all wrong for you, Signorina, being blessed with, ah, sturdy feet and well-balanced toes.'

He rests her foot on his bent knee. Flavia resists the temptation to jerk it away. Still kneeling, the apothecary dips into his doublet for a tiny vial of oil, tips it into his palm and begins rubbing his hands briskly with wet kissing noises.

'In a moment you will be ready to walk upon the floor of heaven.'

He begins smoothing the oil into the sole of her foot, reaching a thumb into the arch and gliding around the base of her blistered heel with astonishingly smooth fingers. Squeezing her hands together in her lap, Flavia thinks of Mona Grazia's peasant prudery, her dislike of pleasure. As her muscles loosen she tries to imagine it is not the apothecary but Tommaso who is pressing his thumb into her sole.

Her hands relax and she sinks deeper into the chair. Scented oil rises like holy unction. The women on the wall smile encouragement.

'This is what it means to be beautiful', they say, 'to have a cushion at your back and a man at your feet.'

A little groan of enjoyment leaves her lips as the apothecary's thumb digs around the edge of each toe. The foot that is still in its shoe throbs jealously. At the edge of her sight the tray of sweetmeats glisten. Before she can stop herself a gush of honey is breaking over her tongue. The woman at the chessboard signals her approval and Flavia reaches out again. This time sugar paste splits crisply in two as she bites down. Her other shoe is off now, and Il Sicofante is vigorously massaging both feet at once, his curls almost touching her lap.

The oil seeps a nodding scent. Sleepily she looks up at the chess player, who pulls her fingers through her black plait until it unwinds. The dancers whirl with ribbons and fingers entwined, their limbs floating free of the plaster as the paint becomes flesh.

She turns back to Il Sicofante, who is asking her what kind of beetles Ghostanza likes to eat for breakfast. His nose and eyes are twisted out of line with his mouth and fade altogether as he reaches forward, pushing a thumb and forefinger into her cheeks to force her mouth open. He lifts up a jug and begins pouring milky cerussa down her throat. She is drowning in the bitter flow as it splashes over her face, seeping into her lungs and coming up through her nostrils as she fights for breath. At the same time there are fingers easing themselves under her clothes, pushing up her thighs, down her undershirt, urgent and cold.

She wakes with a start. Il Sicofante is standing in front of her. His features have not quite reassembled and there is frustration on his brow. Flavia snatches her legs up to her chest. Her feet, still oiled, slide treacherously on the cushion.

The apothecary unlocks his smile and bows a retreat towards the shop.

'Cimon will fetch you more biscuits, as sweet as your little face,' he says. 'And I will bring you such ingredients as will make Ghostanza Dolfin shine like the mother of God.'

* * *

She is lopsided under the pestle and mortar paintings, her arm pulled down by her basket and the good wishes of Il Sicofante ringing brilliantly and briefly in her ears. Her feet don't feel as if they belong to her body any more. A cushion of air lies between her ankles and the cobblestones, as if the magical thumbs of the apothecary have stolen not only pain but feeling too.

The shadows are still short and there is no sign of Madalena in the marketplace. It is quieter now, and broad sections of the piazza are empty. Flavia wanders over to the two-tiered fountain and perches on its lower lip, watching the women traders as they tease a group of little boys and make them gamble for fruit. One of the women is very squat, with patches of crudely cut hair sticking out from under her cap. The others begin laughing at her, saying she gave her hair to a man who ran off without paying her. Another trader with chalky face paint breaking into the creases of her skin grabs at the cap of the squat woman, who then flies at her. Soon the pair of them are wrestling among the waste of the marketplace, their heels scraping channels into flattened vegetables. A fleeting punch sends the squat woman staggering over to the fountain where she coughs and empties two teeth and a wad of blood into the water.

She stumbles away as the others jeer. Flavia stares through the water to the discarded teeth.

'At least they were already rotten.'

The voice by her shoulder is faint. An echo on distant stone. She does not jump this time when she sees the physician's reflection peering into the fountain.

'Who was she?'

Maestro Vitale reaches into the water and plucks out the teeth, brown and burrowed as a worm-eaten apple.

'A *treccola*. They sell fruit, and whatever else they can.'

'How humiliating for her,' says Flavia, her hand coming involuntarily to rest on the patch of cerussa.

'She has saved herself another humiliation. People are only too keen to watch the tooth surgeon at work in the Piazza Piccola.'

When he turns to Flavia his face is thinner than before and there is a new line of worry across his forehead. He looks at her candidly, piercing her flimsy veil as he takes in the crust of cerussa, making the bird feel stronger than ever. Then she remembers how Ghostanza said he was a Jew, and that Mona Grazia once said if you press a Jew's sleeve then blood will come pouring out of it because they worship the night.

This Jew does not smile much, but he did make Ghostanza better, and he did not steal her blood to put into his special flatbreads. She does not like how he frowns at her cerussa but she is not scared of him.

'Maestro Vitale, what is an ornatrix?'

The physician rolls the rotten teeth between his fingers and looks back into the fountain as he speaks.

'It is an old Roman word, from when there were many temples to the goddess of beauty.'

'So why does Ghostanza Dolfin give me such a name now?'

'Because she is educated, and the comparison amuses her. An ornatrix served her mistress in all bodily things. She oiled and braided her hair, and applied such lotions and colours as were thought handsome.'

'So she made a lot of money?' Flavia thinks of Il Sicofante's dazzling red parlour.

'No. She was a slave. Just like her mistress.'

Flavia waits for him to say more. The priest of San Fortunato often talked about things that made no sense, and then explained them so everyone could see how clever he was. But Maestro Vitale does not finish the circle of his thought. Instead his gaze wanders to her basket, perched on the edge of the fountain.

'You have been to Il Sicofante.'

'Yes,' Flavia cannot help the pride in her voice. 'I was there for hours, and there were painted women on the walls. Il Sicofante gave me sweetbreads and looked after my feet.'

It is not just the bird that is swelling under her cerussa. Suddenly she wants to talk about everything she has seen that day, things that Madalena will not understand and Ghostanza will sneer at. But Maestro Vitale just looks ruefully back from the packages in the basket to the splintered cerussa on her face.

'I think you have had a wasted day.'

'Not at all,' sniffs Flavia in annoyance, thinking him less of a friend and more of a Jew after all. 'I got everything I came for. Il Sicofante liked me very much, and now I have all the tools to give grace to Ghostanza Dolfin every day for a month.'

The physician takes another look at the *treccola*'s teeth before dropping them back in the water. They drift slowly downwards, trailing tendrils of blood.

'There is no grace but in the mind, Flavia. Do not look for truth in a smile.' He gets up then and walks down the fountain steps, across the wide piazza, into the shadows.

For Eyes that are Bloodshot

Take the roots of red fennel, stamp them and wring
out the juice, then temper it with clarified honey, and
make an oyntment thereof, and annoint the eyes
therewith and it will take away the redness.

14

Ghostanza purses her lips. They are a shiny deep purple and her mouth looks a bit like a burst mulberry.

She is stretched out on her bed, unable to move because there is a large poultice on her chest, a sticky mixture of gum arabic and boiled fruits from the service tree in the convent garden. She measures the droop of her breasts each month by wedging goose feathers beneath them and counting how many get trapped in the flesh. One breast holds four, the other three. This has not always been the case.

Not for the first time, Flavia wonders how old Ghostanza is. When she is behind the cerussa it is impossible to tell. Other times her face is red raw from scrubbing, or covered in goosefat. The flesh on her upper arms sometimes sags a little, but rich women always have more fat on them. Pia used to say well-born ladies look younger than they are because their husbands lock them away and the sun does not curse them with age.

Flavia tried to find out once by asking Ghostanza how old Corrado Tassi was when she met him.

Too old came the sneering reply. Age gnawed on him.

Old Tassi. A midlander merchant buying silks in the north. No army of children to waste his wealth, just a son and a small daughter back home, for whom she bought mille-fiori glass beads. Tassi was smart enough or she would not have had him, even for all the flexibility of his purse strings. Though he never did step gracefully from boat to land.

This is all Ghostanza Dolfin has to say about her dead husband.

She did not need to add that she could not hope to love him.

* * *

'She's over a hundred,' says Madalena as they trudge over to the courtyard ovens.

'Take this,' she thrusts a tray at Flavia and begins shovelling out little raisin loaves.

'She's not over a hundred,' says Flavia, saliva pooling in her mouth as the scent of cinnamon wafts over her.

'Well, forty then.'

'But forty is an old woman!'

'La Strega drinks a special potion. If she doesn't, her teeth fall out and her hair turns to cobwebs.' Madalena shovels the last of the loaves onto Flavia's tray then slams the oven door shut, her face pinched with fatigue.

'You'll see – take her spells away and Ghostanza Dolfin will shrivel up. Then Ridolfo Alfani will think himself a mighty clay brain for wiggling his jousting stick in her old woman's *fica*.'

* * *

'It is really none of your business.'

Suora Benedetta shakes out an ash-covered mat, ignoring the cries of Suora Umiliana as grey flecks settle on her flower beds.

'She must either marry again or take the veil, and better for her new husband and better for God if she wipes that mess off her face beforehand.'

'That is what her stepson says.' Flavia sniggers as Suora Umiliana takes a handkerchief from her sleeve and begins wiping ash off her rose petals.

'And he is right!' trumpets Suora Benedetta. 'Ghostanza Dolfin may have thirty more years or one more day on this earth, but when it is time for her to pack up her mortal remains she will stand naked as all of us before the Lord. No amount of painting will keep her soul hidden then.'

Flavia shakes her head, trying to rinse out an image of Suora Benedetta's hidden flesh trembling bulkily before the heavenly throne.

'But can a person stay young forever? ... If they sleep in goosefat and sit in the dark?'

She knows she is asking the wrong person even before Suora Benedetta rubs her stubby eyelashes and sighs.

'Child, why would they want to?'

* * *

'I don't think anyone really knows about La Veneziana.' Suora Dorotea is heating soapwort in the infirmary hearth to clean the sheets. Marsh winds have brought dysentery to the convent and Flavia is relieved not to be spooning ginger tisane down the nuns' throats and wiping their backsides with Suora Dorotea's endless supply of thin grey rags. Ghostanza takes up most of her time now but the dispensary sister does not complain. Her dread of nursing Ghostanza herself is so great she accepts Flavia's loss with barely a word.

'But there are so many rumours about her. Madalena says ...'

'Madalena is no authority on moral behaviour. I would

not trust her tongue, much as the manners of La Veneziana make a fine stick for its sharpening.'

* * *

With Il Sicofante's help, there is almost enough powder to cast a life-size figure of Ghostanza in cerussa. Alongside that and the fucus for her lips and cheeks, her dressing table is crowded with salves, pastes and a host of scented soaps and lotions. Though she criticises the coarseness of Il Sicofante's ingredients, Ghostanza still hunches over Flavia's basket every time she comes back from the city, ripping off the wax lids and rubbing the contents between her fingers with savage delight. The cerussa she refined herself, turning it from a grainy off-white sand to something close to her brilliant Venetian shell. She did this secretively, while Flavia was at her other chores.

Now her wrist is better Flavia is demoted to meaner work: removing dead skin, hair and dirt. The more she delves through the layers, the more she realises Ghostanza is far from perfect. The skin on her armpits is grey, the flesh around her knees thicker than a floor-scrubber's. Either side of her belly are a series of wriggling purple lines which will not be softened by any creams. When Flavia innocently asks if Ghostanza's mother looked too hard at some worms when Ghostanza was in her belly, the latter grabs a stick of charcoal and drives it so far up Flavia's nostril she has to remove it with a pair of tweezers.

The worst job is the depilatory bath. Three cauldrons of boiling water mixed with quicklime and yellow arsenic stolen from the dispensary. When the steam pinches her eyes Flavia tests the mixture by dipping in a chicken feather. If it is ready the feather will emerge steaming and quite bald. Because there is nowhere for Ghostanza to immerse herself, Flavia has to carry the cauldrons down to a tiny storeroom and pour it over hot stones while Ghostanza sweats in the steam with a thick cloth wrapped around her head. The mixture burns Flavia's skin when the cauldrons bump against her legs and she wonders how anyone can bear to sit among the fumes and heat. But Ghostanza Dolfin is beyond pain in this regard, rivalling the torment of a martyred saint when it comes to beauty.

Much as Ghostanza despises the hairs on her body, no amount of care is too great for her flaming red curls. As well as rummaging round Suora Dorotea's dispensary, Flavia must sneak into the kitchen stores to cut off hunks of fat and siphon oil and wine, all of it mashed into recipes for softening and lightening Ghostanza's hair. She spends hours boiling mallow roots and cumin seeds in wine to make a rinse, only to discover this is just the first stage in a process that will take several more days and involve at least two more raids on the kitchen. Sulking in her own sweat, she thinks it would be quicker for La Perfetta to grow a new head of hair than wash the existing one.

Nearly all of Ghostanza's lessons are harsh ones, ending with a slap or a pinch when she makes a mistake. The crushing, grinding, sifting, soaking and drying in Maestro Bartofolo's workshop is nothing compared to her new work. When a hide is soaked for the last time the dyer can rest. For Ghostanza Dolfin it is different. Flavia is fast discovering the truth of her new role. The industry of perfection does not stop, and the ornatrix will never have a moment's peace.

15

There is no more circling of the convent wall, which truly has no end to it now. The hole that used to open onto the world is blocked with hard lime mortar.

Ghostanza never speaks of it. Her secrets are as close as the little gold key chain about her neck and she keeps her lips pressed as her needle scythes in and out of a linen napkin, tails of coloured silk flying as she embroiders a little girl with dark hair framed by a pink and white rosebush.

The key definitely belongs to the painted box on her dressing table, because if Flavia so much as rests a brush on its lid Ghostanza will hit her hands and sometimes her face, so she has to walk around with a purple mark on both cheeks and bear the taunts of Madalena.

The box stays shut and the wall stays closed. Some days it seems as if the very soul is being wrung out of La Perfetta. Her temper, never even, threatens to leapfrog sanity. When Flavia casually mentions that two nuns from the Alfani family are in the infirmary Ghostanza lashes out with the chain of pearls she is fixing to her hair and Flavia must duck to avoid the whip of its clasp.

'What do I care about Alfani whores?' she cries. '*Puttane*, they deserve to shit out their own stomachs.' Ghostanza yanks the chain tight between her fingers and slumps back down.

Sometimes she is easier, seeking entertainment. In the evenings she sets out her wooden board games, pours sweet *passito* wine for the pretty choir nuns, and cheats them out of their jewellery by making up her own rules.

'What do you mean you have never heard of the five-dice trick?' Her songbird voice kindles mockery as Suora Maria's cheeks become strawberries to the cream of her headband. 'In Venice, a game of Zara can only be won if a two and a three are thrown together. I am afraid you must pay the forfeit.'

The choir nuns' habits grow plain from gambling – their shoulders pricked with little holes where bright brooches once sat.

Ghostanza shines ever whiter.

In the mornings she rubs linseed oil into the fine lines across her brow, washes her face with kidney beans and malmsey, lemons and honey. Then she paints herself thick with cerussa, because she does not know, unlike country women, that thrift begins at the mouth of the sack. Mona Grazia rationed her grain as soon as it was opened but Ghostanza sees only the autumn harvest and thinks nothing of the winter. She gorges like a friar after Lent, smearing spatulas across her brow until her forehead is a jutting cliff. Crimson salve swells her lips and she takes to painting great swatches of glittering turquoise over each eyelid, all the way from her tinted lashes to the line where her eyebrows once lived.

'They have no notion of entertainment, these midland women,' she complains when the choir nuns have gone. 'In Venice, our actors staged floating plays on giant rafts, and during the carnival fireworks lit the night in the shape of all manner of animals. When I came home my cook would make chocolate meringues to eat warm as the sun rose . . .'

Most of Ghostanza's laments begin this way, boasting to Flavia that everything from her native city is splendour embodied. The beauty salons she attended, the hours spent refining the texture of her paints until they outshone even those of the Venetian alchemists. By contrast the midland citizens are only slightly better than the froth that forms around a horse's mouth. 'To be expected, I suppose, eating all those fatty meats'.

Once the span, shape, buoyancy, colour and height of her hair is approved, she has nothing to do but to pace up and down, chiding Flavia for the messy state of her rooms. Even the pretty choir nuns begin to feel the edge of Ghostanza's tongue, though she stops short of testing their cheekbones with the back of her hand. Their visits become less frequent and the sound of wooden pieces clacking on the games table is replaced by the steady glug of wine as it hits the bottom of the cup. The sweet *passito* makes her remembrances stranger, her face empty as she speaks to the glass oval.

Sometimes the things she talks about make sense: a bridge over water or a street that Flavia can almost imagine, but other times she speaks of storms. A winter of wind and water, restless wall hangings and breached shutters, waves that cuff at stone until the world feels like a ship creaking at anchor. How one morning she stood barefaced on her balcony and watched a boat glide by, how a handsome young man in its cabin glanced from one side of her to the other and did not see her at all.

16

The dandelions send their seeds dancing into air. Flavia plucks one from the ground, its head soft and large. She and Pia used to blow on them and count the number of seeds left for the number of children they would bear. Pia always blew very softly so she had at least twenty left. Flavia would try to puff them all out in a single breath.

Madalena is not with her. She cannot hide behind the servant's big bottom if she gets into trouble but she has enough cerussa to paint her face for a hundred trips to the city and this is all the protection she needs. As soon as she is wearing it her fear of the world slips away like water from oil.

The sun rises fiercely as she walks up to the city gates. By the time they shut behind her she is gasping for breath.

If the convent simmers, the city bakes.

Shade without air. No escaping the sultriness that rolls along the streets, the plumes of rotting waste. Some of the traders and menservants making house deliveries have barely a stitch on, and a group of boys dart about entirely naked, much to the horror of an elderly priest who sits stiffly under a balcony in his jet black *biretta*.

She makes her way through the marketplace towards Il Sicofante's.

She uses the side door now. The tomb white shop with its marble counter is for the rustle of silk brocade skirts and crystal voices: this much the apothecary has told her without saying a word. She does not enter the blushing room either –

her name for the room with the painted women because she cannot think of Il Sicofante's hands on her skin without boiling cheeks. The kitchen is her entrance, and Cimon's lair. The apprentice is always there, shuffling around with his Adam's apple bobbing metrically. Apart from helping Il Sicofante in the shop and making neat triangles of dust with his broom, he bakes hard, flat loaves that belong more to a Jew's table than a Christian's. He never seems to understand a question or give a useful answer.

The kitchen is long, low and dim. Il Sicofante works here on the table, his head brushing against bushels of herbs pinned to the rafters. There are riches in here too: jars of oil, milk and vinegar; fresh and dried flowers; nuts, seeds and spices. Some of them go into the biscuits baked by a woman named Palmeria, but most find their way into the hair and skin of Il Sicofante's customers. There are ingredients for physicians too. Serious-looking men in plain round caps who wait sullenly on the shop bench while the apothecary guides his matrons through the merits of cumin and tobacco in hair dye.

In the corner by the sugar bin is Cimon. Or rather Cimon's buttocks, jutting high in the air. His hands are clasped behind his back like two white spiders in the act of procreation and his head is deep in the bin where Il Sicofante keeps his precious loaf.

'Cimon, why do you have your head in the sugar bin?'

The buttocks purse.

'Because I will not tell a lie,' comes the muffled reply.

Flavia sighs and mops her brow with the edge of her sleeve.

'But what is wrong with your hands, Cimon?'

Cimon eases his face out. His normally hollow cheeks are plump and crusted with glittering sweetness.

'When my master asks me if I kept my hands away from the sugar loaf, I will not have to lie to him. Cimon does not paint falsehood onto what is real.'

'But Cimon, you are lying to him really, if you have gnawed on the maestro's loaf.'

'Fool of a servant,' Cimon rasps, his greenish teeth sparkling at the gums. 'There is only truth and not truth. Cimon never lies. He is on the outside what he is inside.'

Flavia thinks of her father's best sow, slit end to end for curing. Grimacing, she sees Cimon's pale white heart, bobbing intestines and his greasy sated belly.

'I want to see Il Sicofante.'

'He is not here,' Cimon has already stuck his head back into the bin and his tongue is slow with gorging.

'He must be here. He is always here!' Flavia casts about the kitchen, as though Il Sicofante is about to unfold his great thighs from a cupboard and spring out. 'I must see him, Cimon. He has to prepare ingredients for Ghostanza Dolfin.'

'Paaah!'

The sound of particles fired onto the inside of the bin. Cimon drags himself upright, his nose streaming sugar.

'Whores rolling their faces in powder? Sparrows in a dust bath have more sense.'

'Cimon!' Flavia's chest is tight with exasperation. 'Where is he?'

The apprentice's eyes shuffle back to the sugar bin.

'Cimon, you will be telling a lie if you do not answer me, when I have asked you so clearly.'

The apprentice sniffs wetly.

'And because I am honest too, I will have to tell your master that even though your hands were free of sin your mouth was not.'

The Adam's apple wavers, swinging into an involuntary swallow.

'He is painting the face of Mona Bartola at the house of her husband Bruno Sciri.'

'Then you will take me there.'

She speaks like Ghostanza giving orders, leaving no space between them and the yank of the kitchen door for anything like a 'shan't' to slide off the apprentice's tongue.

* * *

The sun has passed behind the towers but the city is still sweating a fever. Cimon takes her back through the Piazza Grande and down the main *corso* before turning into a street lined with elegant sand-coloured buildings. They stop half-way along and Cimon calls up to a first floor window before making a mocking bow to Flavia, leaving her to wait in the patterned shade of the jasmine leaves until a rumpled-looking servant opens a shutter.

Flavia has never stood before such a grand-looking house, much less asked for admission. Mona Grazia once said to Pia that if ever she was lost she should ask for the lady of the house, because a lady would give her a bowl of something hot to eat whereas her husband would put his hands on the parts that only God sees and try and make her his second wife for a few hours.

Flavia looks at her feet and asks if Mona Bartola is at home.

'Mona Bartola?' the servant's sleepy features shift momentarily around her face before settling in their accustomed niches. 'Child, my mistress has been dead these three days.'

Hot and weary, Flavia glares up at the servant.

'That is not possible! I was told by a man who never lies that the apothecary Il Sicofante is painting her face.'

The servant arrests a yawn and grins.

'Ah, that is true as well.'

Up a gleaming staircase a series of small, fussy chambers admit and expel them until they arrive at a set of double doors. With a sideways nod, the servant slouches back to her bed and Flavia steps alone into a sunlit room with a green paved floor. Along the walls are shapes of furniture covered with dust cloths. In the middle sits a trestle table cluttered with dirty brushes and paint-smeared slabs of marble.

Il Sicofante stands behind it. His face is down, shoulders hunched as he mixes small dabs of colour. On the wall behind him is a painting of an elderly man in a high-collared coat. Next to him, a square patch of plaster sparkles with marble dust. The background colours are filled in: purple hills and a little castle in the distance surrounded by trees. In the centre the shape of a woman is outlined. Her robes are Roman, full and folded where fullness and folding are most pleasing. Hair thicker than a jennet's mane tumbles over her bare shoulders. As for her face . . .

'It is perfectly symmetrical.' Il Sicofante looks up, his teeth in the shape of a grin. 'That is the very heart of a woman's beauty.'

'I thought you were painting Mona Bartola's face.' Flavia wanders over to the outline of the woman.

'I am!' Il Sicofante laughs, adding a spot of pale blue to the mixture. 'A wall is no different from skin. White lead will suffice for both. For the reds I always use the best vermilion, for my clients' lips or making a mouth from thin air.'

'You painted the women in the blushing . . . the back room? The chess player and the others?'

A nod of curls, flecked with paint.

'They are my assistants. When Mona Emilia waddles in and finds herself among ladies of such perfection, she cannot help fingering that hairy mole on her neck. And when I arrive a few minutes later with the bottle of Acqua Dolce she ordered, there are suddenly a great many more things Mona Emilia wants.'

Flavia thinks of all the beautiful things the apothecary owns, the sugar loaf Cimon is probably making love to at this very moment. Then she thinks of Ghostanza when her cerussa is heavy and her heart light, and when it is the opposite.

'What did Mona Bartola really look like?'

'You can see for yourself,' Il Sicofante points his brush through a doorway at the end of the room. 'Luckily her husband,' he nods at the elderly man in the other fresco, 'is rich enough to keep her cool in this wretched heat, so she looks as well as she ever did.'

Following the line of the apothecary's brush, Flavia creeps into the next room. The walls are bare and there is no furniture except a table covered with plump grey velvet. On top of it lies a well-dressed corpse. Blocks of ice at either side, head and feet glisten in the heat, half masking what even a beautiful woman must smell like three days into a summer death.

Nervously, Flavia moves towards Mona Bartola.

The dead woman's pose is symmetrical, but she is not. Not blossoming and folding in all the right places. Not harmonious at all. Rubbery-jawed and stub-nosed. It is not possible to blame that on death.

Her hair at least is as Il Sicofante traced it. Thick and full, meandering freely down the front of her bodice. Flavia cannot resist touching it, marvelling as the golden threads slip in and out of her fingers. She does not notice a strand getting caught around a button on her sleeve, and when she moves her hand away the curls around Mona Bartola's temples shift sideways, revealing a bare patch of dark brown scalp.

'Il Sicofante, help! I have broken Mona Bartola!' Flavia wails as a paintbrush strikes the floor and the apothecary rushes through the doorway. Pushing her aside, he leans over and deftly realigns the curls around Mona Bartola's face.

'Don't worry,' he grins. 'Like the rest of her, Mona Bartola's hair is already dead.'

* * *

'Your picture looks nothing like her.'

They are back in the sunlit room. Il Sicofante is still laughing and Flavia is starting to get annoyed at his big teeth. She wonders whether to tell him he has a piece of miniver tail stuck in them from sucking his brush. She is annoyed at Mona Bartola too, for her stupid wig and because she would love to sleep just once on plump grey velvet, living or dead.

'That is not my fault,' the apothecary winches his big shoulders into a shrug. 'In fact, it is Mona Bartola who looks nothing like my painting.'

'So it's her fault?'

'Well, what will people prefer to look at? Bruno Sciri will soon forget his wife's face, but he will always enjoy this image of her. What is more, his new wife will be certain to keep her cheeks smooth lest she make a poor comparison. Everyone is happy.'

'But it isn't her likeness.'

'Mona Bartola never had a likeness!' The smile slips from Il Sicofante's face as he spoons out a line of yellow pigment. 'Her hair belonged to some marketplace tart, her clothes belonged to her husband and her face, such as it was, belonged to me, because it never saw the light of day without my help. I choose to make this painting her likeness, better than she ever had before. When the workmen of tomorrow come with shovels and spades to dig out the family vault for another new palazzo, what will they care for the bones of this woman? It is all in the paint: the cerussa, the fucus. There never was a Mona Bartola without it.'

He pauses for breath, and Flavia is a little frightened of his darkened face. She turns instead to the woman-shaped space that is Mona Bartola's outline.

'Have you ever painted Ghostanza Dolfin?'

'I have not had that honour,' says Il Sicofante stiffly. 'Only maestri from the studios of Venice would be good enough for her.'

Flavia wonders if she dares ask why he is not such a maestro, but the apothecary is talkative now and needs no questions.

'Painters! No better than dogs on their bellies! I did not want to live like a dog. A basket of food for a week's work, maggots in the *salsiccia* and never any soap. Before I was in my skin seventeen years I mixed my first fucus with the leftover pigment of a cardinal's portrait and sold it pot by pot in the Piazza Grande. I made more money in a week than Perugino did in a year. Soon I had enough to buy an apprenticeship with the apothecary Gregorio di Santo and together we turned our skills to the malady of ugliness, which the ladies of this city did not even realise they suffered until we told them so.'

'But you still choose to paint on walls?'

'If I paint a fresco now, it is for the pleasure of knowing that my colours will not be sponged off at the end of the day.

But that is not where the money lies. Only when you make a portrait to be carried on a woman's face will you know a full stomach and a soft bed.'

He works as he talks, filling the skin of Mona Bartola while the plaster is wet. Despite the excitement in his voice his hands are steady, and Flavia can see why the matrons of the city come to sit in the blushing room and give him their faces.

'How old is Ghostanza?'

Il Sicofante laughs.

'Old enough to lose her lover to a younger woman.'

'Was Ridolfo Alfani really her lover?'

The curls bounce confirmation.

'Are they lovers still?'

'Ha! What does it matter? Ridolfo is taken, and neither family will let that match slip.'

Flavia is eager to hear more but the plaster is drying and Mona Bartola will not wait for words. She must content herself with pulling a stool from under a dust sheet and watching the memory of the dead woman take shape under the apothecary's brush.

If she had known to pray for such things at the Casa Nascosta, she would have asked God for what Il Sicofante gives Mona Bartola: wide blue eyes under fleeting golden eyebrows; a nose both straight and soft; lips as sweet and generous as an amarelle cherry. The more he makes up Mona Bartola, the more Flavia understands he is right about the things people will pay for. She would rather have that face painted on her every day than a lie on a wall when she is dead.

* * *

The servant brings in a tray of food as the sun glows orange on the drying colours. With a cup of wine in his hand and his teeth scything fresh bread, Il Sicofante is talkative once more. Flavia says and drinks little, remembering the last time she relaxed in the apothecary's presence – the feel of his fingers under her borrowed dress.

After eating, Il Sicofante leans back in his chair. He draws a silver toothpick from his pocket and digs into the gums around his biting teeth.

'Now, Signorina, I think you have something to give me.'

The miniver hairs have gone and his smile is bright, like Alfeo's mare when she tickled her nostrils with long grass. But Il Sicofante's smiles are never quite what they seem. Flavia tucks her elbows against her ribs.

'No Signore, I came here for more ingredients for Ghostanza Dol–'

'Ghostanza Dolfin was married to one the wealthiest men in the city,' says the apothecary, still smiling, 'so naturally she has failed to pay me for the ingredients I have already given her.'

Il Sicofante replaces the toothpick and examines a fresh blister between his thumb and forefinger. His normally smooth nails are brittle, bright pigment scored into them.

She swallows at nothing. Ghostanza says it is vulgar to talk about money, and Flavia, who has never held a coin in her hand, never questioned how her empty basket grew full every time she came to Il Sicofante.

'You see, when a person – even an insignificant one – walks into my shop, they are signing a contract. Like the peasant who asks the rich man for a loan, you have put your little country name in my book. You made a promise of payment, and that payment was secrets. No?'

The smile that is not a smile grows to a quarter moon, but his eyes are less friendly with each new stretch.

"'If your work is pleasing, Ghostanza Dolfin will dispense some secrets of her own to the improvement of your art." Do you remember those little words?'

Flavia shakes her head. 'I don't know any secrets.'

Il Sicofante picks at the paint around his fingernails.

'No, I think not,' he says. 'At first I thought perhaps a recipe or two, sewn into your undershirt as a bribe, but that is not the ways of our noble matrons is it? To give, if you can get for nothing?'

So those were the secrets he wanted in the blushing room. Ghostanza's, not hers. An odd ripple swims through Flavia's stomach. She does not know if it is relief or disappointment.

'It is well known the rich whores of Venice have recipes particular to themselves. A map, if you like, of how best to enhance their beauty.'

The apothecary leans back in his chair, his face twisted slightly to where Mona Bartola dries on the wall. 'It is beyond imagining the famous Ghostanza Dolfin does not have such a collection.'

'Ghostanza?'

Something must have changed in Flavia's face. The apothecary sees it, the ignorance and the astonishment. There is a look of calculation as he stretches out his long legs.

'A legend she was,' Il Sicofante's eyes reflect the falling light of the sun.

'It is said that when she was fifteen, three Mohammedans built a ship to sail up the Adriatic. When they docked in Venice there was a quarrel over whose black fingers would be the first to put a chain around her neck. By the time they'd drawn knives to resolve the issue Ghostanza's emerald had been cracked a good many times, but her fame never was.'

Flavia looks queasily down at her lap, thinking about Ghostanza's white skin and red brocade dress. Despite her viciousness and her night-time wanderings, she cannot imagine La Perfetta this way.

'I thought she was a lady,' she says quietly.

'Some of them end up that way, given half the chance,' chuckles Il Sicofante, flexing his thighs. 'But whatever she is now, Ghostanza Dolfin will have the secrets of her trade somewhere. Venice isn't like here. Apothecaries, goldsmiths, perfumiers, herbalists, all of them testing new recipes in salons across the city and a fortune they are making too. When marriages are made on the height of a woman's cheekbones, the value of Venetian cerussa cannot be imagined.'

Flavia looks up at Mono Bartola on the wall, seeing nothing but the blank mortar behind the paint. It makes sense now, the sweetbreads and the sweet words, the wide smile and the open door.

'You know where she keeps things, of course?'

Il Sicofante looks hard at her. Flavia turns her bad side away because the muddy cerussa is itching. She feels sick. If she were back at the Casa Nascosta she would definitely crawl under the workshop table.

'There is a box,' she says quietly. 'And a key that only Ghostanza has. It is very pretty, with pictures of little winged boys on it and I'm not allowed to touch it. I thought perhaps she kept tokens of love in there.'

'Unlikely,' sneers Il Sicofante. 'From what I know of her, Ghostanza Dolfin is too boastful to keep signs of adoration hidden. And the key?'

He is trying to keep the eagerness from his voice but his nostrils are big black ovals and his breathing is fast.

'Around her neck. I cannot get it.'

Il Sicofante snorts.

'This neck of hers, is it always holding her head upright? Or does it make an impress on her pillow from time to time? In my experience a lady is not a lady who sleeps less than twelve hours a night and three in the afternoon.'

'She does not sleep very deeply, even when she has taken the *passito.*'

Flavia picks up the end of one of her plaits and crunches it between her teeth. Mona Bartola's new eyes look calmly down at her.

'But if I could get it, what would you give me?'

She already knows what she wants.

The thing she has wanted ever since Ghostanza Dolfin lifted her face to the heavens in the chapel of Santa Giuliana.

But she also wants to know if Il Sicofante is as good at reading faces as he is at painting them.

The apothecary's eyes are thoughtful, the same shade as Tommaso's. Again she senses the tips of his fingers running through her gown, caressing her flesh and the parts of her soul that had never been touched before.

'That mixture you're using on your cheek won't last long,' he says finally. 'Not in this heat. Whatever is underneath it will come bursting through those riverbed cracks and then you will look a bigger fool than if you'd never covered it at all.'

A little smile, real this time, tickles his lips. He dabs a finger into a drying splotch of paint and smears it across the palette.

'If you bring me the secret of Venetian cerussa, my country Signorina, I will give you a proper face.'

To Make the Nails Grow

Take wheat flower, mingle it with honey and lay it to the nails, and it will help them. For cloven nails mingle turpentine and wax together, and lay it on the nail. And as it groweth, cut it away, and it will heal.

17

'It feels odd, Ghostanza.'

Suora Umiliana's dark hair has been stripped right back behind her ears. It rears like a stark hedgerow behind a pin-pricked expanse of scalp. Flavia plucked for so long she wore out a groove in the middle of the tweezers.

Ghostanza smiles at the choir nun.

'In Venice, a woman is only considered beautiful if she has more hair plucked than remaining. Sadly I have a small mole on my scalp which prevents me from achieving a brow such as yours. If it weren't for the fucus on my cheeks you would see they are quite green with envy.'

Someone cleverer than Suora Umiliana might wonder why La Perfetta is so keen to play with her pretty choir nuns, because she is not the only strange-looking thing in Ghostanza's parlour. Suora Lampidia's hazel eyes are as playful as ever but her cheeks are awash with orange cerussa and Ghostanza has drawn matching triangles were where her eyebrows used to live. The mouths of both choir nuns have been replaced by small black slugs taking refuge under their noses.

Both of them look very odd, but who is there to tell them? Not the servant nuns, who have to wash Suora Umiliana's velvet cushions every time her little dog eats sugared prunes. Not Suora Benedetta, who has trodden on a rusty nail and is now oozing puss from her foot in the infirmary, unable to walk but rather proud to be suffering one fifth of Christ's wounds. Certainly not Flavia, who can think about nothing other than finding her way into the painted box on Ghostanza's dressing table.

Suora Umiliana smiles up at Ghostanza. Her plucked hair is tinged with pale green, courtesy of the verdigris Flavia put in her hair dye.

Ghostanza has covered up her oval glass so the choir nuns cannot see how they look, but they can both see each other and are full of praise for their fellow sisters' beauty. Perhaps it is their admiration of Ghostanza, who is positively dancing among them, assuring them that everything is Venetian, perfect. But the curl in Suora Lampidia's lips is not kind when Suora Umiliana's remaining hairs are scraped into a tower and her ears hung with ugly brass rings.

'Will you not try some of this?'

Suora Umiliana passes the pot of black lip salve to Ghostanza, who shakes her head benignly.

'On this day of finery, I will be a mere background. Think of me as a wintry sea against which the colourful ships' masts flutter.'

Ghostanza is aglow with suppressed laughter. She tries hard to keep a straight face but when Lampidia opens her mouth and the black fucus smears over her front teeth she lets out a shriek and collapses, giggling into a chair.

Umiliana laughs too, but Lampidia is quick to point out that her forehead looks as high as Mount Sinai. A bitter argument breaks out, accompanied by fierce rubbings of face and lips. Ghostanza laughs all the while, only recovering her composure when Suora Umiliana jumps to her feet.

'Mona Ghostanza!'

There is fury on her blistering forehead, and another kind of agitation which Flavia recognises but cannot put a name to. The kind of look when someone knows an unkind thing and suddenly aches to say it.

'My dear?'

Ghostanza blinks through tears of laughter.

'Mona Ghostanza you have made pretty work of us today,' Suora Umiliana pulls out her ugly earrings, 'but perhaps you can be forgiven for seeking idle distraction at such a time.'

'Now what are you talking about, my little plucked grouse?' Ghostanza stretches her arms out and affects a yawn.

'My father has written to me . . .'

'Your father can write? Goodness, the skills of the governor have increased no end since I came to Santa Giuliana.'

'He will know well enough how to write RA and GT on a marriage contract when the time comes!'

'What nonsense are you talking about?'

Ghostanza's words are measured but her face is whiter than a dawn frost and her lips burn red enough to make Suora Umiliana take two paces back.

'M–my father writes Ridolfo Alfani is set to marry your stepdaughter. He says theirs will be a blessed union, that Gilia Tassi is called Gilia la Bella by all who see her.'

* * *

Dusk is thickening when Flavia bolts down the remains of her supper, sitting on the roots of the poplar by the convent wall. Down the line of wall she can just make out the circle of fresh mortar. The younger nuns come here sometimes, during the day. They run their fingers round the edges and whisper to one another with their heads bent and their faces hidden, just as Ghostanza once whispered to her lover before the last psalms of the day.

Licking her fingers, Flavia wanders back towards the cloister and the narrow band of orange that spills out of Ghostanza's window when her candles are still lit.

Up the staircase the passageway is pitch black and warm as an oven on feast day. Nervously she feels her way to Ghostanza's doorway, expecting to find her sprawled on her bed or gazing into the oval glass, bitten raw by ill humour. But La Perfetta is not to be seen, either in the bedchamber or the parlour.

The oil burners unfurl a sickly scent.

Flavia peers under the little daybed.

Perhaps Ghostanza is in another part of the convent, but Flavia did not see her out in the grounds and tonight she will certainly not be pulling wishbones with Suora Umiliana in the dining hall. Looking back on it the pretty choir nuns were lucky they left straight away, while Ghostanza still sat dumbly in her chair. Flavia was not far behind them.

A horrible notion emerges. Less in her head than her bowels, which start to fidget and squirm away from their unwanted promotion to an organ of thought.

What if Ghostanza has left the convent?

Suora Benedetta is still in the infirmary and the feather-brained listener nun has been promoted to gatekeeper. What if Ghostanza has managed to threaten a key from her? Even if she cannot go back to her husband's house, she must have friends in the city.

Again Flavia's bowels clench. She hardly dares look at the dressing table, where the painted box ought to be. Ghostanza would not have left without it, not if Il Sicofante is right about her recipes. And if the box is gone it will not be Ghostanza Dolfin shuffling around the inside the wall with no beginning and no end; it will be Flavia di Maestro Bartofolo da San

Fortunato, her stiff plaits drying out beneath her cap along with the bitter white memory of Ghostanza's cerussa.

She turns slowly, her eyes wandering up the legs of the dressing table, in and out of the crowds of perfumed water, salves and powder pots.

The little winged boys are still there, grinning among the peacocks.

Flavia hurries over to the box and eases her fingernails beneath the lid.

Still locked.

She drops her head in relief. The floor gives a waxy reflection, its tiles encroached at the edge of her sight by a hem of deep, cochineal red. A silky trail. She tracks it to the foot of the window curtain where it disappears.

Crouching down, Flavia pulls carefully at the edge of the curtain. Ghostanza is slouched on the stones, legs folded and head tilted to the window casement. Her eyes are closed and her hair falls untidily over her face, fluttering with each parting breath. The cerussa has been refreshed and her lips are a warning vermilion but her jaw is loose and a snail track of saliva runs down her chin.

Even with the cerussa she looks old. Pouched and limp, like an empty purse. The layers of powder weigh on her brow like a lifetime of bad thoughts.

Not daring to breathe, Flavia leans closer. The front of Ghostanza's dress is dappled with sweet-smelling splotches, a trail of *passito* from breast to lap. The collar of her undershirt is loose and the thread of the key chain is fired by candlelight.

She should wait.

Il Sicofante would tell her to wait. The apothecary prepares everything, the same as her father when he is grinding, sifting and stirring.

Patience, Flavia.

But the wall hangings of the blushing room flap in her mind and the soft crack of pastry is on her tongue.

She reaches around Ghostanza's neck and feels for the clasp: two interlocking loops. Gently turned, the chain slackens. Pulling the key up through her undershirt, Flavia watches the stray knots of hair rising and falling over Ghostanza's face. Carefully she draws the curtain over her, creeps back to the painted box, and slides the key into the lock.

A folded pad of cotton, squeezed tightly around the edges of the box. Flavia tucks her fingernails around it and peels it back. Underneath is a collection of hair ribbons. Every colour Maestro Bartofolo ever made and some he could only imagine. A rainbow of interleaving smoothness that Ghostanza never uses on herself. Nervously Flavia ploughs through them, parting the feather soft strands until her fingers find leather. A gasp of relief is blocked by a fist to the mouth. Breathing quickly, she buries her fingers deeper into the ribbons. There are bumps and crevices. The book of recipes must be very old. Her fingers inch around, finding more roundness than squareness.

Cold doubt begins to creep up the back of her neck. Grabbing the nearest candle, she pulls the ribbons apart and scoops her hand in.

The thing she is holding is small, round, stiff and brown. It has a leathery covering, but it is not the skin of an animal.

A tiny head stretches obliquely from the back of the skull. The nose is almost entirely swallowed by a bulbous brow. There is a mouth. The mouth looks human, though it gapes a little where it meets a squashed cheek, like a sleeper trying to breathe when his nose is blocked. The limbs, though twisted and hard, look like something that might once have been unwrapped, pink and warm, from their swaddling bands. It is much smaller than anything she saw at Zia Caracosa's house, and the wet nurse used to get them very young. It is dark too, but skin always goes dark when it dies, unless you scrape the fat off and lay it in the sun. Flavia traces a finger over the stretched skull. Up close the oil burners do not cover its smell, a darker version of a deathbed stench, unusual for something so small and crinkled.

Gently she returns the brown baby to its nest of ribbons, then takes up the cotton pad to cover it. As she beds it down a loud cracking noise fills her head. She blinks very hard because no one told her there was going to be a storm today. Twice more, the smack of something hard on her ear. Her knees send shockwaves up her thighs as they hit the floor. The box, snapped shut, is still in her hands. For a moment she wonders how she has fallen but the clanging in her eardrums makes it hard to think. Another cracking noise and she is flying backwards on her heels, her head rolling up and into the face of Ghostanza Dolfin.

She is brilliant in the flickering light. Candida but golden. Lips slightly parted, relaxed. Eyes clear and kind as a priest delivering the last rites.

Flavia kneels before her with bells in her ears. Blood is coming from somewhere, trickling along the bridge of her nose and down her cheeks.

Ghostanza bends over. Her outstretched thumb gently wipes a trail of red tears from Flavia's cheek. In her other hand is a silver card-case, dented along one side and wet with blood. The only hard edge in the room. Everything else is underwater, blurred. Ghostanza's knotted hair seems to float fathoms under a broken-backed ship. But the hard edge of silver is still there. As she looks down tenderly she raises the card-case in her right hand and brings it scything towards Flavia's skull. A lunge to her right and the case slices across her shoulder, ripping through her undershirt and into flesh. Scrabbling to her feet, Flavia throws all four of her limbs towards the doorway, not caring which one reaches it first. She crashes through, turning as the frame catches her shoulder.

Ghostanza's face is in the oval glass. A swivel of the neck and she is staring straight at Flavia. Her expression is still tranquil, a little inquiring. Flavia does not wait to see what she will do next. Lunging through the bedchamber, she runs into the blackened passage, hammering the walls either side with the palms of her hands to keep herself straight.

Down the stairwell and out into night. She has a sense of something behind her. An evil wind chasing. She does not look back as she streaks through the courtyard, towards the outer wall. Desperately she prays for the solid hulk of Suora Benedetta keeping guard, but the gatekeeper nun is nursing one fifth of Christ's wounds and this wall has no end for her now.

There are footsteps somewhere, gaining with each snatched breath. Whatever beast it is that shivers and rages beneath Ghostanza's blue cape, it is let loose on her this night.

The long stretch of stone marks the end of her escape. The painted box is still in her hands. Her only thought is to get rid of it. With one great heave she throws it high into the air. It thuds softly into the long grass on the other side.

She blinks the blood from her eyes. Pressing her chest hard against the wall, she drives her fingertips deep into the gap around the stones above her head. Arms straining, she kicks off her clogs and does the same with the toes of one foot, then the other, spreading herself flat as she pulls herself up from the ground. Some crevices are deeper than others. She digs in until her nails tear, edging higher, arms strained and burning in a desperate embrace of stone.

She is almost at the top when a cold hand circles around her ankle. With a swift tug she is plucked into air.

To Endure Long Hunger and Thirst

Of the herb called tobacco, namely the juice thereof, and the ashes of cockle shells make little balls and dry them in the shade. Hold one of them between the under lip and the teeth and suck continually and swallow down what you suck, and all the day feel neither hunger, thirst nor weariness.

Gilia la Bella III

Ghostanza still put on her flat shoes and went out of the Palazzo Tassi whenever she wanted, and Jacopo still got very purple about it all, but Antonia never did manage to follow her without being seen. Eventually she gave up on it so all Jacopo could do was tap his stick around the courtyard and shout at anyone who crossed his path.

Ghostanza was happier than Gilia had ever seen her. Clearly she liked having her admirers and at first Gilia was worried she wouldn't be called her summer flavours any more but it didn't happen like that. The happier Ghostanza was, the more she wanted Gilia with her. Sometimes she felt a bit like Parassita, something to be stroked and cradled, but Ghostanza seemed to want more for her than just petting. Lessons for one thing. Not just at the dressing table – which Gilia never understood in any case – but in the little room next to her father's study that hadn't been used since Jacopo huffed through his writing and arithmetic with his old tutor Maestro Alessio. Dancing instruction too. Though Gilia was not as graceful as her stepmother she managed to learn some steps of a salto and a bassa danza. Ghostanza clapped her even when she made mistakes, and when she did it completely right she got a present at the end.

One day it was peaches.

Ghostanza had bought a dozen at the marketplace (Gilia wondered if one of her admirers selected them for her). They sat together in the *sala grande* and Gilia took the topmost one from the bowl and pressed it lightly between her palms, watching the flesh rise again. Ghostanza took hers and sliced it thinly. She brought a piece to her mouth and sucked at its yellow flesh. When she had finished eating she turned to Gilia and ran a curled finger lightly down her cheek.

'Nothing tastes quite as good as this,' she said.

But soon there were no more trips to the marketplace and no more admirers for Ghostanza. When Gilia wanted peaches she had to ask Antonia to fetch them, because her stepmother was always being sick and more often than not she was in her bedchamber (which used to be Ricca's parlour but Ghostanza said that Ricca would be better in a room close to the kitchens, even though it always smelled at that end of the house).

Gilia was allowed to visit her twice a day.

'I must try not to blunt my wits by cotside gazing.' A blotchy Ghostanza reached for her wine cup, which was on a special tray only women like her were allowed to use because it was a pretty reward for doing their duty. It used to be Ricca's but Ghostanza said she wouldn't ever need it.

Parassita had followed Gilia into the bedchamber and was licking her paws on the rug.

'Get that vile little thing out of here,' snapped Ghostanza. Gilia quickly shooed the cat away.

'She only wants to be friendly.'

'So do her fleas.'

'She doesn't have fleas!'

'Even so,' Ghostanza sipped from her wine cup, 'I don't like the way she looks at me.'

Ghostanza smoothed the sheets down over her middle. Gilia tried to imagine it. The stirring of little limbs under her skin.

Antonia said Ghostanza's belly was not the only thing swelling. Rumours, which were bad stories that may be true, were growing limbs of their own that would not be swaddled. Antonia said they would leave the laps of their mothers soon and totter through the streets. She looked very satisfied with herself and Gilia felt a shadow of something quite heavy in the part of her head where Ghostanza had moved so many things around.

There was a large book open on Ghostanza's bed. Gilia looked at it distrustfully.

'How are your lessons?'

Gilia took her beads from her mouth so she could stick out her tongue. Ghostanza didn't like it when she did that but it was her stepmother's fault she had to sit with old Maestro Alessio and his abacus and his fingernails all long and blue around the edges. The words Ghostanza thought she ought to know better were still little black strangers most of the time, and she was relieved when her stepmother pushed the book towards her and it was mostly pictures.

Gilia pointed at one of them: a woman in long robes with a vase under her arm standing outside a tiny church.

'Saints?' she asked.

'Damn your cursed saints!'

Ghostanza laughed and Gilia blushed as much as if Lucia and Apollonia were in the room suffering their hideous martyrdoms in front of her. Ghostanza pulled her down onto her pillow, which smelled of spice and oranges, and propped the book on her knees between them.

'That is Venus, the goddess of love. And that is her temple.'

'Temple?'

'A church, I suppose, but better than our dry old churches, and much better than our dry old Santa Maria.'

Gilia blushed again, and mouthed a silent sorry to Maria, who didn't get cut or burned but who still had to hold her dead son in her arms which was a kind of torment.

'Is the priest in there?' she pointed to the doorway of the little church in the picture.

'There is no priest,' tutted Ghostanza. 'There is a priestess. A very beautiful woman, loved by many men. Her life is given to rituals of improving her charm beyond all others.'

'Fra Michele wouldn't let that happen here,' Gilia giggled. The priest from the Chiesa del Gesu came to the palazzo chapel for family prayers. Ricca thought him very good, though his face was stony and he penanced harshly.

Ghostanza sighed.

'If you knew your history Gilia, you would know it has already happened. Fra Michele and his kind have not long been tenants in our churches.'

Gilia fiddled with her beads. Sometimes Ghostanza said things that were strange. Ricca said she had a malady of the soul.

'Would you like to see a Venus temple?'

Gilia thought for a moment. The words made her think of sparkling fountains on a spring day, and the woman in the picture was very pretty, almost as pretty as Ghostanza when she was a girl, though Ricca did not keep that portrait on her wall and when Gilia asked if she might have it Ricca said no very loudly.

'There is a nice young man of this city,' said Ghostanza. 'He was kind enough to show me the old temple that was found under his father's courtyard.'

Gilia was not sure if Ghostanza was telling her something real or whether it was a story, another one of her strange Da Lezze songs even though she was not singing and Ibn

Yunus was sitting quietly on a chair on the other side of the room.

'They were building a new tower. When they dug into the clay they found plates and oil burners. And then a big hole opened into a very old street that had been covered and forgotten, and when they went down they found the temple and an empty niche where the word "Amor" was cut into the stone, and beyond that a small bathhouse patterned with creatures who were half men, half fish.'

Gilia giggled at this last bit of the story. Ghostanza poked her in the ribs in a way that was only a bit playful.

'You think I am lying? I have seen this place.'

'No . . . but the half fish . . .'

'You know nothing,' Ghostanza dug her fingers into Gilia's ribs again and Gilia thought of Parassita playing with her mice in a way that was fun for her but not for the mice.

'I have seen it,' continued Ghostanza. 'We passed from light to dark, my young friend and I, down cellars and passageways and into an ancient brick street strung with dripstones of hardened water. He set his torch in the place where "Amor" was cut.'

Ghostanza's fingers softened. The digging became more tickling, then stroking.

'Was he an admirer?'

A nice young man of the city. Did he see the world through Ghostanza's eyes?

'Yes, Gilia, an admirer,' Ghostanza sighed in an amused way.

'Is that the end of the story?'

Ghostanza put her cup back on her special tray.

'No it is not,' she smiled.

'What happened next?'

Ghostanza lay her head on the pillow. Her breath smelt of wine and sick.

'Gilia, in that place all things were possible.'

* * *

Though she said it wasn't the end of the story, Ghostanza wouldn't say anything else about her nice young man and Gilia was almost glad of it, because now Ghostanza was sickly there was less reason for Jacopo to shout and her father looked happier too, looping his beard around his fingers and saying we must prepare this and that.

But still there were long stretches between her dead sleep and her morning sleep with only the wood panelling above her head and no Ibn Yunus to calm them. It was confusing then because even though Ghostanza knew how to make those black hours pass quicker she also jostled the order of Gilia's thoughts, so that instead of her dolls and her cat and all the normal things of the Palazzo Tassi there was sometimes just a shifting space in her mind with Ghostanza squatting big and beautiful in the middle of it.

The dark hours turned more often to water. Floating on her raft mattress, Gilia watched the shapes in the wood turn from her beloved saints to visions of her stepmother swimming through the grain, her eyes twin crescents above a smile.

One night after staring for hours at Ghostanza in the panelling, Gilia slipped into a dream of herself at the top of a flight of steps leading down to a long stretch of water. Her toes slipped as she struggled for balance. Antonia was there, and Jacopo and Ricca, climbing onto a big stone further down, their clothes glossy and wet. Gilia tried to lift her skirts clear but the water rose too quickly. It plucked her from the steps and carried her down. She fought against the swell but the water was too strong, dragging without pause.

She woke up with a shout as something dug into her arm. Her breath was short and ragged and there was a frantic rustling of sheets. Parassita was at the end of the bed, her back arched and her tail thick as a fir tree. There was a deep bite mark down the inside of Gilia's arm. She must have rolled onto the cat or been holding her very tightly in her sleep because Parassita looked terrified and sprang off the bed when she reached out to her.

Gilia sucked at the scratch, which tasted of blood and Parassita's mousy teeth. Next to the bed was a little plate and a knife and a plump red-orange peach that Antonia had left for her. Seeing the peach on its little plate made her suddenly thirsty and she snatched up the knife, slicing right down to the stone and tearing it in two. She took one half and sucked on it until the juice bled from the corners of her mouth.

It was sweet and rich but after the first few gulps something about it tasted wrong. She swallowed at the chewed-about flesh but her throat wouldn't open and she had to spit the rest of it into her hands.

She lay back on the pillows. Although she was properly awake the mattress still seemed to shift and sway beneath her.

Gilia prayed to Santa Lucia then, and to Sant'Agata and Apollonia, to come back into the wood panelling and find her a rock to sit on, somewhere high and far from water.

18

'It will come back.'

A voice she remembers.

'You will be as you were before.'

The flesh above her eyes is heavy, pressing them deep into their sockets.

It feels like daytime. Swifts shriek through an open window and the grunt of Suora Dorotea's pestle carries from the dispensary. A hand closes over her own as it wanders among a mass of bandages, gaping in places to her ripped scalp.

A few strands, strangely soft, are all that is left.

She fell for a long time.

The ground thumped the breath from her lungs but she could not draw it back in because there was a hand around her neck. Another pulled her cap loose. Then there was nothing but plucking and pulling, plucking and pulling: the rhythm of a determined rosary.

'Your hair will come back. In time.'

The hand is still on hers. Careworn, hollow-palmed. The outgrown ring worn deep into the skin.

There must have been screams, but she did not hear herself make them. It only stopped when Madalena wrestled Ghostanza's hands away, still clenching the remains of two brown stiff plaits.

Her hand is guided away from her head and settled on the sheets.

She tries her voice.

'I cannot afford to pay you Maestro Vitale.'

A sense of something both dark and light standing over her. The voice that comes from another age, before there was either Ghostanza or Il Sicofante, before anything was beautiful or ugly.

'You do not have to. I am here to attend Ghostanza Dolfin. She injured her wrist again,' he pauses, 'striking you as hard as she did.'

Again her hand travels to her face, prodding carefully around the swollen cheeks and the lip cleaved as fiercely as Zio Alfeo's.

'Flavia, I have spoken to the sisters. They agree that as long as Ghostanza stays here, you should not. Given what has happened here, I cannot doubt that your father will welcome you back.'

Back to the Casa Nascosta. Swollen faced and bald as a turtle. Hiding from Mona Grazia, Tommaso and Pia, the world.

'No.' Her fingers find the underbelly of the bird across her cheek, bare of cerussa. 'Please . . .'

A bitter taste of poppy seeds makes her tongue curl. There is a sludge in her mind but she still has the ghost of sweetmeats in her belly and the painted women in the blushing room might be gathered at her bedside their faces are so clear.

In the dispensary Suora Dorotea's pestle grinds to a halt. She tuts quietly to herself, leafing through her Book of Common Ailments.

'You know, of course, the apothecary . . . on the little piazza near the marketplace?'

A sigh. The pallet sinks a little, as though the physician rests on its edge.

'I know Il Sicofante.'

He does not sound happy. She does not care. The painted women are so close she could reach out and smudge their cheeks with her fingertips. She bullies her face into a smile.

'Will you please deliver him a message?'

'I will do what you ask of me, Flavia, if the message is truthful, and if you think to do good by it.'

Hearing nothing beyond the first words, Flavia seeks his hand once again – the only thing left between her and the Casa Nascosta.

'Tell him, then, that I have found what he was looking for.'

PART FOUR

'Now we arrive at the mouth, fount of all loving sweetness. It is best it should lean toward small rather than
large, nor should it be pointed or flat. And when it
opens, especially when it opens without laughter or
speech, it should not show more than five or six upper
teeth.'

Firenzuola

19

Breathing hard, the mute pedlar heaves the rack from his shoulders and leans it against the porch buttress. If he is unlucky the city marshals will order him to pick it up. Unluckier still, and they will kick it down the cathedral steps and all the pretty things he has for sale will be stamped into the dirt. He looks up to San Lorenzo, asks the saint to give him peace as the first customers wander over to sift through his tiered racks of ribbons and beads.

Sometimes it is men who buy things. Young boys in the first shiver of love spend their wages on a pair of brass buttons for their sweetheart. Old men caper among the paper fans and sparkling bracelets until their eyes light upon the perfect trinket for their brides. More often his customers are women. They smile at him as they wave their perfumed fingers for the value of the coins they will give him, and the mute pedlar holds up his own in reply. They continue to wave hands at one another like two friends at either end of a long bridge until a deal is struck.

The Jew Vitale sometimes sits by the mute pedlar on the steps of the cathedral. On days when the pedlar's sales are poor, the physician buys him food from the marketplace and together they sit and watch the women in their tight bodices and wide skirts. The Jew will turn the tight silver ring on his finger, where the flesh has swallowed so much of it a narrow glint is all that catches the sun.

They seem to trouble him, these women with their wide

skirts and silk smiles. When Il Sicofante's new servant comes to the pedlar one morning and asks to buy two birds, the physician does not gaze longingly at her pretty face with its clear brown eyes. He does not smile or lean close to loop her sun-coloured hair between his fingers where it curls loose from her leather cap. When she opens her finely painted lips to speak he turns away.

'I want two of them. These ones.'

She points to the bullfinches.

The pedlar pulls out a male and a female, then roots among his sack for a smaller cage to put them into.

'No, I want pretty ones, two females with red breasts.'

The pedlar shakes his head but he knows better than to try and persuade this girl that the plainer birds are female.

'How much?'

He holds up five fingers and waits for her to extend three or four in return, but her hand stays firmly on her basket.

'I want them to fight. Will they fight?' She takes the cage and rattles it sharply so the little birds tumble into one another. Their squawks appear to satisfy her, and she tosses the coins at the pedlar. Then she smiles at the physician, showing off a set of small even teeth.

The physician does not smile back. He looks at her sadly as she lifts her basket back into the crook of her arm and walks away.

20

She has lied to Il Sicofante twice today. It does not matter. Il Sicofante lies to everyone. Yesterday he told Mona Lucrezia that she has the loveliest chin in Italy when she doesn't have one at all, and that the bulging veins on Mona Aurelia's ankles are a sign of nobility. The apothecary would paint fucus on a wild boar and marry it to the King of Spain if he was paid enough. Lying is as much part of his household as the staircase and the sugar bin. Palmeria, the maidservant, lies about the flour – she says she gets it from the miller on the Via Appia but really it comes from the Monte del Grano and everyone knows the friars mix their flour with sand. Cimon too, for all his righteous talk, is a creature best suited to crevices. He slithers around the house at all hours, and Flavia, working hard in the cellar, must be still until he returns to bed.

* * *

For months she has been doing this. A cold sweat forms on her back as she strains stone against stone, peering through the candlelight at what she has made. During the day she drags her limbs around, so tired that her tasks swim before her eyes.

She has no choice. She arrived here with the biggest lie of all. After that, the little ones hardly matter.

Already today she has told Il Sicofante she ordered more

cardamom seeds when she actually forgot to add them to the merchant's list. Then she told him she was going to pluck the hairs from Mona Fulvia's toes, but went instead to see the mute pedlar on the steps of the cathedral. Now she must pretend the birds are a present from Mona Fulvia because she took the money to pay for them from Cimon's purse. Il Sicofante is bound to see them because he cannot let the moon lose its belly without sniffing round the painted box with its little winged boys.

The painted box is Flavia's biggest lie. It sits in her room like a stolen chalice, full of ribbons and wrongness.

* * *

Cimon is not in the kitchen so she pulls one of the hooks out of the beam where the apothecary's herbs hang to dry. With the birdcage in one hand, she rushes up to the top of the house.

The room where she sleeps is very small. Half the floor is taken up with dusty storage jars and sacks of grain, but there is a window looking out over the city, a lattice of crossed wood that makes diamond shapes of the corrugated rooftops. On her first night here she dragged her pallet underneath it just to breathe everything in. Now she eases the metal hook into a split in the panel above the window and hammers it in with the heel of one of her old clogs. She does not wear the clogs any more, just uses them for squashing scorpions or throwing at Cimon's backside. She has leather shoes now, just like the ones Pia wore for feast days, except hers have mother-of-pearl buttons on the sides. They are better than Pia's, though sometimes she still wishes she had her sister's shoes.

She loops the birdcage onto the hook. It hangs lopsidedly and the bullfinches flutter back up to their perch. Their heads make little swivelling movements as she puts a few specks of grain in the bottom of the cage. The birds ignore it, huddling close.

Flavia watches them for a moment then goes over to her dressing table.

Cimon laughs when she calls it that – three pieces of wood begged from a scaffolder and hammered together with nails and her ever-useful clogs – but it is covered with as many little pots and jars as Ghostanza Dolfin had. Il Sicofante lets her take what she wants from the storerooms, even musk oil, which she mixes into breath lozenges, and a tiny piece of ambergris, which is rarer still because it is spat out of a sea monster's stomach and is good for making perfumes last.

This is the beauty of the lie she has told Il Sicofante. He needs her still, because she has not yet shown him Ghostanza's secrets. The new shoes are from him, as is the cheerful cluster of peasant hair that now sits on her head. A little darker than Mona Bartola's but curlier and softer than Flavia's stiff plaits ever were. Il Sicofante showed her how to flatten her remaining tufts of hair with wax and seal the wig to her scalp. Then he gave her a silver-framed looking glass that shows her things she never realised she had: spots whose yellow centres erupt from her skin like earthworms in the rain; hairs that sprout where they should not be and sometimes when they cannot sprout become another worm hole that must be plucked and purged.

The glass shows nicer things too. A pair of delicate black lines where once her eyebrows knotted into a scowl, dark-lashed eyes shaded with a smudge of kohl along their lower lids.

Best of all it shows what is not there, because now the bird lives always behind a hardy cerussa of the apothecary's making. She hates taking it off, even in the brief hours of sleep. She is so frightened of being without it she always keeps a little pot of powder in the pocket of her skirt.

In this Il Sicofante has been true to his word – giving Flavia a face that can bear heat and frost without crumbling into dust. Still, it is lumpy and discolours easily. When she puts it on, it does not glide across her face like Ghostanza's cerussa. Both Flavia and the apothecary know it is very far from the Venetian recipe, and it is hard to say which of them wants that particular secret most.

* * *

As the birds hop around their new home, Flavia takes off her wig and combs out the tangles the wind has woven into it. Her own hair has grown back almost to her ears, straight and stiff as ever. She would like to shave it off but it has its uses. There are strands of grey, green and pink among the brown, offspring of her less successful experiments. She cannot try the same things on her face without rousing suspicion.

She picks up a pot of Il Sicofante's new fucus. Blush of Eve, he calls it: a dark pink powder melded with fish glue and gum arabic that she paints on her lips and cheeks every morning. She takes a brush and swirls it around the pot, then trails a line over her lower lip and presses it lightly against the upper one until the fucus makes a blushing reflection of itself.

'Ghostanza,' she whispers, watching the pinkness concertina.

She smiles at the looking glass. Her teeth are whiter now she uses the apothecary's tooth powders. Some of them are

beginning to hurt her, a dull ache that seizes her gums and
makes her cry when she chews on Cimon's hard bread, but
everyone can see how well her mouth looks at the front.
Before, it was just a thing for stuffing food into and complain-
ing with. Now it can do all kinds of tricks. She can smile when
she does not mean it, squeeze her lips together in vexation
when she is not cross. Most importantly, her mouth can lie. It
can say, 'I have something for you,' when she has not, and it
can weave deceit as skilfully as a choir nun embroiders an
altarpiece.

She used it for the lie she told when Maestro Vitale
brought her to the apothecary. A lie like oricello, sinking deep
and wide. The fruits of it are already in their summer shades
because Il Sicofante is greedy for fame and he cannot stop
boasting to the city matrons: Ghostanza's secrets wrapped
around the cheeks and brows of his noblewomen.

Because of this she scours the apothecary's shelves for
hope. Alum, musk, white lead, quicksilver, turpentine, vinegar, cloves. Ground metals and sulphides. Each promising
cure and restoration, though their scents are acrid – little like
beauty. She has watched the apothecary crush pearls and
dried lilies into his cerussa, grind up red roses for his fucus.
Gold and silver he uses as well, for smoothing wrinkles and
keeping the skin in its glowing youth. But she must do more
than copy Il Sicofante if she is to recreate Ghostanza's recipes.
Spices, herbs and oils: all of them known or possible ingredients, but they are dead in their separate jars and nothing she
has done yet has brought them to life.

How to Correct the Ill Scent
of the Armpits

The stink of the armholes makes some women very hateful; especially those that are fat and fleshly. Pound litharge of gold or silver and boil it in vinegar, and if you wash those parts well with it, you shall keep them a long time sweet.

21

The smell keeps her rooted. A vicious stench, loved by no one except dyers and their daughters. Zia Caracosa used to say it was the devil breaking wind.

The fumes drift out of tight air vents. Like Maestro Bartofolo with his head to the vat as he weaved the stirring stick, she travels through them, seeing things that exist no more in this moment. She wonders if her father has ever come to look for her here, if Pia or Tommaso think of her at all or whether they are all like Mona Grazia and her army of trees, trying their hardest to scrub her out.

A young friar flaps past, his nose swaddled in his hood, eyes streaming. No one else is on the path. Further along, the poles stretch at regular intervals outside a long building spewing thick grey smoke. Pieces of indigo-coloured wool catch the high winds and flap on their rungs.

This is what has expelled humanity. The smelliest trade.

A small group of dyers perch on the north side of the city. Plain dyers, not masters of all colour like Maestro Bartofolo. They get their water from the mountains, through the aqueducts that criss-cross the city. The city dwellers do not love them, but then city dwellers do not know the value of piss. They do not realise that it cleans the wool, getting rid of dirt and oil, making it softer than the lamb's first coat. They do not understand that it brings out the colours; they have never seen the stunning violet of the lichen orchil when it has been soaked in it. Piss will fix a dye so that it stays in the cloth and does not drain into the wearer's skin. The staler it is, the better.

It was the same at the Casa Nascosta. They never threw away their own. Maestro Bartofolo even asked the taverner at Avigliano to leave a tub outside his doorway so the customers could fill it on their way home. They took it from Zia Caracosa's infants too, squeezing out the sodden nappies into a bucket. Some say this is the best piss of all because there is no meat in their little bellies. But still it stinks, and still it takes a dyer's daughter to be able to walk past and sniff the air and not lose her stomach on the cobbles. To know that this terrible smell is nothing more than the feet of the swan who glides serenely over thrashing legs. Doing what is ugly for the sake of beauty.

Cimon says the dyers throw acids into the water supply, that the fish are beginning to glow in the dark. Flavia does not know if this is true or not. But already she has seen enough to know that dyers are not the only polluters of rivers here.

*　*　*

A rotten part of town, the streets behind the Via Bontempi. A tangle of steep inclines with no sun between the roof tiles. Grey laundry strung in place of flags, not fluttering because it is still thick with grease. Noises from unseen places: a pair of shutters creaking open and something hit hard against the window ledge; a bucket of something wet emptied onto dirt; and a child crying as a woman's words are spoken sharply. It gets worse from here. The Via del Lupo curls under an archway then burrows beneath the newer streets into a tunnel. Though the rain can't reach it, the grey green walls are never dry. Their cracks spread along the length of the street, spilling rotten straw as rats plop casually through tiny window casements.

Flavia stops halfway down at a well worn door. She knocks timidly and repeatedly until it opens.

A heavily-lined face peers out. Then a hand, bare of flesh but covered with ugly glass rings, clasps Flavia's shoulder and pulls her inside. A gust of foul breath hits Flavia in the face as Susanna sighs.

'What have you done now?'

Muddy footprints litter the hallway, ending with the rise of a staircase that turns unevenly into darkness. A house of women says Palmeria with a sniff, though there are no brooms or mops, no smells of pummelled dough or roasting meat.

Susanna leads her up and into a tiny low-ceilinged room.

'Let me see it.'

Flavia sets down her basket. She rolls up her sleeve to the elbow then eases it over the bandage tightly wound around her upper arm.

'I have not been able to take it off entirely,' she says as Susanna unties the bandage knot.

The cloth is heavy as clay as she unwinds it. It is not how Flavia remembered it at the convent, when she did the same recipe with Ghostanza. It should be almost dry by now.

Susanna sighs another rotten gust into the tallow flame, bunches the bandage into her skirt pocket. When the last pad is all that is left she begins to peel it away.

'No, do not touch it.'

Susanna grabs at Flavia's hand as she tries to smother the seething pain.

Ghostanza's skin never bubbled like that. It was very red

for days after the camphor and the turpentine had soaked her, but the flesh did not ooze and there was no blood.

Maybe the recipe only works on noblewomen.

'This is not good,' Susanna wrinkles her nose. 'I think the physician of the Comune should see it.'

Flavia shakes her head wretchedly. Maestro Vitale has rarely spoken to her since he brought her from Santa Giuliana to the apothecary's house. When Il Sicofante ushered them into the blushing room that day, he kept his face from the painted women on the wall and just looked sadly at Flavia as she sat with the painted box squeezed down into her lap.

She breathes out slowly as Susanna reaches to a shelf above her head.

How many times has she called on her now? Once when a dye burnt her scalp, another time when the famed hair remover itched her eyes until she thought she was blinded.

Bit by bit she is ruining every part of herself trying to rec-reate Ghostanza's recipes, and she still has no idea how to make Venetian cerussa.

Susanna takes a mustard root and begins to chew on it.

'Have you been back to Santa Giuliana?' asks Flavia.

Susanna nods, wincing with the heat of the mustard. She spits it into a bowl. 'Once. I took some ingredients to Suora Dorotea.'

The name of the dispensary sister makes Flavia flinch. Susanna casts her a questioning look.

'Poor woman. She was searching high and low for her Book of Common Ailments.'

'That rubbish?' Flavia tries a laugh. 'It was written in such a terrible scrawl. How could she even read it?'

'Nonetheless, she is distraught.'

Flavia has not told her about the first night at Il Sicofante's, but for all their bloody lacing round the whites Susanna's
eyes are sharp. She senses her friend is crawling inside that
very moment, watching from a pocket of memory as Flavia
excuses herself from the apothecary's presence, shuts herself
in her room and flips open the lid of the painted box, plung-
ing through the ribbons until her nails dig into its little brown
secret.

She hadn't really thought what to do with it. Only Ghostanza knew she had it, and perhaps Maestro Vitale, who waited
for her as she rooted among the long grass on the other side of
the wall, and said nothing at all.

Suora Dorotea's Book of Common Ailments, such a perfect fit. Smooth leather, stamped with Santa Giuliana looking
very pretty, holding her apple for good health.

And an empty space is made for filling, after all. Just like
Zia Caracosa's spice sack doll, all saggy and frayed about the
stitching. A little more hollowing and there was a big enough
space inside it to stow the monstrous thing that had masquer-
aded itself as a path to riches.

* * *

The street seems almost fresh after Susanna's chamber. At
least there is a portion of air in it, and she is careful not to use
it all at once. She walks through the tunnelling houses until
they drop away into the Piazza Piccola.

At the far end a small crowd has gathered to listen to a sermoniser. Clutching her arm, Flavia skirts the edge of the
crowd. The sun glints fiercely on the friar's shaved scalp and
there is a year's worth of dirt between his toes. His voice rings
across the piazza.

'They say the devil hides in the space between a woman's true skin and the cerussa she wears. And was it not Eve who held a looking glass to her face just before she threw paradise away for all mankind?'

Murmurs of agreement from the crowd.

Flavia wanders towards them, feeling in her pocket for the biscuit she stole from Palmeria's tray before she set out.

'Every one of you, if you want to know if a woman is painted you must chew saffron between your teeth and blow on her skin. It will turn a horrible yellow colour if she is falsely fair.'

She takes a bite of moist ginger, then clasps her mouth as a pain shouts out in her back tooth. Pushing her tongue sideways she digs at a wad of biscuit jammed inside it.

'What is a painted face? Let me tell you, it is a truth ill told.'

Flavia cups her jaw and scowls at the friar. The cerussa has hardened in the foul air of the Via del Lupo and she runs her finger along a crack beneath her left eye.

'Flavia di Maestro Bartofolo,' she mutters under her breath, 'you are falling apart.'

'And what ugly pieces remain,' someone whispers behind her.

She spins around. Cimon, his upturned nostrils widening with his leer, keeps his face to the sermoniser. He has several small packages in his hand, plainly wrapped.

'Busy?' he smirks.

'Yes,' snaps Flavia, stuffing the rest of the biscuit into her pocket.

'Not enough. Take these to the Collegio,' Cimon thrusts the packages into her arms. 'Ask for Maestro Vitale.'

22

His room is almost as plain as the Casa Nascosta. Stone walls parenthesised by a wooden floor and ceiling, a window with an iron grille. At the far end is a cabinet and writing desk, and above them shelves that are empty except for uneven parchment edges and a few bound books. A cleanliness which is not sweeping or bitter like Mona Grazia's.

'You are shocked. It is alright.'

'I am not shocked. I have seen stranger things in Zio Anzolo's shed.'

'Zio Anzolo?'

'He cut up the animals for the village.'

'Humans are not animals, Flavia,' says Maestro Vitale. 'The porter should have not have taken you in there.'

There are scratchy ink drawings nailed to the walls, things she has seen after a summer slaughtering at the Casa Nascosta.

She swallows down a wave of nausea, trying not to think of the room the porter of the Collegio first led her to, Maestro Vitale standing there on the blood-soaked straw, solemn over a pale creature sliced from end to end, her knotted hair hanging over the end of the table.

'Pah! There is no difference,' she says stubbornly. 'Except people do not grunt as much as pigs, unless they are carters or taverners.'

A smile. The first he has given her since Santa Giuliana. A stretch of unshaven skin and a crease around his eyes, which is against everything Ghostanza told her about beauty but lovely to look at.

She feels around the edge of her bandage. Susanna's salve has a fiery sting but the lies that blistered her arm seem many miles away now. For the first time in weeks the cloud in her head folds back and Flavia breathes in the quiet scent of nothing.

'Thank you for the medicines.'

She retracts her gaze from the scratchy drawings, smiles cautiously.

'I forget, sometimes, that we serve the physicians as well.'

His straw-like hair hangs over his shoulders and indigo stains the curve of his right thumb, the colour of the dyers' aprons.

The bells of a nearby church run a mismatched toll.

'Who was that woman?' she asks.

'A *treccola* from the marketplace.'

'Did she say you could cut her up after she died?'

There is exhaustion on the physician's face such as holy men wear when their visions keep them from rest.

'They do not always have a choice in the matter,' he says.

'What on earth did you think to find inside her?'

A half smile.

'I was searching for answers. Why a woman might happily sell apples in the morning and cough blood in the evening is a mystery I would like solved.'

Flavia shakes her head. The physician looks inquiringly at her.

'You do not think it possible?'

'I think you are capable of things of which I have no knowledge. But you have claimed to stand against vanity, and here I find you playing the cosmetician yourself.'

She is pleased to see confusion on Maestro Vitale's face for a change.

'I mean, you want to make people well on the inside, and I want to make them well on the outside. Don't you wish your patients had perfect hearts and lungs?'

'Of course, but . . .'

'. . . so how can you deny perfection of the lips and eyes?'

She looks for another smile but the physician turns his head, gripping air into his fists until the skin around his silver ring flushes purple.

'You miss the point entirely, Flavia. Health and beauty are separate. Worse than separate. They fight one another, and if beauty wins it is not a merciful victor.'

The tone of his voice wakes the pain in Flavia's tooth. The sharpness of it makes the shape of the physician merge into his background and she presses a sleeve to her lower eyelid to stop the tears escaping, accidentally peeling away a patch of cracked cerussa. When she looks up Maestro Vitale is clear again and she knows he can see part of the bird poking free. That makes her feel worse, and as quickly as she dabs at the tears they are back again.

'Are you unwell, Flavia?'

The physician's voice is back to normal but he is still as a tomb, and does not offer her a handkerchief as Il Sicofante would have.

She shakes her head.

'Homesick perhaps?'

'No!' she says tightly. 'Though . . . sometimes I miss the smell of woad.'

Now he laughs, and Flavia is startled that something like beauty flashes across his face.

'There are not many who would utter such words.'

This time he does pull a handkerchief from his pocket. She holds out her hand but he does not give it to her. Instead he goes to the cabinet and pulls out a rack of small earthenware jars. Uncorking one, he dips a corner of the handkerchief in.

'If you suck on this, the pain will be less.'

She takes the handkerchief with a questioning look.

'All women who wear the cerussa have pain in their teeth. In time it will loosen them.'

Taking the cloth in her mouth, Flavia shakes her head vigorously then stops in case she looks like a dog at play. The smell of cloves makes her eyes water more than ever but she bites eagerly into the linen, shivering as the oil eases between her gums.

'If you wear cerussa your gums will wither. There are other things too. You must have seen Il Sicofante's clients. Yellow skin, watering eyes, swollen throats. All of these are from the cerussa. Their faces will pucker and fold like a woman three times their years. Then they can never stop painting, because what lies beneath the cerussa will be more poisonous than what covers it.'

She spits out the handkerchief and crushes it between her hands.

'I can never stop anyway,' she mutters. 'And you are wrong about the cerussa. My teeth hurt because I clench them in my sleep. My sister said I would grind them to dust but I could not stop it because I was in my dead sleep and more witless than my uncle Alfeo.'

The physician doesn't laugh this time and Flavia is surprised at how much she wanted him to.

'It is said that Il Sicofante works on a new set of recipes for the Alfani matrons. That the secrets of the Venetians will soon deck the fair brows of the city's wives and daughters.'

He looks at the handkerchief in Flavia's hands. The corner is chewed flat and bears a smear of bright pink which might be blood or lip salve.

'I find this strange news,' he continues. 'It is well known that the only Venetian in the city sits quietly within the walls of Santa Giuliana, her face bare of tincture and no more ornatrix to comb out her hair.'

A jolt goes through Flavia's back tooth and she shoves the handkerchief back into the crevice, sucking and scowling. She knows she looks ugly now, the bird stretching its wings out of the cerussa and her mouth full of cloth. She does not want Maestro Vitale's eyes on her.

She looks hard at one of the pictures, something like a pig's heart with tubes twisting out of it like a maiden's hair caught by the wind. The shadow lines of the grille stretch across the physician's feet.

'Flavia, I will tell you something Ghostanza Dolfin would never have revealed to you.'

Swallowing, Flavia nearly chokes on the oil as she looks eagerly back at him.

'There are no beauty secrets,' he says quietly.

Now it is her turn to laugh. The way Il Sicofante does when Mona Fulvia tells the same joke for the hundredth time.

'Of course there are!' she snorts. 'The women of Venice have books full of them, and the Alfani matrons pay Il Sicofante for his recipes which no other apothecary in the city has knowledge of.'

'No!' Maestro Vitale shakes his head quietly. 'You are giving these women nothing more than a tubful of quicksilver and rotten teeth.'

'You are wrong!' Flavia is on her feet, her voice strained and high. 'Beauty is where the angels are and the nymphs and the little boys chasing boar. It is what we pray to. Heaven is full of beauty.'

The tears are back, hot and angry. She does not wipe them away.

Furiously she tugs her wig forward so the curls cover as much of her cheek as possible.

The physician walks over to the door. His face is half in shadow so she cannot tell if the stretching of his jaw is a smile or a grimace. His arm is outstretched, gesturing her towards him, and out. In the half darkness his stubble is rough-sanded wood.

As Flavia walks towards him, the pain is not just in her tooth and her bandaged arm. Though he is little more than a statue in the gloom, she wants to rest a moment against him, know herself welcome to someone who sees life's ailments through a frown, who will take a knife to cut out death's secrets.

She pauses at the doorway.

'You expect me to turn my back on heaven when I am right outside its gates?'

Vitale does not answer. The shadow of the grille is far across the floor now, falling over the tip of her shoe. Flavia shifts her foot back.

'Heaven is beauty,' she says. 'Ugliness is hell.'

23

The first time she saw Il Sicofante Flavia thought him a spider who brings his mate a fly all wrapped up, so that he can have his pleasure with her while she is busy uncovering it. But there are other spiders, more crafty, like the one that spun his web in the arrow thin window of her old bedroom. This spider brought a sticky parcel to his mate as well, and she was so happy investigating it she let him do what he wanted. It was only when he had crawled back out of the web that she realised there was nothing at all inside it.

When Il Sicofante first took Suora Dorotea's Book of Common Ailments out of the painted box he was suspicious. She was terrified of him then. Something told her there was nothing to stop him cutting her throat for the secret of deflating a woman's double chin, and she sweated hard behind her cerussa, swallowing twice before she said – 'Look, this book is stamped with an image of Venus herself, with the golden apple she won for being the fairest goddess. The writing is very hard to read for it is in the language of the Venetians, which is next to the language of the Gods, so you must be a native of that city to read it. How lucky for us Ghostanza Dolfin taught me the basics before she plucked my head.'

And so she brought the apothecary a sticky parcel with nothing at all inside it.

* * *

Sometimes he is offended, because she snatches Suora Dorotea's book away whenever he is near and shares nothing with him. He waits like the sterile husband whose wife must lie with another man to give him an heir: a perfect translation of Ghostanza's book of secrets, written out by her, tested by him.

As soon as Il Sicofante discovers she can no more whiten skin than she can turn night into day she will be walking home in her old clogs, hairless and faceless, and Maestro Vitale will think that is right, even though he is wrong about everything and cannot preach to her. His only mark is a cloth badge on his cape and he can take that off any time he feels like it.

Her arm is healing but her tooth still aches. One night the pain is so bad it keeps her awake, curled on her pallet under the window and hugging Zia Caracosa's sack doll until the smell of the little brown baby stitched inside is too much to bear. Tossing the doll aside, she digs her hands into the small of her back and stretches her legs up until she reaches the bottom of the bullfinches' cage. With a flip of her big toe she sets it swinging, listening to the percussion of their wings against the bars, and the little dry thud as one of them falls from its perch.

They never fight. The more she rattles them the closer they huddle. This is because they are too plain, and have no long tail feathers to pull from one another.

She kicks the blankets aside and goes over to her dressing table. The silver looking glass shows deep shadows under her eyes, and her skin has a yellowy sheen that does not come from the rising sun. Exhaustion, she tells herself.

Toothache is not the only thing keeping her awake.

It has been six weeks since she started brewing her first batch of cerussa; today it will be ready.

Il Sicofante showed her how he makes it. An earthenware pot filled with sharp white vinegar and three small plates of lead. They buried the pot in the cellar to keep it cool, patted the earth over the rim and marked the spot with a stone. At the time it felt like they were burying treasure, though it was hard to believe cerussa could grow out of something so dirty and heavy. Then she remembered how wine turns to blood when the priest says the right words, and how Il Sicofante performs miracles on his sagging clients that are almost as good.

Leaving her wig on the dressing table, she pulls her cap over her grey, blue and pink hair and wriggles into her dress. Carefully she slides the mother-of-pearl buttons through her shoe straps.

*   *   *

The cellar is icy and Flavia's breath makes the flames curl as she fixes the torch to the wall. The air creeps up her sleeves but it is not cold that makes her tremble as she kicks aside the marking stone and bends to scrape at the ground around the earthenware lid. Soon she has dug a little moat around the edge and can prise it open without risk of sprinkling dirt inside.

A dark sludge, framed by shadows. She digs deeper until the pot begins to loosen, slowly easing it free. Setting it near the torch, she peers again. The sludge is paler now. Hopefully, she dips a finger into it. Floating inside is the remains of one of the lead plates. It is much smaller than before, half melted into the vinegar and thick with a glistening mire. She uses a knife to scrape off as much as she can, then does the same for the other plates, mixing the remains into paste. Again she dips a finger in, traces an off-white smear along the palm of her hand.

It is not as light as when Il Sicofante does it, and his is not as light as Ghostanza's, so now she is two whole shades away from perfection.

Upstairs in the kitchen Palmeria starts making noises with pans and logs. The servant has a large soft chest full of lamentations, and as Flavia wanders up, frowning, with her muddy pot of cerussa, Palmeria pummels her dough and moans about the price of salt.

There is no sound from above, not even the sly patter against the kitchen shutters of Cimon relieving himself from the upstairs window. In quiet panic Flavia stalks around, looking for something that will make the cerussa whiter. She grabs a handful of fine marble dust from a jar and sprinkles it in. The dust makes the cerussa even lumpier but gives it a certain twinkle.

Palmeria's dough is now in the outside oven but there is still no sign of Il Sicofante. He has an appointment with Mona Selvaggia of the Alfani family, one of his wealthiest clients. She will expect the apothecary to be prompt, smart and nodding like a full-seeded sunflower at everything she says. As the bread rises and the appointed hour with Mona Selvaggia grows closer, Flavia sets the cerussa to dry on a windowsill and takes the staircase to Il Sicofante's chamber.

Cimon's pallet is laid up against the door. The apprentice is fast asleep on it, stiff limbed and snuffling on his side like a dog that has not the brains to escape a doorway draught. Flavia puts one leg cautiously over him as she would a pile of slops, but cannot help noticing the smudge of wet jam across his pale cheek. Grimacing, she knocks lightly on Il Sicofante's door and listens for a moment. Legs braced either side of the pallet, she twists awkwardly to reach the keyhole when the end of her skirt is sharply tugged.

Cimon leers between her legs.

'Get away from me, slug,' she whispers.

'It is the ugly servant who spreads her legs over Cimon. He would not choose to be in this position for all the world.'

'You have jam on your cheek, Cimon. It does not suit you.'

'Nor becoming in you is this spying on the master.'

'He is late for Mona Selvaggia, I need to wake him.'

'You will leave him alone. Go to the old goose yourself. She will take you under her wing and smother you with the stench of her armpits.'

Cimon's spidery hands are inching their way up her ankles. Flavia yanks her foot above his face.

'I'll crush your nose into the back your skull.'

Cimon whimpers and rolls his head into the pallet, raising his bottom in the air. An unfortunate sight, with no thread of cloth on it and the skin all grey and goosebumped. If only to spare her leather shoes, Flavia resists the urge to launch a foot right into its crevice.

* * *

Mona Selvaggia is in the heart of the city, but she is not of the city.

The Palazzo Alfani spreads wide, its banks of stone as impregnable as Santa Giuliana's. Several towers fly above the fortified grounds, and it is said that Braccio Alfani once built another one so high a person at the top could have rain hammering his head though the ground below was parched. Braccio's tower fell to an earthquake on Saint Saviour's day, but still the Alfani build up to the heavens, and it is in one of these spires that Mona Selvaggia holds court.

It is strange to find yourself travelling upwards for such a

long time, to know there is only up and down and no sideways because you cannot make a path into air.

Flavia does not climb alone. A servant thuds heavy-
booted in front of her, his staff digging into each triangular
step as they circle a stairwell as tight as a chimney. They are
both out of breath and the servant leans on his stick a moment
as Flavia takes a nervous look out of a passing window. The
rooftops of the city have never been so small; the tonsured
heads of two friars walking past the palazzo are like tiny moving circles on one of Ghostanza's board games. Flavia's body
tenses. Some spirit of madness tells her she can burst from
the window and straight into flight like the screaming swifts.
She ducks away from it and continues to climb.

By the time she is ushered into Mona Selvaggia's presence
there is a pain below her ribs and she can barely wheeze her
thanks to the servant, who flies from the room so quickly she
thinks he might trip on the utmost step and find himself back
at the bottom in no time at all.

In the event it does not matter that she has no breath
because Mona Selvaggia has more than enough for both of
them. Before Flavia has unfolded her perfumed plaits of
yellow-grey hair she has already learned the quantity, weight
and value of every gift that has recently passed between her
family and that of the Tassi household. Mona Selvaggia only
interrupts her race of words to let out little wheezing coughs
and spit into a pot beside her chair.

Flavia is used to this. As soon as their heads are tilted back
and their tresses undone, the little lives of Il Sicofante's clients
spill freely from their lips. In less than an hour she knows if
they prefer sewing to lace making, which Saints they admire
the most, and whether or not they love their husbands. It is
what Il Sicofante calls the perfume of patricians. A blend of

candour and stupidity that makes his nostrils flare and his tongue probe deep into their mollusc brains.

Cimon has already warned her: Mona Selvaggia's cerussa does not come off. Not ever. No one has seen her skin since a violent downpour made one of the aqueducts overflow. Passing beneath it on her way to church, Mona Selvaggia's face melted into a flood of milky water and she stood there sobbing, yellow and puckered as a corn-fed capon. Now Il Sicofante just keeps adding more and more paste to the layers. This is what Flavia does now, mixing up the apothecary's best pearl and silver cerussa and smoothing it over her forehead and cheekbones. Because Mona Selvaggia's jaw keeps moving it does not feel like good work, and somehow she thinks a plasterer who covered rotten walls without scraping the mould off first would not keep his job long.

'Of course we shall be inviting the Tassi family for the Michaelmas feast, well, all except Ghostanza Dolfin. I cannot imagine she will be appearing.'

The spatula digs into Mona Selvaggia's cheek. Flavia is about to apologise when she sees it has only gone as far as an old layer of cerussa, and she is still some distance away from the yellow skin.

'In any case, I hear Ghostanza has all but taken the veil and that really is for the best. My cousin was visiting her daughter only last week at Santa Giuliana and she said that Jacopo Tassi was there, and it was the strangest interview she ever saw. Jacopo was so far back from the grille he was almost outside the parlour, and had to shout everything across the room.'

'And Ghostanza?' Flavia quickly mixes some more paint to fill in the hole made by her spatula.

'Beyond recognition.' Mona Selvaggia plumps the cushion behind her back and resettles herself contentedly. 'Not a shred of colour on her cheeks, and her hair as flat as a cloth iron. Apparently she has been forbidden all her little beauty tricks and no one there will so much as mix up a salve for her dry skin.'

Guilt swirls into Flavia's stomach. Just as it does when she thinks about Pia's wedding cassone.

'Surely she could ask a servant to come up to the city for her?'

But Mona Selvaggia is not listening, and in any case she knows that even if Madalena or one of the others agreed to play courier, Il Sicofante thinks he has no more need of Ghostanza. He will not help her now.

'I rather pity Ghostanza.' Mona Selvaggia dabs a little silk handkerchief to her chest and cocks her head in a poise of sympathy. 'Apparently she was quite motherly towards Gilia at one stage, hard as that is to imagine.'

Flavia thinks of the urgent scraping through the convent wall and the look on Ghostanza's face when she learned that Gilia was betrothed to Ridolfo. But already Mona Selvaggia is off with the speed of a trotting nag.

'Ridolfo is my youngest brother's boy. He adores me, and Gilia is such a charming creature. Il Sicofante has promised me he will make her so beautiful on her wedding day that we shall have to find a new name for her, because Gilia la Bella will no longer suffice.'

Feeling as though she is trying to swallow a pebble, Flavia begins to mix up a fucus for Mona Selvaggia's busy lips.

'But you are quite a little creature in your own right,' Mona Selvaggia swivels her chalk face towards Flavia for the first time. Two small eyes glint inquisitorially, a gatekeeper peering through a weathered peephole.

'Have you a young man?'

'Oh yes,' Flavia keeps her face to the fucus. 'His name is Tommaso and we are to be married next year. I have a dowry of fifty florins and a wedding cassone inlaid with ivory.'

'Well!' Mona Selvaggia tries to arch her eyebrows but they quickly collapse under the weight of the paint. 'That is charming. Fifty florins and an ivory chest indeed. It is a marvel such a wealthy father would send his daughter into the service of an apothecary!'

Her white-lipped smile has the angle of mockery and Flavia grips the spatula hard, squeezing her eyes tight against a picture of her jamming it through Mona Selvaggia's tongue.

'Marriage really is the most glorious time of a woman's life.'

Mona Selvaggia dabs again with her handkerchief, which is a history of different perfumes, fresh and stale.

'There can be no happiness without it, beyond girlish anticipation and the pleasure of recollection should a woman have the misfortune to outlive her husband. Anyway, I am sure you will be perfectly content with your Terenzio, ivory chest or no.'

'Tommaso!' Flavia spits into the fucus and swirls the brush in trembling circles, but Mona Selvaggia has no more ears for her.

* * *

She is still taut with fury when she leaves a plucked and re-braided Mona Selvaggia in the clouds and stomps back down the stairwell. Cursing quietly to herself she almost bumps into a woman in a plain black overdress marching her way up in the opposite direction. Flavia flattens herself against the curved wall and the woman climbs past with an indifferent nod. There is something familiar about the pock-marks on her forehead but Flavia cannot quite place them.

Outside the tower the servant is nowhere to be seen and she is uncertain of crossing the courtyard alone. There is a sunken garden, a row of box hedges and several studded gates between herself and the outside world, with so many bolts Suora Benedetta would be delighted to stand guard at them. This, she thinks, is probably for the best if it keeps Mona Selvaggia from escaping.

Underneath one of the box hedges is a little leather ball with red stitching. Flavia picks it up and squeezes it gently in her palm. After a brief glance around, she tosses it in the air and catches it with one hand. The ball lands with an appetising plop, and she throws it again, higher and higher, past the first and second windows of Mona Selvaggia's roost. It rolls in its ascent, falling hard and flat. Watching it fly, Flavia thinks of Pia, who never could catch a thing until Tommaso turned up at the Casa Nascosta. She wonders if their child has taken his first breaths into a clear chest, or if he is wrapped in a box by the church wall with his little uncles. Perhaps he is something so brown and shrivelled they must pretend he never existed.

With one great lob she launches the ball with all her strength. It barrels clear of the third window before it fades and rolls. It comes down hard but, caught by the wind, veers wide. As she lurches to catch it a small gloved hand reaches out before her and snatches it tight.

'I have never seen one fly so high.'

A young girl stands before her. Her skin is pale and an excess of dark curls fuss over the shoulders of her overdress. Her eyes, black and round as an infant's, are framed with lashes that seem to curl of their own will.

Unmarried hair, too loose for a matron.

The girl rolls the ball between her hands.

'Does this belong to you?'

Flavia feels the old twist of the neck, the slide of her cheek into her cap.

The girl cocks her head inquiringly. Fifteen perhaps, a little younger than Pia.

'No? I am happy to share it, if you will teach me how to throw. Mona Selvaggia says it is not elegant for a woman to raise her arms above her shoulders, but sometimes I must reach to the shelf above my bed if my maidservant is not there to do it.'

Her voice is even younger than her face, sweet but not sickening like Pia making cow-eyed talk to Tommaso. Nor sewer-crystal like Ghostanza's. Bare lips, like her forehead, eyelids, cheeks.

'You catch well enough.' Flavia eases a finger under her wig, her scalp suddenly itchy.

'Oh yes, that is the easy part.'

A gentle laugh sets the curls trembling. Then the girl blushes and looks to the side. She is a little plump, her chin duplicates itself like rising dough.

'You are Il Sicofante's servant. I saw you with him at the feast of Santa Clara. We stood at the balcony to watch the parade pass by my brother's house.'

Flavia remembers it. Fancy dress. Cimon stitched goose feathers to his hose and was almost merry until a stray dog chased him down the Via Bontempi.

'Could you not have come down to the street?'

'Oh no!' A look of shock passes over the girl's face.

'There were ladies there too, not just servants and whores.'

Crimson spreads across the girl's neck and Flavia thinks this is probably the first time she has seen a rich person blush, except when the cerussa is off and their faces are rubbed with pumice.

'My brother would never have let me. Back then my feet had only touched eight and twenty stones in the city: fourteen on the way to the Chiesa del Gesu, fourteen on the way back. Now I come to see Mona Selvaggia, so I have the acquaintance of four and ninety new ones, both coming and going, which is a total I cannot yet count.'

'Don't you tread on the same stones on the way back?'

Another sidelong blush and a rueful smile.

'Oh no, I make sure to meet new stones going home.'

Flavia thinks of the path through the woods of the Casa Nascosta to the river, how every knotted tree root was known to her.

'Would you like to wander about more?'

'Perhaps, sometimes, but I am lucky. When my mother was a girl she had never once walked in the street before her wedding cassone was delivered to my father's house. Her father's chapel was reached by a covered bridge and the house of her cousin – where she dined once a month – connected by a tunnel. So you see, she never had cause to go out, and never met any new stones.'

'But now you have to visit Mona Selvaggia.'

The girl smiles blankly.

'My sister Ricca goes up before me. They talk of things that are not for my ears. My maidservant is at hand,' she points to a tall thick-chinned woman pacing the sunken gardens. 'She will tell me when it is time to go up to Mona Selvaggia.'

'Do you count the stairs up the tower?'

'Yes I do!'

There is genuine delight in her reply. Flavia bites on her cheeks to suppress a sneer but the girl does not seem to notice.

From the sunken gardens the maidservant beckons. The girl ignores her so the maidservant calls out her name and Flavia knows who she is, and wishes she did not.

Gilia Tassi sighs, takes a few steps towards her maidservant, then swings around.

'I nearly forgot,' she calls out. The ball leaves her hand but the throw is short. Flavia lunges forward with arms outstretched, missing it by inches.

Gilia does not see it fall. Already she has linked arms with the maid and is walking towards Mona Selvaggia's tower, her curls bouncing on her shoulders as her feet take little measured strides.

A Recipe to Lighten Freckles

Take galbanum (the plant from which the medicinal juice may be extracted) and grind it into an ointment. When you go to sleep, cover the entire face with it. In the morning wash away with distilled water.

24

Supper in the kitchen. Flavia and Il Sicofante hold their faces to their plates, trying to ignore the smell of boiling rose petals. The apothecary is making soap and both of them have a headache from crushing cloves and lily roots into the sweet-smelling patties. Cimon has a head cold so does not notice the smell. While the apprentice amuses himself blowing balloons of yellow mucous from his nostrils, Il Sicofante plies his fingers through his hair. His doublet is undone to the waist and his shirt collar smeared with charcoal. He does not tidy himself for servants. As Flavia takes his plate she offers him a smile but the apothecary does not give it back to her. Chewing at a hangnail, he pulls a narrow strip of skin right down to the knuckle.

Cimon is talkative this evening, which is bad news because his stories are always disgusting. He wipes his nose on his sleeve and tells them about a holy man from Monteluco who offered his meagre remains to the dissecting table.

'When his insides were cut open they found a stash of jewels lodged inside his stomach. The story spread like pestilence. People said they must have got there by the grace of God. That diamonds are the hardened shit of the pure at heart. Many a rogue took a knife to the gut of a poor friar before the scholars found they had mixed up the holy man with a cavalier who was killed while fleeing the city with his jewel purse jostling in his belly.'

Laughing, Cimon blows a wet balloon from his right nostril.

'Beware the surgeons! They will kill two men for the price of one. I knew one who was so hasty cutting off a soldier's leg he sliced through his own finger. The soldier lived but the surgeon's hand turned as black as the pox. He was tumbled into the lime pit not two days after.'

Flavia pushes her remaining sausage to one side. Cimon seizes it and crams it into his mouth, chewing and breathing agape.

'Most people lose their appetite when they have a fever.' Flavia regards him with distaste.

'Most people lose their teeth when they bathe in cerussa. Happy chewing, little dust sparrow.' Cimon gives a meaty leer over the top of his fork and Flavia kicks hard at his stool, which makes him lurch forward so abruptly the prongs of the fork fly into his forehead. For a moment it is wedged tight and Cimon jumps from his seat, thrashing around the room like a startled frog.

'Enough!' Il Sicofante growls and slaps his palm hard against the table. Still whimpering, Cimon plucks the fork loose, leaving two bright beads of blood in the middle of his brow. He shuffles out of the kitchen and is soon heard in his favourite whimpering hole beneath the stairs, snuffling and sobbing.

Flavia smirks, but Il Sicofante's look wipes her face as thoroughly as a scrubbing cloth. He has a line of fury for every one of the recipes she has not given him. It is a long time since he lined up his tombstone teeth in a smile for her, real or otherwise.

'I hear you met Gilia Tassi this week.' Il Sicofante pulls at one of his oiled curls and loops it round his finger. 'Mona Selvaggia was most distressed to think of her throwing balls around the Alfani courtyard.'

'There are plenty who would like to throw Mona Selvaggia around the Alfani courtyard,' mutters Flavia.

'Quiet!' Il Sicofante slaps the table again. 'You braided her hair too tightly and she was kept awake by pains to her scalp. Next time there is a call to attend her in the middle of the night, you can go.'

Flavia is quiet. She knows Mona Selvaggia's braids were no tighter than her lips, and that some people cannot lie content in their beds unless they have made a servant run halfway across the city.

'No more time wasting, Flavia. I will have ten recipes by tomorrow morning, or that little book of secrets is going back to Venice. I'll take it there myself and have its words unlocked. Do you understand?'

His eyes are colder than the cellar steps as he pushes his chair from the table.

'And Flavia,'

'Yes?'

'Get rid of that filthy sack doll. It stinks.'

25

Dusk. A strange time to be on the streets.

In the black hours she has heard the city savagely alive: a moonlit wilderness you would never find in a peasant's backyard, where drunks roll through the streets, shrieking obscenities and rampantly purging their suppers. It is already beginning: one staggerer appears from a side alley, seeming uncertain whether to empty the flagons of wine from his bladder or his stomach. In the end he does both, reels near vertical and stumbles away.

She sticks to the main streets, skirting the great buildings of the Piazza Grande and past the Merchants' Guild. Two city guards appear from nowhere and she pushes herself into the shadows, waiting for their footsteps to disappear. She is quite near the gates of the Palazzo Tassi. Above, its windows are dim and shuttered. There is a long walkway stretching beneath its roofline and she wonders briefly if Gilia is ever allowed to count the terrazzo tiles from one end to the other.

A pigeon shoots out of the Tassi rafters, oddly pale against the indigo sky. Startled, Flavia breathes hard, her neck twisted up like the Virgin beneath her announcing Angel. In the depth of the walkway she thinks she sees the ghost of a movement: a glancing shadow.

She peers again. The arches to the front of the walkway are still brushed deep pink by the setting sun, but further back it is midnight. There are shapes among the gloom, statues perhaps, but there is no more movement, no sound.

An anxious flicker goes up her spine. She curses herself for it and moves on, away from the main streets and down into the alleys and the tunnels of green stone, hurrying with her face to the ground until she reaches Susanna's door. Knocking as loud as she dares, she huddles close to the worn wood and counts the steps as they come towards her. The plea is already on her lips when the door is opened by Maestro Vitale.

* * *

A matt of coarse hair is all there is. Otherwise she is just a shape beneath a single blanket, shifting slightly with each fluted breath.

'Is she very ill?'

Maestro Vitale tilts his head towards Susanna.

'She will recover I think, but she cannot live in this place. The convent was better for her.'

'Why did she come back here?'

The physician passes his fingers through his hair, which is badly cut to the line of his unshaven chin and neither curled nor oiled.

'I suppose for the same reason we all go home, sooner or later.'

He pushes a stool towards Flavia, who shakes her head and perches on the foot of Susanna's bed.

'It is late, I know,' her voice holds little apology. 'But I must talk to her. When will she wake?'

'You cannot speak to her now. If your tooth needs attending . . .'

'My tooth is fine!' Flavia snarls. 'I just wanted to ask Susanna . . .'

'If she knows how to make Venetian cerussa?'

A slap of cold white on her cheek. A sting worse than mercury. She is too shocked to deny it.

'Or perhaps some other concoction, just as bad,' he says, 'something you think she may know and you do not.'

Maestro Vitale cups his hand around the back of his neck, rubs where it meets his shoulders. He does not make accusations with his eyes. He looks too tired to argue in any case.

'I am sorry Flavia, but I don't think Susanna holds the key for you. She is a healer, and for such beauty treatments I have known her to make, the recipes are simple. The ingredients can be found in any housewife's stores.'

'I think she knows a little more than you give her credit for. Or perhaps you just want to keep her recipes from me.'

It is a mean response. She has grace enough to say it to the floor. Ghostanza would slap her for such words, and that would be alright because it would make things even again; but the physician has a dyer's patience where insults are concerned, and this only makes her more angry.

'I have to give Il Sicofante something tomorrow because I said I could do it, just like the spider with nothing inside his gift. I must find out how Ghostanza Dolfin makes herself beautiful!'

The truth at last. She had not meant to speak it.

The physician rubs again at the muscles of his neck, pushing at the knots that are made when a person must lean constantly forward. She remembers the last time she got angry with him. How he stood in the doorway with his face closed tight. She does not want him sealed off again but her tongue has only one direction. It follows her thoughts like a dog at heal.

'I must have my cerussa.'

She has no other words. The deathbed drunk who cries out for his wine has greater conversation. If he could just see how beautiful it is. The pure whiteness, flexible as skin, light as air. A mask that is not a mask, saving her from a world seen through woven threads.

She wonders what Ghostanza would do.

Vitale still has a hand on his neck. If she pulled it away and wrapped it in her own would he jump back as he did when Ghostanza stroked the wool of his cape? Though he is close to her, she is certain the air between them cannot be passed through. Certain that her breath is foul from her rotten tooth, her face ugly and her cerussa even uglier to his eyes.

'I only want what everyone else has,' she says quietly. 'You choose to live in such a way with ... with gruesome pictures on your wall, talking only to cadavers, but I would have everyone know who I am and see me truly.'

Vitale shakes his head. Refusal or submission, she cannot tell. His eyes seem to be searching for the edges of the missing bird. He takes his hand from her neck and lets it hover, not quite dropping to his side. The thin band of silver round his finger stares out of the gloom.

'To each their own mask,' he says.

PART FIVE

'But all this would be nothing if the beauty of the teeth
did not concur, being small but not minute, square,
equal, separated in an orderly way, white, and above all
else like ivory. By the gums – appearing as borders of
crimson satin more than red velvet – they should be
bordered, tied and held.'

Firenzuola

26

There is a ring of pigeon blood round the bottom of her sleeves. Scrubbing with lye water has not brought out the stains.

White pigeons. Cimon fattened them, gleefully forcing apple kernels down their throats as they clawed and flapped. When they were well plumped, he and Flavia wrung their necks and did away with the heads, the guts and the feet, and distilled what was left in a limbeck with three hundred leaves of silver and gold foil. Finally they added an *etto* of breadcrumbs steeped in milk. The resulting soap is now sealed in little terracotta pots that Il Sicofante sells for a florin each. He says it will bring freshness to the cheeks of a woman even if she is on her deathbed. Flavia tried some on her own face. It made her itch.

Il Sicofante is growing desperate. He scours the hillsides and the market stalls for anything that is white or glowing and pounds it into the cerussa. So far he has tried cauliflower hearts, flint, the jawbone of a boar and sheep's eyes. But the cerussa is not Venetian. It does not speak to the heavens. It is as flat as the lead that goes into it. Good enough for an artisan's wife but the apothecary has pledged his soul to the Alfani matrons.

They must shine.

* * *

Three things Flavia no longer has: her shoes, her wig, Suora Dorotea's Book of Common Ailments.

The day after she went to Susanna's house, the apothecary summoned her to the blushing room and demanded ten recipes. She gave him two, both of her own making. One was a face wash designed to even the texture of winter-roughened skin; the other a digestive tonic to cleanse the breath. Il Sicofante tried both of them on Cimon, who woke the following morning with screaming diarrhoea and a boil the size of a quail's egg on the end of his nose. Flavia protested that Cimon was an unfair subject, being closer to a toad than a human being, but Il Sicofante was furious.

Her heels are now hardening themselves on her old clogs. She has been careful to put them to good use whenever Cimon's skinny bottom hooves into view. The wig was surrendered along with the shoes. She has seen it since, at the market, sitting pompously on the head of a banker's wife. Instinctively Flavia put two fingers into her mouth and whistled like a herder to a straggling goat. She imagined her wig springing lightly off the banker's wife's head and romping back to its proper mistress, but it seemed happy where it was. Perhaps the banker's wife combed it out more than Flavia did, maybe she picked out the fleas. Either way, Flavia has no time to dye or curl her own hair, so she plaits the fading coloured strands beneath her cap and tries not to think about it.

As for Suora Dorotea's Book of Common Ailments, it is cloth wrapped and strapped in a courier's saddlebag, trotting its way to a scholar in Venice. The scholar will doubtless write back to Il Sicofante, berating him for wasting his time with the ravings of a scatterbrained dispensary nun.

* * *

Flavia spends more and more time away from the apothecary's house. She takes whatever messages or packages are thrust at her. Despite her losses she is glad to breathe in the city for hours on end. It feels familiar now. The Piazza Grande and its two-tiered fountain, the smart streets and the grubby ones, all of them more like home than the Casa Nascosta ever was.

She begins to forget she is country born, and thinks her father a fool for ever leaving the city of swinging black capes.

But she does not understand the dangers. One day she is cutting through alleys behind the Via Bontempi when an unknown man steps out of a doorway, his yellow teeth shaped in a grin. Without a word he pulls her towards him and swings her round until her back strikes wood. Tangled odours, feral and stale, rush into her nostrils as his head smothers the half-light of the alley. There are lips, tongue, teeth around and inside her mouth. A rush of saliva, not her own, which she can neither swallow nor expel. Her head is gripped in his hands, two mouths in bitter duelling.

Though her back tooth is burrowed through, the rest are good. She used them to smile at Vitale in the marketplace; now she uses them to bite hard on the tongue that does not belong inside her. There is a squeal that seems to be of her own making because he is so far inside her mouth. Fresh blood mingles with his spit and the tongue darts away like a lizard under a rock. Everything she can gather in her mouth she pools and fires at his face.

She runs. Out of the alley, through the tunnelling back streets and up into the Piazza Grande. There she leans and gags against the fountain.

* * *

She is used to feeling dirty on the outside. Powder under her nails and a ring of dust where her face meets her hair: she once stayed filthy for weeks until Mona Grazia dragged her to the trough with a bucket of lime water and a brush.

The mark on her face, that is outside dirt as well, put there by God or the devil – she is not sure which – but it is still outside dirt. At confession she might sit on a little stool and say she threw a pebble at Zio Alfeo or coveted her sister's woollen stockings, but there was nothing to make her want to take the lime water to her insides as she does now.

It is time for mid-morning prayers and the door to the cathedral is open. Nervously Flavia creeps up the steps, into sudden darkness and the quiet air of a tomb.

A vast sanctuary of stone, pillars spreading higher than oaks towards a distant ceiling. Like the steady grind of pestle and mortar, the cool interior of the apothecary's shop. No alteration, no decay. Her breath slows until she does not notice it any more.

A long curtain is strung deep along the nave: a wall to separate the men from the women. On the women's side there are only two others: both black shawled, facing the altar. Seeking comfort among the sparseness, Flavia takes a seat a couple of rows behind them. There is still a foreign taste in her mouth and she sucks on the end of her sleeve, which tastes of dust and pumice and a bit of pigeon blood, all of it better than the saliva of the yellow-toothed man.

In front of her, the taller of the black heads stretches from side to side, the shoulders rising as a yawn is suppressed.

Flavia looks over to the priest.

His flesh is failing him; it can barely hang onto his skull. If he were in the blushing room she would take both cheeks and pull them tight to his ears, just to see what time has done.

Much better looking is the statue over his head. The elegant suffering of the Lord, his body twisted in pain. The lacquered paint picks out the stretched sinews and his ribcage glistens in the rough altar light. White and red are Christ's colours. His naked flesh and vibrant wounds. Il Sicofante says no one can blame the city matrons for their love of cerussa and fucus when they are the colours most found on the body of our Lord.

Again the shoulders belonging to the taller head in front of her rise up. A hissing yawn escapes in the pause after the prayer of absolution. The priest looks blearily from the altar, his lower lip a sagging line of laundry. Something in the redness of it, fleshy and unstrung, coincides with the hiss from the black head and makes Flavia's heart tap softly at her insides.

There is something here, under this shawl with its covered boredom. Something even worse than the yellow-toothed man.

Flavia begins to ease her way back out along the bench. Halfway along, her foot catches on her skirts and twists them sideways until the pocket where she keeps her little pot of cerussa falls open. She leans down to grab it, striking her knuckles against the bench. The sound echoes loudly and the tall black head swings round.

Red lips and white skin. The two tones of Ghostanza Dolfin.

Flavia scrabbles to the end of the pew. Hurrying up the nave her clogs strike at the stones and echo between pillars. Behind her the priest's words are cut in two by an angry bark of laughter.

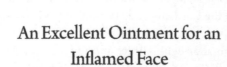

An Excellent Ointment for an Inflamed Face

Take an ounce of the oil of bays and an ounce of quick-silver, and put them in a bladder, with a spoonful of fasting spittle. Then rub them well together, so that nothing of the quicksilver is seen. Take of this oint-ment, when it is made, and annoint the face therewith, and it will heal it well and fair.

Gilia la Bella IV

The silver brooch wasn't the only thing her mother had left her. There were two drawings of Santa Lucia that she wasn't allowed to touch any more because her fingers had worn so much of the ink away. The first one showed Lucia punished and strapped to a team of oxen. She was looking to the heavens as a pagan came towards her, his knife drawn and ready to cut out her eyes because she used them only to see God.

The second picture showed Lucia in the clouds, holding a plate with two big eyes sitting in the middle of it like a pair of poached quail eggs, because what she had lost in life the heavens had been given back to her twofold. Eyes to replace the ones she had lost, and an extra pair for healing all those who wander blindly through their lives.

* * *

Ghostanza had got a bit fat but she had stopped being sick, which was very useful because Gilia needed help in making a tableau of herself like Santa Lucia strapped helpless to the oxen (in this case four of her larger dolls) with the peace of martyrdom on her face. When it was finished, Ghostanza looked at her lying on the floor with hair ribbons looped about her wrists and said the enactment of suffering was Gilia's only true talent, which was cruel sounding though she said it with a smile. Gilia sulked a little as she undid the ribbons. Parassita chased the ends of them around, her paws skidding on the waxed floor until Ghostanza picked her up by the scruff of the neck and threw her out into the passageway. Gilia cried out when she saw it, and then bit on her lip to stop herself saying Antonia thought Ghostanza was a strega and a curse layer; that nobody in the Palazzo Tassi except Gilia and her father liked her at all.

Ghostanza didn't say sorry about Parassita but she did take Gilia to her dressing table and ground up some powdery red dust which she mixed with water so that Gilia could have Santa Lucia's tears. Ghostanza dabbed a wet brush down her cheek and sent her along the passageway with her eyes dripping crimson. Gilia felt happy then, because her stepmother was calmer and not always swinging between anger and amusement, and there was no more talk of admirers which brought all the wrong colours to the Palazzo Tassi: Jacopo's purple face and her father's grey one, and the dark shades that couldn't really be seen but crept sometimes inside Gilia's head among the moved-about furniture.

She wandered wet cheeked towards the kitchen, thinking of Lucia and her extra eyes, but also of the Venus temple and the torch that lit the word 'Amor' which Maestro Alessio said meant love, until the clatter of plate and the screams of Antonia brought her back to herself.

It was the wrong time for games said Ricca, sending her to bed. Jacopo was in her father's study all day. Household accounts, said Ricca. Names, said Antonia. Marcello Sciri, Paolo Corgna, Ridolfo Alfani. All young men of the city, all unmarried, grinned the maidservant slyly, taking Gilia's hand and saying, 'you are near fifteen after all,' which seemed like an obvious thing to say until she realised what Antonia meant. Then she was all over her maidservant and pulled at her apron

and her cloth cap until she hissed her be still so she could tell
her that Jacopo and her father talked longest around one
name, which was Ridolfo Alfani.

Gilia was very quiet then and her breath stopped entirely,
because Ridolfo Alfani was said to be the best in everything.
Not just the look of him but in hunting and riding and all the
things young men were meant to be good at. Antonia said he
was the best too, though Jacopo murmured things around his
name that she could not hear. After that she said they talked
of Ghostanza, and every so often her father said no and sometimes he cried. Gilia asked then if her stepmother was still her
father's legend of emeralds and water and Antonia laughed in
a short harsh way.

Afterwards she curled herself around Parassita and
thought about Ridolfo Alfani who was the best, and a bit
about Ghostanza's gold dice and her ivory combs that she kept
in her painted jewellery box. She pushed her hands under her
pillow, snuck between the cold linen to the ghosts of the beads
her father hid there when he came back from the north to tell
them about a woman so beautiful she made the stars pale.

For the first time, Gilia was not sure if she was happy her
father had married Ghostanza.

Without knowing exactly why, she suddenly wished he
had brought back someone like Ricca. A woman with bad
skin and a nothing face.

* * *

The engorging of sin is always painful. So said Fra Michele
when he heard her confession in the Chiesa del Gesu.

She looked at her hands, which were still pink from washing away Santa Lucia's tears. Fra Michele gave her ten Our

Fathers but she never did them because later that day she was sick down her dress and Antonia said she must be still and not fuss Parassita or even look at the wood panelling above her bed. She asked for Ghostanza to bring Ibn Yunus and sing for her but Antonia said it might not be safe, which was strange because, although they were often gloomy, none of her step-mother's songs had sounded dangerous before.

Sweating through her third undershirt of the night, she heard the slap of waves against stone.

*　*　*

The next day there was a strange man in her room. Antonia said he was a physician and stayed right beside her so she wasn't afraid even when he took the bedsheet away and put his hands on her head and her throat. Then Ricca came to the doorway and asked if he might come to see Jacopo too. After he left Gilia stared up at the panelling and saw Apollonia writhing in her flames and knew exactly how she felt. She pulled at her undershirt until the parting threads scratched at her ears. Antonia was saying, 'Stop, please stop,' but all she could hear was Apollonia screaming and the plucked strings of Ibn Yunus.

Sometime later she woke and there were no more sounds except the physician and Antonia talking quietly to each other. He came to sit by her bed and said she should not look so much at the ceiling. She said it was easier when Ghostanza played for her on Ibn Yunus, and he looked thoughtful then-said perhaps he could tell her a story instead. She tried to nod, though it hurt the back of her head. He asked what kind of story and she said a dark one like Ghostanza's songs. The physician said he would give her both light and dark in the tale of two sisters. Were they saints, she wanted to know, and he said no he could not say that, although one of them was very good.

Lailah and Lilith, he said. Twins of comfort and ruin.

Lailah. Midwife of souls, they called her. When the soul was very new she lit it a candle and taught it all the other places it had been throughout time. When it was finally ready to come into the world, Lailah lightly struck her finger to the child's lip, as if to say 'shh,' and the child forgot everything it had learned in its mother's belly, because knowledge must be gained, not given.

Lailah was light.

Lilith, darkness.

Lilith was the strangler of newborns. The night hag they called her, sucking their blood. A demoness howling in the desert and in the night. La Strega, the witch. Demon of lust, destroyer of life.

Antonia did not like this part of the story. She shushed the physician then and he said he was sorry, it was a story his uncle told his little cousins and there was nothing really in it. Gilia told Antonia to be quiet because she wanted to hear more about Lilith but then Ricca came in again and the physician asked if Jacopo was worse, but it was not Jacopo.

* * *

Antonia said Ghostanza came early to the birthing stool.

Gilia's first thought was Lailah and Lilith.

She asked Antonia which of them had been at the birth. Lighter of souls or strangler of newborns.

Antonia said neither.

27

There is no secret to it now. Ghostanza Dolfin's return from Santa Giuliana is rarely off the lips of Il Sicofante's clients.

She has been seen in the marketplace and on her way to prayers. Painted, plucked and proud. Il Sicofante himself ran into her along the Via dei Priori. Panicking, he bowed so low he grazed his forehead on the cobblestones. Immediately afterwards he sprouted two white hairs in his forelock, which he plucked out in the blushing room, his great thighs squeezed tightly together.

The apothecary is nervous because of the stolen book, which never was Ghostanza's, but he doesn't know that. Flavia can only set his mind at rest by revealing her trickery, but she will not do this while there is still a chance of finding the secret of Venetian cerussa. Besides, Ghostanza is furious with Il Sicofante anyway because he refused to send her any more ingredients after Flavia came to him, reason enough to thrust something heavy and sharp in his direction. No doubt Ghostanza will hurt him when the time is right, even though he was not the one to steal her monstrous baby in its painted box.

As for Flavia, she is often on her chamber pot at all hours, gripping her ankles as a flush of warm shit splatters the earthenware, because this is what she has been dreading most.

Ghostanza Dolfin, freed from Santa Giuliana. A wolf's eyes on her every move. For the first time she wishes herself back at the Casa Nascosta, hidden by trees and Mona Grazia's shame.

* * *

'Message for the dust sparrow.'

Cimon leers at her over the kitchen table.

'She is to go to the Palazzo Tassi,' he sniggers, his Adam's apple convulsing with delight.

'Ghostanza?' Flavia swivels a look of terror to Il Sicofante. The apothecary looks grim but he cuts her fear in half when he shakes his head and says, 'Gilia.'

* * *

Hugging the shadow of Gilia's maidservant all the way from the Tassi courtyard gate to the roof terrace, Flavia sweats right through the bodice of her dress. Out of every doorway looms Ghostanza's face. Cerussa and fucus: the pale skin and beating blood of Christ's wounds on the devil before her.

Gilia sits on the roof terrace. Her dark curls bubble out of a hole in the middle of her straw hat, hopeful that the sun will bless them with flecks of gold.

'It is my first time up here,' she confides, nodding her head sideways.

Though her breakfast is about to crawl out of her stomach, Flavia tiptoes towards the parapet and peers down to the street.

A group of young men flit about like freshly hatched butterflies, their family colours on the breast of their doublets.

'Paolo Corgna,' Gilia points to a boy with dark-honey hair.

'And there is Marcello Sciri, look!'

She points in a style Mona Selvaggia would not approve of. Straight and eager.

'There!'

She guides Flavia to a tall, thickset boy.

'A fine man, Signorina.'

'Yes he is,' laughs Gilia. 'Though not as fine as Ridolfo. I often think if you took all of them and melted them in a pot you could not make anyone so joyful to look at.'

There is no denying the beauty of these men in the street: urgent and vigorous. Il Sicofante always says women are beautiful at rest; men in movement.

'You have seen him these past days?'

Gilia nods in a childish, exaggerated way.

'We met by chance outside the merchant's guild. He asked me if I was well.'

'And what did you reply?'

'Oh I did not speak to him then. My sister Ricca was with me and she answered on my behalf that I was suffering a wet cough. I would have preferred she gave him a prettier reply.'

Clearly Gilia's new parcels of freedom come with tight strings. Flavia watches as she hugs one arm to her side and blushes. The apothecary says cheeks higher than the colour of a dog rose are not approved of. He has already suggested Gilia be cut, so the blood stays in her heart and does not spring so eagerly to her face.

Flavia shudders to the think of a knife biting into Gilia's arm. She hopes Ghostanza is not the one to do it. Gilia's maidservant said Ghostanza is visiting friends on the other side of the city but Flavia's ears are still primed for the sound of sewer words in a crystal voice. When Gilia finally pulls her hair out of her straw hat Flavia does not tie her braids very well for shaking.

'Why is it that I can love a man well pleasing to my eye, but not one who has the teeth of a rabbit?' Gilia pulls a loose curl to her lips and brushes the tip lightly over them.

'For the same reason he loves you,' replies Flavia with forced gaiety. 'Because a soul should have a pretty house in which to live, just as a lady inhabits a fine palazzo. With such a pleasant dwelling, the soul will surely wish to stay at home for as long as possible.'

It is Il Sicofante, word for word. He does not just sell cosmetics to his matrons, but long life too.

Gilia smiles at her, the same as peasant children when the priest offers them honeyed fruit after a lesson they have not understood.

'Can anyone be beautiful, do you think?

Flavia considers the question a moment.

'I suppose so, yes.'

'Can a Moor be beautiful, or a Jew?'

She stops braiding, clenches her fingers.

'I don't see why not. As long as they are symmetrical.'

Again the lost smile.

'Never mind,' Flavia soothes. 'It is enough to know that a woman lacks much who lacks beauty.'

'That is what Ghostanza says.'

Flavia's breakfast does another little dance around her insides. She leans against the parapet. Down below the men are playing a game of tag. One of them scampers up and down the street with a tail of ribbons flying from his belt as the others try to catch hold of them.

Flavia takes a big gulp of air, ready for the question that has been digging at her insides ever since she found herself staring into the face of La Perfetta.

'Signorina, why did your stepmother come back?'

Gilia's lower lip fills slightly.

'My brother said she might return to us for a while, seeing that she has kept herself quietly at the convent these past months.'

Her voice is small, a speaker in an empty room.

'And is Ghostanza allowed her deliveries as before, from Venice?'

A nod and a half bounce of curls.

'Provided she goes daily to mass with my sister Ricca. It gives her great pleasure, receiving her packages.'

Of course it does. La Perfetta, happy and greedy, gorging on her powders again.

'Does she not let you to watch her while she makes her cerussa?'

'She does not now.' Gilia's voice fades almost to nothing and her eyes, though open, seem to seal over any thoughts she might be having.

'But she must know that Il Sicofante is working on new recipes to rival her own. Has she spoken about that?'

'She laughs. She says no apothecary here has the skill, and that the Venetians never share their secrets to such people. Mona Selvaggia and Ricca say the Venetians are cunning creatures but I do not know if that is true.'

A little frown appears on Gilia's brow and Flavia senses she has pushed her too far. An ornatrix should never ask such things. Still, she cannot help hazarding one final question.

'And what will happen to Ghostanza after you are married?'

The frown eases and Gilia's mouth slips back into its natural curve.

'Jacopo says she will go back to Santa Giuliana, although he has not told her yet and I am not to say it either. I think she must be happier there with the nuns though. I would like to live with all the good sisters and sing songs beneath the peach trees ... as long as I could have Ridolfo with me as well.'

'Will you not miss her? Mona Selvaggia said you were friends.'

'Oh we shall always be friends,' says Gilia lightly, though her hands are squeezed tight around the brim of her straw hat and her voice does not entirely track her words.

'Signorina Gilia ... do you really want to wear cerussa on your face?'

Gilia turns her half-plaited head. Her eyes are double curtained as she blinks slowly, her lips twisting an attempt at thought.

'It is what all married women wear. Mona Selvaggia and the other matrons will think me a little girl if I go barefaced to my own wedding feast.'

Down below, one of the men catches hold of the ribbon tails and lets out a whoop of delight that ricochets off the surrounding buildings. Flavia watches as he tucks the ribbons down the back of his own hose and sets lightly off down a side alley with the others in pursuit. The cheers grow fainter as the chase takes them further off, leaving the street empty, except for a stray dog with a bloated belly lolling in the shade.

To Keep the Teeth Tight in the Jaw

Take a cup of plantain water and boil in it these things: tragacanth putty, one ounce rock alum. Make very fine powder out of all these and boil them for half an hour in said water, and with said water wash the gums frequently.

28

It is the season of games. Seamstresses mend the flags of the richer families so they can show their colours from tower and horseback. The strong men of the city flex their muscles and lift children from the ground with one hand. Banners are strung between opposing balconies, while the trumpeters set about cleaning their instruments, and the streets are cleared of the worst of their filth.

In the apothecary's kitchen, Flavia munches her third biscuit of the morning, a spray of crumbs bearding her chin. From his seat by the fireplace Il Sicofante gives her a look of distaste. She wants to shout at him that it is not her fault she is graceless. Instead she takes another biscuit and eats it in two bites.

Palmeria and Cimon are talking about the horse race that will be held along the main street, debating whether to bet on Marcello Sciri's grey or the chestnut courser of Ridolfo Alfani. Cimon has made serious work of it, stalking the stables and interrogating the grooms in turn. He is determined his precious *scudi* will not drift and fall on the winds of fortune.

'Ser Marcello looks heavy around the girth,' says Palmeria, spooning a mound of flour onto the worktop. 'I will put my bet with Ridolfo Alfani. He is a good rider, for all his book reading.'

Palmeria makes a well in the heap of flour and cracks two eggs into it. Il Sicofante slaps his fur stole onto the table and pulls himself heavily from his chair.

They are all exhausted. Every rich woman in the city would break through iron gates for a chance to show herself off at the games. Even Cimon has been forced into action. He was charged with perfuming Mona Aurelia's wig until he was overcome by the fumes and fainted head first into her lap. By the time they'd brought him round it was hard to know which of them was more appalled. Il Sicofante beat him for that, and Flavia approved because Cimon does not so much court disaster as ask for its hand in marriage.

It is a good time for the city, between the stony dead of winter and the broiling heat of longer days. It should be a good time for the apothecary as well. Winter played havoc with the delicate skin of Il Sicofante's customers and they would happily rub slugs into their cheeks if he said it would restore them. His strongbox holds as many florins as ever, but some things are harder to measure. There are grumblings from the Alfani household. Mona Selvaggia had a nasty fit when he scrubbed her face with alkaline salts. When he tried to revive her with a raw egg tonic she retched all over her new brocade gown and the apothecary discovered his entire stock was sulphuric. He beat the *treccola* who sold them the eggs, but by then the damage was already done.

At the same time, the sermonisers in the Piazza Piccola openly denounce Il Sicofante as a man who earns his living smearing filth on the modest matrons of the city. Though he laughs at the friars' prudery, the shine on the apothecary's conker curls is not what it was, and as he stalks out of the kitchen with his great shoulders drooping a little closer to the ground, Flavia almost feels sorry for him. But then she remembers the wig that would not come back when she whistled for it, and the calluses around her toes where her clogs rub at her skin.

She thinks of Mona Grazia and the Casa Nascosta with its army of trees. Now there is a different kind of army: one made out of fear of the lie she has told. Of things promised that she cannot deliver. Once she thought it was only God and Mona Grazia who saw through her lies, but their eyes were never as powerful as the ones lurking behind a brilliant cerussa, bound to the moon but stronger than the August sun. These eyes see the flaccid skin that hangs below a matron's chinline; the uneven shape of her nostrils or the bulbous veins on the back of her hands.

Ghostanza Dolfin sees all weaknesses, she knows the things that are made to cover them up. Flavia cannot help thinking she is waiting for the right moment to show everyone the lie Flavia puts on her face every single day.

* * *

The last day of games and the Piazza Grande is packed. Above the crowds squeezed around the two-tiered fountain, large wooden platforms line the edge of the square, giving their occupants a good view of the sand-covered arena in front of the cathedral.

Flavia has to push her way to where Il Sicofante and Cimon are eating skewered chicken and looking askance at the country wives and daughters in their thick-stitched dresses. Standing on tiptoe, Flavia watches a walking puppet show, its wooden players bloodthirsty in their wielding of red-painted swords. She vaguely scans the crowd for Susanna or the yellow badge of Maestro Vitale until Il Sicofante jogs her ribs and points to the platforms. Most of the nobles have taken their places. Gilia Tassi is up there next to her brother Jacopo and his wife, her hands clutching a feather fan and her eyes as big as plates as she waits for Ridolfo Alfani to appear in the arena for the archery contest.

Flavia trails along the platform until a tall shape blots the edge of her sights. Ghostanza stares straight at her. Too late she buries herself behind the apothecary's shoulder. She would like to shrink deeper into the crowd, but thinks it safer to stay with Il Sicofante and Cimon.

'They call her Gilia la Bella, but she is not beautiful.'

The apothecary is still looking up at the nobles' platform.

'She is pretty, but that is not the same. Round eyes and soft cheeks are all very well for a baby, but her nose does not have a sufficient curvature and her chin is lacking by a finger's width.'

In spite of her nerves, Flavia cannot help smiling. Il Sicofante is happiest when debating how far a woman's neck should extend above her shoulders or the proper distance between her brow and hairline, and a happy Il Sicofante is much to be desired these days. His great teeth are enjoying quite an outing this morning, and they salute the crowds once more as he joins in a cheer for the archers making their way to the arena.

Curiosity gets the better of Flavia and she peeps over Il Sicofante's shoulder again. Ridolfo is there in the colours of the Alfani, his slender figure sheathed in a leather doublet. He waves briefly to the crowd, a little shy behind his silk curtain of hair. It is the first time Flavia has seen him close up and she doesn't really know what she expected, but there is softness in his eyes and a quiet beauty to his movements. She can easily imagine how he turned Ghostanza's well-groomed head.

The competitors take their instructions from the judge. Over on the platform, Gilia beams and whispers to her maidservant. Flavia risks another glance at Ghostanza, whose wedged heels raise her head and shoulders above her step-daughter. She wears a peaked butterfly headdress and a new gown the colour of a ripe peach. Her face is peerless white and she is stiller than a portrait. Only her eyes seem to have the power of movement. They have released Flavia and are launched into a steady pendulum movement between Gilia and Ridolfo. Otherwise there is nothing, no sign of hate or anger or any of the things a person is supposed to feel.

Ridolfo and the other archers take their positions for the first rounds, flexing their arms and crunching their brows in concentration. Each thud of an arrow into thick leather meets with applause, and Flavia comments that they look well skilled.

'As is to be expected when men have no proper work,' sniffs Il Sicofante.

Ridolfo makes a good effort in the final rounds and his arrows meet the inner markings more often than not, but it is Paolo Corgna who wins the prize calf and the ecstatic cheers of Cimon, who has placed a large bet on him. Up on the platform Gilia makes a sorrowful little shake of her head and Ghostanza's mouth develops some faculty of movement, flickering slightly when Ridolfo leaves the arena.

Next is a race of men and women on donkeys around the edge of the square, a sport for the lower classes says Il Sicofante, though he laughs with everyone else when old Gianfranco, an idiot from the Porta Eburnea, falls spectacularly over the head of his steed.

'No racing of the Jews unfortunately. There we fall short of the bigger cities.' Il Sicofante must shout over another great roar.

'What do you mean?' Flavia raises her voice to match his.

'Our Roman cousins make the Hebrews run in red cloaks every year in the carnival season, quite an event by all accounts. Unfortunately our Jews pay a tax to avoid the same happening here, though I think some would be happy to keep their money and run the race.'

So that is why Vitale is not at the games. In spite of the tax he might be pulled forward by the crowd – made to take a turn before the nobles. Flavia shakes her head when Il Sicofante offers her a chicken claw to suck, and she does not enjoy the wrestling match, which only has one real contender: a blacksmith made of the same material as his hammer. Cimon is again calculating his winnings on his scrawny fingers before the final challenger has crashed into the sand.

Finally the horses, all of them draped in as much finery as the matrons of the city. The riders wear plumed helmets, some set with jewels that flash in the bright sunlight. Ridolfo is on his chestnut courser, his silver helmet mirroring the sky.

At the raising of the banner the horses twist their heads, skittering sideways and turning full circle with unspent energy. The banner flutters down and they race away as one body, powering to the end of the piazza before whirling from sight along the main *corso* in a mass of plumage, flying tails and dust. Cheers from further along ripple back towards them like a human bell toll, fading then growing again as the horses round the far mark and fly back up towards the Piazza Grande, making their second circuit before tearing once more down the street.

Three times the cheers rise and fade. Up on the platform, Mona Selvaggia falls into a dead faint and has to be fanned by her maidservant.

'It is not excitement,' sneers Il Sicofante. 'She insisted on wearing her auburn wig though it has shrunk too tight for her head.'

Gilia seems not to have noticed Mona Selvaggia's distress. Her hands are clasped to the rails of the platform and her eyes are fixed on the place where Ridolfo and the other riders will ride back into the piazza. The only person on the platform with no look of panic or hope on their face is Ghostanza, frozen in her brilliant white shell. Every time Flavia looks at her, something buzzes fretfully through her mind like a fly that has come in through an open window and cannot find its way back out.

The riders explode back up the *corso*, urging their horses towards the finish.

First is Marcello Sciri, his colours streaming out behind him. Cimon has put a large sum on Marcello, and his teeth work away at his lower lip until a circle of blood begins to bud. Ridolfo is a little behind. His helmet has gone and his horse's caparison is ripped but he still has both feet in the stirrups. Three others follow them. As they round the corner one of them slips and crashes onto its side, hurling its rider into the crowd. No one cares about the fallen man or the twisted neck of his horse because Ridolfo is levelling with Marcello and the piazza fills with cheers as he urges his horse past the line, the white blaze of his chestnut edging ahead of his rival.

All Cimon's winnings are lost on this final race. As Ridolfo's horse circles to a halt, the apprentice launches a wad of spit towards the finishing line and sinks to the ground. Il Sicofante laughs and drags him upright, though Flavia would happily have left him there.

Across the piazza, Gilia scurries the length of the platform. The others are too busy tending Mona Selvaggia to stop her squeezing through the crowds towards Ridolfo, and Flavia is quite certain she does not count the stones from one place to the other. A few heads swing back to Ghostanza, but she does not move. Even when Ridolfo shyly takes Gilia's hand, she stays tight within her cerussa.

The courser twitches as flowers are thrown about its neck. Ridolfo is presented with a little crown of laurel leaves and the piazza erupts in a great cheer. Still Ghostanza does not move. She has both Gilia and Ridolfo in her sights but her limbs are obedient to restraint.

'I will offer my congratulations. Are you presentable?'

Il Sicofante looks carefully at Flavia, notes the newly starched cap and the clean dress, the shoes she has begged him to return for the day and the acceptable state of her cerussa.

'It looks better to be attended. No, Cimon!' he waves away the apprentice as he shuffles forward, a bulge of saliva christening his chin.

'Keep behind me.' Il Sicofante turns and marches off to where the riders are gathered, between the sandy arena and the cathedral steps.

Flavia stays close, her throat narrowing with each pace. She would much rather stay on the other side of the square, away from the cold fire of La Perfetta's eyes, but if the apothecary is wary of Ghostanza he does not show it.

Ridolfo and Gilia are packed tight among the well wishers. Il Sicofante eases much perspiration through his brow to make his flattery more lively than the others. Eventually he gets the ear of the winner, and Gilia beams wildly as he makes extravagant promises about the beauty he will give her, even though the bride suffers from the terrible complaint of unimpeachable perfection, by which he, poor savage, is invariably struck blind whenever he lays eyes on her.

Ridolfo looks bemused by the apothecary's words but no one has yet been able to silence Il Sicofante when the goddess Venus is his subject. Flavia's hands grow damp and a bead of sweat tickles its way down her spine. Up on the platform, the shadow in the corner of her eye tells her that Ghostanza is still there, watching.

Il Sicofante talks, Ridolfo frowns, Gilia beams.

A minor shortening of Ghostanza's shadow on the platform, as though a head is slightly inclined.

A signal.

Flavia swings around as two thickset men push through the hordes of people towards her. Startled, she turns back to Ghostanza up on the platform. La Perfetta's smile is broad and her shoulders tense as a hunter, ready to strike. Flavia tries to move away from the approaching men but she is hemmed in by the crowd, and before she can squeeze through them there is a rough hand on her neck.

She is pulled backwards and the breath is punched from her stomach. Her feet leave the ground as the cathedral rises at a strange angle in front of her. Her lungs have nothing in them though she gulps for air.

The men have a tavern smell to them, and their breath is hot.

A great thump and she is down again.

Not a hard landing. Sand whooshes up and her hands sink down as she tries to steady herself. Her skirt is up to her knees and she snatches it down before her arms are grabbed again and she is pushed onto her back.

For a moment there is only sky. Then a fist, thick and brown, bigger than a child's head. It hovers above her face, the little finger curled into three sides of a square with a black hole in the middle. The hole opens and a fine trickle of sand hits her forehead, nose, cheeks. The grains dive into her eyes. She squeezes them tight, sees in the blackness Ghostanza's timer on her dressing table, the specks running through its tiny glass waist.

The sprinkling becomes a deluge. She twists her head but someone rips her cap off and holds her tight. Her nostrils fill up. She snorts sand into her throat but does not dare open her mouth. Then the pouring stops and a great palm is slapped onto her cheeks, rubbing and scouring with a vigour she has not known since Mona Grazia tried to scrub the oricello stains out of her bedroom floor.

She feels it come away. Not just the cerussa, but the skin itself. The sand begins to moisten and meld. More is pushed in. The pain is so fierce she thinks the bird is being scraped from her cheek.

Her eyes are still tight but she senses a pack around her. Tighter than the trees of the Casa Nascosta. Laughter of all pitches, a few voices less cruel. Somewhere an argument starts, feet scuffle as though someone is being pushed. A harsh tug at her arms, then the hands that held her are gone.

She lies back, her face on fire and her ears buzzing with a hundred voices. Something soft is pressed against her cheeks, and what feels like a small thumb reaches round the curves of her closed eyelids, ferreting out the sand with little tutting noises.

'Oh they have marked you.'

A doll's voice, followed by a little giggle.

Gilia, lightly concerned.

'Look, Ridolfo, they have made the shape of a bird.'

'That is not our work.' A gruff sound, coarse as the sand. 'That is her own mark.'

She jerks away from the last voice. There are still grains in the back of her throat and she starts to retch, turning onto her knees and digging her fists into the sand as her body spasms. When the last of her stomach pockmarks the ground and the tears have washed her eyes clean she rolls back onto her heels.

A lot of feet.

Then skirts or hose or long capes, and, high above them, faces she cannot read all at once. On one side of her, a group of men keep the crowd back. On the other, Ridolfo Alfani stands and Gilia kneels, her hair floating forwards like an angel from a church ceiling.

Flavia twists her head a little. Il Sicofante is hovering nearby. His mouth frames an awkward grimace.

'She is your servant?' asks Ridolfo.

'She is from the convent.' The apothecary's voice is quiet. He does not look at her.

'Perhaps she should be handed over to the Podestà for trial.'

A new voice, cool enough to freeze iron.

No need for thrusting candlesticks now.

Ghostanza's headdress flutters as she moves forward. Her lips are blood rich, and her eyes dig past every layer of Flavia until they are scraping bone and sinew.

'The Podestà's office is best placed to deal with strays and lunatics. Not to mention witches.'

Somewhere overhead Jacopo Tassi's voice hushes her, but not before rumbles of approval spread through the crowd.

Ridolfo tries to keep his eyes from Ghostanza, but she gets them all the same, by twine and by hook. She reels him in, working her jaws.

Il Sicofante is nowhere to be seen. The apothecary has slipped into oblivion and there is a new cleft on the face of Gilia Tassi – a deep frown on her empty brow.

Ridolfo manages to dislodge his gaze from Ghostanza. He digs his heel into the sand and draws it in a backward line.

Flavia hates them all. These people who will not part. She wishes their eyes sealed with bark.

The bird is pulsing. It wants to spring out of her skin and take to the sky it has been hidden from. Not that it ever can. Not unless Ghostanza opens her mouth wide and takes it all, biting and tearing until cheek and eye are swallowed down and she has a whole new monster in her belly. But she will not grant such a favour. La Perfetta only bites and tears at things which cannot be seen.

She has perfected the dance of vengeance without smearing the paint on her lips.

29

Her dreams tell her not to dig any more.

They tell her she will chip the Venetians into oblivion before they show her the truth.

Always they begin with Mona Selvaggia.

She is in her tower, sitting in front of a looking glass with her head tilted back. Flavia stands behind her with a thin pointed spatula at her cheek. She presses the spatula until a crack appears in the cerussa, then digs in until there is a small well in the middle of it.

In the dream she looks at the face in the glass, but it is not Mona Selvaggia staring back at her. It is Ghostanza Dolfin.

La Perfetta is calm. She does not seem to mind that her ornatrix has cut a hole in her face. There is no blood.

There is nothing else to do except keep on digging. Flavia tries to level the hole; chiselling around the edges until the cheek is smooth again. But now Ghostanza's face is lopsided. She starts on the other cheek, hacking into it furiously. This too melts away, but she does not reach flesh. Forehead, nose and chin: all are struck and chipped and loosened like aged lime mortar when the rain has gathered behind it.

Ghostanza's face has become absent. Worse than absent. It has gone beyond the *tabula rasa* and into a space that can never be refilled. All that is left is a chalky pit with not even a skull inside it. The cerussa is nothing more than a pile of white flakes on the floor. Flavia sweeps them into a neat pile with Mona Grazia's whisk broom and throws them into the wind.

* * *

Someone is scraping out the hen house. The boy perhaps. A bunched up creature with puckered skin and a monkey face, he is given small tasks beyond his strength.

The raking sound sets Flavia's teeth on edge. She turns her face to the wall.

There is an itching somewhere above her ear. Running over her scalp, her fingers close around a small rubbery lump. She pulls, and the little popping sound releases the fattened body of a tic.

Maestro Vitale will be cross about that. He will have to a put a candle to her scalp so the head comes out too, because tics are made that way. They can lose their heads and think no more about it.

The tic has left blood under her nails. Flavia wipes her hands on the blanket, adding a red-brown smear to the other stains.

If anywhere harbours the spirit of Zia Caracosa it is this house. The filth does not merely inhabit every surface, it takes command of it. She thinks longingly of her little room at the top of Il Sicofante's house with her dressing table and its clustered jars and bottles dearer than any gathering of friends, the window looking over the city and the birdcage gently rocking.

The finches never did learn how to fight. She was fond of them in the end, and hopes Palmeria remembers to give them a crust now and then. After the day of the games she realised straight away: she did not want to see anything being pecked at ever again.

* * *

Through vellum-thin walls she hears what this house has to say: mothers and daughters, bastard infants and a hundred husbands who come to spend their wages and more besides on its damp pallets. Shouts of lust or loathing or whatever it is that makes men cry out like hounds before the chase are all the sand timer she has.

Flavia has come to know them by the sounds they make. Some puff away as if they are trying to unwind a jammed olive press until a final grunt unleashes the screw. Others try to muffle their yells, or laugh, weep and call out to their true loves or Santa Caterina, Sant'Urusula, Santa Maria, mother of God. Some are as speedy as Ridolfo Alfani's chestnut courser, racing to the finish before the door has barely clicked shut. Others make their *scudi* last, and will forever stop and start and talk in between times and get up and piss out of the window as though they are at a game of cards and must make their hand last the night. Whatever the rhythm, the creaking of boards has become her new lullaby. The whole house groans through the night as though it would unshackle its moorings and pitch into a dark ocean.

Vitale says she must not go out. For once she agrees with him. Ever since Susanna found Flavia on her doorstep, her cheeks a mass of raw meat and her shirtsleeves torn by the hands that tried to stop her fleeing the arena, she has barely left this room. Her face is still scabby from the sand and could not suffer any cerussa to cover it up, but that is not the reason for Vitale's concern.

He thinks she might be arrested.

He says the eyes of Ghostanza Dolfin still watch over the city and Flavia must be more fearful than before, because she can no longer return what she stole from her. His face is hard when he talks about the possibility of her arrest, his unshaven chin pale between the bristles.

He knows everything now. How she stole the little brown demon of Ghostanza's lust, thinking it a secret store of recipes that would bring her salvation. How she took Suora Dorotea's Book of Common Ailments and told Il Sicofante it was the work of a Venetian courtesan to stake his reputation on. He says she must leave the city and although she cannot bring herself to agree, part of her knows she will soon be on the road back home, lucky to escape with the wretched possession that is her life. The Casa Nascosta will be black with rain, and Mona Grazia will stand before her and sigh, and blow out all the light that is left.

* * *

The street has no light to it by the time he arrives.

Susanna shows him in. As she straightens the bedding Flavia thanks her for the hundredth time, watching as she walks wearily out of the room, her clogs dragging on the floorboards. She knows Susanna has been far kinder than she deserves, and the women she persuaded to let her stay here, all of them are at risk if she is caught.

A flinch crosses Vitale's mouth when he tilts the wounded bird to the light.

'Keep using the salve.'

He is kinder when she suffers than when she smiles. She wishes the injuries were worse, so he would have to stay there longer, his dusty cape strung high between her and the eyes of strangers.

Vitale drags his feet almost as much as Susanna as he brings a stool towards the bed.

'Il Sicofante and his apprentice have been arrested. They were taken from their house the night before last.'

A shivering in her stomach. She almost laughs out loud.

'Why?'

'Denunciations were lodged with the Podestà, I don't know by whom.'

'La Strega,' she says under her breath.

Perhaps Ghostanza thought Il Sicofante was still sheltering her. No doubt she hoped to get all three of them arrested at once.

'Flavia, there are charges of witchcraft against them.'

'Witchcraft?'

Her mind begins to spin. She thinks of the friar in the Piazza Piccola telling the crowds how the devil hides in the space between a woman's skin and the paint she wears, but Mona Grazia scoured her face so hard she always thought the evil was in her mark. How could Il Sicofante be blamed for making it go away?

Vitale's hands are limp between his knees. The knuckle above his ring finger swollen from the blood that gathers around the strip of silver. She imagines him this way in the Collegio infirmary, sitting at the side of patients who will not rise again.

'What is the punishment for witchcraft?'

She already knows he will not answer this question.

For a Stinking Breath

Take two handfuls of cumin, stamp it to powder and boil it in wine. Drink the syrup thereof morning and evening for fifteen days, and it will help.

30

It is strange to feel the wind. No corners to trap it; no walls at all. The sky isn't parcelled here. Outside of the city the road twists backwards, dead skin rolled off a snake's back.

Her veil is pinned up now the road is clear. Picked-at scabs shrink against the cold air but she wants the light on her face for as long as possible, before the branches over the Casa Nascosta scratch out the sky. Her hat is a scuffed velvet chaperon, a parting gift from Susanna. Her cloak bears the badge of the Jews. Vitale frowned when he saw it and said he was sorry to give her such a mark. He doesn't realise how easy it is to wear.

Is there guilt about Il Sicofante, and the wretch Cimon?

Susanna heard it from one of the arresting guards, a regular visitor to the Via del Lupo. How they went into a small room at the top of the building and talked of stealing the pretty painted box and the chirping birds in their cage. How they argued about who should have what until something else as good as tapped them on the shoulder.

A smell.

It came from under the eaves. A dusty corner by the window where a tangle of sheets were piled on a small pallet.

A wicked smell, such as is made when the devil farts after chewing on a sinner's flesh. The guard thought himself a pious man (Susanna laughed at this point) and well versed in the arts of heresy. He knew of those who wear the false mantle of our Lord, and with needle and thread fashion lifelike instruments to place a curse on their living counterparts.

The sackcloth doll did not look like anyone in particular, but it bore signs of ill use. He picked it up. It spilled part of its belly through a hole in the seam. Tearing it open, the guard watched in horror as a little brown demon dropped out and landed on the floor.

* * *

The horse is jittery. A gelding, he snaps at the bit and the swish of his tail cuts the air.

She sat on a goat, once. A calf when she was bigger.

Vitale is cautious. A walker, too, she thinks. He keeps his seat well enough but grips the reigns of his packhorse with knuckles raised to white. He is cleaner than usual. She sponged the dust from his cape this morning, his badge as well. She wonders if her father will regard him as a Jew or a good man.

The road seeps away on a rain-washed bend. They ride single file over lumps and craters – a peasant's path. No Tassi shoe would ever plant itself here.

Their horses are breasting again. Vitale unties his water flask and puts it to his lips.

'When can I come back?'

Vitale pauses, takes a slow sip.

'Better to ask how many miles to your father's house. That is something I can hope to answer.'

'Not enough,' Flavia grunts.

She dips her head when he offers the flask and rests her lips against the rim, soft and curved like a first smile. Vitale took a risk getting her out of the city. She has not thanked him for it.

The road twists into woodland, the banks either side veined with tree roots and windflowers. A hare shoots across their path, making Flavia's horse skitter and kick up dust.

Vitale leans across to grab the reins but the animal wears its leather mouth with pride. Flailing into the mane, Flavia slips her feet from the stirrups and makes a graceless landing, grasping a nettle thicket as the horse kicks and rears.

* * *

They are one piece now.

Melded as the worn saddle, she sits behind him. The gelding is calmer now its back is empty, happy to walk along-side and nudge the packhorse, nodding and lifting its head to the sky.

A dry wind turns Vitale's cape over his shoulders, flexing the cloth like crow wings on the edge of flight. He dips his head to his shoulder and smiles at her, close enough to see tiny red tendrils round the curve of his cheekbone. Frost webs, Pia used to call them, grimacing.

What can he see of her? A bead of blood where she has picked at a scab; sediment of spittle on her lower lip.

She looks away.

'Still thinking about your cerussa?'

'No,' she lies.

'Whatever will the Alfani matrons will do now?'

She senses the dip turn of his head again and glances back.

An eyebrow creeps up and she knows he is tickling her servant brain for amusement. She digs her heels into the horse's belly, making it snort.

'You think my work with Il Sicofante unimportant, but we brought great happiness to our clients, and to all those who must look upon them, just the same as if they were in a great church admiring the wonderful pictures around them. No one likes to look at a bare wall.'

'I do.'

His eyes are back with her. A glint of mischief in them, which she does not like. She shrugs off the hem of his cape, which the wind has placed on her shoulder.

'Jews are different. They do not understand what is important.'

It is only what everyone else thinks. The way they cook silly flat bread in separate ovens, their tuneless singing and the strange words that carry from their temple in a plain house on the Via Vecchia. All 'achs' and 'hles'. They do not understand what light is. They have no Santa Maria to love in all her beauty because there are no paintings on their walls.

She only spoke the truth. She cannot understand why the words bring heat to her face.

He is silent then. His back, which felt warm and comfortable as the worn saddle, turns rigid and the cloth of his cape is a barrier not only to his flesh.

He is silent, and she is sorry.

* * *

They lost time in the city, getting the travel passes checked and re-checked, having their lies accepted. By the time they stop at a village to the south of Marsciano the sun is already slipping into the hills.

The taverner makes them sit outside. It begins to rain, large drops bursting on the tabletop. They stand for a while in a nearby doorway, then the taverner shows them through a side gate and points to a storeroom on the edge of a courtyard.

There is no space to lie down. They sit with their backs to the wall and their knees bent. Flavia scoops handfuls of straw around her backside and tries to rub off the ache in her thighs.

Vitale has not spoken to her since they were on the road. At first she thought he was angry. Now it feels like there is no one there, that the cape of the physician is a husk from which the soul has flown, as empty as the cerussa mould of her dreams.

His breathing is quietly measured, a child hiding from a quarrel. Their shoulders are nearly touching, but she is careful to keep the space between them. She senses him straining to be away from her.

Rain hammers on the roof. Vitale tightens his eyes and his jaw begins to move from side to side. The muscles of his cheek tremble, flexing the scattered stubble.

She starts to talk. Softly, as if one of Zio Anzolo's goats had strayed into brambles and she had to keep it still while unhooking the thorns from its long belly hair.

She tells him about Zia Caracosa and the infants who urinated on her lap and died in their cribs.

About Tommaso lifting her out of the figs, and Pia's ruined wedding chest.

The painted birds on her bedroom floor.

Vitale says nothing.

She tells him about Alfeo's willowherb and the chewed wads that got stuck in the roof of his mouth.

About the priest at San Fortunato who made them draw a circle in the dirt with no beginning and no end to it.

Maestro Bartofolo and the stirring stick that cuts through the steam. His indigo apron and his pale moon face.

Still he is silent.

To Mona Grazia and her whisk broom. Scrubbing the stone that covers her two dead boys until her fingers bled.

The packages of altar dust. Her own bitterness in drinking them, her mother's bitterness in watching her drink. How she never understood Mona Grazia until she saw Ghostanza's dark blue cape trembling beside the wall of Santa Giuliana and heard a scream inside of her that could not be freed.

Vitale's jaw stops moving and he turns to her with his eyes that peer from dark places, just like her own.

In the fading light they tell her his soul has come back to roost.

He twists the silver ring back and forth. It moves slowly, pulling the skin with it.

Already Flavia has an image in her mind. A woman with long black hair, plaited into a single braid. It swings between her shoulder blades when she walks.

But Vitale says nothing of his wife's appearance. Instead he speaks of things that cannot be guessed from a worn wedding band. That she liked to pet stray dogs and could not sing in tune. How she believed women had greater discernment than men, and pointed him to where it said so in the Talmud. How she always woke up before he did.

These things he can still remember.

They lived together for seven months, in two rooms that smelled of fresh cedar wood, above his uncle's bank. She found it strange there. Her father's house was large and she had never heard a stranger's cough at night. She baked good matzo and had a special recipe for roast lamb dressing. She piled his plate high and watched him eat.

Flavia leans her head against the wall. Her mind takes up the story.

Still the black plait, looped over her shoulder now, as she stands with bowl and spoon. Pretty, with bangles on her arms and olive skin. She is Zingara, or maybe Stella.

The ring stops turning. Vitale digs a heel into the straw, scrubs out the image she has made. His wife thought herself very plain.

Their first winter together. Smaller, paler each day. She cooked vast stews that fattened him and sickened her.

He saw her afterwards, inside and out. Her lower limbs were swollen; he found traces of clotting in the legs. Otherwise the organs were healthy. The child too. Though it was too small to live it carried no deformity.

They left such a slight mark upon the earth. The dress she was not buried in was given to a cousin. Her earrings disappeared one day when Vitale was out, along with a lace handkerchief and some other small pieces from her dowry.

He still seeks her in prayer. Tries to stop the fragments drifting. Sometimes he sees a part of her, a line from jaw to collar; a small waist with a hip bone ledge for the resting of a palm. But these are nothing more than shapes to be measured with callipers.

'The rich men of the city have their dead wives painted on a wall or set in marble,' he says quietly. 'I always hated that.'

* * *

She takes her seat behind him again. They talk of inconsequential things. She is careful not to pick apart the threads they have begun to re-weave to each other.

The mood lightens with the deepening blue above their heads. By mid-morning the hill ridges make hazy folds of the horizon.

Known land. Seen differently now. She had not felt the newness in herself until this point.

Her arms and legs grow loose in their joints, her eyes open

to the pulsing sky and, nearer, to a strand of hair twisting free of Vitale's cap, the end still wet from the taverner's trough. The heat is clean. Country scents drift around her nostrils like the tickling of pampus grass.

Soon they are at the shrine where she stopped with Alfeo on the way to Santa Giuliana. Once the furthest corner of her world, it is now frighteningly close to home. They pass the small painted statue of the Virgin with the chip on her nose, fast behind her grille. She has aged. The black hair is faded to terracotta in places, the cheeks mottled and pock-marked. No timeless beauty for this Santa Maria, though she is loved still; a brace of small violet flowers woven round her feet.

They eat up the remaining distance. Past broken shutters and skin-stretched cattle. Low houses gather like shepherds crouched at a hillside fire, their backs to the night. Everything is crooked here. No walls meet harmoniously. New props are nailed into old ones to keep roofs from collapsing. Tiles over-hang in peeping curiosity, a wind's breath away from falling. The road tilts with the hillside, no purpose to it now the city is just a foggy slant on a distant hill. Order lost to the whims of nature.

They ride on, time measured by hoof-fall to packed earth. Gilia Tassi would be thrilled, having so many steps to count, but Flavia is not counting upwards. Every step since the city gates closed behind them is the tap of the mason's chisel on a tablet already too small to take another cut. Soon she will be at nothing.

Thought will not live long at the Casa Nascosta. Not with the ivy thick around the windows. Tomorrow she will be gulping down the stench of the woad in her back-to-front cape. There will be steam in her eyes and a fog in her mind.

She slips a hand into her pocket and feels the little pot of Il Sicofante's cerussa. Her last spoonful, kept safe since the day of the games.

'Is this the place?'

They are on the ridge where the road forks into a little swoop then trails back up towards San Fortunato.

The village is in front of them. Sleepy as an old hog, its chimneys breathing soft woodsmoke. But something else is missing. Or rather, something is there that should not be seen.

It takes a while to understand it.

The island of trees is gone. Squatting among splintered trunks and the stubble of burned shrubs is the Casa Nascosta, clearly visible from the road, the village, from miles around.

PART SIX

'Elegance is the observance of an unspoken law, given and promulgated by nature to you ladies for movement, bearing and use of your entire person and particular limbs with grace, modesty, gentility ... such that no movement is without regulation, without measure or design.'

Firenzuola

31

The oricello birds still haunt the floorboards. Just. They are faded by lime water and the larger ones are sanded down to the grain, little more than faint bloodstains at the scene of an old quarrel. Nature has bleached them as well. The arrow thin window has been opened up and the oak tree that once stole the sun is chopped and stacked in the wood store. Standing in front of the window Flavia can look to the city towers and know exactly where Mona Selvaggia is scraping the grease from her armpits, her gallipots of pastes, paints and oint-ments ranged around her: faithful retainers who will never spill the ugly truth. Beneath the bell tower of San Domenico Mona Fulvia will be tucking her springy hair under her wig while her youngest daughter takes up her first spatula of fucus and makes an uneven smear of her ten-year-old lips.

The light casts itself across the floor and makes the dust glitter in the air. There is a lot more dust now. On ceiling beams and stickily settled on the wax seals of jam pots.

There is only one spotless room in the Casa Nascosta now: a gift to Mona Grazia.

She goes down to the *sala*. Little Tommaso is at Pia's feet, his cheeks shiny with butter. Pia gives him a distracted look as she hoists the new baby further up her hip and turns a spoon around the stockpot. A smell of something greasy as the steam curls round the hood of the hearth. Out in the court-yard Maestro Bartofolo and Tommaso scrape the fat from a huge boarskin.

Pia does not roast; she boils. Indiscriminate herbs are rolled between her palms and thrown into the scum. Meat, fish or foul: it all slithers onto the plate, pale and pinched and hard to swallow. And her hairs often seem to find their way into the stockpot, ending as a wispy ligature around the tongue in the midst of chewing.

At least Pia does not sigh when she says Flavia's name, and for that she forgives her sister's dreadful cooking, and because it was Pia who brought light back to the Casa Nascosta. She made Tommaso and Maestro Bartofolo cut the trees and take their billhooks to the brambly cats' claws. Shrubs were put to the flame if their roots ran too deep, beating the island into rough-hewn trunks and blackened grass.

When Flavia asked her why she did it, Pia shrugged and said she just wanted things different, and Flavia nodded because she remembered feeling exactly the same when she ruined her sister's wedding cassone. The only difference was Mona Grazia wasn't able to punish Pia for destroying her beloved trees; Flavia isn't sure if her mother even knows about it.

When Pia hands Flavia a basket of peas she takes them without a word. Picking up a stool she goes outside, sets the basket in her lap and begins running her thumb down the ridges. She cracks the peas open one by one. Across the court- yard Maestro Bartofolo raises his head in her direction and smiles in a vague way. They don't speak much these days. It used to be Mona Grazia whose eyes glazed around Flavia's chinline but now it is her father who cannot look straight at her. It isn't because of the mark; he never really cared about that. It's because he lied to her about Christmastide and Eastertide and all the times she thought he would send for her to come from Santa Giuliana and he never did. She still doesn't know if he's happy to have her home now, but she does know he's ashamed of himself.

Flavia is rarely in the workshop now. Her father is making a blue dye for Ser Aldo's wife. Indigo and madder; the colour of the dress she wore to Il Sicofante's that first time. Once she would have been happy to watch a stain soak into pelts on the tip of the hog hair brush, but not now. It isn't her father's shame that keeps her away, it's the thought of trying to make something beautiful again.

There is not enough ornatrix left in her to do that.

Thumbnails scything pods, Flavia watches the two bent men and the curved knives juddering down the stretched skin. Their noses are almost touching the green fat and their chests are swollen with the task of keeping their breath. Maestro Bartofolo cleaves cleanly, but Tommaso's knife takes too little fat in one sweep, then gouges the hide with the next. Tommaso grins across at her as if to say he knows he's an oaf but what can he do about it? Sister, he calls Flavia now. Sister this, sister that. He is warmer than the others at the Casa Nascosta and it's easy enough between them, as though the kiss and the kick and the rotten figs never happened. But still he is a lumbering fool and she is miles away from the jealousy that stamped oricello birds onto her sister's wedding cassone.

Pia says her husband is clumsy because he is worked harder than the mule, but if Tommaso is a mule it is one with two extra saddlebags of grain to carry. His stomach overshadows his hose and all things being equal his brain gets lighter as his gut grows heavier. If his skull were not screwed down Flavia thinks it would probably take flight.

At one time she would have said all this to her sister. Pushing her breath deep into her stomach, she would have loped around in front of Pia with her eyes crossed, twiddling a stick in her ear and laughing at Tommaso, the loggerheaded fatbelly with a lard-bloated footfall. Not now, though. They share the chores that are meant for a woman's hands, speak few words in anger and none in tenderness. Sometimes Pia seeks her confidence but Flavia's ears are stuffed with wax against the peevish flotsam of chatter.

'Take this to Mama.'

Pia is in the doorway, holding a bowl of parched looking fish.

Flavia is about to refuse it but then she remembers: these days Mona Grazia likes to be served by her.

* * *

There is no need to ask if she can enter. Even if Mona Grazia heard it, she could not answer.

Fading chestnut plaits, thinning at the back, where her head lies on two stiff pillows. Pia sometimes tugs a comb through them and ties them back up in a single ribbon.

The room is pale – Maestro Bartofolo has pinned a square of white cloth to the window frame that turns the yellow sunlight the colour of frost. The bedsheets are starched with lime water. White, smooth and crisp.

Looking at her mother's face against the linen, Flavia recalls the fiercely hot day years ago when the dyer's wife made a jelly from the hooves of a calf that would not set. She sees the flatulent jelly turned out of its mould, trying and failing to remember what held it together. A finger pushed into her cheek would find itself swimming, because Mona Grazia's cast is gone.

When Flavia first saw her mother stretched out on her bed with no more strength in her limbs for whisk, broom or crucifix, she wanted to pull the starched sheet up to Mona Grazia's hairline. To veil her seemed only right. Veil her in sheets, and perhaps – the thought took a turn around her head – press them against her nose and mouth until the world grew dim and the grey slopes of purgatory reared from the fog.

That was before Vitale left her on the riverbank. When she was still an ornatrix, a believer in beauty.

Now she can look at her mother calmly. Mona Grazia is pale but not candida. The pallor of the sickbed will not pass for heavenly light. Floating among the flesh there is still some green in her eyes, circling the iris before merging to grey. These eyes are on Flavia's face whenever she comes to her now, wandering from the bird's beak to its tail and back again. The gaze of an infant staring bleakly from a forgotten crib.

There is pity here. Pia parts with numerous tears every time she tends her mother and Maestro Bartofolo still rolls quietly into bed beside her each night. He is sometimes overheard speaking gentle words, as though his wife still has laughing green eyes and a talent with the wool spindle.

The dyer is still a patient man.

Flavia takes a piece of fish and softens it between her teeth before putting it into Mona Grazia's mouth, shuddering as her finger glides over a pool of saliva.

Mona Grazia's cheeks turn hollow. Her tongue is good for sucking but has made no words since the feast day of San Sebastiano. They found her then, knelt on the floor. She was clutching her scrubbing brush, fingers so rigid they had to prize it free. When the last finger was loose she sprang away from them, her head twisted to the ceiling as though an unseen ecstasy was about to carry her straight to the Lord without any need for an earthly burial. Then she was seized by a series of violent jerks, and when she fell back among them her eyes were turned into her skull.

Had she been thinking of her two dead boys, or the daughter who left Santa Giuliana one day and disappeared into the city?

Flavia would have known the answer once.

When Mona Grazia swallows the fish Flavia takes out of her skirt pocket the little packet of altar dust, the last one her mother sent to Santa Giuliana. From the water bowl she scoops a cup and mixes the dust in, swirling her finger round until the water turns cloudy. Holding the back of Mona Grazia's head, she brings the cup to her lips.

The dyer's wife takes a sip, her eyes slowly closing. The water rises to the corner of her lips, trickling down her cheeks and onto the pillow. In Flavia's mind the cup takes on a steeper angle, flooding Mona Grazia's mouth and lungs with altar dust until the crisp white sheets are streaked with grey.

She takes the cup from her mother's lips, blotting a drip on her cheek with the hem of her apron. Mona Grazia's eyes are open again. The grey-green murk and bloodshot white give a single instruction.

Flavia puts her lips to the same curve of the rim and drinks the rest down.

To Rejuvenate

A water that will make a person renewed,
and bring the dead to life.

Take cloves, nutmeg, ginger, peppers both long and round, juniper seeds, cucumber zest, leaves of sage, basil, rosemary, marjoram and mint, elderflowers, red and white roses (and 20 other ingredients, including dried figs, raisins and honey). May all things be well pulverised and added to aqua vita. Put in a tightly sealed bottle and leave for two days, then place in an alambic and distill five times over heat, to release a very rare and valuable water.

Gilia la Bella V

Ghostanza named him Clandestino.

He was not like other babies with their white-blush cheeks and silk drifts of hair.

He dried quickly, turning from blue to purple to brown. Gilia watched as her stepmother rolled him round in her hand. She thought he looked like a monstrous turd but didn't say that out loud.

She asked if Ghostanza needed anything, because that was what Antonia had been saying to her stepmother all morning and she seemed to find it soothing. A biscuit perhaps, but Ghostanza smiled in a slurring way and said she wanted to glide through calm waters and torchlight. She wanted to float face up with no fear of the swell. Gilia wondered then if Ghostanza had climbed inside her own dreams, if she clung at night to the same raft-mattress.

Then Ghostanza asked for something normal, which was her painted jewellery box with the little cherubs on it. Gilia brought it happily to her bedside and Ghostanza took out her gold dice and her rings, the ivory clasps and her lovely sapphire pin. She cleared a space among her hair ribbons and put Clandestino to sleep in it. She christened him with a dab of musk though Gilia knew there was no Lailah to put a candle at his head so he could see from one end of the world to the other. There was no light at all.

* * *

It was not Clandestino that made the servants speak softly. Jacopo was better but her father had got sick like the rest of them, though it was worse for him. Both Jacopo and Ricca said Gilia must visit him and she stood for the first time in his bedchamber and held his thin dry hand. He was still awake then, his eyes soft and spongy yellow. It didn't seem to matter at the time but later on when she was back in her room the bells of the Chiesa del Gesu seemed to ring all at once from Terce to Sext to None and she had no memory of what had passed between them, except that she was looking at her drawing of Santa Lucia in the clouds, holding her plate with the poached egg eyes in it, and her fingers had rubbed over the ink so many times Lucia was hardly there any more.

* * *

Later on she danced. She had made up a new salto and showed it to Ghostanza in the courtyard. Her stepmother sat on the bench with her puffy waist bulging under her overdress while Gilia span around with her thumbs jammed into the small of her back. She didn't do it very well because she was too busy trying to keep her feet inside the stones and Ghostanza didn't clap her at the end.

Breathless, Gilia went to the pink and white rosebush and picked a handful of petals. She crushed them between her fingers and lifted her palms to her face, sniffed them once before poking out her tongue and licking from wrist to fingertip.

'What are you doing, *stupida*?' Ghostanza's eyes were red around the edges.

'You told me we should only eat beautiful things,' said Gilia.

Ghostanza looked at her the same way Antonia looked at Parassita when she was a very little kitten and didn't do her business in the right place. Normally Gilia would have been upset when she did that but not now, because Ghostanza didn't know as much as she thought she did. She didn't know Antonia had overheard Jacopo and her father talking about a match with Ridolfo Alfani – who was best in everything. She was glad she hadn't told Ghostanza. Somehow she knew that if her stepmother found out about it she would reach right into Gilia's head and pluck Ridolfo out so she could have him for herself.

'Here,' Ghostanza took a biscuit from her pocket. It was the shape of an angel and covered in pink sugar paste. 'If you really want something beautiful to eat.'

She snapped it in two and passed half to Gilia, who took it because she could never resist sugar paste. They sat together and sucked on the pieces. When Ghostanza had finished her half she ran a finger over her lips and said:

'It is a trick of beauty to be baked in the oven every day without drying up. You must be fresh every time they desire it.'

* * *

In the evenings they heard the sound of cockfights in the piazza. Dying birds who shrieked and clawed and shrieked again. The house was quiet and the shutters closed all the time. Fra Michele was there, though her father didn't need him now and there was no more penancing to be done, harsh or otherwise. Ghostanza didn't cry once though she looked sad and often worried. She was many hours at her dressing table, plucking at her eyebrows though they weren't there any more. Gilia sat beside her, stiff in her mourning clothes and the smell of Ghostanza's paint sharp in her nostrils.

'Do not pity him,' Ghostanza ringed her lips with a little pointed brush. 'Death only happens once to a man. A woman must bear it each time a shaft of sunlight strikes her unkindly and she sees her face remapped without permission.'

Jacopo had already told Ghostanza to pack up her little pots and her brushes and sponges. There were three large chests open in her bedchamber though Ghostanza had not put anything in them yet.

'Of course I could make my own way, set up home on the Via Deliziosa with its pretty arched windows. A flash of silk bodice behind flowering vines. Another old fool would doubtless come to my door with a weary proposal . . .'

Her mind seemed to house Maestro Alessio's abacus, the beads briskly clicking from one end to the other.

'. . . but I am too near the end of the loaf. I might be dipped in milk and chewed a little longer, but eventually I will be thrown to the pigs.'

At one time, if Ghostanza had said she was leaving the Palazzo Tassi Gilia would have held so tight to her overdress she would have had to drag her along with her. Now she wasn't so sure. Ghostanza wasn't always kind and she took up a lot of space, not just in Gilia's head but in the Palazzo and everywhere else. Even the air was full of her scent.

'Why Santa Giuliana?' she asked.

It seemed strange, Ghostanza leaving when she was still puffy and sickly, and her father not yet in his new stone bed.

Ghostanza patted her lips dry.

'Certain names have been mentioned . . .'

Admirers. Gilia was starting to understand it more. Why

KATE HOWARD

Antonia followed Ghostanza, why she stopped being her father's legend of emeralds and water.

A young man of the city, Ghostanza had said when she spoke about the Venus temple. Ridolfo was a young man of the city. But he was also the best in everything. He would never let himself be owned by a married woman.

'Really,' sighed Ghostanza, 'is a matron unable to play a game of cards in this city without charges being laid against her?'

No, Gilia would not hold on to Ghostanza's overdress when she stepped through the courtyard gate.

'I suppose it is normal to speculate. The winter was particularly long and dull.' Ghostanza picked up her tweezers again. She plucked and plucked, pulling her brow up towards her scalp.

By habit Gilia looked around for Parassita, but she was scared of Ghostanza now and never came near her.

'It will be intolerable of course,' continued Ghostanza. 'I may have to call on you, Gilia, when I have truly had my fill of it.'

The words had a threat about them. Gilia said nothing.

'And you, little chicken. Will I pack you up in my trunk along with Ibn Yunus and my other treasures?'

'Jacopo would not like it,' she mumbled.

'Damn Jacopo,' spat Ghostanza, suddenly furious, 'and damn your little pouting face. You are fortunate Gilia,' she jabbed at her brow with the tweezers, 'children often get stolen away and baked into loaves. Some people think their flesh lends youth to the consumer.' She flashed a horrible grin in the oval looking glass.

'I wonder, would I refuse a portion of Gilia pie?'

* * *

The next morning Ghostanza left, and that evening Gilia lay for a long time under the wood panelling. When she finally slept she dreamt of strong winds and doors rattling in their frames. She tried to wedge them with cloth but the rain lashed against them and the damp crept up and up, blistering the walls and sneaking into her slippered feet until they oozed water.

Then she was on the steps again, leading down to the water that lapped and swelled. She looked down the stream of it. Further along she saw Ghostanza sitting on a high rock, her long overdress splayed around her. Beside her was the shape of a young man, his features blanked out except for his mouth, which was wide and laughing.

She woke with a start, legs flaying and a fist striking the headboard. Antonia wasn't there and the candle was low. She looked around for Parassita, worried in case she had frightened her again.

Then she remembered. Parassita was dead.

They had found her that afternoon, under the pink and white rosebush. Two red pools where her eyes used to be. A witch's work said Antonia. Even Ricca wept over the little curled up body.

Jacopo said it was Ghostanza's cruel farewell. He told Gilia not to look, but she did anyway.

32

The stitching up the back of the gown is loose. It is used to being stretched at the waist, and on Flavia the wool hangs in a shape of its own making.

Mona Grazia disguised it well, the largest and best of the oricello birds. In green and yellow thread she fashioned a sea monster with bulging eyes and a bottle nose in place of a beak. Its scales rotate in decreasing circles along the length of the bird's tail feathers.

Flavia gathers the monster into her lap and settles on Pia's bed, watching as her sister digs around, back bent and head lost inside the chest, throwing what she does not want onto the bed. More oricello birds, given different shapes by Mona Grazia's needle of Genesis. Flavia can imagine her, needle swimming through her creations of oddly-shaped turtles, fish and flowers. Each thread tightened with a bitter tug.

Little Tommaso is propped up next to her. He roots inside his nostril for morsels that are carefully inserted between his budding teeth. The baby fidgets in its cot, sliding its feet up and down like a frog at swim.

Flavia smooths the sea monster along the length of her thighs. Pia's nose wrinkles as she looks at her old wedding dress.

'Are you sure you want to wear it?'

Her pretty face has a puffiness that will one day spread from her cheeks to her eyes, swallowing them into country distrust.

Flavia sits quietly as her sister continues discarding pieces of linen onto the bed.

'I don't know what Papa is thinking. How will they speak of us in Avigliano?'

Flavia takes the sea monster's head between her hands and folds it until the eyes join one another and the long bottle nose rears obscenely upwards.

'It is what I want.'

'No, it is just stupid. Mama would never have let you.'

Pia stops her rooting for a moment, drags out a large handkerchief whose oricello bird has been fashioned into an oversized beetle, and presses it to her cheek while exercising her nose in a delicate sniff.

Little Tommaso looks up at his mother and beams.

* * *

The route to the village is clear now. The errant mule track still twists and turns, but there are no thorns to catch at her ankles and fewer nettles to stitch red splotches on her forearms.

There is less birdsong in the stripped woods, though somewhere above a woodpecker still taps into bark. Buckthorn, cypress, oak and holly: all isolated from one another now. The straggling survivors of Mona Grazia's army. When winter comes they will shiver in a lonely frost.

Still Flavia ducks her head, avoiding the phantom branches. Moving out of the thinner woods and into the valley, a warm wind slaps at her cheeks and lifts her skirts in a country dance.

He is ill today. Bad air. Mal'aria, in his chest.

An ugly chest he has. She has often seen him naked from the waist up, ribs jutting through his baked skin and a tattoo of grime along his shoulders. On his back, a patchwork of scabs where he rubs his spine on tree trunks to ease a rash. In the middle of his chest is a mole, forever crusting and splitting like a sickly third nipple.

She could almost wish him dead of this mal'aria. Pia's ruined wedding gown folded back in its chest and her little dowry used to buy a new mule for Maestro Bartofolo. Instead she has made him a tonic of cinnamon and chamomile, one of Susanna's recipes.

Her first act of wifely love.

At the edge of the hemp field is the little hedgerow where he sets his string traps. He will not have been to check them today. Flavia stops to root among the bushes, now and then closing her fingers around a little feathered breast, tugging it free of its noose and re-laying the circle. Three finches and a thrush. Small roastings, the ants already busy on them. The thrush is damaged, perhaps as it thrashed against the string. Its beak is snapped at the tip and a little greyish tongue peeks through the gap. She stuffs it deep into her pocket, catching her finger on the broken beak.

In the city the finer houses have a special rose on their balconies. Its petals merge from white to pink and back to white again, like the cheeks of a virgin on watching her betrothed walk by on the street beneath her. In San Fortunato there are no balconies, because no one would want to look at Zia Dolce picking the ash from under her eyelids. There are no coats of arms and no badges above the doorways because everyone knows who is who and where they live. A wallcreeper may sprout some rustic flowers, and the occupant pretend they have designed it so, saying, 'Look, are they not prettier than the great blossomy thing Ser Aldo's wife put in her cap at Michaelmas?', but the villagers are ignorant of real beauty. Flavia can just imagine Ghostanza's horror if her wedged heels were forced into contact with its single rutted street, its houses leaning forward like drunks contemplating their beds at the end of the evening.

She walks through the musty late summer breath, past the contented gabble of Zio Anzolo and his cousin, their heads patterned with the shadow of vines as they crouch around a game of marbles. The wooden balls strike one another with soft clacks.

Flavia wanders up towards the church, past Zia Caracosa's house. The wet nurse is sitting outside her door with a new infant. She takes out a mottled breast, purple and veined as a sheep's stomach. The infant is onto it quicker than a tic burrowing into fur. Zia Caracosa leans back, her splotched lap splayed wide, one foot tapping the dirt.

The women of the village have no sense of the poise that makes a woman enticing. Zia Marietta sits with her legs crossed, which a refined woman will never do, and Cousin Paola flaps her hands around when she talks. The peasant women move about with purpose, loose limbs and eager strides.

Zia Caracosa gives a long, gaping yawn. Flavia does not stop to talk to her. She continues up the street, past Zio Anzolo's house and through a long tangle of garden crumbling into an olive grove. Further on is a small gathering of outhouses: stores and pig sheds built from offcuts of stone and packed with everything from corn husks to crow's nests. Rotten sacking makes a pathway through broken barrels and terracotta shards. Flavia picks her way to a doorless opening in the largest of the outhouses.

'Alfeo!'

She puts her head through the opening. On a corner pallet is the shape of her uncle. Invalid hair, greasy and erect, peeps out from a collection of old shawls.

'Wake up you ungodly lump.'

The squashed head pivots in her direction. One puffy eye creeps open. The other, plastered in yellow rheum, keeps its own council.

'Zio Alfeo . . .' like Mona Grazia, Flavia has learned how to sigh and speak at the same time, '. . . there is a goat on your bed.'

A brown and white she-goat, perching on the foot of her uncle's bed like an incongruous lapdog. Alfeo grins and shoots a foot out, striking it hard on the ribcage so it falls to the floor with a startled bleat.

'I've brought you some tonic for your chest.'

She had planned to help him drink it. Hold the squashed head in one hand, perhaps even try and place a kiss on some part of his face that is less disgusting than the rest. But the room is moving in and out of focus. When she looks at the hair sticking from his scalp her tongue wilts in her mouth.

She takes the flask from her pocket and puts it on the table, next to a pot with its lid askew. Down the sides and across the table an army of snails are slowly surging to freedom. Flavia plucks them one by one and tosses them back in.

'Aa–ee–aa.' Alfeo staggers upright. He is wearing an undershirt too short to hide his thighs, which are thin and hairless where they rub against the seat of his cart.

Flavia leans against the table as he wanders hopefully towards her, pushing a palm into his rheumy eye and rubbing it around the socket.

She takes a full breath before he gets too close. Alfeo's undershirt is thick but it does not lie flat below his waist. His body is preceded by a swaying half-eager thing that she recognises and does not want to.

'I have spoken to Papa.'

She speaks tightly, conserving her air.

'The priest is not coming back for a while.'

Fra Bernardino fathers many scattered villages. They can either save their vows for his return, or carry on as if there was no church. Mona Grazia was the only villager to insist her penitence fell on black cloth.

'We can wait, of course . . .'

Alfeo's other eyeball has surfaced and he is looking at her the same way he looks at a flagon of wine after a long journey. His lips are wet and there is a slight rattle when he breathes, but not like a dying man, when castanets trip against the ribcage and the patient cannot even gasp for mucus.

He reaches towards her, puts a hand on her thigh, squeezing until she feels the beginnings of a bruise. He shakes his head.

Flavia pulls away from him, moving to the doorway so she can breathe again.

'Well, we are betrothed. That is enough. When Fra Bernardino comes back he can make it right with words.'

This is what she wanted too. Get it done as quickly as possible. Today even.

But today she feels a little sick, and he has the mal'aria after all.

Then she remembers the birds. Pulling them out her pocket, she throws them one by one. A last lifeless flight sees them safely into her uncle's hands.

'You will come to the house then, on Saturday?'

Alfeo's thumbs rifle breast feathers and he nods. His undershirt is now well and truly parted from the rest of him.

To move her lips might bring forth the little breakfast she has eaten. She turns and walks quickly away through the garden.

Saturday, then.

Better it were sooner; better it were over.

Poor Pia, so confused. Tommaso, too, shaking his head like a failed gambler and Maestro Bartofolo, lifting his moon face in wonder from the fumes. Mona Grazia does not know.

None of them have asked her why. She would happily tell them if they did; there are no more secrets in her life. Not since what happened with Vitale on the riverbank, when both of them cast off more than they meant to.

She is not marrying Alfeo. She is divorcing beauty.

How Warts May be Taken Away

There is a kind of beetle that is oily, in summer you shall find it in dust and sand. If you rub that on the warts, they will be perfectly gone, and not be seen.

33

The river rises halfway up the bank, mosquitos drifting lazily over its surface. All around the scrubby earth is steaming.

Further south the swamps have not been drained. There the mal'aria shrinks the lungs of the peasants so they never get to grow old enough to hold walking sticks with knotty hands.

A wet summer is a sick summer, Mona Grazia used to say.

Flavia comes here often. Walking the banks to the place where Vitale showed how to cast things off, the day she came back to the Casa Nascosta.

He didn't stay long. The dyer poured wine for him and Vitale wetted his lips from politeness. Pia's eyes were like two giant daisies as she looked from Vitale's badge to Flavia's scab-covered face. Tommaso grinned stupidly and Flavia looked at him and wondered how he had ever made her stomach flip over like a newly-made *crespella*. Alfeo was there too, his forehead twisted as he picked at a split thumbnail.

Maestro Bartofolo sat at the head of the table, his thoughts far away though odd glances to the ceiling spoke one thing clearly. Thank God Mona Grazia had already had her seizure.

Before leaving, Vitale asked Flavia to show him the river. She led him through the blackened bushes and they walked slowly to a little spit of pebbles and sediment branching into the water.

Vitale pulled a purse from his cape. Flavia looked quizzically at him.

'This is the day we cast off our sins,' he smiled.

He upended the purse and a few coins splashed into the river, gliding slowly through the water and settling in a cloud of silt.

'I have been careful to empty my purse of all but a few *denari* for this ritual.' A self-conscious smile. 'Only a magician can travel with no funds at all.'

Flavia peered over to see where the coins had landed.

'Why throw in anything at all? Why not just empty your purse of everything before you came here?'

'Because the man does not exist who has nothing to cast away.'

Vitale's face was the same as when he watched the *treccola*'s teeth sink to the bottom of the fountain.

Flavia looked down again, into a floating portrait. The bird among its flock of scabs. Putting a hand in her pocket, she felt the edge of her pot of cerussa. Her fingers crept tightly round it. Just enough there to have her face back for a day.

'Something weighing you down?'

The clenching of her fist inflated the front of her skirts. Without knowing exactly why she did it, Flavia pulled the pot free. They both looked at it.

'A memento,' she shrugged.

'Will you cast it off?' He knew what was in there. 'Whatever Il Sicofante told you, this colour is not the making of us.'

He put one hand towards the pot. The lid flipped off, sending a little shower of cerussa to the ground. Flavia watched it dust the petals of a pale blue flower.

Then Vitale closed his fingers around hers. He was not pulling, just holding them steady. He looked almost tenderly at the bird, as if he really did not mind what God drew on her face in an idle moment.

She understood him then.

On this day of casting off, he was making a deal with her.

If she threw away her shell, he would break his own.

She laughed out loud. Not a sneer or a grunt. The leather strap from his cape flapped in the breeze. Instinctively she reached for it, pulling it towards her. Twisting her fingers like a fool on a rope she inched upwards to the edge of his collar.

She pulled herself towards him, wrapping her arms until her hands met one another in the small of his back. Pressed herself close.

He was still. No breath.

She waited for him to make his half of the embrace. Her back grew cold under the sun.

A shuffle of limbs, such as when an undershirt is put on the wrong way round and must be corrected from the inside. Vitale reached round behind himself, took hold of her wrists and pushed them slowly back to her side.

Impassable air between them again. His eyes rested around the line of her chin but she did not need them to tell her. Kindness had led him this far but he had suffered the embrace.

Anger, hot and familiar, spread across her skin. She could turn away more violently than he could. His hands were still on her wrists, holding her back from him. She wrenched her arms up, smashing the pot of cerussa against his chin so it split in two and sent a great arc of powder over his face.

They stumbled apart. Vitale shock white, a floury waste across his cheeks and his eyes black and wide. He did not look angry, though he breathed hard. A small twitch of his lip. Daring her to laugh? He might go that far, a joke among friends, but he would never step out of his shell, not even a wriggling toe's width. For all his messing with the surgeon's knife and the ink monsters he put on his walls, he found her as ugly as she knew herself to be.

In fury she struck him. He reeled, brought a hand to his face then let it drop. A little blood spurted out of his nose and ran into the white.

She laughed then. Hard and bitter, just like she was ruining Pia's wedding dress again. She called him all the filthy names a Jew has ever worn alongside his cloth badge. She cursed him as a child murderer, drinker of blood, killer of Christ.

Vitale hung his head. He waited until her temper had run dry and she was just a foolish thing in his path, red cheeked and open mouthed. He took a corner of his cape and wiped it over his cheeks, blending the powder and the blood into pale pink. When he spoke, it was to the water and the coins still poking out of the river bed.

'Remember what I told you, Flavia. There are no beauty secrets.'

A light twist of the shoulders, and he was gone.

34

It is too early for morning sounds. Still thick from dreaming, Flavia weaves to the water bowl then decides not to wash. Plucking at her undershirt where it sticks to her chest and back, she looks down at Pia's dress crumpled in a heap where she tore it off the night before.

It was supposed to happen then, her wedding night. There was no priest, no feast. Just a small gathering of family and disbelief.

Alfeo turned up in a pair of yellow hose borrowed from Zio Anzolo, his hair flat with cooking oil and his hands clasping the last of the gifts: a string of green glass beads, mottled and misshapen. The blower's rejects. Alfeo tied it around her wrist and Maestro Bartofolo tried to smile.

She was fidgeting with nerves that sent the embroidered sea monster on Pia's wedding dress into strange convulsions. Pia had offered to help her, tying a bunch of violets to the little crucifix over Flavia's bed. She had some rustic powders, berry grindings from the dyer's workshop to brighten the cheeks. Flavia shook her head. She had not washed her hair nor combed it. It was so filthy she could pile it on top of her head and it would stay put, moulded by its own grease.

She sat at the table in a plain white cap, her eyes ringed with sleeplessness and a sore budding on her lower lip. Maestro Bartofolo looked at his hands a lot. Tommaso was quieter than usual, even Pia had little to say. Alfeo grinned from ear to ear; drank one cup of sloe wine, then another, then a flagon more. Sometime later he slipped quietly from his stool and began snoring under the table.

He is there still. The snores catch in his throat and wake him for a moment of mumbled nonsense before starting up again.

There is a dull ache in Flavia's belly, a tickle of something running down her inner thigh. She parts her legs and sees a drop of blood splash into the floorboards, scoring a red eye on the largest of the old oricello birds.

It doesn't have to be now. They could still wait for Fra Bernardino, make it right with words and wine. But really it will never be right, and no priests or feasts can make it anything other than horrible, so it may as well be now. Even though she's bleeding today she will go downstairs to him and take him somewhere they can't be seen, and someday soon she will puke and swell and then squat on the stool while Zia Caracosa pulls out her very own monster baby.

Would Ghostanza laugh or weep if she saw it?

She does not wipe herself. There will be enough blood afterwards to clean away. She shrugs on the wedding dress and goes barefoot downstairs.

* * *

He is curled sideways on the floor, his head cradled in a bowl half full of mutton stock.

Outside it is raining and there is a terrible stench coming from the workshop. Maestro Bartofolo has three vats of woad on the boil, enough sheep's piss to fill a Roman bathhouse.

Flavia pulls the bowl free and shakes her uncle briskly by the shoulder. Alfeo grunts, coughs, and launches a wad of greyish bile onto a table leg. There are bits of gristle in his hair.

Without a word she beckons him. Not up the stairs, but outside, through the muddy courtyard, into the workshop.

It is the ugliest place. Next to the open vat and its violent stink; among the steam that cuts the eyes and throat.

She turns away from Alfeo and raises her skirts, the same as when she squats to take a piss in front of him. He has seen her all down there, front and back. It is nothing. She kneels on the flagstones, squeezing her kneecaps into the gaps where the edges are sharp. Her arse is facing him, just like Zio Anzolo's goats when he lets the billy at them. It is quick for them, seconds really.

Two thumps as Alfeo drops to his knees behind her. There are noises from where he is, like someone searching through their purse for a coin. She presses her forehead to the side of the vat until it begins to scald, and wonders if she will vomit now or afterwards.

Alfeo reaches a hand around her side and squeezes the nearest breast, which is hanging and tender. She still has fingerprint bruises on her thigh but does not tell him to stop. He pulls on the breast with one hand as the other travels slowly up the back of her leg, the long nail of his little finger catching the skin.

A rush of nausea as the vat gives out a belch of steam.

There is more rustling through purses and the feel of a wet dog's nose nudging between her buttocks. A knee-stagger against the flagstones as he steadies himself.

Flavia squeezes her eyes tight against a sudden burst of pain.

He is fully inside her. His hip bones digging against her cheeks. A gaping squeal of pleasure behind her.

It feels wrong. Worse than something being pulled out:

her hair plucked at the root, her rotten tooth plied loose in the Piazza Piccola. She tries to twist around to where the grunts and the shoves are coming from, but can only see as far as the workbench. At the far end there is an iron pestle stuck in a granite mortar.

Then she understands, and shouts at him to stop. But Alfeo is deaf and soon it does not matter. He pushes deeper and she feels her bowels begin to part until the smell of fresh shit mingles with the woad. A series of excitable squawks accompany the final jerks and Alfeo falls onto her back, his willowherb breath hot in her ear and his heart kicking against her spine.

They are like that for a while. Two battered halves joined by rough edges. Equal after all.

A grim pride in the gracelessness of it all. Fury too that it is not yet done.

Alfeo begins to cough afresh as he slides out. He wipes himself on his borrowed hose and Flavia pulls her skirts back down, unwedges her knees from the flagstones.

Neither of them hear the thud of horses' hooves coming towards to the house.

* * *

Her first thought is Ghostanza. The stewing of a new punishment.

The rain patters against the mud. Somewhere inside the workshop Alfeo begins to cough again. The groom stays well back with a sleeve pressed to his nose but Ridolfo Alfani walks right up to her. His eyes are streaming but he does not seem to mind.

Flavia twists her neck to the door jamb, looking at him

from her right eye only. His mantle is incredibly stitched in a swirling pattern of peacock feathers, pearls studding the thread.

A gloved hand is pressed on hers.

'Please,' behind the woad tears Ridolfo's eyes are wide and urgent and she can think of only one thing that would make him dead to this stench.

'Ghostanza?'

He blushes when Flavia says her name, but he is not the colour of conspiracy. For all his urgency he is shy behind his black hair. He does not look like a man nosing through his lover's traps to see what broken-necked thing he can bring her.

'My aunt.' He blushes again, more softly this time. 'She will kill me if you do not come back.'

So it is Mona Selvaggia who wants her. Strutting her tower room, unbraided hair flying indignantly as she finds a crevice in her cheeks so deep she can poke her little finger through to her gums.

Alfeo is behind her now. One hand on her shoulder, squeezing a new set of thumbprint bruises.

'They should release Il Sicofante,' she says quietly.

Ridolfo's eyes are red-rimmed from the smoke.

'They did! The apothecary was sent home three weeks ago.'

A hint of Ghostanza in his voice, incredulous she should not know such a thing.

'The Podestà had the happy misfortune to knock a candle onto certain charge sheets,' he adds with a sheepish grin. 'It was only a matter of time. After all, he has a wife too.'

Of course. The matrons of the city. Pimpled and vein-flushed at mass. Imploring their husbands to end the cerussa drought. The apothecary back with his mortars and minerals, smoothing his unctions onto patrician flesh with his gilt tongue firmly in his cheek.

'It is solved then,' she says. 'Il Sicofante can do what is needed.'

Ridolfo looks grim.

'The apothecary will open his door to no one except his maidservant.'

She can feel Alfeo's breath on her neck. His fingers are still tight on her shoulder, the smallest one digging deeper than the others, pinching the flesh under her collar bone. For the first time she notices another horse, tied to the groom's. Its saddle is empty.

'How did you find me?'

She does not trust him yet. Vitale would not give her away but Ghostanza might well know about San Fortunato.

'My aunt has more spies than the Pope,' Ridolfo shrugs and she sees for the first time how beautiful he really is. Not just the shaping of his features but the way he inhabits them. No fanfare, just a quiet grace she has not seen in other nobles.

Behind her stands the gargoyle form of her husband. The pain of what they did by the woad vat is a dull repugnance inside her. Inside the house she can hear Pia slurring instructions to Tommaso; her father's sluggish descent into the *sala*. She twists out of Alfeo's grip, turns to face him. His willowherb breath brings last night's supper to her throat: a decision-making bile.

She tells him very clearly that he must go into what is left of the woods and look for a small blue flower with pink tips, as the gentleman would like to see them.

'They are called Eden flowers.'

Alfeo screws up his forehead and shakes his head.

They are very, very small. She smooths down a tuft of hair at the back of his head. He will find them if he looks hard enough.

'For me,' she says.

Not a proper goodbye, but it is more than she gives to anyone else.

How to Take the Scent Out of Gloves

If you repent yourself of perfuming them, boil a little rose water or aqua vita and while they be hot, put the gloves in, and let them remain there awhile. This will take away their scent. And if you steep other gloves in it, and dry them, they will imbibe it.

Ridolfo Alfani stroked the ears of his hunting dog, which was very big and black but had friendly brown eyes and didn't look at all like it would rip a deer apart with its bare teeth.

'He is Ciccio. Don't be frightened.'

'I am not,' Gilia leaned over to stroke the dog. His fur was the same colour as Parassita's, but rougher. Over by the big fireplace Jacopo smiled at her. He had been watching her all morning, tapping his stick on the black and white floor-tiles of the Palazzo Alfani's big hall and sometimes frowning but also very cheerful when Ridolfo's father gave him a gold crucifix set with nine rubies – a lucky number, he said. Jacopo's hands were damp when he tied it around Gilia's neck and he tugged on the clasp of her bead necklace and said these must go, but she said she would wear them both all the time and everyone laughed as though she had made a splendid joke.

Ciccio sniffed at her skirts and she decided she liked him quite a lot, though not as much as she liked Ridolfo. Whenever he looked at her she felt her heart kicking and a sick feeling in her stomach, which was the strongest she had known since she saw Parassita laid out beneath the pink and white rosebush.

'My cat is dead.' She pulled on Ciccio's ears because he seemed to like it. Ridolfo made his mouth look sad and said, 'We shall get you a new one.'

'Will its eyes be pretty?' she wanted to know. 'Parassita's

eyes were the most lovely colour, the same blue as the corn-flowers that grow out of the wall by the oil store.'

Ridolfo smiled at her, but a bit like Maestro Alessio when she gave him the wrong answer and he couldn't say it was wrong because Ricca told Maestro Alessio to never upset her. She blushed and wished she had paid more attention to Maestro Alessio now, because a lot of what Ridolfo said was clever, and ever since she saw him she had wanted him more than anything, even more than her biggest and best doll Micola whose hair she brushed so many times it started falling out in big clumps.

She tried to think of something less stupid to say but then Jacopo tapped up with his stick and said it was time for her to go home, and he would send for Antonia because he needed to talk more with Ridolfo's father. Ridolfo asked would Jacopo like some wine and Jacopo grunted no, though he probably did, and Gilia wondered again why he wasn't friendlier to Ridolfo, even though both he and Ricca said that he was the best, richer than a Corgna or a Sciri and his uncle a cardinal and maybe higher one day.

She fiddled with Ciccio's ears again because she didn't want to leave but Jacopo pulled on her sleeve and she blushed again and tripped on her skirts as she walked away so Ridolfo smiled at her again like she had got the answer wrong.

* * *

The note was delivered that same afternoon to the Palazzo Tassi by a fat maidservant with a thick coil of hair and dirty skirts. Antonia said she was a cousin of one of the servants so she was allowed to sit in the kitchens until Gilia was brought to her.

If Jacopo had been at home he would have taken the note away from her but he was still at the Palazzo Alfani and Ricca was at prayers. Gilia was almost sorry they weren't there because she was still not good with letters, despite all Maestro Alessio's trying. The haughty little jig of the 's' as it peeped over the rest of its companions, the lope of the 'q's tail. They were like the noisy gathering of urchins at the feast of Santa Clara, kicking rotten fruit around and splashing mud. Gilia liked little children, but only if they were as calm and beautiful as her dolls, keeping their hands crossed one above the other in the lap of their miniature gowns.

Now she had to deal with these inky urchins. Unknot the swirling loops as she held the parchment flat at either end. Some of the words were too difficult. The quill pressed so hard it spluttered ink over the next line. But there were words in bold too, their letters separated to stamp out their meaning.

'I must be out of here, Gilia. Ridolfo will not contest it and your brother will surely approve if you insist upon it. He has never refused you any gift.'

Further on . . . 'It is my love, Gilia, that makes me want to be with you as your wedding draws near, to bring you such comfort as can only be had from two women joined in splendour.'

Gilia laid down the letter. Ghostanza's scent was on the parchment. A crimson burst of memory.

Her hands trembled.

'Ridolfo will not contest it . . .'

A shadow of those rumours and their little limbs, caught in her nostrils like a drifting stench. Ghostanza and Ridolfo, stamped together like a seal on wax, sitting on their great dry rock while Gilia was sucked into the rising water. She remembered her stepmother's belly bumping against the dressing table when she sat down to her powders. How her father had cried in his study, how Jacopo was never very friendly to Ridolfo even though he was the best in everything.

There was a fog in her mind. It was there more often now, even though Ghostanza wasn't there to shift all the familiar things around, because her stepmother could calm the waters just as easily as she could ruffle them. With Ibn Yunus she was the only one who made the dark hours pass, cradling Gilia's head against her shoulder as the shapes in the wood panelled ceiling took a life of their own.

Gilia looked back at the urchins on the parchment.

Still they would not behave. She wanted to tear them up but there was a blackness at the bottom where the words had been written over many times.

The urchins sat in a row and made no further mischief.

'I will give you the best wedding present, Gilia. I will give you Venetian cerussa.

'You will shine.'

35

They stop and rest on a stone bridge where the river separates. Already they have passed the Santa Maria with the chipped nose, the gloss-coated horses brisk and eager in the clear morning air. Ridolfo spreads out his cloak on the bridge wall and signals to Flavia. She perches beside him, empty-stomached and queasy. She thinks of Alfeo, picking his way through nettles to look for her Eden flowers. The scrape of his fingernail on the back of her thigh.

When Ridolfo lifts his flask to his mouth there is a passing scent of vanilla.

He smells like a child should. Not the sickly infants in Zia Caracosa's cribs, but a boy without poverty or vanity, running by the water's edge with a bow in his hand and a light in his eye. He is how she imagined her brothers would look now, if they had not tripped up so early on the path of life.

Mona Grazia would have loved him.

'You say the Podestà destroyed the accusations against Il Sicofante ...'

A question she could not have asked when her husband stood behind her.

Ridolfo nods, his eyes already guessing what will follow.

'Do you know if ... if all that stood against him was destroyed as well?'

Ridolfo looks into the well of his flask before he answers her.

'It was thought best that the cause of the apothecary's

imprisonment was disposed of. Everything concerning the case was burned.'

She realises then, the pity in his voice is not for Il Sicofante. It is for her. He thinks the brown monster baby was her own child. A dire melding of Alfeo's and her own deformities.

Flavia kicks her feet against the base of the wall, driving her heel into an edge of flint to stop herself laughing. Then she looks at Ridolfo's beautiful face and laughs anyway.

She wonders how it started, this beautiful boy and Ghostanza. La Perfetta on the cathedral steps perhaps, flashing her brilliant smile across the Piazza Grande. Or a gathering in one of the palazzi, Old Tassi nodding into his dinner plate while his wife scanned the room for someone, anyone, else to talk to. How easily she must have drawn him in, a fish hooked on silk twine.

Now he has to settle for poor little Gilia, who loves him more than Ghostanza ever could. She prays Gilia doesn't know what happened between her stepmother and Ridolfo. That he will come to love her even though she will never be clever or brilliant, because it is good to perch here on this bridge with her empty queasy stomach and thing of at least someone getting what they deserve.

Ridolfo tilts his head, passes his flask to her. Soft pigskin gloves, pulped and squeezed and pulped again. She imagines his young boy's lips reached down to a painted cheek that could hardly feel their touch.

He is too good for Ghostanza.

Before they leave the bridge she asks him for a coin. Immediately Ridolfo takes out his purse and empties a handful of silver into his palm. One of them is thicker than the rest. He tells her it is an old Roman piece he found poking out of the rubble when his father was building a new tower.

There are marks on the back, and the front is stamped with a woman's face in profile, a fuzz of crimped hair springing from a square tiara.

'Ceres,' says Ridolfo proudly. 'A goddess.'

Leaning over him, Flavia pushes the silver coins out of the way and presses her finger to the Roman one.

Ridolfo pauses. She knows it is not what he would choose to give her. Then he looks at her shapeless dress with its bizarre sea monster, and hands her the coin with a rueful smile. Without a word of thanks Flavia leans over the edge of the bridge and throws it in the water.

The coin drifts through the clear water to the river bed. A plume of white silt settles over the face of the goddess.

PART SEVEN

'Of the temples there is not much to say, except that they must be white and smooth, not hollow, nor raised, nor damp, nor so narrow that they appear to press on the brain, which would imply a weak mind.'

Firenzuola

36

There was no messing about with hot irons, which can burn the careless torturer as well as the prisoner. The *strappado* is favoured in the city.

On the first application an eager young guard tied weights to his ankles as he hung from the ceiling, arms twisted behind his back. His shoulder wrenched free from its socket and he passed out.

Twice more they used it, tying his hands behind him then looping the rope into the rafter. The second time he was winched from a standing position and suspended above the floor. Pain shot through his body until he heard his shouts recoil around the room. The third time they stood him on a stool and tightened the rope to lift his arms out horizontally behind him. Then they kicked the stool away.

Until that point he imagined the worst thing about falling would be the lurch into nothingness. But the moment of release was nothing compared to the sudden, breaking conclusion. The cord snapped tight as his arms lurched succinctly upwards, his shoulders screaming at the weight of his body. Never had he felt pain like that.

Lucky Cimon only had the *strappado* once. He shat himself as soon as the rope was pulled tight, then danced a few string-puppet jerks before his heart burst and they cut him loose, still and dead.

* * *

The day after the apothecary's release, the courier returned the book of secrets he had sent to the Venetian scholar. Tucked inside it was a short, acerbic reply.

He laughed out loud when the courier left, tracing his fingers over the embossed image of the woman with an apple in her hand. One by one he tore out the pages of scrawled writing and lay them on the fire.

He slept, resting his head on the kitchen table.

The next day he wandered the house. In his bedchamber there was still an imprint of his head on its pillow, a chair knocked over by one of the guards. In the hallway was Cimon's pallet and blanket, a glitter of sugar dust in its creases.

Passing the storeroom where Flavia used to sleep, he heard a scuffle.

In the little birdcage above the window the two finches panted on the floor of their cage, beaks open.

Il Sicofante tapped a finger against the bars. The cage went into a rocking motion and the birds rolled with it, too weak to resist. He went back down to the kitchen and tore into a piece of stale bread, splitting his gums so the chewed end came out of his mouth flecked with pink.

Sometime later he filled a little pot from the ewer and swept breadcrumbs from the table into his hand. He took them upstairs and put them on the floor of the finches' cage.

He slept again, upright, in a high-backed chair.

* * *

It is Palmeria who lets them in. Ridolfo Alfani, his groom and the girl who has broken him with her lies and her filthy witches' doll. Her forehead is pepper red from the sun and the stain on her cheek pulsates as though it would like to break out of her skin.

The apothecary gets up from his chair.

He could strike her. Even with his broken shoulders he could meet her in two short strides and smash her skull into the wall. Were it not for Ridolfo Alfani.

It surprises him a little, but Il Sicofante still finds his calves straining at the nexus of a low bow.

Nobility is still nobility.

37

An autumn heat is in the air, sleepy, like a passing fever.

It is strange to be in the shop again. The marble counter with its ashes melting into cream. Spotless as an altar, ready for the performance of new miracles. Sweetmeats and sugared prunes sit under netting to keep them from the flies. The floor smells of beeswax and vinegar and the dust is swept not just from one side of the shop to the other, but right outside.

Cimon would be appalled.

Palmeria does all their cooking now. She piles onion stock and spiced chicken onto slabs of bouncy thick bread. She will not cook it flat, though the apothecary prefers it that way. She says yeast is one of God's great creations, the most likely ingredient in Christ's resurrection. She insists on it though Il Sicofante scowls and bites his thumbnails. How else could He have risen?

They eat pork ribs on Sundays, beef on feast days. Palmeria's friend is employed to clean the shop, the back room and the kitchen. Another woman comes to turn out the rooms and take the laundry.

There are others too, friends of the curing woman Susanna. Their hair is a forest of dyed feathers and their skirts are hitched above their ankles. At busy times they walk up from the Via del Lupo to work on the soaps and scents. The women in the kitchen often follow their own recipes, simple as butter into flour, appalling in their homeliness, their lack of mercury or metals. As they work the straight lines of the apothecary's kitchen melt into curves of backs, breasts and buttocks: a place of womanly flesh.

Il Sicofante grunts that he might as well be in a butcher's shop.

The apothecary does not like it.

He has no choice.

He has been saved from the flames by the city matrons. Now he must repay them. Even without her fabled book of recipes, Flavia has brought industry back into the apothecary's house and florins back into his strongbox. She is the one who brings in the dyed-feather women who fill the shop with soaps and pomanders. Though he hates to admit it, she is quick and clever, and best of all she is as good a liar as he is. She can sell a myth of beauty to the ugliest women in the city and he is the one who is paid for it. For all his suffering at her hands, Il Sicofante is still a man with silk wall hangings. He will have no more maggots in the *salsiccia*.

The apothecary is given small jobs, filling out the labels for the perfumed salves they sell in sealed jars. Each one is signed with his name and stamped with his brand: the small purple shape of a bird in flight

This was not his idea either, but Il Sicofante knows he is not in charge of beauty any more. His great thighs have shrunk through lack of bounding and his right shoulder bulges beneath his doublet. Pride has been shaved from his bearing and his hair hangs limp to his collar. He has no apprentice and no desire train a new one. The best that can be done is the girl with her purple mark who knows nothing about Venetian cerussa and everything about concealment.

Flavia is as kind to him as her guilt allows. She understands that pain has come to live inside the apothecary's
body. It may venture out for a day or two when the weather is
fine, but it never moves far beyond the boundary wall. There
will be no more painted women made by his imagination on
stucco or canvas, on the city balconies or its church pews.
Sometimes she catches his eye as they work. It speaks more
plainly than the rest of him. The apothecary hates her. Not
with passion, which is after all the curdled cream of love, but
with a quiet disgust. It should trouble her more, but they are
too needful of each other to linger over it and besides all creatures must hate the thing to whom fate alone binds them.

During the day he sits by the counter and gives instructions. Though she cannot follow the apothecary's shorthand,
Flavia is slowly learning how to brew the elixirs and potions
the physicians require. He greets the customers, naturally. He
is Il Sicofante still, a man of polish.

Together they work on the cerussa. Flavia is surprised to
discover how much she despairs that it is still thick and
chalky. They discuss how to break the news to Gilia that she
will not have what Il Sicofante promised for her wedding day.

*   *   *

When there is a mist over the city towers the apothecary sits
in the blushing room and twists his face as he massages the
ruined muscles of his shoulder. Sometimes he lurches into
the kitchen and orders a tutting Palmeria to flap the flour
from her hands and walk down to the Collegio.

At this point, Flavia scurries away.

She wishes Il Sicofante would find another physician,
but Vitale is the only one who seems to understand his

pain. Instead of trying to beat it off with a stick, he simply unlatches the door and invites it to leave, for a while, of its own accord.

She does not like hiding from him. It reminds her of the other things she is hiding from: the memory of white powder mixed with blood and the vile words she said to him; the thing she did with Alfeo on the floor by the woad vat.

These are secrets to keep locked tight in a box somewhere, with a key around her neck that can never be stolen, though the tile edges still dig into her knees and she knows she cannot go back to the place where she was; her forehead mashed against the hot barrel and her uncle at his cleaving, not caring which pestle goes into which mortar.

So far they have avoided each other. If Vitale arrives through the shop door, Flavia keeps her face to the shelves behind the counter. If he enters the kitchen, she goes down to the cellar. It is as though they are in two separate worlds running side by side, or in the same world separated by a matter of hours, so that in passing neither one sees the other. Still, her hands tremble whenever his voice penetrates the wall, and when they see how she is with him the other women whisper. They understand it, and are sorry for her. Even if the law did not forbid such a match, Flavia would still be too ugly for him. Working in the shop, she wears a blue apron; deep woad like a peasant. The apothecary tells her white is a better shade for shop work but she is resolute. He has even offered her another wig, so she might be more pleasing to his customers. But her hair stays straight and stiff as a mule's tail, clipped piously beneath a little blue cap to match her apron. Her dress is a dull brown thing from the market, a trade for Pia's ruined wedding gown.

Flavia wears no paint on her face. She bares her mark fiercely, staring out across the marble counter. She is, if not entirely wed to plainness, on very good terms with it.

Il Sicofante shakes his head whenever he sees her. He cannot understand why, when cerussa is hers for the asking, she does not wear it.

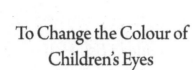

To Change the Colour of
Children's Eyes

You shall do it thus. Anoint the fore part of their heads with the ashes of the shells of hazelnuts and oil. It will make the white eyes of children black, if you do it twice. There are many experiments to make white and grey eyes black, and to alter the colours.

Gilia la Bella VII

Jacopo said no and no and no. Ricca said it more times than that, and even Antonia shook her head and said it would never happen. Gilia spent all that day and the next in her bed looking at the wood panelling. Parassita was up there as well now, dancing through the grain. Sometimes she had her lovely blue eyes with her but sometimes it was just holes and sunken cheeks, the way they found her under the rosebush the afternoon Ghostanza went to Santa Giuliana.

Everyone said what a terrible ugly thing it was, but they didn't understand the true secrets of beauty.

Still Jacopo said no and no and Ricca said it the same number of times, which was double (Gilia had learned her abacus now). On the third day Jacopo said no again but Ricca looked at Gilia on her bed and said maybe, and Gilia knew then that Ghostanza would come home and she was happy for a while, and then less so, and then not at all.

Because she could not remember by then. Was Ghostanza a Lailah or a Lilith? Was she the angel who lights up the world or was she the demon of lust, destroyer of life?

* * *

Ghostanza came back from Santa Giuliana in her dark over-dress. She did not let Gilia listen to her fierce beating heart. She did not speak to anyone at all until her little packages started arriving from Venice again. Then she was white and smooth, and a lot happier because she could go out of the big courtyard gate and be seen again. But when she finally came to Gilia's bedchamber she did not feed her capers and pistachios nor the sweet mostarda of quinces on her favourite plate. She did not talk about the wedding or Ridolfo. Instead she walked in circles for a long while then sat down suddenly and said:

'I suppose I must thank you, Gilia. Who else was there to drag me out of that place, spluttering like a fool on the end of a boat hook?'

She laughed in a cold way, her skin whiter than sugar loaf.

'And all for this . . .' she ran a finger around her smooth white face, ' . . . only for this,' she added quietly.

'For my wedding,' corrected Gilia. 'You said I would shine.'

Ghostanza pulled her lips between her teeth. She wasn't a Lailah for all her whiteness.

'You said we should be joined in splendour,' said Gilia.

'Yes I did,' said Ghostanza, her voice firm then, like Jacopo when he talked to Ricca about the household accounts and wanted to be sure everything added up.

'So now we both have what we want, after a fashion,' she said. 'I am free of those wretched nuns and you can plaster yourself in so much cerussa even your new husband won't recognise you. Let us agree to it then.'

She stood up then and Gilia thought she would leave because she still looked cold and unfriendly. But then Ghostanza came over and reached for Gilia's hands and pulled her towards her and it felt from the movement of her chest as though she was crying.

38

It is a quiet day when Gilia comes to visit.

The only customer is Mona Emilia of the ringed eyes, one bag for each of the ten children she has given birth to. Eleven, rather, for she has just squeezed out another with barely a pause in her game of cards, and though her undercarriage is bleeding she wants rose honey for her receding gums and quicklime for the coarse grey hairs on her crown.

Flavia looks closely at Mona Emilia. The matron's dress is cut below her collarbone and there is a strong smell coming from the glaze of the egg whites fanning across her cleavage. Sitting in his usual chair, Il Sicofante takes a sprig of dried lavender from his pocket and waves it under his nose. He does not like eggs, or breasts for that matter.

Flavia thinks of the flagging teats of Zia Caracosa, who have suckled so many infants she often forgets to pop them back into her drawstring undershirt. She would be amazed at all this squeezing and tying and stuffing with sculpting rags beneath a woman's bodice to make them stand proud; the plucking of nipple hairs and the sponging and painting until they look as white as a stucco ceiling rose.

Beauty and ugliness: they are no longer separate in her mind. Monsters sleep in the bellies of the beautiful, and she is now certain there will be a fusing of light and dark when the rings of Tassi and Alfani pass from one house to the other.

She has just finished wrapping Mona Emilia's packages when Gilia walks into the shop accompanied by her maidservant, a wooden doll tucked under her arm and a pale pink flush on her cheeks. She is allowed out to the marketplace now. Flavia has seen her browsing excitedly among the stalls, bouncing on the balls of her feet and sucking at her beaded necklace. Mona Emilia turns her eggy cleavage towards the door, her rimmed eyes goggling and her tongue shaping questions even as Flavia ushers her out of the shop.

'A gift from Mona Selvaggia.'

Gilia holds out the wooden doll when she returns to the counter. It has a round flat face carved from olive wood and a shock of real hair stitched into its scalp. Feathery eyelashes lay flat upon its cheek, as though it sleeps. It looks like a very young version of its owner at rest, and is so beautifully made that even Il Sicofante rises from his chair to peer at it.

'Look,' Gilia turns the doll upright and both Flavia and Il Sicofante jump as the closed lids suddenly roll open to reveal a pair of glossy blue eyes.

'Isn't it clever? My brother says it is all done with weights. He says it is possible to make a doll move entirely through its insides, which is better than a puppet because you cannot see who makes the strings work.'

Il Sicofante tries to close the eyes of Gilia's doll, but each time he takes his fingers away they spring open again, gazing stubbornly at nothing.

* * *

'Is everything ready?'

They are alone in the blushing room. Gilia flings the doll onto one of the chairs and unbuttons her cape.

'You needn't worry,' says Flavia.

Gilia paces the room, picking up the little trinkets Il Sicofante scatters like breadcrumbs for the jackdaw curiosity of their clientele. She pauses beneath one of the painted women, her eyes travelling over the chess player with the deep red mouth. A little frown and a sideways movement, the kind Flavia used to make when someone looked at her mark.

This is new for Gilia. Ever since she has been allowed to count more steps in the outside world her eyes have opened to other women. Only yesterday she was moaning how Francesca Sciri's chestnut hair springs in greater abundance than her own, and that her cousin Marzia has infuriatingly well-shaped feet. Gilia is fast discovering the unhappy truth that if you put a pretty vase among a whole shelf-full, it will be judged by comparison.

Gilia looks away from the chess player and toys for a moment with the trim of her sleeve.

'I think we should try my hairstyle once more.'

Flavia cannot stop herself groaning. Her hands are stiff from the last dressing, fingertips blistered from the little spiked needle she used to dig numerous plaits into place, some wrapped tightly around Gilia's brow, others making loops below the nape of her neck and yet more forming a flat bun on the top her head. Twists upon twists.

'Please, Flavia.'

Gilia can say it like that. As though Flavia really has a choice about being her ornatrix, because that is what she is now. The disaster at the games is forgotten; scrubbed out with sand and covered with expediency. Flavia can just imagine Ghostanza's fury. The girl with the devil's mark, forgiven by a city that cannot do without her. She will even be on call during the wedding banquet, standing quietly in the shadows with paintbrush and hair comb.

At least Gilia is a sweet child. Even if she is beginning to know the hunger that makes women pace behind high walls at night, she has yet to christen Flavia in broken terracotta and piss.

She takes up a brush as Gilia settles into a chair and begins chattering about the silk overdress her brother is having made for her. Flavia listens with less than half an ear.

'I cannot wait to have a daughter to dress in a matching overdress and a tiny pearl bridle around her forehead . . .'

She lets Gilia talk on.

'. . . and when we have a son, the carpenter on the Via Appia will make him a rocking horse, so we can have it painted the same colour as Ridolfo's courser with a leather saddle made to match.'

She parts Gilia's hair down the middle, then into sections of four, eight and sixteen, pinning each section until just one long strand hangs loose. This she divides three ways, and begins to plait.

'. . . of course our children will have proper ponies as well on the Alfani estate, but how nice for them to ride inside in the winter months . . .'

Gilia la Bella's children, gathered charmingly around their mother when she pays a visit to the nun's parlour. Will her ornatrix always be there to pull them clear of flying candle stands?

'Does Ghostanza know yet?'

'Know what?'

'That she will be sent back to Santa Giuliana once the wedding feast is over?'

A long pause. She can almost hear the straining of Gilia's thought.

'Well . . . I think she will trust in the good council of my brother, and be content with her quiet life there.'

Poor Gilia.

'Strange that she should have been allowed out of the convent at all.'

She has gone too far. Gilia's shoulder's tense and she speaks in a quiet, tight voice.

'Please do not speak of it . . . Not when there is so much happiness coming to me.'

'I'm sorry. Here.' Flavia reaches for Gilia's wooden doll, placing it gently in her arms. Gilia shrinks around it, lifting the wooden eyelids with two fingers then watching them roll closed again. Her shoulders ease and her voice brightens.

'The most exciting thing yet – I completely forgot to tell you – we shall gather the night before the wedding feast in the old temple they found beneath the Palazzo Alfani. We will all be in ancient costumes and I shall lie on cushions like Nero's wife, so you will need to make sure my hair doesn't flatten.'

The foolishness of noble weddings. One of the plaits slips out of Flavia's hand and begins to unfold. She muffles a curse.

'Signorina Gilia, if you don't mind me saying, young women lying around when there are gentlemen present . . . even if your maidservants are there . . .'

'No, *stupida*,' Gilia giggles and another plait tumbles loose. 'The gentlemen will not be with us. It will be just us women, paying homage to the goddess of beauty all together in our very own temple.'

These are not her words. She is not clever enough to think of such a thing, few of the matrons are. There is only person who would talk like that. The same person who must have cursed her stepdaughter a thousand times since her betrothal to Ridolfo Alfani.

Flavia takes a deep breath. Distracted as she is, Gilia will not be pleased at what she has to say next.

'Signorina, you remember how Il Sicofante promised to make you a new cerussa for your wedding banquet?'

'Hmm?' Gilia's head wobbles a little as Flavia unpins another section and begins plaiting again.

'Well, we have not quite perfected it, and we think some milder powders, perhaps, with your beautiful clear skin, which everyone will want to see . . .'

'No!' A flash of anger, startling in its abruptness. 'No,' she repeats more quietly. 'I will have my cerussa. You said yourself the Venetian paints are the best.'

'But, Signorina, we cannot . . .'

'Oh that is not for you to do.' Gilia flicks her fingers dismissively. 'I know Il Sicofante cannot make it half as well as I require it.'

Flavia loops and tucks Gilia's braids, waiting to hear more. But Gilia just rocks her new doll, stroking a finger gently around the circle of its face.

Gilia la Bella VIII

The deal was made. Ghostanza was going to make her white and smooth and all she had to do in return was let herself be pulled inside the long overdress once more.

It was black inside there, darker than Parassita's fur when it was bunched between her hands. Hot too, pressed up against that fierce heart. At first Gilia thought she might struggle, but instead she went limp like Parassita used to when she was very little and Gilia held her by the neck and the bottom, and again on the night before Ghostanza left for Santa Giuliana, when she was still and lifeless.

Gilia still didn't quite know how she had killed Parassita. She remembered being curled around her and staring straight into her eyes all glistening and beautiful. Above them the panelling made a shape of Santa Lucia and her plate flying up to heaven. Ghostanza was there too, floating face up with no fear of the water.

Gilia held Parassita tight. The smell of peaches drifted towards her from an unseen place, moist and sweet. Her breath grew short, and the terrible thirst that never seemed to leave her throat crawled up into her mouth. She closed her hands around Parassita's skull, looked deep into her corn-flower eyes, moist and clear.

Summer flavours.

If you pressed your fingers into them they would rise and rise again.

39

Ghostanza takes them down.

Away from the smell of the campfires dotted around the Alfani courtyard and the gentle strumming of a lyre as the wedding guests tune their voices.

Gilia's shoulders rise with each breath. Her curls are tucked beneath a lace cap and her dress is plain linen, tied at the sides in a country style.

They pass the kitchens, the rolling smell of roast suckling pig and the floral tang of rosemary. Then a staircase, tight and windowless.

'Where are the others?'

Gilia turns to Ghostanza, who makes her little sideways smirk and lifts a torch from its bracket.

'They are waiting. Mona Selvaggia wanted everything to be perfect for you.'

Ghostanza runs a hand round Gilia's waist and swings her face around. Catching Flavia's eye, her thickly painted lips part in a smile. Flavia shifts her gaze to the floor, her ornatrix supplies wrapped tightly in her skirts.

Ghostanza moves on, her torch raised for Gilia but her own feet certain of their path.

Flavia has been watching her all day. From the portico of the Palazzo Tassi where she stepped out into bright sunshine, her bare head shaded by a fringed silk parasol, down the main *corso* where the crowds came to watch Gilia count the stones to her new home, her bridal chest carried by four cousins of the Tassi family.

The crowds cheered for Gilia, but Flavia's eyes were on Ghostanza's sapphire hairpin, glinting in the sun. She walked beside her stepson, calm and proud in a dark red gown that was cut low at the back, leaving a triangle of painted flesh exposed. Flavia followed as close as she dared, trying to read the twist and tilt of Ghostanza's neck, the burgeoning cheekbone as she graced her acquaintances with a smile. Looking for any small clue to her thoughts, wondering if she could possibly be enjoying Gilia's day of splendour, or patiently waiting for her chance to ruin it all.

The red fucus neatly blended into the white of her face. Her hair was plucked well back along her scalp, rising in a tidal shock of russet and crowned by a bridle of little gold-mounted pearls.

Flavia's eyes clung to those reds and whites. She wondered if she knew the shades and the shapes of Ghostanza Dolfin better than any lover.

* * *

A tunnel. Black stones braced against the weight of the buildings above them. The smell of ages past drifting on a cold breeze. Archways to the left and right breed further passages, dark and silent except for the drip of an ancient leak.

'My dear, welcome to your temple.'

A shadow of light on the turning tunnel wall. Never has Mona Selvaggia's voice been so welcome. Ghostanza's hand tightens on her stepdaughter's waist but Gilia turns her hips and slips away.

* * *

'Why is there a Jew at my wedding feast?'

Flavia curls another plait around Gilia's ear and pins it tight.

They are in the ancient bathhouse, a few steps past the temple from where Mona Selvaggia and the other guests can be heard laughing drunkenly. Gilia sits on a lip of marble that surrounds the empty pool. Mosaicked mermen, faded and dusty, twine their tails around her feet.

'It is not uncommon,' Ghostanza yawns from the opposite edge of the pool. Her hair is undone and she sprawls full length on the marble, tracing a toe around the head of a merman striking a giant fish with his spear.

'All noblemen have a physician on hand when they have a hundred guests to keep healthy and whole. You know nothing of household matters, *idiota*.'

Something inside Gilia sinks. When she stands for Flavia to take off her dress her shadow on the wall seems smaller than before.

'You are very harsh, Ghostanza.'

'My poor child,' – is that a hairline crack in the crystalline voice? – 'leave your ornatrix a moment.'

The slap of a palm on marble, another hand outstretched across the empty pool. Gilia's head begins to turn towards her stepmother.

Flavia does her best, holding tight to the strands she has started to comb out either side of Gilia's forehead.

'Really, Gilia, how could you trust someone like that to give you beauty?'

Gilia twists around to look at Flavia, who feels the bird stretching its wings across her cheek. A quiver of distaste, part of the new Gilia, as she wriggles herself loose, stepping daintily in her undershirt over the mosaic to where her stepmother lies: a beautiful red spider with poison in her mouth.

Ghostanza lifts herself to a sitting position and Gilia settles by her side.

'There. Are we not better alone?'

Gilia bites her lip and looks down at the floor.

'No need of that creeping creature.' A vermilion leer towards Flavia.

'But I will need her. For my hair, and for when you go back to . . .'

'Go back where, little chicken?'

Poor Gilia has nothing to hide behind. Her cheeks are fierce and the tips of her ears glow crimson.

'To Santa Giuliana . . .' she whispers. 'I will need her when you go back to Santa Giuliana, because Ridolfo will want me to be graceful every day and you will be sewing altarpieces with the nuns.'

A laugh, clipped and sharp as an arrow.

'I do not think so.'

'But Jacopo said you must go, and Ridolfo only said you might be at the wedding feast for the love I bear you.'

She stops talking then, because there is a hand on her throat. Not tight, but close enough to hold Gilia still as Ghostanza leans towards her. Flavia's legs are coiled springs but something checks their release. Is this a kiss of love, or death?

Ghostanza's lips brush past Gilia's, barely touching, and nuzzle instead to her ear, uncovered and ripe for corrupting. Her jaw moves solemnly, there is no breath to part the light. All of it goes into Gilia.

Ghostanza sits back, brushing her skirts and enlivening her hair by twisting the ends around her pointing finger.

Gilia has not moved since she took her stepmother into

her ear. She has a strange look to her, a fight in her eyes as information battles ignorance.

They are quiet for a moment.

Ghostanza leans back against the marble, a look of bitter triumph on her face.

'I want it now.' Gilia speaks quietly, her voice trembling.

'Are you sure?' Ghostanza replies.

'All those women in there . . .' she murmurs, looking at the doorway towards the temple, 'all of them painted and me with nothing.'

Ghostanza reaches deep into the pocket of her gown, pulls out a glazed pot sealed with a wax lid.

Flavia eyes it warily.

Ghostanza pulls off the lid and sets it down on the marble.

Brimful of Venetian cerussa.

'Signorina . . .' the comb slips from Flavia's hand. 'I really think you should wait until . . .'

'No!' Gilia's cry strikes the mosaics. Flavia jumps and even Ghostanza seems to waver for a moment. 'Perhaps . . .' she begins, but Gilia shouts out again, and although Ghostanza tuts her like a naughty child she still takes up the pot.

Cold and white. Flavia cannot shake the idea that there is something more than just cerussa in it. But when Ghostanza snaps her fingers she still finds herself automatically rooting through her supplies for a dish and a clean sponge. A jug of water has already been brought in by Mona Selvaggia, and she takes all these things to other side of the pool.

Her hands are shaking with fear of Ghostanza, the cerussa, what it might contain, but already she is enthralled by its magic. She cannot take her eyes from the melting powder as Ghostanza adds the water and begins to mix.

Gilia's forehead is damp. Ghostanza wipes it with the edge of her skirt then takes the sponge in a steady arc above her eyebrows.

Forehead, nose, cheeks, chin, neck, breast. Mother's milk.

She mixes and smooths, dries and applies again, slowly encasing. Flavia takes up the little glazed pot with the remains of the cerussa, feeling the strain of her knuckles as she closes her hand around it.

This is the end for Gilia as well as the beginning. Even if Ghostanza hasn't played some foul trick on her, from now on she will know what it is to die each night when the paints are sponged away, her happiness as full as the pot of white lead on her dressing table. White in the crib, black upon the bier; but in that moment Flavia thinks cerussa might just be the colour of death.

'How do I look?'

Gilia's eyes, suddenly small and lost in the sheet of cerussa, have a sheen of quiet frenzy.

'Beautiful,' says Ghostanza.

It is the only answer they ever want.

* * *

A large dish of oil simmers above a brazier. The air is heavy with spiced incense, separating into plumes as the women fan their faces.

Mona Selvaggia is outstretched on a spread of cushions. Her wig is higher than the tower she lives in, and her tunic badly tied so when she leans to pull a grape from its cluster a dark brown nipple hangs loose.

Mona Fulvia sits beside her. Her sandals are fastened so tightly her ankles bulge at the sides like burst sausage skins.

Jacopo's wife is not here – no doubt she was horrified at the thought of this pagan place – but Mona Emilia has no such qualms. Her forehead glares egg white and her cheeks are redder than the hot charcoal. There are younger women from the Alfani family too, but their faces are so thick with Il Sicofante's cerussa they cannot be parted from the matrons. No maidservants, Flavia notes anxiously. Was that Ghostanza's idea too?

Gilia sits above them on a little gilt chair that has been placed at the head of the Venus temple. She is dressed in the white robes of a priestess: a tunic fixed around her waist by ribbons and attached at the shoulders by two bronze disc brooches. On her head is a three-cornered diadem forged by the blacksmith at the Piazza Piccola. A purple brocade shawl loops across her breast.

Ghostanza sits further back. She wears the same red gown as before, though she has refreshed her lips and repositioned her exquisite sapphire hairpin. Her face is expressionless. Flavia finds it impossible to tell whether she is crushing a moonlit howl of fury or laughing like a demon at the thought of her cerussa poisoning its way through Gilia's skin towards her heart.

Wine is flowing fast and the chatter races to catch up with it. Flavia squats all the while behind Gilia's chair, desperate for a taste of fresh air. It is boiling hot in the temple, the brazier too stoked and too large, but Gilia insists they keep it burning.

'It is our sacred fire, and as priestess I must guard over it,' she says as Mona Selvaggia pours her another cup of wine.

Flavia's eyes begin to water as more oil is added to the dish, but she keeps them on Gilia, and on Ghostanza watching Gilia with the same terrible inscrutability that makes her breath grow short.

'Ornatrix!'

Gilia whispers behind her shoulder. There is a ferment on her breath and her lips are trembling.

'Do my lips look pale? I have seen a lot of red on the rim of my goblet.'

'A little. We can go back to the bathhouse if you like.'

Gilia rises unsteadily from her chair. Springing up to help, Flavia grabs her elbow, accidentally tipping her cup so it splashes wine down the front of Gilia's robes.

'Oh!' Gilia grabs at the edge of her shawl and scrubs frantically at the running stain.

'We must soak it,' Flavia hurries her out of the temple and into the bathhouse, swiftly followed by the flapping hands of Mona Selvaggia. There she unloops the shawl and begins to unpin Gilia's shoulder brooches, but her hands are quickly pushed away.

'Let Mona Selvaggia do it. She is not such an oaf as you.'

These words are more stinging than any of Ghostanza's slaps. Dazed, Flavia stands aside for a tutting Mona Selvaggia.

The stain is now a great damp blush. Gilia is close to tears, plucking feverishly at the front of her tunic.

'How do you find the cerussa?' whispers Flavia, as Mona Selvaggia lifts the tunic over a wriggling Gilia's head.

'I do not know. I feel it all around me. It itches a little.'

Her heart starts to race. Il Sicofante's cerussa itches sometimes but she can't remember if Ghostanza's ever did.

'We can always wash it off, if it offends you.'

'Certainly not!' Gilia spins towards Flavia. Her pupils are two black holes and her face has an outline of rage, muted only by paint.

* * *

There is only one person here who knows poisons but will not use them.

Flavia slips away while Gilia and Mona Selvaggia fuss over the wine stain. Back through the buried street, up the staircase and out into the fresher air of the Alfani courtyard.

The night is thick now, made of shadows and fire. In the sunken garden a tent has been strung with banners of the Alfani colours. Ridolfo is standing among a group of men, his hair newly clipped. Jacopo Tassi is there as well, leaning heavily on his stick and looking very drunk.

Flavia moves among the revellers, searching.

Away from the garden a short passageway leads through to a smaller courtyard, lit with a couple of torches but quiet except for the trickle of a fountain. At the far end is a deep *loggia*, sunken into stone and night.

Eyes that peer from dark places.

She is unsurprised when a foot scrapes into view.

'A little late for a walk, Flavia.'

She can just about see him, sitting on a worn and pock-marked bench. Darkly cocooned in his cape, his hair twisting into long tails.

There is just enough fire on his face to know the air between them is passable again. He shifts for her to sit beside him. As she does so Ghostanza's pot of cerussa clinks in her skirts and she presses her knees together.

'I am here because I want something.'

'I know,' he says simply.

She takes out the pot of cerussa, nervous of Vitale's closeness but thinking mostly of Mona Grazia's old goose, who rolled her eggs round and round her pen and was cleverer than any fox but still got served up in a raisin sauce at Michaelmas.

'Please, Maestro Vitale . . .'

'Yes Maestra Flavia,' he mocks her gravity. 'You are worried about contamination.'

'Poisons, yes!' she exclaims. 'What do you know of them?'

Vitale leans back against the wall of the *loggia*, folding his arms beneath his cape.

'I know they can take many forms.'

'And poisons through the skin?'

'Anything can be contaminated Flavia, but I think your worries about Ghostanza are ill-founded. I believe she truly loves Gilia, and Gilia is the only one who really seems to care for her. Besides, Ghostanza has her wretched powders back now, she has no further cause for mischief.'

'What do you know about it?' An echo of the old anger. Flavia softens her voice. 'They say Ghostanza Dolfin cursed her husband, that she killed a cat and took out its eyes.'

'I have heard those rumours.'

'It wasn't a rumour. The cat belonged to Gilia. She still cries when she talks about it.'

'The Tassi household is a large one, Flavia. Any number of people could have done such a thing.'

He takes the pot of cerussa, sniffs, and dabs a fingerful to his lips.

'I hope it looks better than it tastes,' he says. 'But I think there is no greater poison here than the ones we already know to be in this powder. Gilia Tassi may well die of it, but not today.'

A little relief, but not enough.

'Poisons aren't Ghostanza's only method. Did you not know she tried to spear her stepson when he came to visit her at Santa Giuliana?'

'I had the honour of attending him after that particular visit.'

'Then what do you think she will do now she knows she must go back there?'

Vitale turns the pot of cerussa slowly in his hands.

'Ghostanza may not willingly re-enter the convent, but I believe Jacopo Tassi will agree such terms as make life bearable for her there. To do otherwise would likely create misery for him as well as her. No doubt she will be allowed enough cerussa to ensure her true skin becomes a puckered memory.'

'And what about Ridolfo Alfani?'

Vitale is silent for a moment.

'Of this I have no certain knowledge. Ghostanza is a beautiful woman and I do not doubt she could have captivated Ridolfo Alfani if she wanted. But from what little I know of her she is too self-serving to take such a risk, to place her heart so far out of reach, in the keeping of a young man whose family would never contemplate a marriage between them.'

'But I saw her the night she learned about Gilia's betrothal, all slumped on the floor with splotches of *passito* down her front.'

Vitale gives a low chuckle.

'I think we both know it is possible to envy another's good fortune, to fear loss or change, without resorting to murder.'

'Pah,' Flavia's neck shrinks into her shoulders at the hint to Pia's ruined wedding cassone. 'Ghostanza is a *strega* all the same. She will not just lie down.'

'She is not a witch.'

'Why do you defend her?' Flavia says harshly, annoyed because Vitale's words are quietly pecking away at her suspicions. 'Why did she pull the hair from my scalp, if not for the monster I found in her pretty box?'

Her hands are shaking as hard as her voice as she snatches back the pot of cerussa.

'Gilia needs me,' she snaps.

'Will you cover me in cerussa again?'

These words steal her anger. She slumps back down beside him.

'No. And I would not say those things to you again.'

She leans against the wall, her head turned towards the crook of his neck. The smell of dust and blood is on his cape. One hand still holds the pot of cerussa. The other has somehow become palms and fingers intertwined, his calluses matching her own.

'I threw a coin in the river,' she says quietly.

He shifts his shoulder away to look at her.

'When Ridolfo Alfani brought me back from the Casa Nascosta. I threw a coin in. I think it was a very old one. He was not pleased.'

When Vitale laughs she does not mind. She knows now that he will sometimes laugh when she wishes he would not.

'So you performed a casting off?'

'There were things I wished I had not done.'

She does not tell him about Alfeo and the woad vat. The wrong pestle in the wrong mortar.

They sit together. Not bodies in the way an ornatrix knows them. Salves and cleansers and standing upright and being candida, perfect. There is a darkness where his face should be. He does not flinch when she puts down the cerussa and brings her hand to his face. Already she knows the shape of him. Creases and bristles, rough cheeks and a frown-scarred forehead. A human terrain.

Above them the torchlight plays against the roof of the loggia, lighting a relief of scrolling vine leaves. A line of swallows shuffle on their ledge and tuck their beaks close.

His lips are dry. The crack of stale bread at communion. She can feel where the skin has started to peel. Warm like the river bed in drought, it brings moisture to her own mouth. Greater than any church rite. The long bristles of his upper lip stray into her nostril and make her want to laugh. His mouth leaves hers and he begins to kiss her brow. Small blessings, his fingers lightly on her neck, under her chin. Around her left eye, tracing the mark.

An arm around her waist, an easing together. His hand rests lightly on her back.

Her flesh is something to be dragged and pushed into work. Legs to scurry down the stairs, a neck to turn her head left and right as she steps out into a sea of other bodies, all of them in the grind and swing of their own mechanics. That the poor might love as the rich do, this is new to her. But if she has to make a choice, staying down here on the bench or flying away from it, she knows exactly what she will do. Because Ghostanza is wrong. If need be, the body can be left to writhe or rot as the soul shoots into the stars.

The shout that has been inside her since she first saw La Perfetta, wrapped in teeth and tongue then buried by cerussa, is moving up her chest. A joyful fury, clenched to strike clean through bone and flesh.

Then she hears it. Once again. The perfect note that came to her on her first night at Santa Giuliana. It soars above the *loggia*, twisting skywards, higher and higher, into another person's scream.

A Good Trick

Place a decoction of boiled chameleon in the bath-water, and it will turn the bather's skin green.

40

Flavia is stumbling, tripping over the darkness.

Her vision is still laced with stucco vine leaves and the shape of the stars.

Some of the other guests have heard the screaming too. They stagger blearily across the sunken garden, so slow they seem to be swimming.

Waves of pulsing blood in her ears and the footsteps of Vitale behind her.

The tunnel is glowing, much brighter than before. Somewhere a fire must be out of control because there is a rancorous smell of burning and a dancing screen of smoke which fills her mouth and chest. A shadow moves behind the smoke. Two hands push through and a figure tumbles forwards, her skirts snatched high and one hand clamped to her towering wig.

Mona Selvaggia. She weaves towards Flavia, her cerussa powdered with smoke and her eyeshadow seeping dark rivulets down her cheeks.

'Do . . . do not . . .'

Flavia pushes her aside and dives through the smoke towards the temple.

* * *

The screaming has stopped.

The women stand in a circle, outwardly unaware of the fumes that clutch at Flavia's throat. The brazier of sacred fire lies on its side, the dish of oil spattered pungently over the floor.

They are looking down at something. Someone.

Face down, smoke rises from her blackened crown. Her white robes are singed across her back and the flesh of her right shoulder bubbles.

Flavia shouts at the women. Pleading words in no order. None of them move.

Shock bleaches some cheeks, reddens others. But is that a haughty look on the face of Mona Emilia? And what about Francesca Sciri's grimace of disgust? Why will they not help?

Vitale moves past her. Kneeling down, he puts a hand to the white painted neck. 'We must carry her away from the smoke,' he says.

But Flavia does not hear him.

She has just seen Gilia Tassi sitting primly at the head of the temple, her ankles neatly crossed. She wears Ghostanza's red gown and a vague smile.

'It is an offering,' Gilia says in her little girl's voice.

In one hand she holds Ghostanza's sapphire hairpin. The other is closed in a fist. Both are stained as red as her gown.

'God,' whispers Vitale.

They look back at the scorched figure on the temple floor.

Gently they turn her over. The cerussa is melted. It runs in milky tears across her cheeks. From her high forehead it parts over the bridge of her nose before trickling into two deep red wells where Ghostanza's eyes used to be.

Vitale rests his head against her chest. Though she seems to breathe, she does not move.

'She will not mind. I told you, it is an offering.' Gilia stands before them now. Because of the cerussa her face looks blankly peaceful but her breathing is fast and there is something more frightening in her eyes than Flavia ever saw in Ghostanza's.

Gilia fidgets with the sapphire pin and squeezes her red fist in and out.

'A bride is allowed anything she wants,' she insists.

She holds out her fist, straightens her fingers.

The wolf's eyes in the palm of her hand.

They sit together like two Venetian marbles, pointing straight at Flavia.

'She taught me,' says Gilia, her voice a melding of frenzy and delight.

'Inside and outside, there is only beauty.'

Cupping her hand, she brings the eyes up to her mouth and swallows them whole.

A Woman Deflowered Made a
Virgin Again

Make little pills thus: burnt allome, mastick, a little vitriol and orpiment. Make them into a very fine powder; that you can scarce feel them. Make the pills with rain water, press them close with your fingers and lay them on the mouth of the matrix, where it was first broken open. It will there make little blisters; which when touched will bleed much blood, that she can hardly be known from a maid.

EPILOGUE

'Have you come at last, *bruttina?*'

A head of pale blond hair, coiled into a Grecian bun. It does not move as the hands work their way around the dressing table, neatly replacing lids and lining up brushes. Flavia cannot see her face, but she senses the words are spoken with a smile.

'Do you remember where things are?'

'Always.'

A pot of cinnamon water cools between them. In the gilt cage the two finches that once belonged to Flavia sit quietly on their perch. The brilliant exotic birds didn't last the winter but the finches seem happy enough. Ghostanza has been told they are oriental thrushes with silvery feathers. She is very pleased with them.

Flavia watches as Ghostanza pours for them. Again her hands work by memory, just as they do when she selects her jewellery by the cut of the stones. One could be forgiven for thinking she had been this way since birth, so smoothly has she learned her new way of seeing, a mere five months from the Venus temple.

Ghostanza passes her a pretty glass drinking cup, gold vine leaves etched around its rim.

She is the only one at Santa Giuliana allowed such things now. When the new bishop was appointed there were bonfires at the convent. Dresses, looking glasses, fans, jewellery:

anything that was left in the cells when he made his inspection was piled in the middle of the cloister and set alight. Suora Umiliana's rosebushes were used as kindling.

Not for Ghostanza Dolfin though. No one would have dared set light to the belongings of a woman who survived the sacred fire of Venus to emerge more beautiful than ever.

La Perfetta. La Strega.

She has never been so admired.

Flavia takes her cup and slurps noisily. Ghostanza smiles and the light catches a slight bulge in the lid of her left eye. Vitale sewed it well, the place where Gilia dug with her stepmother's sapphire hairpin. The eyes could not be recovered, though Flavia insisted on sifting through the milky spawn of Gilia's chamberpot for two days afterwards. In their place sit two finely crafted orbs from Ghostanza's home city. The glass blowers of Venice did their daughter proud, mixing the swirling waters of their lagoon into a deep vivid blue that glistens against a peerless cream, never reddening with woodsmoke or weariness.

Her burned hair has also been replaced. That was Il Sico-fante's doing. He took himself to the marketplace for days on end, scouring the crowds until he spotted a peasant girl with a tumbling brown mane that glinted to copper as the sun set. He gave her a florin and shaved her to the scalp. Flavia dyed the hair a silvery blond – Ghostanza was tired of red – and delivered it to a wigmaker in the Piazza Grande.

Ghostanza was very pleased with her new dead hair. She ordered more wigs, and Il Sicofante was surprised to find himself enjoying his pursuit of long-haired maidens around the market. In all he and Flavia presented her with five differ-ent coloured wigs, for which Ghostanza has paid them not a single coin.

There are scars still. The burning oil seared through the skin on Ghostanza's shoulder and back, making a cobweb of raised purplish skin. But her face is saved and La Perfetta could, if she wanted, still sit on a balcony as young men stand beneath with a lute and a song written for her ears alone. Perhaps that is all that matters. She never came into this world through the sloppy chance of nature. She does not live by its decree now.

Ghostanza sips her water and rolls her head towards Flavia. Though pretty, her eyes cannot move so she must always twist her neck fully to make it appear as though she is looking.

'Let me have it.'

Flavia unwraps the painted box and passes it to her.

'It is undamaged. But, and I am sorry Ghostanza, it is empty.'

The brown baby, burned in the oven to free the apothecary.

A sneer stretches the red lips. Sometimes Ghostanza's mind appears to seep through the glass so you can look into the Venetian blue and know her exact mood.

'It was always empty, *bruttina.*'

'Of course . . . I mean . . .'

'You mean what?'

'I . . . took it because . . .'

'You took it because you like pretty things. You took it because you are plain and greedy,' says Ghostanza, her voice gently instructive.

'I wanted to steal your recipes,' says Flavia quietly.

'Then you are more stupid than you look. The Venetians are not imprudent enough to spill their recipes onto vellum.'

Vitale's words come back to her. No beauty secrets; just an empty box.

'I thought the key, around your neck . . .'

Ghostanza lets out a sharp laugh and shakes her head.

'You would have needed a key to my head.'

Flavia does not need to ask whether such a thing exists.

A swoop of disappointment, realising that part of her still wants what such a key would unlock.

'Does Il Sicofante know his servant is a thief?' Ghostanza snaps suddenly. 'I suppose he is not beyond a bit of thievery himself. I would not be surprised if he put the idea in your little country head to begin with.'

Time to turn the conversation.

'Can I ask you one thing?'

A sigh. 'Yes, *bruttina*, but you must be quick. Paolo is coming to read me his sonnets and I must prepare.'

Flavia cannot help smiling. First Marcello Sciri, now Paolo Corgna. No end to the young men who sit longingly behind the grille in the nun's parlour. Not just to love, but to worship.

'I wanted to know what you said to Gilia, that night in the bathhouse,' she swallows dryly, aware that Ghostanza is still within striking distance.

'Oh, that,' the vermilion hovers for a moment, the mouth not quite closing.

Flavia already has a fraction of what happened in the temple, Gilia growing more agitated as the evening wore on, fretting tearfully about the stain on her robes which was worse for Mona Selvaggia's sponging. Ghostanza offering to swap clothes. The stain didn't matter to her. She paced the temple, enjoying her role as its new priestess, revelling in the look on Gilia's face as she tied the purple shawl around her hips and began to dance. She was too beautiful that evening. Lost in the song, her voice swelled to the roof of the temple.

'Very well, as you failed to get my recipes I will give you this one little secret.'

Ghostanza's hands squeeze the rim of her cup then soften again.

'I said that Venus decreed there could be just one beauty in a person's life. I said Ridolfo would see only my eyes when he took her to his bed.'

Ghostanza puts down her cup slowly. The liquid barely ripples when it touches the table top.

'It was an ill-timed remark.'

Her voice is flat but her eyes do not make sadness any more and Flavia cannot tell if Ghostanza is sorry that Gilia Tassi will never count any more steps than those from one side of her bedchamber to the other.

'Do you miss Ridolfo?'

She cannot help herself. She would never dare ask if Ghostanza still had her wolf's eyes.

'Ha! I see. No, no,' Ghostanza twists one of her rings with thumb and forefinger. 'He has married, I hear. A widow from Assisi. Quite a troll apparently.' She laughs, suddenly. There is real mirth in it.

'But the wall . . . the hole . . .' Flavia is skimming La Perfetta's choppy patience, a glint of front teeth as she seems to consider whether to smile or strike. In the end she fiddles with the lace of her sleeve and turns her blank eyes towards the oval looking glass.

'Ridolfo was never on the other side of the wall,' she says quietly. 'Nobody was.'

'But Jacopo said . . .'

' . . . what everyone thought. That I had thrown over my situation for a sloppy encounter. No,' she says firmly, 'he was just a nice young man who followed me around the marketplace a few times. An admirer. Not the first and not the last. It is a game often played in my home city, to let a young man sit at your feet and talk of love, but nowhere is it written that you must repay him with anything more than a fan flutter and a kind word. Perhaps Ridolfo thought differently but I am not responsible for the daydreams of others. He took me to see the old temple under his father's palazzo. It was a little adventure but my only act of foolishness was to think myself still in a place where simple flirtation is understood for what it is.'

'I don't understand,' Flavia frowns into her half empty cup. Ghostanza has rarely answered her honestly before and she is far from thinking them friends now, keepers of one another's secrets.

'Why cut a hole in the wall if there was no one there?'

Ghostanza flicks her hand with irritation.

'Do you of all people really need to ask me that?'

Behind them, a swish of skirts and a light tread.

'Suora Lena.' Ghostanza's eyes turn with her head towards a young choir nun standing in the entrance to the parlour. She has a small, heart-shaped face and a tender smile.

'My new ornatrix. Such a pet, so much easier to teach.'

Flavia gets up from her chair.

'I shall leave you to your preparations.'

'Yes, run back to Il Sicofante, the rogue, and chirp in his ear all that Ghostanza Dolfin has said this fine morning.'

A slight adjustment to her wig and Ghostanza stands, arranging her skirts so they fan out evenly, and walks back to her dressing table. Suora Lena waits patiently as La Perfetta arranges and rearranges the little pots and vials then ploughs her fingers through a rich pile of powdered fucus. In the mir-

ror her face is calm. The eyes meet the glass oval in mutual
appreciation and a smile creeps into her lips.

* * *

Flavia stands on the other side of the wall. The stone Ghostanza once cut free is circled with clashing white mortar. She
lifts a finger to it, tracing around until the loop is complete,
finding no beginning, no ending. She tries to imagine Ghostanza's face on the other side, staring out at the night, her hand
reaching into an empty space.

When Flavia looked through the hole on her first night at
Santa Giuliana she only saw what was there. But Ghostanza
was always looking for something else. If not Ridolfo, then a
city of bridges and fireworks. A balcony where a woman can
stand and be seen by those who pass beneath her.

'How is she today?'

Vitale, behind her. He rests a tentative hand on her arm.
She shrugs it away, smiling.

'Not unhappy.'

'And you?'

Flavia rubs the mortar dust from her fingers.

'Not unhappy,' she says.

They walk up the dirt road, towards the Porta Eburnea and
through the city gates, climbing the see-saw streets. They pass
under the shadow of Mona Selvaggia's tower as they skirt the
edge of the Palazzo Alfani.

Always when they walk this way Flavia thinks about the
noblewomen who did nothing to help Ghostanza that terrible night.

'You know they have buried it, the Venus temple,' Vitale nods to the Palazzo Alfani. 'They had it filled up with earth.'

Flavia shrugs. Some things are best covered over.

They walk on, Vitale moving a little ahead as the streets grow busier.

She passes Mona Fulvia of the hairy toes, pursing her fucus-heavy lips and patting her cheeks with a red-powdered cloth. Il Sicofante says she is the ugliest woman in the city though Flavia's money is on Mona Emilia.

None of it matters really. There are much worse things to see, most of them lodged deep under the skin.

Goodness and beauty. Mona Grazia always said they could not be parted.

Flavia looks at Vitale's cape, its shoulders dusty and its cheap dye patchy in places.

She reaches forward and pats at the dust. The fragments drift away, catching the light.

AUTHOR'S NOTE

My route to this story came largely from two sources, separated by hundreds of years but sharing a common theme. The first is an obscure sixteenth-century dialogue on the perfect female physique; the second a canonical twentieth-century feminist work on the exploitative nature of idealised beauty.

Agnolo Firenzuola's 1548 *Discorsi delle bellezze delle donne* (*On the Beauty of Women*) is set during a summer outing in which a man leads four women in a discussion of the ideal woman. Celso, the male adjudicator, has a Pygmalion-like obsession with the female form and his various decrees for parts of the body are quoted throughout *The Ornatrix*. Skipping forward to Naomi Wolf's *The Beauty Myth*, Celso (or Il Sicofante) could well be reincarnated as an advertising executive for the too-big-to-fail cosmetics industry: airbrushing in place of pigment.

Wolf also discusses the Germanic instrument of torture known as the Iron Maiden, a cage which held its prisoners in the dimensions and painted features of a beautiful woman. The connection between this form of torture and the modern entrapment of women in the pursuit of an unattainable ideal is brilliantly expounded in *The Beauty Myth*, and this in part forms the basis for various characters' relationships with cosmetics in *The Ornatrix*.

Further research led me back to the Renaissance equivalent of modern magazines and beauty bloggers: numerous treatises for women on creating the perfect home along with the preparation and use of beautifying products. The recipes quoted here are all from sixteenth- and seventeenth-century Italian and English manuscripts, except 'A Good Trick', which comes from Pliny. The recipe sources are Hannah Woolley's *The Accomplisht Ladys Delight in Preserving, Physick, Beautifying and Cookery*; Caterina Sforza's *Gli Esperimenti*; and Giambattista della Porta's *Natural Magick*.

My understanding of cosmetic use in Renaissance Italy is also much indebted to Farah Karim-Cooper's excellent *Cosmetics in Shakespearean and Renaissance Drama*.

In terms of location, 'the city' is largely based on Perugia in Umbria, and the names of various noted families such as Alfani and Tassi are Perugian. San Fortunato and Santa Giuliana are fictional, although other places such as Pesciano and Avigliano (Umbro) are in the area I imagined San Fortunato to be. The Casa Nascosta can be found – if you look very hard – just outside Pesciano.

I want to offer big thanks to Norah Perkins of Curtis Brown for her unwavering and plentiful support for *The Ornatrix* and for ensuring Flavia finally gets to show her face. Also to Nikki Griffiths and all at Duckworth Overlook and their associates for their enthusiasm and solid guidance throughout the editing process.

I am also immensely grateful to Emma Reece, Tessa Whippy and Ingrid Howard for reading through various drafts, and to Mark Bristow for the author photo. My thanks also go to my wonderful neighbours in Mezzanelli, providers of friendship, warmth and very strong coffee, to Charles and Philippa Seditas of Casemasce for their unstinting generosity, and to Francesca Bonacina – who always had the best recipes. My family have also been immensely supportive and encouraging throughout the many years of writing and rewriting.

Most of all, thanks to Andy. For the belief, and the cakes.